I0633006

The Brook of Tears

Charlene Lassig

Edited by Judy Mobile
Cover illustration by Joshua Frazer—www.jkfrazer.com
Medical advisor James Toniolo, MD

"The Brook of Tears," by Charlene Lassig. ISBN: 978-1-60264-609-4 (Softcover); 978-1-60264-615-5 (Hardcover); 978-1-60264-622-3 (electronic).

Library of Congress Control Number: 2011913850.

Published 2011 by Virtualbookworm.com Publishing Inc., P.O. Box 9949, College Station, TX 77842, US. ©2011, Charlene Lassig. All rights reserved. No part of this publication may be reproduced, stored in a retrieval system, or transmitted in any form or by any means, electronic, mechanical, recording or otherwise, without the prior written permission of Charlene Lassig.

Manufactured in the United States of America

Also by Charlene Lassig
The Scroll of Deuel
www.charlenelassig.com

DEDICATION

In memory of the Angels God called home.

Leah Page Kiley
June 4, 1991 – December 12, 2009
Kyle Vincent Ippoliti
February 11, 1989 – May 22, 2010
Ruhim Abdella
October 22, 1979 – May 22, 2010
Bradley Allen Dower
September 30, 1987 – September 29, 2009

I did not know during the course of writing *The Scroll of Deuel* and *The Brook of Tears*, that your lives would be taken from us so unexpectedly. Your shining stars beckon us to remember the good times and strive to carry your torches. There is nothing in the world that can fill the emptiness left by your passing, but we will take comfort in knowing someday we will be together again.

I pray God's peace and blessings will be upon your families and friends.

Charlene

CONTENTS

I have heard your prayer,

I have seen your tears;

surely I will heal you.

II Kings 20:5

PREFACE

I fear I will drift away in the darkness, only you can bring the light. I see you in the stars, your eyes shining bright. I feel you in the wind, your essence is near. I knew you before, it is all quite clear.

I felt your breath; I have heard your sigh. Tell me the truth from loneliness did I die? I know you are there, from me you cannot hide. I can feel your presence, your essence, and my soul are tied.

It is all too familiar, the things I know. I can't hold out any longer, you are all I was meant to hold. Don't turn away from me; I must feel your caress. You complete my life, my soul, and all the rest.

Your kiss still lingers on my lips, your hands upon my face. Your arms secured around my waist, hold me tightly in your embrace.

My mind is never clear when you are gone; my heart, it fails to beat. I can't stand the emptiness when we are apart, I lay my dreams at your feet.

Are you here with me forever now, within these castle walls to stay? Has Heaven answered my prayers, or will you leave me again, one day? Believe what you may, or call it what you must. I know what brings us together is fate; in this I put my trust.

Like a flower that withers away, without you, nothing is right. Light the torches to point the way, our love is worth the fight. The realms of Heaven and its majestic Angels proclaim. He has made us one in unity, in His holiness God reigns.

1.
WAVERING THOUGHTS

Guardian Realm—unmeasured time

Today was a calm day, whose beauty seemed enhanced by the singing of sparrows and the elegant patter of butterfly wings. The mellow breeze blew through the window of Mataya's chamber, filling her room with the aroma of roses. Her visions had not surfaced in several days, leaving her mind filled with memories of darkness. A void had developed in her mind because of the life stolen from her since the arrest of her brother Mateo. How strange it was to find her mind empty and feeling so alone in his absence. The evil workings of a fallen Guardian compromised her brother's mind, and Mateo's actions would be felt for many years to come.

She imagined that this is how the Head Elder must feel with the loss of his Esprit de corps. Mataya would find some reprieve should she choose a mate, there was no escape for Josiah, because his mind would never know the thoughts of another.

Why me? She thought to herself daily, fighting to find some sanity in it all. *Why must I endure such pain and emptiness?*

Lost in the emotions of self-pity, she ignored the unnatural signs forming around her. At that moment, a strong wind blew the chiffon curtain across her cheek. Her body became cold, and she gasped impulsively, recalling the responses of the humans she became so fond of observing. There was no way to stop what was about to happen. Mataya could only hope that her thoughts were not carried out, bringing a form of destruction to her people and her world. Too many times Mataya had jeopardized what she and Beck had started out to do. She prayed that this was just a memory and not a vision full of fear. Mataya closed her eyes, subject to whatever the next few moments brought her through.

A vivid memory played in her mind. She saw herself standing in the Abilene Chamber on Callisto with her brother. Before her the Head Elder knelt on one knee with his head bowed, holding the Scroll of Deuel in his hands. The chamber filled with the beautiful sounds of the scroll's music. Then a sense of discord washed over her.

Josiah's presence was replaced by that of his father and best friend, Jaleel. Her brother was inches away, but his mind wasn't with hers. Jon leaned over the Scroll of Deuel that was spread across the table. A light born of energy radiated from Mateo's fingers toward the piece of parchment. She watched the scroll flutter in the energy's force. The music of the scroll didn't fill the room with peace, for it was silenced by the anger emanating from her brother's essence. She heard Jon's words of request to decipher the scroll, and she wanted to comply. Nevertheless, the meaning now remained void to her understanding as panic and uncertainty filled her mind. There was something peculiar happening that had brought this once confident Great Elder to a plane of desolation.

Before she could clarify what she was experiencing in the chamber, another vision flashed in her mind. This time she stood by a rippling brook watching a brown-haired man swishing his hand in the silky blue colored water. She sensed a unique power emanating from around her. It grew more intense the longer she stood there. A strange tingling sensation traveled through her hands and then up both of her arms. The power appeared to consume her every thought, blocking her mind from assessing that of the knelt stranger. Then in the stillness of unmeasured time, the energy consumed Mataya pulling her essence into its center. She felt both nervous and safe at the same time. Her previous visions had taken Mataya to unfamiliar places, taunting her mind to think the unthinkable. Today she visited a place her mind could never have imagined existed.

Mataya heard faint whispers flowing from the stranger's beautifully proportioned lips. His eyes met hers, projecting a calmness that diminished her nervousness. She questioned if the man was aware of her presence, or if this too was part of the hallucination. Scenes of a time past and of days to come flashed in her mind. Mataya didn't need the visions explained to her by words; her keen mind gladly absorbed their companionship.

She watched as the figure leaned closer toward the water, extracting an object from the brook. It was a silver heart—shaped box secured by a golden chain. As the chain dangled in the air, it caught Sol's rays and shined magnificently. The peaceful stranger removed the chain from around the heart-shaped box and opened it. Then he picked up two stones that lay along the brook's edge putting them into his pocket. He removed a stone from his other robe pocket dropping that stone into the silver box. Then reaching inside the box, he removed a brown piece of parchment tucking it under his arm. In a graceful motion he placed the chain back around the box so swiftly that Mataya's keen eyesight nearly missed it. Before she knew it, the box was back in the water.

With great care, he began to unroll the parchment holding it tightly so that it didn't blow away in the wind. The tall Guardian began to read from the parchment in a language Mataya had known well. When he finished he looked at Mataya and motioned for her to approach him. She complied, advancing without hesitance, and she took the parchment that the Guardian held out for her. As she touched it, a burning sensation rippled through her essence. The fogging affects that incapacitated her twin and hindered her own actions disappeared. In that moment, her mind found the clarity it had missed for so long. The meaning of the Scroll of Deuel once again intertwined with her thoughts. The intents of Mateo were exposed and a hidden secret revealed. Her next course of action became very clear.

The Guardian took back the scroll, placing it in his robe pocket that contained the stones. He nodded his head, glancing back and forth from Mataya to the Brook of Tears. Without saying a word, the man faded from her sight and was gone. Mataya too, found herself back in the chamber executing the plan that had filled her mind by the peaceful brook. Again, the wretched stare of her brother's twisted essence called to her to help him. His eyes begged her to release him, but she knew the consequences if she had. Mataya reassured herself that her actions were accurate and continued forcing her subduing strength upon her brother. Even when several Keepers of the Courts personal arrived to take Mateo into custody, she couldn't immediately release him. A power she didn't understand cried out to her, demanding that she give retribution for her brother's vile actions.

2.
DIRTY DEEDS REMEMBERED

Earth Realm—1926

The wind whipped violently on this cold December night. The foul entity approached slowly, stopping at the tree line to remain hidden. The falling snow glistened from the moon, lighting up the woods around him. The glowing aura of his essence added to the night's beautiful radiance.

He hated being on Earth. Even the serene view couldn't make him second-guess his assessment of Earth and its inhabitants. This place reminded him of how vile his life had become. All for the sake of power he would soon learn, he didn't have.

The wicked Minion concentrated on what he needed most, to look human. In disgust, he willed his essence to create an image mimicking a human form. It resembled that of a well-known resident of the small community of Silver Lake, Wisconsin. If he were seen in this form strolling through the woods—many would question his appearance, and more would run. His essence was strong, but tonight's dirty deed weighed heavily on his conscience. He laughed to himself trying to shake a new feeling of guilt, a human emotion he didn't bargain on experiencing. A hate crime is what humans called it. No matter what the title, murder is what this fallen Guardian was willing to commit.

The snow crunched below his human feet that were bare from lack of ingenuity. The cold didn't bother his exposed skin. Unlike the shell the Head Elder Josiah created, there was no connection between his essence, and the counterfeit body moving undercover of the night.

This time, his cursed actions would conclude its deed much quicker than on the tiny plane he sunk in the future. He didn't have to wait at the scene of the crime to see the outcome. Tonight his human hands would finish what he started. There would be no mistakes afforded during this second chance, and no witness left alive. Just two innocent souls were to perish this night, unlike the ten who called for redemption from their deaths in Good Hart, Michigan.

The Minion didn't count the lost essences from his earlier battle. The foolish Watcher, who attempted to deceive him by disguising himself in a human form, meant nothing to him. Although he appeared normal and resembled the human Clement perfectly, destroying him came easily. The struggle on the platform was over before it began. The weak Watcher couldn't convert back to his natural state before the attack.

No regrets plagued the fallen stranger then, and his choices to take the living now, were made without doubts. At least this is what he told himself, while he shrugged off the guilt that bore through his evil exterior.

He briefly dismissed the thought of who his next victim

would be. His Master Tarik, an evil Demon from a distant world, was very adamant about how the Guardian of the future was to die. This pawn in the Demon's game would be the only challenge left to face after tonight's deed—but he knew the death of that Guardian wouldn't go unnoticed. Surely, the Minion who secretly walked through the woods would have to be very cunning to avoid capture.

As he neared the dimly lit cabin at the edge of the woods, he saw her standing by the window. He knew she remained there, faithful like a dog. She still wore the long floral dress from the dreaded afternoon at the icehouse. Her posture showed her defeat and loneliness fed by her grieving.

The Minion laughed again, realizing this was going to be easier than he predicted. Swiftly and silently, he could overtake her without a struggle. No more power from his essence would have to be wasted than actually needed to fulfill his vile plan. He glanced around to ensure he was alone, and then he approached the cabin quietly. Naomi met him at the door summoned by his light knock. Her eyes red from crying, lit up at his welcoming smile.

The moonlight shone brightly through Naomi's cottage window. The light didn't wake her, for she had not slept this night or the two nights before. She moved about her home like the *undead* during the last few days. Naomi functioned with barely just enough strength to care for her little precious two-month old baby girl. Rebekah is the tiny angel who stole her father's heart the day she was born. Clement's love for his wife and baby girl showed strongly in his expression. He wore a smile too beautiful for words to describe.

New to the community of Silver Lake, Naomi had no other family besides her daughter and husband Clement. The frail teenager had left her parents behind in Arizona the previous spring. She moved from Arizona to start a new life with the man she vowed to love for the rest of her life. A vow she promised to honor until death would make them part. Four days ago right before her very eyes ... death called, and Naomi saw the man she loved die.

Silver Lake had become a large venue for the ice business. Trains arrived regularly to export the harvested ice to Chicago. After Clement and Naomi arrived early in the fall, he took a job at the start of winter working at the icehouse as a stocker. When the men completed the grueling task of chiseling the chunks of ice from the lake, they formed the ice into blocks. Then the blocks of ice were loaded onto the shipping trains for delivery.

The temperature was below zero that morning, and the dock was very slippery from the previous day's warmer weather. The temperature had reached 40 degrees melting the thin layers of ice on the docking platform. The welcomed warmth made working conditions dangerous.

Tragically, Clement slipped off the docking platform after loading a block of ice onto a boxcar. The crews made sure the planks were secure, but the platform was just too slippery. Clement lost his footing and then slid off the dock helplessly, landing under the boxcar that a work crew was busy hitching up for shipping.

The memory of the accident haunted Naomi. She pleaded with God, begging him for answers. She had to know how this could happen to the man who was her whole world. Her grieving heart replayed the events in her mind torturing her very being. He was several feet away from the edge of the dock, smiling at her, and waving as she approached him. Naomi was sure his back faced the train as he walked toward her. Then all of a sudden, Clement disappeared.

She clutched her baby tightly in her arms, as she ran to the edge of the dock. She felt the wood planks bounce and shift beneath her feet. With hazel eyes full of fear, Naomi searched frantically until she found Clement. He was lying beneath the rail car with his body across the cold iron railroad tracks.

Her fears were answered by his horrifyingly twisted expression. Clement's dark pupils screamed of terror as his eyes seemed frozen in a fierce glassy stare. Naomi nearly fainted while watching his body convulse and jerk violently. His arms thrashed wildly at his sides making deep impressions into the snow.

Two work hands that saw him fall to the ground came to his rescue and jumped down from the platform to get him off the tracks. The ground was covered with ice, and the work hands slipped while trying to reach Clement. Then without any warning, the train lurched forward crushing him as it rolled over his torso. The two work hands leaped out of the path of the rolling train, narrowly escaping with minor injuries. Injuries that would mar their dreams forever, forcing this event to haunt them until God called them home.

The heavy steel wheels cut Clement clean through, pressing his sheared spine deep into his deathbed. Clement's blood flowed from his body staining the crystal-white snow a deathly dark red. Naomi didn't remember screaming or letting go of little Rebekah. Even as her husband's best friend ran to her side to console her, the scene faded from her mind. She didn't comprehend that reality; the new one surrounding her at this moment was much more pleasant.

"Naomi?" Clement beckoned her to join him at the doorway. He had whispered her name so tenderly, that even the saddest memories no longer mattered or inflicted her grieving soul. His eyes were not as loving as she remembered, but his smile welcomed her discouraged mind.

He held out his arms to embrace her. The air passing between her lungs reminded him of how fragile a human body really was. He thought about what a waste of the Creator's resources it was for her to use the precious oxygen the trees produced. Yet, the waste went beyond the air consumed by humans. It expanded far past the planet they called home and the space this sphere occupied in the outer realm of Heaven.

"Clement, my sweet Clement," she spoke softly under her sobs. "I knew you would come back to me. I knew they were wrong, my love."

Tears began to fall from her eyes and the warm salty water splashed onto his wrist. He almost imagined the tears of sorrow burning into his essence, branding him for all eternity as a murderer.

Clement loved to take walks, and tonight the cold wouldn't hold them back. "My beloved, come for a walk with me," he asked so tenderly, "and enjoy the beauty that this place has given us."

"Yes, my love. I will gladly take a stroll with you this evening. It has been too long, and I miss them so badly."

"I have also missed them, my beloved."

Naomi joyfully turned to grab her wool shawl from the coat hook. In the bassinet, little Rebekah whimpered. Did the sound of her daddy's voice awaken her, or had she perceived the discord about to be brought down upon her and her mother?

Clement reached in removing the child from her warm bed. The eyes of his adoring wife followed his every move, as if she feared he would leave her again. He sensed her eyes following him and laughed to himself. What a devoted little puppet this woman proved to be.

With a mischievous grin, he clutched his daughter in one arm and his wife in the other. He led them blindly from the warm cabin into the blusterous weather. They began their peaceful stroll down the winding path off to the left of the empty cottage.

"Oh, Clement, the night is so lovely."

"Yes, indeed it is," he agreed falsely.

"Please, tell me that you will never leave again?"

"I promise you, Naomi, that as long as your heart is beating, I will never leave you."

Naomi smiled, never sensing the danger around her. Her mind felt only the love her heart so dearly missed. "I believe you with all my soul, my love."

"Did I not pledge my allegiance in our vows? Did I not promise you, until death do us part?"

"Yes, you did, my love." The blusterous wind muffled her voice, but the cold didn't bother Naomi, for she was warm with her husband at her side.

Rebekah fussed as the cold penetrated her blankets. The vindictive imposter silenced the child with his essence. Her mother believed it to be the special bond Clement had with his daughter that calmed the cooing in the night.

No kerosene lantern was needed to guide the family down the snow-filled path. The Guardian knew it well and lit their way with his essence. Naomi didn't question the lack of a lantern or abundance of unexplainable light—her mind just processed what his essence would allow. He found the lake without difficulty or resistance from his prey. Both victims existed void of understanding because of his mind control.

Even in the clearing as the snow danced off the glassy sheet formed above the lake, her admiring smile stayed fixed upon Clement's dark expression. Naomi's smile never left her face, even as the ice shifted and pinned her beneath its layers. Neither she nor the baby struggled, facing their death like sheep led to slaughter.

The deed was done now, and his Master would be pleased. In triumph, the Minion began to convert his form back to normal. As he turned to leave he felt a strong presence surround him. Behind him, an aura appeared shattering through the outer surface of the icy lake. Before he could react to its appearance, an apparition floated from the frozen grave, and the baby's body disappeared. He squinted, trying to focus through mystical lights and flying debris. All he had seen was the dead woman staring at him. Her skin was ashen while her lips were blue and lifeless. He didn't hear her heartbeat, but he swore her voice called out for vengeance.

"You promised, my love. Until death do we part?"

Caught in the middle of his essence's conversion he reacted too slowly to her appearance. The remnants of her human influences hindered his celestial mind, and he was not able to discern the spirit that crept up on him. Trying to sense the location of the surviving baby became impossible for him to determine. He left Earth in a hurry, cautious that more entities would come, or perhaps the Keeper of the Courts would arrest him. Deimos was never to see the likes of him or absorb his essence.

3.
STARTING OVER

Earth Realm—four months after Earth's re-birth

It had been years since Jon took on an Esprit de corps. His position on the counsel as Keeper of the Courts traditionally kept him on Sol. Times had changed and so did the practices and laws for all Guardians. The excitement of a lifestyle outside of the courtroom intrigued him. Jon enjoyed his service to the Council and took pride in upholding the laws of his people. He never doubted his path to serve all entities of the Guardian realm and those beyond his—but he had a different perspective now than in his youth. He realized his essence always belonged elsewhere traveling the universe for the cause of humanity.

To Jon the day he bonded with his wife Kiersten always remained his favorite memory. The life they made together in the Guardian world made them happy in many ways.

Even though Earth's people didn't know what happened that awful day the Abyss was opened in Camp Lake, Wisconsin—it was a day Jon and Kiersten would never forget. The fear and loss they felt never left them and served to increase the human emotions each acquired. Emotions enhanced with Guardian essences and bound spiritually forever.

His excitement at traveling to Earth in the service of an Esprit de corps soon turned to discontent. Unwanted fear darted through him when he realized where his Esprit de corps would take him. Jon's mission began in Silver Lake where he had to aid his reckless Esprit de corps.

The village brought back many painful memories for Jon. Here a lifetime of happiness faded from his son, stolen by a cruel fate. Stolen by one so evil Jon cringed at its thought. He knew Markian and Dinah had perished in Deimos for their role in the destruction of Earth and for opening the Abyss. For some reason, their punishments didn't bring him comfort.

Although Mateo had been brought to justice for his part in the plane crash that took Tori's life and the other innocent victims—Jon questioned his true involvement. When Jon went back to the crash site to look for the hidden Scroll of Deuel, he sensed the essence of a Guardian. Several times during the trial, Jon questioned if Mateo actually was the evil presence on board the plane. Mateo had no clear recollections of any of the events that Markian coerced him into performing. Nonetheless, he held the position of Great Elder, and shouldn't have allowed himself to be compromised. The evidence against him was strong, and Jon's suspicions were not enough to build a case in his defense. Mateo knew Markian had acted irrationally, and his duty was to bring him to trial before Markian prevailed. Mateo's choice to wait and observe

Markian's behavior for his own benefit cost him his life in the end.

For Jon to act on his instinct and search out the truth, indeed benefited him nothing. His conscience pressed for him to investigate further, except his love for his son diminished his will. Jon witnessed the unnecessary emotions that plagued his son. To allow them to surface once more in an investigation that would have no bearing for him personally seemed to be immoral.

It had been no more than a few human months since the great battle. The time passed unannounced to the residents of Silver Lake, but too slowly for this Guardian. Brendon Franks was an actor on location in the small village making a movie. He preferred to do his own stunts and often got careless. Jon had to keep him safe until he fulfilled his destiny. In thirty years, Brendon Franks would become the next President of the United States. One who would be responsible for preventing World War III before it began.

This service guaranteed Jon a substantial amount of time on Earth. He didn't mean to revisit the dreadful street, but how could he not? The sign called to him as if it were a beacon in the night. He stared at the piece of ground where he lost his essence saving his wife from the wrath of Azazel. The place his son's life would change forever. It was here on South First Street, the Chosen One would begin a new life to benefit his people. A life that wouldn't make him complete. A life he would sooner give up than continue living.

Jon thought this would be another usual human day, and then his essence alerted him to a young woman riding her bike. She coasted rapidly down the hill trying to free her pant leg that had become tangled in the bike chain. She was approaching the bottom of the hill on County

Highway SA and couldn't stop. It was not a large hill, but Silver Lake Road below was busy. If she avoided the oncoming traffic then she would collide head-on into a metal road barrier designed to stop a moving vehicle. This meant certain death for the young woman.

Jon saw the girl's distress and willed her bike to stop. She lost her balance and crashed into the path of an oncoming car. Jon maneuvered the car so it avoided hitting her. Then he rushed to her side transforming his essence into the image of a human before he reached her. Every fiber of his being shook in disbelief as the situation affected him intensely. Jon stood surprised not believing whom he had saved.

"Here," Jon called out to her, "let me help you."

He knelt down pretending to adjust the chain so her pant leg would be released. He noticed the girl's right hand and elbow were bleeding. It didn't seem to faze her—she was just grateful for the help.

"I am so glad you stopped to help me. With the filming of the movie this place has been so busy. I thought for sure that the car was going to hit me."

"That is exactly what I thought. Are you okay?"

She looked down at her arm feeling her elbow tingling. "It seems my arm is a little banged up. But I am fine."

"Forgive me, miss, for staring, except you look very familiar. Are you with the movie production?"

"No, perhaps you have seen me around Silver Lake?"

"Perhaps, may I ask you your name?"

"Oh, sure," she said happily, "my name is Raina."

Jon's essence cringed. How could this be? The Sentinel assured Josiah of her safety. He and his son believed she would never return to Silver Lake. There was too much danger for her here, and they assumed the Sentinel would have hidden Raina away in some other country for her protection. Yet, now she stood before Jon strangling his essence.

Josiah was in his study preparing for a court session when he sensed his father's great concern. Immediately Josiah left Sol and came to assist his father on Earth. Josiah materialized a few blocks away from where his father was, mimicking a *familiar* human appearance. Cautiously he ran to his father's aid not knowing what he would find. The moment was so powerful, and his human lungs couldn't breathe. His human eyes fixed intently upon Raina sending a jolt of pain through his body. A large lump appeared burning his throat, and his heart began to race uncontrollably.

Jon felt the anxiety maturing inside of his son. It was almost more than he could take. There in front of his son, stood a ghost from Josiah's past.

"Raina—this is my son, Josiah."

"Hello," she said, and then smiled. "It's so nice to meet you."

"Thank ... you," Josiah managed to say with slurred words. "I am glad to have this chance to meet you—as well."

Once again, this human held him powerless to look away. His desire to reach out and embrace her consumed him like fire. The urge to touch her cheek, as he had done so many times before, overwhelmed his essence. Without his permission, his hand raised toward Raina's face. He pulled his hand back, pretending to adjust his shirtsleeve. His fingers were so close he almost felt the warmth of her body.

Raina didn't know who Josiah was or what they once meant to each other. She couldn't possibly understand what emotions or memories were flowing through his mind. If he were to act on any part of his desire, it wouldn't be fair. What they shared belonged to another lifetime. A life the Sentinel made clear no longer existed.

Josiah's face caught Raina's immediate attention. She stood there looking intensely at him almost mesmerized by his features. There was something familiar about Josiah's eyes. Raina had recognized them from a life she didn't remember. It was unclear to her just who she was looking at, but her stare was not missed. It was more than Josiah could take in.

There before him were the blue eyes that once held his gaze, except the meaning and their life together were gone from them. This Raina was not the girl who once loved him. She was not the one he was destined to spend his life with on Earth. That girl died four months ago in Lake Michigan. At least that is what Josiah told himself. It was easier to think of Raina as dead than to know she was in reach and yet untouchable. Was this meeting now an accident? Surely, the Sentinel would make sure they never met again.

Jon had crossed her path accidentally while assisting his Esprit de corps. It was once written in another era that a Guardian should never interfere with one who was not an Esprit de corps. Their belief behind the law was because human lives were important only when one's destiny was assured for all humanity. Therefore, acting on a cause of other than the need for an Esprit de corps' safety was prohibited. Then on that heart-wrenching day for Josiah, the Sentinel had instructed all Guardians to assist any who were in need.

"How do you like living here in Silver Lake?" she asked, trying to be friendly.

"Oh ... I have never lived in a village like this before." Josiah struggled, breathing in deeply as he tried to find the words to speak. "The scenery and the people are so different here."

"Well, I hope you like it. I have lived here all my life. My parents were raised here in Silver Lake, too. You'll have to meet them some time. My dad is really cool. He's a doctor and thinks he is a comedian. My mother is everyone's best friend. Sometimes" —she laughed, displaying some of her father's humor— "I think she favors my friends more than me."

Josiah sighed softly, still forcing his perfect expression. "I cannot wait to meet them."

"Yes, perhaps another time soon," Jon interrupted, as he brushed the dirt from his pants. "We must finish packing first. We have to get back to our home in ... Colorado."

"You're moving away?" Raina asked hesitantly.

"Yes, with my employment Josiah and I travel a lot. Our stay here has been temporary."

"I guess that's why I have never seen you before today. Where did you go to school?"

"It is much easier for Josiah to be home schooled," Jon interrupted again, wanting to spare Josiah his pain. Josiah nodded his head ignoring the fact that his human heart was breaking.

Raina smiled bringing her cheekbones to meet her eyes. It was one of Josiah's favorite features about her face. "Well, thank you again for fixing my bike chain. The walk around the lake would have been a very long one. With this heat I'm sure I would have gotten dehydrated."

"Anytime," Jon said. He stood in awe examining this ghost before him. "Let us go now, Josiah," he insisted. Then putting his hand on Josiah's shoulder he urged him to leave. Jon knew how difficult this must be on him. Jon's own essence burned from the intensity of the moment. He couldn't possibly imagine how it was affecting his son.

"Well, I hope you have a safe a trip back home," she said. Then bidding them farewell Raina got on her bike and started to leave.

Josiah remained silent staring off into the street as Raina rode out of sight. He sensed the comfort his father was trying to offer through the hand that never left his shoulder.

John tried to assure him gently. "She is safe now, Josiah."

"How can this be? The Sentinel said she would be safe forever. There is no safety for her on Earth," Josiah blurted out angrily. "Why is she here and this place of all places to be?"

"Josiah, you heard the Sentinel's words. The life of her parents has been restored. She is healthy and happy. Any danger posed to her I just stopped. Your meeting was coincidental. Make no more about it, Josiah. I feel your human pain and confusion. You must put this past you."

"Past me! How can you suggest such a thing?" he shouted, feeling the pit of his stomach wrenching. "I have seen the only one I ever loved before me—alive."

"Yes, she is alive ... and in her world. Raina lives a normal life without the dangers your presence presented."

Josiah felt his anger burn once again because of his father's ignorance. "Dangers—do you forget it is I who kept her safe until the Sentinel was to emerge? Do you so easily forget what I went through, what I suffered to agree to let her go? I had a choice, and the one I made in the Abilene Chamber has haunted me ever since. I regret that I did not allow human selfishness to rule my judgment. All I have gotten for my trouble is pain. Now you dare tell me I caused her dangers!"

"Son ... you know that is not what I meant. Perhaps you should return to Sol. Your human side is taking over, and it is leading you astray."

"Leading me astray!" he shouted, clenching his fist tightly. "The only thing affecting me is the absence of Raina. Do you not understand that she was ... is my whole life? Without her, I am nothing."

Jon stepped closer to his son. Before his very eyes, he watched their Leader begin to crumble from the tormenting human emotions that intertwined with his essence.

4.

SILVER LAKE

Earth Realm—two years after Earth's re-birth

"1920s.... Things were so different back then. Our town was small, and the folks were very friendly. We stuck together, and folks were there for one another. Not like it is in that big city of yours, in California." Netamae grinned.

She had lived in Silver Lake all of her life. She called this village her home and never desired to leave. As the world evolved around her and her community, Netamae took pleasure in the simple things in life. She had so much and never asked for more than she needed.

Her husband Enoch took her to be his wife when she was seventeen. Although young in years, Netamae had great wisdom and a heart of peace. Until Enoch had moved into her parents' boarding home, she was promised in marriage to another. His appearance changed everything.

Enoch worked hard at the icehouse, taking on the status of foreman. He lived right and treated everyone fairly. In his mind, the world offered more than he could obtain or deserved.

"Silver Lake," she continued, "was a proud community, and it still is now. Oh, sure times changed, and business left, but we had each other. Folks thought when the icehouse closed our town would fall apart, but the railroad kept bringing us more excitement. Many new folks arrived from all over the world to begin a new life here. Just like the day, a very special couple arrived on the train. The day I met Clement and Naomi Wood changed my life forever."

"Grandma, why were the two of them so special? What happened to make you believe that?"

"Why, they gave me a special gift." Netamae turned to look at an old faded portrait on the table next to the porch door. Her smile widened, enhancing her velvety gray eyes. "I didn't know it when Naomi stepped off the train, but she was pregnant. When I found out, I was glad they had set up board at my parents' rooming house. Now your grandfather also boarded with my family. Oh, my how he was special. He and I became very good friends. Your great-grandfather was nice, too. Such a sweet young man he was. My parents pledged me to another, but that didn't matter. Your granddad caught my eye." Netamae gently cleared her throat. She continued, but her voice still sounded raspy from her old age. "After a couple of months, Clement had finished a small log cabin by the lake. He wanted to be close to the icehouse and to home, for when it came time for Naomi to deliver. The harvest was already completed so the whole town came out to help. I especially appreciated all your grandfather did to help them. Well, the weeks came and went, and then finally the joyous day arrived." Netamae sighed softly. Then her smile faded from her face. "Sadly, their lives changed for the worse."

"What happened to them?" her great-granddaughter asked. Her curiosity grew with every second that passed.

"I felt so sorry when I heard about the tragedy. Clement was working with your grandfather up at the old icehouse just a few weeks before Christmas. Naomi had weathered the cold with little Rebekah to bring Clement some lunch. She always took his fancy; you know how it is with young love." She winked, patting her great-granddaughter's hand. "Well, he was so excited at seeing her that he got careless. Clement lost his footing, and slipped between the dock and the train," Netamae said. Then she paused to look up at the cloud-filled sky. Her expression changed slightly, but she remained in control.

"Oh, no," her great-granddaughter gasped.

"Before he could be pulled from out of the way the train jerked as a car from behind was being loaded. Oh ... his poor wife. Naomi just about died right there. The site of her mangled husband was too much for her to take. She handed her child to Mr. Krause, who was another icehouse foreman, and walked away in a sure daze. Your granddad went chasing after her to make sure that she and little Rebekah got home safely. After that, the women of the town checked in on her endlessly over the next few days. My parents even tried to get her to move back into the boarding house until winter had past—but the poor child refused my parents' offer.

"There was no closure to Clement's death because she couldn't bury him. The ground was too frozen to dig his grave, so he had to be held over until spring. His body was stored away in the cellar of the icehouse. What a dreadful thing it was. Naomi had nothing to do, but to stare at that building day after day—right out her own living room window. She certainly wasn't the same anymore either. Folks said that she had sunk into a great depression, being a new mother and all.

"After Naomi missed church the following Sunday morning, the Reverend went down to the cabin to see her. He came back from the cabin white as a ghost, holding the child in his arms. He could barely speak to anyone in the church. He just mumbled incoherently about Angels. After that, no one saw Naomi again. The Reverend contacted the child welfare services, and they came and took the baby to an orphanage in Chicago. I cried so hard because Naomi was my best friend, and I had lost them all."

"Oh, Grandma Mae—that is terrible," her great-granddaughter exclaimed, wiping the sweat from her brow.

Netamae looked back at the faded picture again. It had been eighty-four years since the accident, although her memories were like yesterday. "It is, my child, except look at what your grandfather and I received because of that tragedy. He loved me something awful, but hid it from me at first because he knew of my parents' wishes. However, after the accident, I had seen his love come out so strongly when he consoled me. I remember it so clearly. His embrace felt so tender, and his words were very comforting. I could have stayed in the shelter of his arms forever.

"I didn't know at first, but your grandfather had petitioned to be young Rebekah's guardian because he was going to ask me to be his wife. He told the judge that since he was Clement's best friend, it was best he should raise the child. His Christmas gift to me was his hand in marriage."

"Oh, Grandma, I didn't know you were married on Christmas day. You've never said anything at our family gatherings."

"It didn't matter to us. The wedding ceremony was nothing elaborate besides, who needed that. We took a fancy to one another, but we both agreed little Rebekah needed our care. My parents had hoped for me to say no to Enoch, but for some reason, they changed their minds and backed us all the way. So, on Christmas morning, 1926, I became Mrs. Enoch Christian." Netamae smiled, patting her great-granddaughter's hand.

Then she poured her a glass of cold tea from the tray. With a shaky hand, she held the glass out to her great-granddaughter. Fatigued from the afternoon heat, she closed her eyes then leaned back into her rocking chair. Enoch came out to the porch at that moment giving his pride and joy a peck on her cheek. Netamae kissed him back, still mesmerized by the attraction they held for one another after all of the years they spent together.

"Your grandfather was so happy when the state car came down the road. He just about broke his neck running down the stairs. He hollered so loud, he darn near couldn't speak for a week."

Enoch chuckled. "I believe it was almost two, but look at what I had. God gave me the world's two loveliest ladies to share in my life together."

Netamae smiled again, with the same poise of her lips that forced Enoch's heart to beat for nearly ninety years.

"Oh, you stop that now, Enoch, you are just being silly," she said. Then blushing slightly she continued her story. "Anyway, from inside the car the county nurse crawled from out of the front seat. She was holding a white bundle of linen in her arms. It wasn't until I heard a whimper that I realized what she held in her hands. Three weeks after the accident I was holding Rebekah in my arms."

"Grandma Rebekah," the young woman whispered amazed.

"Yes, honey. We brought your grandmother into my house and received the world's greatest blessings. Oh, how I cried when I held her. She made our life complete. Enoch and I kept her birth given name as an honor to her parents. We felt it right to carry on the dream they had started."

Enoch's body stiffened from nervousness at that moment—he knew the words Netamae was thinking. She had told the story only a few times, and each time, he acted the same.

"Well, when spring came we decided to have a service to put Clement's body to rest. When the men went into the cellar to bring up poor Clement—he wasn't there anymore. No one knows what happened to his body. Some believed that Naomi mustered up enough strength and carried his body away. Others swore they had seen her and Clement walking in the woods a few days after he had died. Ghosts they said—waiting and watching—to be sure that little Rebekah was cared for properly. Oh ... what foolishness some folk's minds were playing on them." She laughed, attempting to make her next words seem less severe than they really were. If she pretended as if she didn't believe in her words, then it would make them untrue.

"I hate to admit it myself, but once, when your grandmother Rebekah was about four years old, I awoke in the middle of the night to find her rocking in her rocking chair. She was just sitting there carrying on a one-sided conversation. I almost thought for one moment that I saw Naomi sitting right next to her. A little boy who looked just like Rebekah sat opposite of her on the floor. I'll never forget the smile on his face as he stared at little Rebekah. I opened my mouth to speak, but no words came out. Instantly, the woman and the boy were gone." Netamae cast her eyes to the floor and paused for a moment.

Enoch wondered what Netamae thought about each time she recalled that summer night so long ago. His curiosity was strong, but his will to obey stronger. He forced a smile to his lips to remain in his charade. In truth or falsehood, it was his destiny.

Netamae looked back to her great-granddaughter and sighed. "So ... isn't this the most foolish thing that you have ever heard someone say?"

Her great-granddaughter said nothing. Her half grin sufficed as a response.

"Well," Netamea continued, "in the spring the body of a woman was found at the bottom of Silver Lake. The tattered remains of the woman's dress resembled the dress Naomi wore the day Clement died. Folks had many stories going around about the dead woman being Naomi."

"Wow, Grandma Mae, that brings shivers to my spine."

"Do not dwell on it too much. God works in mysterious ways. Besides, if I wouldn't have known your grandmother Rebekah, I wouldn't know your mother. You would have never been born ... and we wouldn't be sitting here now reminiscing."

"Grandma, it all seems like a story book," her great-granddaughter said. Then leaning forward she rested her head on her hands. She pretended to be searching for a comfortable position, but her great-grandfather knew differently. He didn't miss the twitching of her hands, and he knew her flushed complexion was from more than the hot sun.

"A story book ... well that's what life should be. Your grandfather and I have been a record testimony to prove it. We have spent the last eighty-four years together completely in love."

"I'm just amazed at what you two share. How did you two do it, Grandpa? How is it that you and Grandma could be married for so long?" she asked, smiling at him curiously.

Enoch cleared his throat smiling triumphantly. The words he spoke flowed with the hum of a melody, covering his concern for his great-granddaughter's health.

"From the first day I looked upon your grandmother at the train station; I fell in love with her. Through the good times and the bad times, we stayed strong and faithful to one another. There is nothing that life could have thrown at us to make our faith waver.

"I will never forget that day. Oh, how she was spouting off at the mouth to the conductor. A group of orphans came through on the train. Their parents had all died in a mining accident at a camp out west. The children were en route to Chicago, where they were to be placed at the orphanage there. The rail car was a mess, and the children were all hungry. They had not bathed in days, and there was no light in the rail car to see by. There were not enough blankets to keep the children warm at night and no fresh water for them to drink.

"Before your grandmother was done with that poor conductor, the train was delayed a whole day. She petitioned for the town's folk to provide a bath, food, clothing, and blankets for the children. I knew from that day forward, your grandmother was meant to be a mother-type figure."

"It is love child, pure love," Netamae said, fixing her eyes upon her soul mate. "From the moment I saw the look in your granddad's eyes, I knew he was mine. I'll never forget the striking green glare of his eyes when he smiled at me. Heck, it is a surprise I saw them at all, through that shaggy brown hair of his. Would you believe that a million men beg to keep their hair at fifty? And your great-grandfather has a full head at one hundred and three."

Netamae's great-granddaughter chuckled at her words. How good it was to be in the company of her great-grandparents. Their presence seemed to make her anxiety fade—dissipating the chronic headaches that hindered so many days of her youth.

"Grandma, is that when you and grandpa started the home?"

"Yes, child. Well, it was far from what it is now. My parents went out east and gave us the big boarding house. We hired a few good people and took in about thirty children. Of course, with time things changed, and politics took over. However, I finished what I started out to do. The foster care program gives so many children new hope."

Enoch grasped Netamae's hand and smiled. "You look so tired, honey. You should be getting some rest."

"Yes, Enoch, it is a might bit warm, and what a long day it has been. I think I'll be lying down for a little while." Netamae reached over to hug her great-granddaughter. "Now run along, child. I am sure you have some packing to finish." Then waving her hands in the air, Neteamae gestured toward her great-granddaughter's car.

"I do," she said, tucking her golden curls behind her ear. Then leaning forward, she kissed her great-grandmother on the cheek. "I'll catch you later. I love you both very much." Smiling she embraced them with a hug full of compassion and peace.

"Oh, honey," her great-grandfather spoke, with words that flowed like silk in the wind, "we love you, too. Now you listen to your parents and to your heart."

"I will, Grandpa, don't worry."

"Now listen to me, child. You will face many difficulties in your life. To survive them you must do what you know is right before the Creator. Let no one stand in your way. Remain firm in your course, and do not waver. Life is too short, child. Live your life to the fullest, always remembering to serve those who are in need. Remember, child, no sacrifice for humanity is too great. Do you understand this?"

She smiled, widening her powdered blue eyes. "Yes, Grandpa, I understand. I will. I promise you both," she said, kissing the two of them goodbye again. Her curls bounced as she trotted down the porch steps.

"Oh, wait, child," her great-grandfather called after her. "Your grandmother and I want to give you something."

"Oh, that's right." Her great-grandmother laughed. "I sure would have felt silly later, dear."

His great-granddaughter returned curiously, taking her place beside her great-grandmother. Enoch opened up the screen door and went inside the parlor. Carefully, he opened the right drawer of the bureau reaching to put his hand inside it. He retrieved a silver heart shaped box with squiggly lines etched upon it. He opened the lid, listening as the sound from within the box filled the tiny room. It was a beautiful song too low for any human to hear.

Inside the silver box was an engraved locket. The sunflower forged upon it was made with love and determination. Enoch examined it once more. He recalled the steps he took and the choices he made to retrieve the forgotten locket. Then he grinned envisioning the one who held the seeds that formed this trinket of love. Sadly, he wiped away the drop of water that rolled down his cheek.

Enoch returned to the porch seconds later, carrying the shining silver jewelry box. His deep green eyes widened as he held out their gift. With a smile, he opened the box and handed it to his great-granddaughter. Inside the jewelry box, resting on shimmering red cloth was a Black Hills gold locket.

"Here dear, we wanted you to have this."

"Oh ... it's so beautiful. Please, I can't take this. It must have cost you a fortune."

Enoch frowned. "Do not dwell on material prices. Dwell on the thought behind the gift instead. We are so proud of you."

"Thank you so much, Grandpa, and Grandma. I just love it; the floral engraving is so detailed. Where did you ever get such a remarkable locket?"

"Open it, child." Netamae insisted smiling.

She clutched the locket gently within her fingers, gracefully snapping it open. Her eyes formed tears as she focused on what was delicately displayed in each oval framed slot.

Inside the tiny locket, the young woman found a picture of her great-grandparents on the left side of the frame. Her grandparents, Rebekah and Isaiah, were on the right side. She flipped the hinged frame over to her left and found another picture. That picture was one of their great-granddaughter. She was younger posing with her mother and father. On the right side of the picture frame, the window remained empty. She rubbed her finger across the blank window, and Enoch's eyes went wide.

"I am sorry, child, about the locket, it has one small defect."

"No, don't say that—it's beautiful, Grandpa."

"No, child, it seems to be broken. The right window appears to be welded shut. We could not put any pictures in it, but we just knew it was right for you, so we bought it anyway."

"I don't care about the last frame. It has the most important pictures inside of it already. Where did you ever get them?"

"Your grandfather found a shop in town that shrunk the ones we had. The man sized them perfectly."

"Oh, he did a wonderful job. I just love this, you two. It's really great," she said, fastening the chain around her thin neck.

"I am glad you adore it so much, child," her great-grandmother whispered softly.

"Yes, I do. I'll never take it off. I will always cherish this. Thank you both."

"We know, child," Enoch said, patting her shoulder. "Now run along. I know you have better things to do than hang around with a bunch of folks older than time itself."

With that, she hugged them both one more time and then headed toward her car. After waving goodbye, she drove away twirling the locket in her fingers. The box continued to play the melody filling her car with peace. She loved her great-grandparents dearly. Enoch and Netamae had been an important part of her life. When her grandparents Rebekah and Isaiah suddenly moved to Michigan several years ago, Raina missed them so much. It was good for her to have her great-grandparents so near to ease the burden.

Enoch sat down in the rocking chair proudly next to his wife. With a smile, he hummed their special melody taking his bride's hand into his. Gracefully, he held the hand of the only woman who could keep him on Earth. Together, they both closed their eyes feeling the love of a lifetime flow through their touch. Enoch left his human mimicked life for the outer realms of Heaven that day, never to return to Earth. He vowed an eternity alone when he bonded with Netamae and now her soul found its rightful place in Heaven.

5.
ESPÉRER

Guardian Realm—two years after Earth's re-birth

"Josiah, my brother, and my friend," Jaleel had announced, as he knocked firmly on the door of Josiah's study. "Are you up for a visit?" he asked, as he glided through the doorway.

"Of course I am, Jaleel. Please come in and join me," Josiah said. He stood up setting the binder that he was holding down onto his desk. He could never refuse the visit of his dear friend.

Jaleel and he were united in a bond of friendship since their essences were willed into existence by their parents. They called one another brother, confirming that their camaraderie went much deeper than the words. The camaraderie they shared strengthened as the natural forces around them evolved. The aging process means nothing to the Guardian entities. Their celestial bodies are designed in such a way that the universe's molecules and their existences work together. They constantly absorb the universe around them adapting to their surroundings. This benefits their needs and those of their Esprit de corps.

Although the death of a Guardian is rare, it is expected. The molecules and power that produces life for Guardians, eventually diminishes through the forces under Heaven. For Guardians, death is viewed as a natural event. There are no emotions or tears linked to their deaths. This is not the case for the other life forms that the Creator calls His children. For many death seems unfair, cheating the entities of their life's work. The emotions that develop from death became very strong. Some entities cannot bear living through grief and it destroys their lives. This is not what the Creator wants for His children. However, in the interest of free will, He stands by patiently waiting to aid them when they asked.

"Please, make yourself comfortable," Josiah said, motioning to the chair in front of his desk. Then he sat down himself.

"I must say, Josiah," Jaleel began to say, as he took Josiah's offer to sit onto the chair, "that you are looking a little 'blue'." He laughed, trying to show his friend and Leader how mastered he had become in human dialogue.

"No, Jaleel, I am not 'blue'. I think the color black describes me best."

"Black?" Jaleel questioned. "I must have picked up some of the humans' confusion along the way. I am sure I learned that the phrase 'blue' meant 'up in the dumps'."

"It is 'down in the dumps', Jaleel, and outside of that you are correct. The phrase is 'blue'."

"Then, why did you say you were black?"

"Because black is a gloomy endless color with no honor or intriguing values surrounding it."

"If the color black is so miserable, why do you compare that color to yourself?"

"Jaleel," Josiah retorted, "I have held my seat on the

Council of the Twelve since Earth's rebirth. I serve our people with saddened honor and regret—that I am not even sure I can hide. My election to this position has come not without a price. The cost for this position is too great to give me any peace—or reason to rejoice. There is nothing in this new life of mine that brings me comfort."

"How can this be, Josiah? You have wisely overseen our people and in a just manner. The respect given to you is immeasurable."

"Jaleel, my essence has improved in strength and wisdom—just as the Sentinel had promised. Her predictions are correct concerning the acceptance of our people; however, she is wrong on the other matter."

"What do you mean, Josiah?"

Josiah moaned leaning forward in his chair. "Jaleel, since the day I took my seat on the Council, I have done as the Sentinel has instructed me to. I know that our people look to me as a strong Leader. Our people have followed my words obediently without question and without doubt. We as a whole community have worked to revise our laws—so that these new laws benefit all of humanity. Thus, they ensure the Creator's desires are completely fulfilled for all entities."

"Do you find an issue with the course of past events, Josiah?" Jaleel asked, still dense to the emotions that plagued Josiah.

"Do you even feel a need to ask me that question? Jaleel, what do you think I do in this study with my *free* time?"

"I beg your pardon, Head Elder. I assumed you spent your time developing new ways to assist our Esprit de corps in communicating with each other. I thought you were working with the other Elders—to enhance those powers that were bestowed upon you by the Sentinel. Perhaps, even creating links of communication with the entities the

Creator calls His children."

With guidance from the other Elders, Josiah learned he had developed many more talents than he thought he possessed. He believed it was the Scroll of Deuel that imprinted the powers upon him. However, Elder Mataya had assured him that they were always his talents. Devine powers ... held back for the esteem in correlation with the Creator's plan. A constant reminder of the life he would never live again.

"No, you are wrong," Josiah corrected. "Jaleel, I can take no joy, but only sorrow in developing my talents as you have proposed. I function just doing what my essence tells me is right for our people. I have learned to forsake my desires, Jaleel, for those of the outer realms of Heaven—"

"You will never let this go will you, Josiah?" Jaleel interjected, surprised at his friend's resistance to his new life.

"Let what go, Jaleel?"

"Earth ... and that girl ... Josiah, let them go. Will you not accept what our world has to offer you here? The Creator has granted us so much."

"Is that all she is to you now, Jaleel? Is she just some human female without a purpose or—"

"Josiah—do not put words in my mouth," he interrupted again. "I know what you believe existed between the two of you. Do you not remember that I fought for you, and for her? Do you forget what role I played on Earth to watch over her in your absence?"

"No." Josiah stood up, and then walked around his desk to stand in front of his friend. "No, I do not forget. I owe you my life in exchange for hers. The care and kindness you gave her can never be repaid by me."

"Josiah, I ask for no repayment. I acted as I saw fit in allegiance to you, my friend. What I did at that moment, I would gladly do again. However, it is time to let go. It has been two human years. Move on, Josiah, and stop torturing yourself over what you cannot change."

"So, you will use her human timelines to remind me of what I no longer have?" Josiah retorted.

"Yes, I do, if it is the only thing that will make you see what you are doing to yourself," Jaleel replied, crossing his arms.

Josiah opened his mouth to speak, but choose not to. As much as he hated to admit it, Jaleel was correct. Then giving in to the sense of leadership he so carefully practiced, Josiah changed the conversation. He had learned this technique well since his appointed role to the Council.

"Jaleel, our friendship has remained strong even after our duties have taken us along different paths. I value your dedication and I know that without your friendship ... I would be lost."

Jaleel laughed. "We spend much of our time together recounting our youth. I do value you as well. So, as long as we are being open, do you grow tired of my ramblings about my mission to the Prometheus Universe?"

Jaleel recruited the assistance of Yakira to help save Josiah. What began as a rescue mission turned into a unique situation. It developed rapidly involving more than the circumstances of Josiah's safety. She later counseled Jaleel to assist with the discernment of his powers. In the midst of it all, he had learned a great deal about himself from Elder Yakira.

Josiah knew Jaleel's real purpose for their talks was his infatuation with Yakira. The connection between the two of them formed immediately. She found herself unexpectedly attracted to Jaleel also. Yakira couldn't ascertain what caused the fascination that consumed her mind. Perhaps it was because she could feel his virtue and strength of will to save his dear friend. The driving force behind his determination was met with unanticipated emotions buried deep inside of Yakira's mind.

The day their minds linked had changed each other's lives more than either one could possibly understand. The Great Elder was destined to live isolated from others for the sole purpose of retaining her mental purity and powers of guidance. Jaleel had consumed so many of her thoughts that day. His whole presence incapacitated the mind she worked all of her life to develop.

Her twin brother Yakir sensed the impact Jaleel had upon her. Yakir was concerned that he would never be able to break their link and bring her back to reality. What neither of them knew was that this connection formed a bond between Yakira and Jaleel. A bond that was strong enough to change their destinies forever.

A love affair between the two of them would be as welcomed as the one Josiah once shared with Raina. The attraction that day became unbearable, drawing the two of them together in secret meetings. Jaleel now understood how powerful love can be, and what it truly meant to exist filled with unanswered hope.

Josiah chuckled, shifting his weight against the desk. "I could never grow tired of your *ramblings*, as you call them. You make my days interesting with the risks you are willing to take. Therefore, if you are up to more risks, this evening we shall meet in the Great Hall. There I will allow you the opportunity to try and win back your title as chess champion."

"Allow me the opportunity you say," Jaleel said. Then he laughed to himself as he stood up. "The last time we played a game, Josiah. I do believe you concocted some story of galaxy obliteration to distract me for an unfair advantage. That, Josiah, is the single reason you won."

"Jaleel, your mind causes you to remember what has not really happened. Is this a scheme of yours to diminish your guilt of loss?"

"Guilt, Josiah, is for humans. I am a Guardian and I live on determination and truth."

"Is that so? This is what you believe then?"

"No, Josiah. It is not what I believe, but what I know."

"What you know ... then tell me if you will win tonight's game?"

"You, Josiah, will have to wait and see for yourself." Jaleel laughed again, and then he darted out the chamber door. "At the turn of Sol, I will be there waiting," he called back, his voice echoing through the hall. "So, do not be late!"

Josiah smiled, and then leaned back into his seat. His study presented itself distinguishably decorated in the fine arts of many cultures. The walls were lined with many shelves containing thousands of books, much like the ones in the Great Library.

Displayed on his desk, rested a special novel bound in leather and trimmed in gold. On the cover, a dazzling sunflower laid delicately etched and painted in an array of yellow blends. The golden-tones shone brighter than Sol itself. The words inside the book contained a beautiful narrative about an impossible love story. It took his essence just a few human seconds to will the story into existence. Somehow, it didn't seem to do the story justice.

So Josiah transformed into the dark-haired boy who once played football. With a shaky human hand, he began to pen the greatest love story ever known to a Guardian. He called it "Espérer" for its title means to hope. His only hope in life was to embrace his beloved once more. He knew this hope was born out of foolishness and yet his mind encouraged what his Guardian heart would never feel. As always, he gently brushed his fingers across the leather cover, tracing the delicate etching. He allowed his mind to wander, and he dreamed of meeting her again. A thought he tried hard to dismiss for in all pretenses, she was dead.

6.
FORGOTTEN MEMORIES

Earth Realm—present-day

"The pain is supposed to fade when you hit it straight on."

At least, that is what Josiah heard his Esprit de corps lecture in Biochemistry this morning. Professor Gordon Russell, Ph.D. became distinguished for his academic research in Biotechnology. His extensive role in humanitarian aid while striving to cure disease made him a well-known icon in the medical field. His research spanned beyond Earth looking for new organisms on other planets to assist in his experiments. He lived life optimistically accepting the knowledge of divine intervention. Often his lectures would begin with a philosophical note.

Besides teaching the scientific aspects of his research, Russell taught compassion for humanity. He reminded his students daily that without compassion, research no longer has its place in their world. For if, there is no cause behind one's efforts, then they are done in vain.

Professor Russell's destiny is to discover the cure for one of humanity's deadliest diseases. It is through his study and exploration with molecular biophysics and bioengineering that a cure is to be developed.

Josiah's responsibility has been to keep him safe until the important date arrives. Josiah followed Professor Russell to the remote areas of the world in his search for the cure of cancer. He believed that using cellular engineering of organisms found in space debris and fallen meteorites could restore health. Often, Russell was met with obstacles from bureaucrats and diplomats of foreign countries. Each official claimed to have a willingness to assist, however, their true goal was to preserve the findings of their own research teams. Their *willingness* to act just ensured that their scientist could make the discovery of these living organisms and proclaim the cure in the name of their country.

Josiah spent much of his days like this one, traveling back and forth from his study on Sol to the desert. His dislike for the surrounding smog-filled cities grew daily. While the desert brought him only unpleasant reminders of a time in his life, he wished dearly to forget. Fortunately, Professor Russell was near to his discovery. This may be one of the shortest roles as a Guardian that Josiah would serve.

In years past, those on the Council didn't take charge of an Esprit de corps. Josiah believed it was a necessary task to remain in-tune for what their cause should be. Thus, offering Guardians a chance to learn and guide compassionately in complete tolerance of all entities.

However, for Josiah it helped to pass the time. Time that

seemed to move too slowly for him. Time ... no other Guardian measured and time that only mattered to humans. Sadly, he was reminded that the earth seconds, which passed him by, was time he no longer spent with Raina. The woman he pledged his life to and the Esprit de corps who he joined with forsaking his Guardian life. Josiah's unknown destiny played-out as a protector of the Sentinel. She was the one sent by the Creator, to save humanity while discreetly claiming residence in the small Village of Silver Lake, Wisconsin.

Josiah didn't find amusement in creating dancing flowerbeds as he had long ago. He didn't stop anymore at the sound of rain and admire the uniqueness of God's universe. Instead, he found himself immersed in a strict pattern such as he had during his days spent in Vienna with Beethoven. At that point in time, Beethoven's music captivated Josiah. Nothing about the cold lecture hall of Professor Russell called for his attention.

Even the strange junior who sat in back didn't intrigue him today. He felt her presence, and he knew she was special. He could feel the energy that swelled from within her, but he couldn't discern it accurately. The quiet girl never spoke to him, nor did she acknowledge Josiah. Once, in a different life, he may have sought after her and investigated her purpose. Now there was nothing that she could threaten him with or take from him. If her intentions were dishonest, and his existence grew distressed—let it be so. Perhaps, this entity would end his life, and then in peace, he could have his only *hope*. He would have his Raina and the life he lived with her on Earth.

Lost again in Russell's lecture, Josiah faded away to a time long ago. He allowed his mind to be consumed by the memory of the day he asked Raina on their first date. He recalled their first kiss, and then painfully, his last embrace. The thrill of playing human didn't inspire Josiah anymore, as there was nothing to gain from it. He was one of Russell's worst students, and unbeknownst to him, the brightest one. The clanging of the chair next to him interrupted his memory or daydreams, as he liked to call them. He supposed that it was Professor Russell attempting to wake him again, so he paid no attention. The soft whisper of the voice asking for forgiveness stole his breath.

"I am sorry. I dropped my pen, and it rolled under your seat. I did not mean to trouble you."

Josiah's human heart skipped a beat. The entity from the back of the room now stood next to him. Her friendly smile asked for his acknowledgment, but all he wanted to do now was to leave.

"Ah, no. You are not troubling me ... here." Josiah reached under the chair and picked up the pen. He handed it back to the young woman feeling her energy blaze upon his fingertips. The look in her eyes told him that, she too, felt the energy.

"May I sit here, please?" she asked, catching the angered stare of their professor.

Josiah nodded at the girl, but he said nothing in response to her question. Her vigor troubled him more now than ever. He sank further down into his chair, and tried to ignore her. This was something that was not easily obtainable for Josiah. For the first time in many years, his human curiosity got the best of him. He glanced inconspicuously as he studied the girl sitting next to him. She appeared to be as unique up close as she was from the back of the classroom. Josiah attempted to assess this suspicious entity, almost regretting not doing so before.

His essence sensed her power, but he couldn't establish her power's value or her life force. It had a familiarity about it, yet the power remained unclear to him. He believed she must have sensed his intriguing behavior, because she quickly turned her head to look at him. Her sudden stare broke his concentration. Alarmed by her actions, he tried pushing her presence from his thoughts in hopes that she wouldn't try to investigate who he was.

Josiah attempted to revisit his daydream again. If one could call it that. Guardians didn't dream, but it was something he wished he could've done a million times. Josiah longed to dream of Raina and experience endless tales with her at his side. Until today, he had not been afforded this liberty, except, this dream was not one of his pleasant imaginations. This dream drove him to the edge of insanity.

The room began to dim as the professor's voice faded away. Raina's fear ate at him. Helplessness to comfort her swarmed over Josiah, crippling his thoughts. He had to find away to free her. If Raina could just absorb his essence as she had done in Silver Lake, then her fear could subside.

"Raina, can you hear me? Are you all right?" he asked, bewildered at her frail image before him. The woman he loved sat huddled in a dark corner.

She scrutinized him with her inquiring eyes. When she saw him materialize in the dark shadows, she knew she should run, but something called to her, telling her to remain. She opened her mouth to speak, but couldn't. Josiah began to panic. What kept her from responding to him? Was she hurt? Was he too late?

He stiffened, afraid for her well-being. "Raina, answer me please. Are you all right? Please, Raina," he pleaded.

The only voice to answer him in the darkness was a wicked laugh that echoed through the cavern. Josiah crouched defensively, slamming his weight into the coarse rocks. His body shifted the loose chips and they crumbled to the ground. The aroma of mildew lingered, stinging his nose and his essence cringed at the evil that radiated in the cave.

"Who are you? What do you want from her? Let her go—she is of no use to you," he demanded, shouting from human fear.

A hoarse voice answered his plea. "What do you know of her usefulness? How dare you trespass into my realm? I reign here and will take what I please."

Josiah looked back toward Raina startled by her troubling appearance. His escalading fear for her life began stealing his rationality. Josiah knew he had the power to take her from this awful place. He had the power to save her from the evil lurking in the cave. If he reached out and grabbed her hand, he could take her to another place by using time shifts. He had done this once before when an evil entity tried to harm her in Silver Lake several years before.

He had to think, something about the darkness, and the stench clouded his human mind. Josiah knew he had to get her away from that place, except his desire to act abnormally diminished. The urgency strangely faded leaving Josiah content to remain in the musty cavern. Even the soft whimpers coming from Raina had no effect on him.

The cloaked figure crept closer, and his stench turned Raina's stomach. With shaky hands, she covered her mouth holding back her scream. Josiah reached out to take her hand to pull her from the Demon's view. As he turned his head to look for her, he tried to scream warning her to flee.

"Raina, run—"

"Mr. King, wake up," Professor Russell demanded. "This lecture hall is no place to recover from your late night drinking binges!"

Josiah looked in all directions blinking the sweat away from his eyes as he surveyed the room. Just a few seconds ago, he crouched in a darkened cavern beside the love of his life—now he found himself in the well-lit lecture hall. His last vision of Raina still terrified him. Disoriented, he grabbed his books from underneath his chair and fled the room. Each step to reach the door seemed endless as his knees wobbled. He felt the eyes of those in the lecture hall follow him almost piercing through his body. Josiah's shell was in great physical condition, therefore the panting came because of a reason other than his desire to leave so quickly.

He stood outside the room grasping the doorframe for balance. Sweat still streamed down his face, and his hands trembled. Josiah's knees weakened, and he slid along the wall collapsing to the floor.

An intense fear welled up inside of him as he realized his visions were not over. He panted harder, and then closing his eyes, he tried to will the thoughts in his head to disappear. Josiah had seen this vision once before in the Abilene Chamber, the day he received the Scroll of Deuel from the Great Elder Mataya. A day he tried hard to block from his mind, but now after his dream, the dreadful day seemed so vivid.

"No!"

Exasperated he pounded his fist onto the tile floor feeling the tiles crack beneath his knuckles. The crashing sound ricocheted loudly off the cement walls in the corridor. He drew in another useless deep breath, trying to clear his mind. Josiah couldn't allow himself to recall the thoughts that crept so painfully into his head. He began to lose the fight as a pain shot across his temple. Josiah grabbed his head and winced in agony—fighting to free his mind of the vision forcing itself to appear.

Josiah found himself bowing at the feet of the two Great Elders, Mataya and her brother Mateo. Their grace and glory shone brightly within the magnificent Abilene Chamber. Elder Mataya held a small box in her delicate hands that hummed with a pleasant melody. Elder Mateo stood next to a table that had carvings of musical notes notched deeply into the finished oak. The distinctive song of an Angels' chorus erupted from within the box that contained the Scroll of Deuel, the scroll of God's knowledge.

It was on this day, he learned he would lose his Raina. Since he was her vessel of protection, Josiah knew that she harbored the Sentinel. The Sentinel would eventually emerge to take her place, dissolving Raina's life. This would leave a lonely Josiah behind. The thought of existing alone scared him. Her life couldn't end taking away what they had become together. His selfishness boiled over into the chamber. Immediately his mind recalled Raina's birth and their relationship, reminding him only of the death of her father. He couldn't lose her even after Mataya opened his mind and showed him the future.

"There must be another way, Elder. I love her ... she is human," he pleaded. "You must be in error to speak of the things you do at this moment."

"No, Josiah. You know the truth. You have always known it deep within your essence."

"The truth is that Raina is human. She is my Esprit de corps. I am to watch over her until she has fulfilled her destiny."

"Yes, young Josiah, and her destiny is to be the Sentinel. Raina's body harbored the Sentinel and that is her true propose. Any other life, any life you propose ... shall not and cannot be."

Josiah clinched his fist, the truth that was so clear before him, remained clouded in his mind. "You are mistaken. Trust me. I am with her day and night. She has no powers, she is not a Guardian."

"Josiah, you must listen to reason. It is her destiny. She will save Earth from destruction, and when her time comes, your Raina will be gone."

"No!" He raised his fist to his chest. "Do not say that. Raina is under my protection—"

"Josiah," Mataya interrupted in a strong voice, "take my hand. If your mind has been so polluted by your human emotions ... then allow your Guardian mind to hear mine."

Obedience is the only thing that kept him from fleeing the chamber. Hesitantly, Josiah stood up and then stepped forward. He took Mataya's outstretch hand into his trembling grip. Her fingers grasped around his tightly securing her grip. Josiah pulled back slightly, but Mataya prevailed. His fingers became locked within hers as her power fused their hands together.

His mind began to wander as his thoughts mixed with Elder Mataya's mind. The urge to pull away dissolved, and a new desire emerged. Her words began to flow gently into his restless mind soothing his anxieties. All sensation of weight and control left him as his essence succumbed to the power of Mataya. His mind became one with hers as their thoughts joined, becoming one thought, and purpose.

Josiah, do you hear my voice?

Yes ... Elder.

Do you understand what is happening to you now?

No, I have never felt such an experience before.

Do not be concerned, young Josiah. I have entered your mind removing all the uncertainty that you suffer from. The residual effects of your human encounters have been dissolved. At this moment, it is just your essence and mine. Nothing in your world or hers—matters to you anymore.

He felt Mataya's calming peace move through him. It was a sensation he had not experienced in many years. Mataya offered him a peace he had unknowingly missed. A peace replaced long ago by the earthly contentment to accept the sins and darkness of a world away from his. To Josiah it was always a welcomed trade to have his Raina. However, this trade didn't come without penalty and severe consequences for Raina and him. Raina changed his priorities and his assumptions about humans. Her soothing personality and undying compassion covered his dislike for her kind. Because of Raina, he no longer despised the humans who gave too little and took too much.

Josiah, Mataya said, as her delicate voice danced in his head. *Listen to my words and understand their meaning. Raina's destiny was always to save humanity. As the Creator had Lexis search the purest minds on Earth for his wife, Lina, he also sought out the purest soul on Earth, the soul of your beloved Raina. Lexis found her in the future at the same moment of her conception. He secretly placed his daughter's essence within her to lay in wait on Earth. It was his power calling to you that spring morning—singing to you from within the child's mind. Lexis believed he had performed his final task in secrecy, except the evil one saw his intentions and plotted to destroy her.*

Josiah winced at the thought of Raina's life being in

peril. Mataya ignored his reactions and continued.

Lexis' spirit compelled you to guard her in a realm outside of ours until this day. This task you have done faithfully. If Lexis had not ceased to exist, then I know he would be pleased with your efforts. Now you must understand the events that have come to pass this day. The evil seeks to overtake the Sentinel. You are aware of this I know ... by the dangers that have fallen upon your Raina. He has come into power, and you alone can no longer guard her.

The evil one's actions will soon torment Earth until it is destroyed. The Sentinel must emerge sooner than predicted by the scroll's account. Your time with Raina is almost complete. Shortly, the Sentinel will emerge led by the Creator to stop the evil. She will grant mercy to the universes around us, saving them from the destruction of evil. When she does, the child who harbored her will be no more.

No, Josiah's mind shouted, *that cannot happen!*

Josiah, please listen to me and do not interrupt, she ordered, ignoring his protest for Raina's life. *The Sentinel, at the wish of the Creator, will guide her soul. You need to trust in the events that are to unfold, and do not interfere. The Creator has chosen a new destiny for you, Josiah. You must be patient, and obey His commands.*

Josiah heard her words, but his faulty rationality twisted them in his mind. He was neither ready to believe them nor ready to let her go. He contemplated what life would be like without her. What would happen if he stole Raina away to Callisto and lived with her there secretly? The thought of an old legend now crossed his mind. Could it be possible ... could he petition to become human and live with her, subject to a human's life?

Josiah knew the answers to all of his questions. Raina could never live without fear of the evil one, and he could never live the life of a human. Josiah knew then what obligation he had to Earth. He must guard her at all cost allowing her transformation to occur, knowing his life with her was over. Knowing ... that he would never see her again.

A soft voice interrupted his thoughts pulling Josiah back to reality.

"Are you well, do you need any help?"

Josiah's words flowed slowly, broken by his deep reparations. "What—what did you say?"

"I asked if you are well."

"Why do you ask that of me?" Josiah questioned her, still unaware of his disturbing appearance.

"Because, Josiah, you look really awful right now. Can I get you some water or something?"

Josiah shook his head trying to concentrate upon the girl before him. She stared at him waiting for his delayed response. Human impatience didn't affect her judgment. This allowed Josiah the time he needed to recover and think more clearly. What was this girl's purpose? Who was she and why was she here? If her intentions were honest, then why did she not present herself sooner instead of hiding in a human form?

"Oh," he said weakly, scurrying to get to his feet. "No, I am fine ... thank you."

"Are you sure?" she questioned, still concerned by his demeanor.

He cast his eyes down to the floor looking at his pile of books that lay near his feet. He moved his body forward slightly, desiring to lean over and grab the books with his extended arms. All of a sudden, the room began to spin, and Josiah's shell lost its balance. Unable to stop himself he fell into his petite classmate. She caught him gracefully in midair supporting Josiah's weight with ease.

"I think you had better sit down," she said, looking over her shoulder as if to gesture toward the bench along the opposite wall. "Here let me help you."

Josiah's shell was not functioning as he had willed it to perform. He couldn't control its reflexes, or command his shell to obey him. Without resistance, Josiah allowed his classmate to escort him to the bench. Fear had begun to intertwine with his confusion, celebrating at his expense. The only time his shell ever failed to follow his commands was when an evil entity held him under the water two years ago. That day Josiah almost failed to rescue Raina from the icy clutches of the Fox River—this time there were no excuses that his mind could fully comprehend.

His classmate stared at him seeming speechless and then spoke to him with an uneven tone to her voice. "Man, you look like you have seen a ghost. Are you sure you do not need to go to a hospital?"

He wiped the sweat from his forehead. "What—no thank you? I will be fine. Please, just give me a moment."

Josiah leaned forward resting his forearms on his knees. His breath began to steady itself, but his mind still raced. He couldn't process any reasons as to why he was suffering from these episodes of distress. Josiah couldn't think of anything he encountered that could have caused his shell to fail. His essence didn't conceive or sense any rationality behind the vision that disturbed him so badly.

"Sure," she said, ready to lend a hand, "but hey, listen. I am done with class for the day. If you like, I can carry your books to where ever you have to go next."

Without waiting for his reply, she walked back over by the door and pick up his books from the floor. When she stood up the stranger turned her head to face him. She smiled wide with stunning auburn eyes and said, "I promise. It is no trouble at all."

He nodded his head slightly. "Fine—actually, I am done as well. I think I will go back to my dorm to rest for awhile."

Josiah didn't need to rest; however, it was essential to discern what was affecting him. Not only did his shell suffer from this rare event, but his essence had as well. Josiah knew he had to go somewhere secluded until he was sure of what was happening to him. He had to concentrate to keep his essence contained in his shell. If his essence released against his will it would draw in the molecules around him producing a large amount of energy. This would unwillingly put everyone near him in danger. His dorm was the safest place to go. Locked inside of those walls he could shed his shell and return home where his life seemingly flourished without complications. Home was a good place for Josiah to revive himself and evaluate the situation.

"I am sure that is a good idea. Shall we?" she insisted, holding out her arm for Josiah to grab a hold of for stability.

He stood up slowly feeling the blood of his fabricated shell rush to his head. With a slight stagger, he moved his foot to take a step. Then the room began to swirl slightly and dark spots flashed before his eyes. Josiah's hesitance to continue was eased as his newfound friend guided him from Chandlers Hall.

The walk to his make-believe dorm had become too consuming upon him. The previous vision had passed leaving him terrified and distraught by the human emotions he couldn't control. He had to know more about the girl who carried his books in pure silence. She was a stranger, but her utter presence recalled a long forgotten melody to Josiah's mind. Her presence intrigued Josiah, except his shell's state became of greater concern.

The fresh air did little to help his shell recover. His solace came from the trickle of energy he imagined flowing from her grip. It was impossible for this energy to be real, yet his mind calculated the reasons for its existence. He knew she was much more than the entity from the back of his classroom. He considered the consequences of exposure against his inquisitiveness for discovery. Even though it was a great risk to pursue the truth, he had to know who she was, and why she was on Earth.

His classmate continued to hold onto Josiah as they walked through the college grounds. At times, his knees grew weak, and he stumbled relying on her far more than he would have liked to. His clumsiness never seemed to bother her; she just kept on supporting him, remaining very quiet.

The dizziness Josiah experienced had returned, plaguing his thoughts with uneasiness. This clouded his mind blocking his concentration. It seemed as if every time he questioned her identity, he appeared to grow weaker. Josiah felt sure that it was not this girl who caused his misfortune. He sensed she truly was there to help him, but if that were so, then what was the cause of the episode?

Exhausted, Josiah looked helplessly at the stairs leading up to the student housing. Disgusted with himself, Josiah sighed and stopped walking. The staircase seemed too enormous for him to conquer at this moment. Josiah realized she must have sensed his uneasiness, because she pulled him closer into her body adjusting his weight. This allowed her to guide him up the four flights of stairs easily, urging him to press onward.

The cool hall almost felt soothing to him, providing a shelter from the Sun's heat. Normally, Earth's temperature never affected him, nor did he give any thought to its effects on any human other than his Raina. Today the atmosphere around him had an emotional and physical impact that should have been irrelevant to a Guardian.

Josiah removed the key he never used from his pocket. With his shaking hand, he fumbled with the doorknob trying to insert the key into the key hole. He moaned appalled by his weakness as he dropped the key onto the floor mat in front of the door. Bewildered, he took in a deep breath and tried to bend over to pick up the key. Without any warning, he lost his balance and staggered once again. Josiah's classmate caught him in her grip and propped him against the wall. Her smooth and graceful movements amazed Josiah. His human stature was much larger than she was, and yet she seemed unaffected by this.

She smiled trying to be comforting. "Are you sure that you are okay?"

"Yes ... thank you," he said shaking his head. "I am just a little dizzy. It will pass in a moment, I am sure."

"Well, I think you need to go to the infirmary. There are many illnesses going around campus right now. Maybe the doctor can give you something to help with the dizziness."

"No—really, I am fine. I just need to lay down for a bit."

He knew this wasn't true, except he couldn't offer any other excuses for his condition. He certainly couldn't share his vision with her, for he didn't even know what was happening to him.

"All right," she answered softly, inserting the key into the locked door. The flimsy wooden door snapped open making a creaking noise. His Good Samaritan easily pushed the door completely open, making way for them to enter the room.

His dorm room was dark and cool. The curtains were drawn, and the afternoon sunlight didn't shine through. He staggered past the dusty computer desk, kicking the chair with his foot. That made him stumble sideways several times, but Josiah finally gained his balance. He made it across the room flopping himself down onto the bed. His classmate followed him stopping just past the desk.

"Here, let me get you some water to drink," she offered kindly.

Before he could respond, she was already at the sink with a glass in her hand. The running water caught his attention recalling his vision from earlier. Yes, he had heard the sound of water flowing faintly over the revolting voice of the mischievous spirit inside of the cave.

"Thank you," he said weakly. His hand trembled as he took the glass from her and he watched embarrassingly as some water splash onto the floor. He grinned angrily.

"Do not worry ... I will clean it up," she said.

Josiah nodded and then set the glass down on the nightstand. Humanly exhausted, he propped himself against the pillows. Then he lay back covering his eyes with his arm. After a moment of silence, he realized he was being rude. Sitting up to speak with her, he found his dorm empty. The only sign that she had been there was the glass sitting next to the folded kitchen towel on his nightstand. She had left discreetly, closing the door without Josiah noticing. It troubled him that he acted so oblivious to her being there.

What is wrong with me? He thought. *Why is this happening to me?*

Then he scooted off the bed and stood closing his eyes. As he released his essence into the room, Josiah emerged from his shell illuminating the room with his aura. His existence as either human or Guardian didn't come without a personal price. In one simple thought, he dematerialized from the room appearing in his study.

Josiah moved fluidly around his mahogany desk to the recliner in the corner by the window. When he caught his reflection in the oval shaped floor mirror, he stopped to admire his image. Now in his true form, no human could see him. A glow at best is all that could be seen, if the human's eyesight were keen enough. Yet, here he stood in the same image as the Creator. The same image humans would see as their own reflection.

Mimicking the human body gestures that became so natural for him, Josiah kept staring at his reflection. He had indeed learned very carefully and with great precision to act human. Guardians moved with grace and without thought. Every desire of a Guardian was met with ease, existing naturally as one with their surroundings. Humans were afflicted by the immortal bodies that required their environment to help sustain them. Air to breathe and food to eat became necessary to survive. Guardians' celestial bodies required nothing to exist. They chose to enjoy the benefits the Creator developed for the worlds of other entities and accepted them in appreciation.

Josiah closed his eyes and sighed, imitating a human response. Almost floating onto the chair, he positioned himself at his desk. Josiah sighed once more from boredom and then began tapping his fingers on the mahogany wood armrest. Without meaning to, he hummed along with the taps, creating an old familiar song. When he found himself lost in the beat, he broke out into an a cappella swaying his arms into the air. It was here, in the music of her world where he felt the most content. In the time that had passed since Raina *died*, Josiah didn't allow the music to enter his heart. Tonight, the music seemed to come to Josiah without regret and sorrow.

All of a sudden, a sharp pain shot through his celestial body. Josiah jumped up from his chair as the room turned black. Instantly, he found himself in a large ballroom. The music of Beethoven played loudly throughout the room. Josiah didn't have to see Beethoven to know it was he. In his many years of watching over this famous Esprit de corps, Josiah had learned the distinct rhythm of Beethoven's body. This allowed him to imagine the notes before they were played.

He closed his eyes and allowed his essence to float with poise through the crowd. Lost in the music, he became distracted. Then without any warning, he bumped into something. This startled Josiah, because his celestial body should have fluidly moved through the object without hesitation. Josiah opened his eyes to find the single thing that could ever render his essence incapable of functioning normally.

There before him stood Raina, dressed elegantly in an eighteenth century gown. Her eyes were fixed steadily in his direction, yet he was sure in his state he was invisible. As he reached out to touch her, the room grew dark, and he fell to the floor in his study. Physical changes normal for a human to experience and against the spiritual nature of a Guardian, flowed through his body. He lay there breathing rapidly as sweat steamed down his face. His vision blurred, and a throbbing pain traveled through his temples.

Josiah's mind raced as he tried to process what was happening to him. The ballroom and the music he had witnessed before, except this time, it wasn't real. The reality of another lifetime, and the unexplainable dreams he suffered from, blended supernaturally into another realm. This realm mysteriously existed parallel with the present.

7.
DWELLER BY THE BROOK

Guardian Realm—present-day

It had been years since the young apprentice began visiting this brook. He loved to come here and listen to the melody of the birds. The warm breeze invited his senses to get lost in the sound of the water's tranquil flow. Yes, a most satisfying retreat Beck had made for himself. Here he formed a secret garden. The Creator's entire splendor existed in this place ... magnified by the emotions of humans and the discipline of a Guardian.

Beck's last sojourn brought him to this place on a mission of protection; one filled with hope for what he knew then would be humanity's fate. Beck grew strong with Guardian wisdom and strength. Even without the guidance and counsel from his peers, Beck developed unique powers. These hidden powers were as strong as those the fallen Guardian Markian harbored. However, unlike Markian, Beck kept the desires and wishes of the Creator in the forefront of his ambitions.

He literally saw visions of the past and the present. Beck dreamed dreams never experienced by a Guardian before. A simple human function Josiah wanted very badly. He believed if he could dream of his Raina, then his human heart might still beat. Dreams of course, were unnecessary in the Guardian world, and none had ever dared to imagine the possibility. None, except the young Beck.

He found at an early age, he unwillingly linked with the humans on Earth. This link pulled him into the dreams of the sleeping. In the humans' dreams, he felt their love and their fears. These dreams created endless boundaries that were not hindered by the earthly realm. These boundaries had no limits, where one's imagination controlled the actions of everything in the dream.

Josiah imagined ... remembered his life with Raina and allowed his mind to wander. In his thoughts, he corrected the bad events and continued their love story. Only, they were his thoughts and not the daydreams he believed them to be. He was not as fortunate as young Beck.

Beck created this invisible retreat in his dreams and his powers made this place real. He soon found himself to be the keeper of this realm and the guider of human tears. Within himself, he found the compassion and strength to endure the sadness and fill the brook with the Stones of Fayruz. As the years of the brook's existence advanced so had the waters of the brook.

His service to the Council of the Twelve as an apprentice to Councilman Jaleel allowed him to sit in on court sessions. The most important session he had ever participated in was the trial of Josiah. Jaleel had instructed

Beck to hide a second set of charges secretly to clear Josiah's name. Beck hid the list of charges in a valuable book he had discovered as a young Guardian. Beck found it in the floorboards of an abandoned cottage belonging to his father's past Esprit de corps. They were on the planet Elara checking on the deceased's wife. That morning the book seemed to glow through the cracks in the floor catching his attention. Beck reached under the floorboard and pulled out the book. The very feel of it within his fingers sent a tingling sensation through his hand. The cottage was to be burned down for commercial development of the countryside. He knew without any doubt that this book shouldn't perish in the flames. While he held the book, he read the title "Dweller by the Brook." The narrative told the story of one who walked beneath the layers of water collecting treasures of the lost souls.

As time passed, he removed the charges from the Library and brought them here. In the brook, the faded charges were not the only thing buried beneath the layers of calm waters. Beck also protected another item of greater importance, an item that many would give their soul to have, and no Guardian's essence could refuse.

In the beautiful forest where the Brook of Tears flowed freely, he harbored the special entity Mataya charged him to watch over at all cost. A mission she assigned him during one of her visions. She believed it to be her imagination ... a wish of what she wanted most and didn't know her actions in this world were implemented. Mataya immediately forgot the entity's presence in the brook, just as she had with her other adventures when she returned to her reality.

As with many of her visions, Mataya sought after the quest of another lifetime. She desired the comfort of hearing her brother's thoughts in her head once more.

This yearning drove her to find a way to free him and their Head Elder. Josiah deserved much more than an eternity alone. He too, desired to hear the voice of love in his mind.

She knew the crippling loneliness he felt and the burden placed upon him. It was her determination that formed a plan of peace, but its effect was devastating. In her thoughts, she went back in time to change history. Mataya wanted so badly to have the stability of her brother in her mind; she vowed to do anything necessary in order to make her desires come true.

While her superior mind tended to the matters of reality, her subconscious mind developed a strategy lost deep within her thoughts. There she carried out a secret mission of what she believed to be of hope and of human love.

Mataya's mind created many scenarios to ensure the outcome of her plan. The most certain method of execution for her was to stop Markian before he coerced her brother. It was ingenious; all she had to do was prevent Lexis from finding Raina. If he absorbed his child, then the evil wouldn't come against them at all. There would be no Sentinel birthed for Markian and his daughter to locate and destroy. Thus, Markian wouldn't need his little puppet, and Mateo's mind would remain pure.

However, that plan left no reasons for Josiah to find Raina. She would have her brother, but Raina would be lost to Josiah. Again, she subconsciously mastered another scenario. In this one, Josiah stumbled upon Raina, and her purity alone called to him. However, that wouldn't be enough to drive Josiah to forsake his ways for a human. Yet again, Raina would be lost to him.

The only strategy that her subconscious mind could carry out in which Raina and Josiah could be together—

would be to allow Lexis to find Raina undetected by the Demon before Lexis' journey began. For this to happen, Mataya would have to be sure any clues leading to Lexis' intent and the birth of his daughter Rayna remained a secret. This included diverting the Demon in the wrong direction. Her plan was to send him to another universe in a completely different time. With the clues covered by her actions, the Demon would never know the human Raina existed, and he wouldn't come to Earth searching for her.

Mataya exited the forest in awe of her surroundings. The view before her remained serene calling to her senses. By the rippling brook, a cloaked figure knelt onto the ground. His hands swayed in the water carelessly moving with the current's force. As he looked up at Mataya, she caught his green eyes. They cast a glow of reassurance, welcoming her appearance. As she approached, the figure stood up to greet her with his extended arms.

"Mataya, my sister ... I see you have concluded your journey to this place."

She smiled unsure of her surroundings. "Yes, thank you."

Beck smiled back with a slight nod of his head.

Mataya cast her eyes downward to examine the water. Her reflection magnified the brook's beauty. Truly, Mataya had never seen such translucent waters in all of her years.

"What is this water that fills the brook?" Mataya questioned, kneeling to dip her fingers into the cool water. "I can feel the pain and the joy trickle through my fingers. It reminds me of the waters that flow from the tears of the Angels after the Great War on Earth."

"What you feel are the tears of grief from the entities of many realms. The humans' tears fill this brook. When they cry out from anguish ... it is here where their tears come to rest. It is what feeds the brook ... what covers our emotions. It is this water that the Creator bathes His children's broken dreams in, draining their sorrow so they can feel renewed and at peace."

"What is the darkness that lies beneath the colored stones?" she asked hesitantly, examining the reflection of the colors dancing in the rays of Sol.

"That," he said, motioning with his hand, "is the substance of their broken dreams and their pain. The crystal-clear water's surface displays the regeneration of hope and life. The beauty of life and love swirls here for the Guardians to see."

"I do not understand why this process takes place."

"Elder Mataya, the Creator does not want His children to feel pain or the burdens of sadness. He welcomes His children to cast their cares upon Him. When His children do, the tears of their burdens flow into theses healing waters. The sorrowful repentant tears of one human wash the failures of another."

"Please, Beck, tell me why such a place would need to exist?"

"It is not to be questioned, Mataya ... just the miracle of its meaning proclaimed."

Beck glanced back toward the brook just as a mist blew over the water. It began to dance forming musical notes that hummed in a dreadful tune. Then the musical notes fell from the air fading into the brook. The mist soon dissipated, and the music stopped.

At that moment, a shimmering reflection of a silver object pierced through the water. Mataya focused on the glare curiously in awe of its magnificence. She examined the reflection's shape, recognizing it to be a heart-shaped box.

"And what is the meaning of the box that lies within the peaceful waters?"

"That, my sister, is the dwelling place for the scroll of hope."

"What is this scroll of hope you speak of?" she questioned, curiously anticipating what his answer would be.

"Come and sit, Mataya, and I shall tell you. I know you have many questions, and I have many answers."

Mataya followed Beck to a bench opposite of where they were standing. She rubbed her hand over the smooth metal, and then she proceeded to sit down on the cool stone seat that was fastened to the steel bars. Beneath her feet, the plush grass flattened making the impression of her tiny slippers in the grass. She followed the path of her steps from the brook to where she sat on the bench admiring the beautiful dark green shade of the grass. She glanced off to her left, she saw the beautiful meadow whose occupants danced in the gentle breeze. Their sway enhanced the luxurious colors of the many flowers. She had come to know the aroma the meadow offered. Mataya had sat upon this bench once before in another vision she saw. Like today, Beck returned her curiosity with reasons for more.

"The scroll of hope is known as the 'Scroll of Espérer'. Inside the scroll, many secrets are written to find happiness. If the bearer believes with their entire mind that a wish can come true, then the scroll's magic will allow their wish to come true. The scroll knows no partiality to good or evil."

Mataya shifted her eyes looking intently at Beck clearly void of understanding for what he was saying. He paused looking at the perplexed expression upon her face. He continued hoping to clarify the matter for her.

"Clearly, it is a wretched tool that plays on the lost. It makes many stray from belief in prayer. I found it one day as I entered the dream of an archeologist stationed on

Mars. He spent days trying to translate the cryptic writings. He had an overwhelming desire of greed, and in his mind he knew what happiness power would bring to him. Since the scroll gives the bearer their truest desires, I feared what his corrupt mind could do with the scroll's power. I removed the scroll one night from his possession and brought it here. I secured it inside the silver box that I fashioned after a heart. Ironically, humans associate the shape of a heart with love. Then I bound it with a magical chain and tossed it into the brook. There I have guarded it each day as I attend to the brook."

"Is it right to hold it to one and not share it with others?" Mataya asked, questioning the right of Beck's ownership.

"I can answer only by saying, is it right to leave this tool unguarded?"

Mataya didn't answer his question. She looked around, focusing on a large tree and then glanced back down at the carved bench.

"Mataya, do you recall this place?" he asked softly, with a glimmer in his eye.

"Yes, I have been here before, have I not?"

"Indeed ... however, do you remember when?"

"I am not sure ... this place is very familiar, except I do not know why. It seems natural for me to have found my way here and to speak openly with you. However, it should not be. This I know for sure."

"Mataya, I brought you here a very long time ago. You were in your study waiting for news of the Demons' war against our universe. Markian and Dinah were still at large causing massive destruction upon Earth. Elder Jon and Councilman Jaleel were on Earth searching for the Scroll of Deuel."

Mataya didn't take her eyes off Beck contemplating the meaning of this place. The day he spoke of seemed like yesterday, but in her memories there was no visit to the brook. She nodded her head slightly waiting for the cloaked Guardian to continue.

"You were by the window looking upon the meadow, when briefly you felt beside yourself. Perhaps you were somewhat at a loss for your identity?"

"Yes," she whispered, "the mist blew in through the window. It was cold, and yet I felt an odd sensation of warmth swarm over me. It was the same just now before I saw you in the clearing."

"Yes, you are correct."

"Why have you brought me here?"

His words began to flow fast, almost mesmerizing Mataya with the even tone of his voice. "You sensed the interruption in your brother's essence. He had changed somehow, and you could not clearly ascertain his new behaviors. You have a keen mind, Mataya; however, your mind flows with the same thoughts as your brother. Markian clouded his thoughts, and each time he fogged Mateo's mind, you too, were affected. Unbeknownst to you, your brother led a secret life. That life cost Mateo his own in return."

Mataya moaned at the memory. Beck was right. Her brother had destroyed his future whether willing or not.

"After the summons to the trial that you and Mateo disobeyed, I knew I had to intervene. Markian disrupted your memory as to cover the secret actions of your brother. That is why you found yourself lost to the harmony of the Scroll of Deuel. It was that moment when I brought you here."

Her eyes lit up enhancing her high cheekbones. "I remember," she whispered, "one moment the scroll was unclear. I did not hear the music filling the Abilene Chamber. My mind felt dark, and then suddenly it all became so clear. I knew what was happening and what must be done."

"Yes, Mataya, that is when you subdued your brother and linked your mind with Jon's mind. The connection allowed him to learn the significance of the scroll's meaning. He knew what course he must follow to stop Dinah. You acted righteously by binding Mateo and delivering him to the Council for punishment."

Mataya looked away. This was a very unpleasant memory for her. She loved Mateo dearly, except she knew right from wrong. Forsaking the love she had for her brother, she made the choice to bring justice to humanity.

"Together we read the scroll analyzing its meaning. The hidden secrets of the scroll were exposed. They directed you in the course of action that was needed so the Abyss' location could be found. In the writings, we discovered the Demons' weaknesses. You went throughout the realms of our universe warning our fellow Guardians. They fought vigorously and defeated the Demons. Then you sent Elders Yakir and Yakira to Earth to meet Josiah and help seal the Abyss. After you directed the Elders to act you followed the scrolls instructions and joined our fellow Guardians on Prometheus. You were there when the Sentinel emerged."

Mataya closed her eyes lost in thought. This story seemed familiar to her; however, she didn't recall the events exactly. "I remember what you say to be true ... except I do not know why I chose to bury them deep within my thoughts."

Beck moved to sit next to her. The aroma of her floral perfume swirled in his head bringing his desires to the surface. He had already acted against the nature of his conscience when he gave in to them and made his wish. He knew it was his duty to protect the future against Mataya's dreams. He had to change the damage she caused to the past timeline. That duty alone kept him from expressing his thoughts to her. Her knowledge of his feelings could be more damaging than her actions to the future he vowed to keep safe.

"Mataya, you suffered much. It is normal for you to want to forget what causes you the most pain."

"You speak as if I am a fragile human with emotional difficulties. I am not, Beck. I am a Great Elder. My mind has surpassed human emotions and intellect. No Guardian born without a twin can even comprehend the workings of my mind."

"If that were so, then how do you suppose Markian manipulated your brother so efficiently?"

She looked away speechless. Beck chided himself for speaking so openly. He knew how much his words had cost her.

"Please, Mataya, I am sorry. I did not mean to be so rough. I just meant to give you an example. Once again, I have hurt you."

"Again ... what do you mean? When did this happen?"

He sighed. "It was a long time ago in another dream that you had created during one of your episodes."

"Another dream—episodes? What are you saying? I do not dream, Beck. No Guardian dreams, you know that."

"Mataya, the loss of your brother has affected you greatly. More than you can ever know. The plans you create in your head to free your brother have come true."

"My plans—that is impossible. They are just thoughts and wishes of what I want to happen. They have no relevance."

"You are incorrect, Mataya. Your mind has indeed followed through with each plan you concocted. Your thoughts have not been your own. They have affected our universe."

"I do not believe you. What you say is impossible."

"Mataya, this realm has certainly known and carried out each plan you buried within the solitude of your mind. Those plans created an alternate universe where your desires have come true. Here in this brook lie your broken dreams and desecrated thoughts. They call out to the Creator for help."

Mataya stood up alarmed stepping away from Beck. "I do not believe you. How can you know these things to be true?"

Then briskly, she began walking toward the brook's edge in a sure panic. Beck could sense her uncertainty and knew what his honesty was doing to her. Beck stood up to follow her.

"Send me back to my study now," she demanded, breaking into a run.

Beck ran after her catching Mataya by the edge of the brook before she slipped in. He grabbed her left shoulder forcing her to turn around and face him. Her eyes met his, and she saw something there behind his green stare. Something in his eyes once again seemed familiar to her.

"Please, Mataya. You asked how I once hurt you. It was just like this. I put too much upon you, and I did not give you enough time to absorb my words."

Her trembling hands caught her attention. Guardians didn't experience fear or sorrow. Any reaction that pulsed through Mataya's body now was unthinkable. Mataya tried to ignore the human characteristics that somehow seemed to slip into her every day demeanor.

"Beck ... how is what you say this day possible?"

"I believe it is the same situation that allowed me to make this brook. A new source of power we do not yet understand courses through our essences. Surely, a power the Creator has kept from our people for His own benefit." His voice broke, and Mataya could see his uncertainty.

"A power? What kind of power do you mean?"

"Perhaps He has given us this power because He has deemed us worthy enough to know the mysteries of His world. However, Mataya ... your thoughts have begun a dangerous cascade of events. We must change them now, for humanity is at risk once more."

Mataya winced. The thought of her causing destruction was overwhelming to her superior mind. Her life was created to protect the realms and the entities she watched over, not to be their demise.

"I do not understand. What is it you believe I have done?"

"As I have said, you have created alternate universes where events are radically different. We must find the universal timeline that is the key player, and force it to unfold to our advantage. I believe if we can find it, then we can set into motion the true events. Together we can change what has gone wrong."

"I do not believe you. Show me evidence of what you say I have done. I am a Great Elder. There is no deceit within me."

"Mataya, I understand how this all seems impossible to you. I myself had questioned this theory, too. It was only after I evaluated all of the facts carefully, did I know my theory to be true."

"I am not a fugitive, Beck. How dare you stand there accusing me of causing disruption in the Creator's finely fashioned realm?"

"Mataya, you misunderstood me. I accuse you of nothing. I know there is no deceit in your essence. You have not purposely willed any misgivings on the entities of any realm. It is the power within you acting as the Scroll of

Espérer does. I can sense you mean goodwill to others, too. It is just that you have no control, as you have not learned it. That is why the events have unfolded as they are now. Together we can stop the fluctuations and restore order."

"You are mistaken, Beck. I have never held the scroll in my hand or made a wish upon the scroll. How could my desires be fulfilled with the scroll?"

"You have held the scroll, but it was not you who physically touched it with a wish."

"Then who touched it willing my desires to be?"

Beck lowered his head in shame. His actions were just as much at fault for the time shifts as Mataya was. Had he not removed the scroll from the brook the day he grasped her cheek in his hand, then he wouldn't have dreamed her desires to come true for saving her brother.

"It was I, Mataya, who touched the scroll. I meant no ill fortune to befall you."

"How could you do this to me, Beck?"

"Mataya, I am very fond of you. It is my friendship with you that grieves for you."

She looked away embarrassed. "Beck, how are you so sure that your so called desires for my happiness have affected my thoughts? How could your desires bring this curse down upon me?"

"I just wanted what was best for my friend. I know what I speak of is true, because I have seen your actions in my dream world. I have watched your desires play out before my eyes. I know the pain you have inside of your essence. I can feel the determination to link your mind with your brother's mind once more." He lowered his eyes, sighing from his own embarrassment. "I am sorry this has happened to you, however, do not worry, Mataya. We can fix this."

Beck turned toward the brook and dipped his hand into the water. The luxurious mist had appeared again, forming translucent musical notes. They floated above the fast moving current, almost dancing in rhythm to the sound of the water smashing against the rocks. When Beck turned back to face Mataya, he held a shiny object in his hand. The musical notes swirled through the air, darting from the brook into the shiny object. It began to glow, and a humming sound sang from it.

Beck extended his hand toward Mataya to show her what he held in his grasp. "We can do it with this."

Just as Mataya reached out to take the shiny object from Beck, she faded from the brook. At a simple thought, he sent her away from his dream world. She would never know his confession or that his dealings caused great ramifications for her—and their realm.

8.
GUARDIAN SECRETS

Guardian Realm—Earth's timeline 1926

Unexpectedly, Mataya found herself standing at an open window. The chiffon curtain tickled her cheek as it blew in the breeze. Mataya was back in her chamber conscious of the environment around her. Her chambermaid addressed her questioning if she needed anything. Before Mataya could respond to her maid, a yellow light expelled from her hands. The fire once again warmed the chilly air around Mataya, and then ... she was alone standing next to an unfamiliar window. Off in the distance she heard footsteps. She turned around to see whom they belonged to, and when she did, she found the owner of the rhythmic taps standing three feet away from her.

"Who are you?" Lexis questioned, shocked by her arrival. The human emotion of fear he unwillingly developed nearly consumed him. "I have not seen you before. I do not recognize your spirit."

Mataya immediately recognized the stout Guardian. She had never met him personally, but his essence was familiar to her. "Lexis, my name is Mataya," she said, with compassion in her tone. "I come from the future."

"The future—why do you break our laws? What business do you have coming here and bringing damnation upon me?"

"Elder Lexis, please believe me. I bring nothing except peace."

"How dare you say peace?" He shook his fist. "The very action of time travel is forbidden. It will bring discord down on anyone whom you associate with."

"Do not fear, Lexis. I have concealed my travels, and no one knows that I am here."

"Deception as well. What do you want from me?"

"The same thing you want, Lexis. I want to ensure safety for your daughter."

Lexis gasped in surprise as his human emotions appeared stronger than he anticipated. "What do you know about my daughter? Where have you gotten such a notion?"

"I told you—I am from the future, and there are others who know of your human bred child as well."

Lexis became defensive. Many had sought after him to stop the completion of the Creator's plan. He guarded the scrolls of Deuel and Sychar with his life. Even after he lost the Scroll of Sychar, Lexis continued obediently risking his essence and the life of his wife, to keep their daughter safe. Day and night, he eagerly pressed on until he would be guided to the vessel his daughter was to dwell within spiritually.

He knew the other Guardians would never understand what he was trying to do. Their hearts and minds were always opened to the Creator, except Lexis' people would never understand the concept the Creator was forming. Just as humans, some Guardians allowed the sanctity of their fellowship with the Creator to diminish. They needed to see signs or material objects before faith and trust could replace what they really knew to be true. That was not what the Creator had envisioned for His children, but the dark one crept in, and planted the seed of doubt.

The faithful servant knew he had to give his all. He was to ride the storm and turbulence waiting for the light to shine. Lexis didn't fear for his own life, just the lives of his wife and daughter Rayna. However, fear had no place in the plan, and in the end, sacrifices and choices were to be made. Lexis wouldn't receive material rewards, and he knew that. His reward was spiritual, and the redemption of this gift was to come after the loss of his life.

Lexis bowed his head knowing there was no chance to cover his actions. The power of the woman before him reigned more supreme than of those who came against him. Dignity and respect no longer mattered to Lexis, but he knew lying to her would be deceptive on his behalf. He didn't feel the need to be secretive or hide his actions from her for fear of his daughter's existence. The truth was the only way to confront the mystery before him.

"I acted out of duty and loyalty," he said. His voice sounded triumphantly through the chamber. "My actions were part of a plan. What reasoning do you have, Mataya?"

"Elder," she began. She felt confused by his sudden strength. "I just want to offer the safety you are having difficulty providing."

"What makes you think I have difficulties with her protection?"

"I told you, I am from the future. I know your child has been prophesied about. I know what spirit develops within her ... and I know others search her out."

"How could you know these things? I do not believe them to be true."

"Lexis, will you add human lies to tarnish your service to the Creator?"

He tried to remain focused by showing his boldness, except he was never good at playing games. "Speak the truth, if you claim to know these things. How did you acquire this information?"

"I know these things, Lexis, because I am from the future. I have told you this."

"You can tell me many things I may not believe. Now why should you expect me to trust you if you have claimed to know my child is in danger? How do I know that you are not the danger I should fear?"

"I can see how you would question that, any father would. Nevertheless, discern my reasons, and you will see I speak the truth."

"Discern your reasons, how can you propose such a thing? One would have to read minds, and you know only Great Elders have that gift bestowed upon them. To say one could read another's mind is blasphemy."

"I do not just speak the words, Lexis, I can prove them."

"I do not believe you ... Mataya."

"Lexis, please allow me this. I have another purpose for the safety of your child. I have the safety of my brother Mateo to consider. Together we can save them both."

He examined the tiny female Guardian before him. Her auburn eyes delighted his curiosity. Her high cheekbones intrigued Lexis' desire to understand her reasoning, and his determination to search out the truth of her claims.

"Your brother," he said cautiously. "It is rare that you should have a sibling. How did your parents acquire another?"

"He is my twin."

Lexis immediately fell to the floor bowing. Never in his two thousand years did he have the opportunity to be in the presence of a Great Elder. Now, one stood before him prophesying about his life and offering the shelter for his daughter that he couldn't provide.

"Please, Lexis, rise." Mataya motioned with both of her hands. "We are equals at this moment. We share a common journey, and without one another we will both fail."

Lexis didn't stand. He remained in awe of the Elder before him. He had broken their laws and deserved to be punished. His people would never forgive his actions. For the Creator's reasons remained a mystery, one that bound him to silence. Yet, now before a Great Elder, it appeared he had found grace.

"What is it that we need to do?" he asked, obediently of Mataya.

"Lexis, please rise. Our conversation will be better suited should we make eye contact."

Lexis hesitated to raise his eyes to meet hers. He got to his feet keeping a respectable distance from the Great Elder.

"I know you propose to keep your daughter Rayna hidden. Just as I know with the passing of your wife, Lina, this task becomes harder with each new dawn."

"Yes, Elder. The loss of my wife has complicated matters severely."

"I know that you have fought many battles in secret to avoid capture from the wicked one who defiles all the

Creator has designed. You have not lost him. He will strike again."

"Please, tell me, Elder Mataya. What must I do to keep my child safe?"

"I have seen into the future, and you believed your only way to protect the scrolls and the Sentinel was to consume her essence."

Crystal drops of water filled his eyes. He had contemplated her death for days. If the evil one took her, she would be tortured and turned. If Lexis consumed her, she would suffer no more in the hands of the vile one. Still, he bonded with Lina vowing a life of loneliness when she died. With Rayna's death, he contemplated a life of isolation. If he absorbed her life and then was caught and tried for her murder, Lexis would lose his essence to Deimos.

"Elder, please do not think harsh of me. I have lost everything even one of the scrolls to keep her safe. I have no other choice. I love her too much to watch her perish from the evil one."

"Lexis, what I propose to you will bring her life."

His eyes widened, and his human heart skipped a beat. "Life ... how?"

She smiled at him as she sensed his essence grasp the shredding strings of hope. "In my future an evil Guardian found your child in the fetus you placed her within on Earth. He was ruthless and spared no one in his vile plan. He searched from the outer realms looking for an accomplice. His name was Markian, and he became a most despicable Guardian. Markian also bore a human daughter of his own. However, unlike your daughter, Dinah was tarnished and unworthy of life. The child was born with an essence and a soul, but both grew dark with lust and greed.

So dark that the light could not shine through and she was lost to the evil.

"Together he and his daughter sought after more riches and possessions—allowing their greed to consume them. Others became pawns in their plans. Markian secretly controlled the minds of respected Elders to profit from his erring ways."

"How was he able to do this? Was he a Great Elder such as you?"

She shook her head hesitant to reply. "No. In his endeavors, Markian destroyed the human father Nolan before Raina's birth. He and his daughter later succeeded in killing the human mother before your daughter emerged as the Sentinel. Fortunately, your spirit was strong and it called to a passing Guardian. Your essence encouraged him to claim the infant as his Esprit de corps."

"Who was he, Elder?" Lexis asked. He was barely able to stand still from the anticipation of knowing who his daughter's savior was to be.

"His name is Josiah. He is a gallant Guardian whose essence recognized the human child to be more than human. Josiah did not understand that there was a distinction between the two, your daughter, and the vessel. I believe that as the shell he created loved the human protector, his essence loved your daughter."

"Human love," he whispered.

"Yes, Lexis. Human love. Then just as the scroll had predicted, the revelation unfolded. Unfortunately, at a much sooner time than anticipated. Markian recruited the assistance of my brother Mateo by fogging my brother's mind. He forced him to send an innocent Guardian to Deimos. In my future, Dinah found the Scroll of Sychar that you hid in the Adrastea Universe. Lexis, she opened the abyss on Earth unleashing the Demons."

Lexis gasped terrified at the actions he heard. "She found the Abyss!"

"Yes, and when she brought the Scroll of Sychar back from Adrastea—she brought another form of evil we have never encountered."

"What kind of evil?"

"I am not sure. I have never felt its presence. I am not sure if the two of them did either."

"Such treachery you speak of, Elder Mataya."

"I know, Lexis." She frowned. "It gets much worse. Markian and Dinah used the occupants of the Abyss to destroy Earth."

"What!" he exclaimed in disbelief. "How could they have such power to annihilate a whole planet?"

"They got it unknowingly by the evil from Adrastea. Josiah had expelled Markian and his daughter Dinah to Deimos. Then the Sentinel emerged and restored the destruction they caused. She returned the human Raina to another life wiping the evil event from the timeline. The gallant Guardian now rules our people." Mataya sighed. "My brother now serves a sentence in Deimos, and our Head Elder lives a life of loneliness. I come here today because I propose a plan to change the outcome for Josiah and Mateo."

"How, Elder, will this help my daughter now?" he asked, seeming too confused for a Guardian. His years of dwelling as a human affected his supreme thoughts.

"I have devised another scheme. My plan is to hide your daughter in a secret location and place the essence of a special Guardian child in Raina's great-grandmother. Your daughter's essence will be safe, and the Guardian child will be raised as a human child. Then when the time is right, we will pass her essence along the bloodline of Raina— secretly under Guardian protection of a Watcher. When the Earth has rotated bringing many seasons, and the appointed time of Raina's conception has come, then I will switch the essences of both children. I will place Rayna into the womb that carries Raina, and I will send the Guardian child back to her home.

"Time will not expose our methods, and your daughter will be safe. The future will then unfold as originally predicted, and the life that harbors the Sentinel will not be forsaken. Thus, Markian will not have sensed your daughter's existence, and he would not have coerced Mateo. His daughter will have had no reason to search out the Abyss. What I propose will allow your daughter to live and give me back my brother."

Lexis remained very quiet surveying the woman before him. Her words seemed too incredible to believe. Yet, his desire to save his daughter outweighed any unbelievable facts. Lexis would do anything to protect his daughter's essence from destruction.

"How do you know that placing my daughter's essence in an earlier vessel will work? What proof do you have that history has already been changed?"

"Because ... Lexis, I have seen it."

"What—how?"

"Lexis, the day the terrible events unfolded, I found a peculiar sense of loss within myself. It troubled me greatly. It seemed as if the things I knew before were lost to me, and the things I had no knowledge of previously danced in my mind. It was not clear to me at first what was happening to me until I entered the Abilene Chamber.

"It was there that Jon, our Leader's father, had the Scroll of Deuel in his possession. I had held it many times before as I sang the songs hidden deep within the writings. Yet, as he was before me, my mind was blank. I fought to concentrate and search out the truth. It was at that point when I realized I had suffered many episodes of this displacement for a great length of time."

"What do you mean, Mataya, by displacements of time?"

"I can explain these episodes only as being fractures in space that consumed me. Vividly, different realities flashed in my mind until I caught a vision of my earlier visit with Josiah. It was then when I knew I once had the secrets of the Scroll of Deuel locked deep into my mind. It was then, when I felt an odd cool wind blow through me, and my essence dematerialized from where I was to a beautiful garden. It was there where I learned my thoughts were not my own, and buried secrets surfaced."

"More secrets," Lexis mumbled. "Secrets cause deceit. How sure are you that you are not affected by this deceit, Elder?"

"Lexis, many good Guardians were affected by Markian's evil. Their minds became so twisted and clouded that right and wrong no longer meant anything to them. Their Council meetings turned into situations to benefit just Markian. He used his persuasion to cover his horrendous deeds and prosecute the innocent."

"What you say seems improbable," he interjected, cautiously examining Mataya's reaction.

"I knew this to be true after I remembered my Council appointed summons to witness at Josiah's trial. A summons neither my brother nor I honored. We simply forgot to attend his trial. Even worse, no Keeper of the Courts personal pursued the matter of Mateo and me not appearing in court."

Lexis continued to stare at Mataya as if she were insane. His uncontrollable nodding of his head alerted Mataya to his disbelief in her claims.

"Your ramblings are preposterous. Elder Mataya, I think you need to seek a healer. You have become delusional with human emotions you cannot contain nor control."

"I know I sound mad to you, Lexis, but please believe me. I have already traveled to the past before."

"You are mad, Mataya. There is no way you could have accomplished what you speak."

"Do not doubt me, Lexis, for I know the truth."

"How—how do you know this? What makes you so certain that you would risk my daughter and me?"

"Because, Lexis, I have a witness."

"Show me this witness, that I might believe you and your tales."

"I cannot because it would be too dangerous."

Lexis sighed with severe impatience. Every moment he listened—this one before him increased his dangers of being stopped. Her delusions put them both at risk.

Mataya could sense his disbelief and yearning to leave. "You must have faith, my friend. Allow your human heart to guide you. Lina bestowed upon you many human treasures that I know you preserve *secretly* to honor her memory. It is there where you will find the comfort to trust me and save your child. I cannot expose any more confirmation of what I speak. As I have said, it is too dangerous. Please, Lexis, for the sake of your daughter ... you must trust me."

9.
HONOR AND DREAMS

Guardian realm—after Earth's re-birth

Beck learned years before that he could see the dreams of humans and pull those dreams into his reality. This is how he made the peaceful brook and its beautiful surroundings. Soon after creating the brook, Beck journeyed off on an adventure of a lifetime. In one of the dreams he observed, Beck found a small child playing with several brilliantly colored stones in the sunflower garden by a strange brook. Their earth tone, turquoise, and blue shades of color and unique shapes caught his attention. She carried them in the pocket of her robe removing the stones often to sing to them. One night when he visited the dream of the child, she presented him with a stone. Remarkably, he felt a rare connection to it. He sensed a power emitting from the stone that he had never felt before. This stone became a treasure Beck valued.

While sitting along the edge of the brook after his dream, he rolled the stone between his fingers. He accidently dropped the stone and it fell into the brook. As it splashed into the water, he heard a song play from within it. The melody was like none he had ever heard before. It sounded mightier than that of the chorus of God's Angels—who were sent to cover the multitude of anguish—in the realms outside of Heaven. Faintly above the harmonious song, he could hear the whisper of the child's voice.

Guard the Stone of Fayruz, and tell no one that you have it.

"What?" he called out amazed at hearing the voice.

Tell no one you carry the secret, the voice instructed him again.

"What secret?" he asked again perplexed.

Then as suddenly as the voice came with the song, it was gone. Beck continued to look around to see if the voice came from somewhere other than the stone. He knelt down, putting his hand into the water and then scooped up the stone. The swishing motion of the water gently pushed against the stone, and the music played again. Surprised, he dropped the earth tone colored stone back into the water—and when the stone stopped ricocheting off the brook's floor the music ended.

Beck realized at that moment the swooshing motion of the water encouraged the song. He rejoiced at hearing this new gift. Beck jumped into the brook and began wading with the stone in his submerged hand. The music flourished once more. Then Beck began to pray that he would find more stones, believing the chorus would grow into a song fit solely for Angels' ears to hear. With each new prayer, came the opportunity to find the child in her dream. Daily, for months to come, he visited the child gladly accepting a new stone from her. Before long, the brook's bottom had filled with the stones, and the song filtered into the air.

One day, as he sat relaxing next to the brook sifting the stones with his feet, he noticed something about the chorus had changed. As the tune turned from its angelic pitch that he loved so well, Beck was startled and jumped from the water's edge. He felt the air begin to cool, pacing itself with the thunderous roar of trumpets. The sound grew louder pounding fiercely inside of his chest. The sensation of fear and anxiety began to fill his mind. Then off to his right, Beck caught an odd vision of a white mist. It began to close in around him so thickly that he felt as if his essence would suffocate. Flashes of light developed from the mist streaking across the sky. Beck's retreat had never experienced this side of Mother Nature. His brook was always calm and tranquil. Now the mist had brought a new emotion to his place.

As the thunder began to diminish, a new sound swirled in the mist. He heard voices, but they were not tender like the child who gave him the stones. These voices screamed frantically with cries of sorrow and pain. Beck could taste the salt of their tears as they began to rain down from the mist. Alarmed by this new occurrence, he reached into the water to grab a handful of stones to flee from the brook. As he stepped onto some of the stones, they rolled along the bottom creating a new song. Instantly the mist that surrounded him darted into the brook. The stones began to glow in fluorescent colors absorbing the cries of the invisible guest.

Beck exited the garden feeling remorse and helplessness. It was not the same as what he felt from the waters of the brook moments before. This time they had a new meaning to them. This time the pain was real. His essence took a claim upon the pain he felt, for he now knew truly, what it was that filled the brook with sorrow this morning. The vision that captured his mind while he waded in the brook wasn't a dream created in someone's imagination. Beck had seen the horrible death. The shadowy view of the face of the Guardian who lost his essence burned into Beck's memory.

His superior mind processed the nightmarish images that the vision brought at an incredible rate, except the meaning behind the vision he couldn't decipher. This was nothing new, for there were a few times Beck had believed he knew the meaning of the vision before it came true. Today, like the other times, he prayed he was wrong and regretted that his mind held any knowledge of it at all.

Beck heard the plea of the one who deserved no mercy and felt the evil rejoice at his victory. Had the Guardian lost his essence on Deimos—thus receiving his rightful punishment for his heinous actions—then the brook wouldn't have absorbed the remnants of the Tracker's crime. For nothing lost on Deimos flows over into the other realms. Yet, for some unknown cause, the Stones of Fayruz must sift the sullen emotions absorbed by the Tracker's victim and burn them into Beck's Guardian heart.

He summoned Mataya through the mist to join him—looking for solace from his unexplainable emotions.

"What is it, Beck?" she asked, as her form appeared within the mist.

"Please come and sit with me. I would like to talk awhile ... if you will permit me to do so."

"It will be my pleasure to join you." She beamed. "I have always enjoyed your company, as rare as it is."

Beck motioned for her to sit with him by the bank of the brook. Gently, he assisted her as she knelt to the ground. Beck held her hand to help steady Mataya as she positioned herself closely to the edge. Mataya removed her shoes to allow her feet to dangle into the warm water.

"Please, Beck, tell me what is on your mind."

"Mataya, I have not completely shared the occurrences of this place with you. I have felt a need to keep its existence a secret." He paused, focusing his attention on the way Mataya held her posture. As always, she presented herself with elegance and grace.

"Go on," she encouraged, catching his admiring glance.

"Mataya ... I am troubled, and I am not sure why."

"What do you mean?"

"Many of the humans' dreams I witness are so vivid, that at times, I question the truth of their situations. I find myself analyzing them for clues. Some of the time, the dreams seem too strong to be just that. I have realized many of the dreams are much too intense to be born of one's imagination.

"When this occurred to me, I began to evaluate the scenario of the dream—and the dreamer's subconscious emotions that drift into this world with the dream. When I did this, I realized that the similarities I have witnessed in the dreams—and the events I have watched unfold in other realms are too coincidental. What I am afraid to admit both alarms and intrigue me. For I soon came to realize I not only saw the dreams of humans—but I have also seen visions of the future as well."

"Beck, that is impossible. Future detection solely exists when in guidance of an Esprit de corps. How can you even think of seeing the future in any other instances?"

"You are correct for the most part, however, what I speak of is true. I have seen beyond the dream world into one filled with reality. I have seen visions fit for only the prophets of the Creator."

"Beck, do you understand what this means?"

"I am not sure yet, Mataya. Learning to decipher between the two of them becomes, at times, a burden for me. For in His perfect world, I walk the stone-lined paths and stroll through the forest of young trees. In my meadows, the aroma of roses and wild flowers always linger in the air. Here, in this serene refuge, I feel happy. Although, not the same way as a Guardian who has no real need for emotions does, but the way a human feels happiness. For me to sense any other emotion in this world troubles my essence greatly."

"How does it trouble you, Beck? Is there any way that I may help you?"

Beck remained silent for a moment because admitting that he, a Guardian; felt troubled by any issue meant certain weakness for his kind.

"Beck ... you do not need to shy away from me. I do not find you less powerful because you have chosen to honor the Head Elder's commands at experiencing human emotions."

"Mataya, you misunderstand me. I shy away from no one. I have taken pride in the glory of feeling life outside of my essence. It is the uncertainty that comes with what I experience in this brook which has me, perplexed."

"Please, Beck ... forgive me. I meant you no dishonor. It is just that I have trouble relating to what this place really is. I am void of understanding the magnificence you have created here."

Beck reached up and patted her shoulder. "Mataya, you have not dishonored me in any way. It is my fault that I have not clearly explained this place to you. Forgive me, please. It is not that I do not trust you, for I do with my life. However, I must protect this brook and its gardens. It is the urgency for protection that has made me act so discreetly."

"Beck, I will not ask you to act against your instincts, however, I have learned the value of discretion and practice it well myself."

"Of course." He grinned, removing his hand from her shoulder. When he continued it was in a tone of voice Mataya had never heard. "Before I summoned you I saw a vision. It was like nothing I had ever seen before. At first, I discovered many years ago that I could enter the dreams of other entities. I found the humans to be the most intriguing. Their minds were not as advanced as other entities, and there their imaginations ran wild. I enjoyed observing the dreams and bringing objects from them back here with me.

"One day, a most peculiar event unfolded. A female entity offered me a token I had admired greatly. It was a beautiful stone that is called The Stone of Fayruz. This token brought wondrous music to the brook. Its chorus so magnificent, that I visited her frequently to ask for more. Soon ... I had so many stones they overflowed the water in the brook. I learned that the movements of the water made the stones sing. The song, my dear friend, is beyond any describable words in our language."

Mataya felt amazed at hearing his words. "I shall look forward to listening to the music."

"Yes, I am sure you do. However, you must understand that the song does not come without a price."

"A price ... what do you mean by this?"

"A mist appeared from out of nowhere and hovered above the brook. As the mist formed into a thick haze, it brought with it a terrible sense of pain and fear. I heard the peaceful song change, and the musical tune became dark mannered. The dreadful song produced violent emotions deep within me." Beck winced before he said the awful words. "I heard screams and wretched cries of suffering—from afflicted humans through the mist. Then the Stones of Fayruz began to absorb the vile music—filtering out the gloom and silencing the humans' cries. The stones expelled the remnants of the music returning it back into the mist, as a melody of hope. I watched as the mist drifted away from me, and then it disappeared."

Mataya opened her mouth to speak, but then she chose not to. Whether it was a loss for words or the expression on Beck's face, she kept silent.

Beck continued ignoring Mataya's brief interruption. "I still felt the helplessness and despair brewing within me, so I too, jumped into the brook. When I lay myself down onto the Fayruz stones, I felt the darkness leave me, also. While laying there in the water my mind began to grow dim. I had no control of myself or of my desires. My eyes became heavy, and I believe I fell asleep. For when it was blacker than night itself, a tiny light appeared very far away from me. I could see the mist carrying the melody of hope toward the light. I followed the mist and found myself in a brightly lit room."

"Where were you, Beck?"

"I am not sure where I was. I believe it was on Earth. Beside me, hunched over in a chair sat a man weeping across the chest of his dying son. The child was injured somehow and screaming in horrid pain. I felt so much compassion for the father to have to see his son in such agony. The pain of the child darted through my essence bringing back the darkness of my moments before lying in the water. I felt weighed down and overwhelmed by sorrowful emotions."

"Oh, Beck," Mataya whispered.

He just nodded slightly and continued. "Then the mist began to swirl around the room invisible to the humans. Without warning, the mist entered into the boy's body. Immediately, his cries stopped, and his heart beat one last time in peace. The father seeing the child's newfound peace wept no more and collected himself. He arose from the bedside, went to his wife, and comforted her.

"It was then that I realized I had just witnessed the purpose of the mist. It seeks out the humans' afflictions and draws them to the brook. The stones cleanse the pain returning hope to Earth in a magnificent song. Somehow, I knew at that point if the stones were in the wrong hands; they could return the evil and sorrow back to Earth. The devastation it would release could drive the humans mad."

"Beck," Mataya said in a low and uncertain tone. "This is an incredible story. How did you ever survive the rash emotions of those humans?"

"I am not sure of how I did anything that day. I just knew with instinct, if you will call it that, what was expected of me at that moment."

"Expected of you?"

"I do not know how else to explain it. I thought I created the brook for my pleasure, except now I know this has been another plan of the Creator's. Again, a few days later the mist appeared bringing more anguish from Earth. The stones, like before, had pulled the sorrow from the mist returning more music of hope. As this continued, I felt a change in my essence. I grew weary and confused. I bathed in the brook allowing the stones to absorb the bitterness from my essence.

"I believe now that I am a vessel chosen to help remove the grim emotions from the disrupted humans' lives. Therefore, each time I enter a humans' dreams, I take with me their uncertainties, and pain. I bring them back to the brook and bathe in the waters of sorrow. Because of this, I can balance the emotions when I walk in the humans' dreams. They no longer weigh me down or stop me."

Mataya's expression changed. Beck sensed her disillusionment for his story. He could feel the human compassion brewing inside of her.

"Please, do not be dismayed, my dear friend. Do you not understand what powers are at work here? Because of the Stones of Fayruz, I can take away the human children's nightmares and they trouble no one anymore. It is because of this, I can distinguish between the dreams of the sleeping and the visions of the Creator."

"Beck," Mataya managed to say, "how can you be so sure that what you see are visions? Can they also be the magic of the evil one?"

"I am sure they are visions because of the voice that echoes in my ears from beyond the dream world. I have seen the one who held the stones before I did. I have heard the soft whisper of her instructions. Although at first, I nearly missed them over the sound of the swishing water. Her words are always clear to me and I remember them well. How can I not, for they are burned into my celestial mind and are with me day and night."

"Beck, how can you say that these events are not a burden? I find no message in your words to make me believe that this is of the Creator. He reigns supreme and knows what is and what shall come to pass."

Beck's eyes went wide. The denial of the truth he heard from her made him feel uneasy. "It is not for us to question the working of the Creator, my sister."

"Do not misunderstand me," Mataya's voice squeaked with concern for his statement. "I do not question the Creator at all. It is you whom I question and this ridiculous notion you have presented to me today."

"Mataya, you have not offended me by your apprehensiveness. If you were to walk in my shoes, then perhaps, you would easily understand what I speak of to you. If you were to feel the emotions I have come to enjoy—or feel love's touch in a realm outside of ours—then you would see how other entities demonstrate their love for one another.

"The people of Naiad glance into the eyes of their mate with reverent certainty. This action is their greeting and their expressions of devotion. The people of Pan continuously whisper melodies of lengthy poems that are used for more than communication in their society." Beck paused, and looked off into the distance as if he had heard something.

"Beck," Mataya spoke, requesting his attention, "are you well?"

"Yes." He grinned, with a low chuckle. "As I was saying to you ... just now. Please consider the humans as I speak of love. They battle daily a turbulent storm of fear, sadness, and joy all rolled up into the heart the Creator designed for them. They are a nation made in the Creator's own image and allowed to have free will. The humans' emotions are what intrigue me the most about their cultures and existences. How joyous it is to know that what one does can make an immediate difference in the lives of those around you. I cannot make you understand any of this for I am not sure how to explain it myself. I can only tell you about the emotions—and wish that you had the opportunity to experience what I do.

"With the same heart, they can love themselves and hate humanity. They can watch a stranger starve homeless in the street with no remorse—yet cradle their child at night. And of course, that same heart can commit murder and still ask for forgiveness from the Creator. It fascinates me to see how one human can tolerate and expel so many emotions—while the bearer retains his or her sanity. It is ..." Beck trailed off again looking into the distance.

Mataya watched him silently, observing the expression upon his face. Had her curiosity not been so strong—she could have observed him for hours—lost in whatever reality had taken his concentration.

"What were you doing just now?" she asked, gaining his attention.

"Listening," was all he offered her.

"Listening to what?"

"Can you not hear that, my sister?"

Mataya leaned closer toward Beck straining to hear what he heard. "Beck, I hear nothing except the ripple of the brook. I do believe the water flows more forcefully today."

He chuckled. "So, you have noticed that?"

Mataya looked at him strangely. "Of course I have."

"Well, Mataya, it is the song within the water that I hear today. The chorus sounds more triumphant than ever before," he stated confidently.

"I do not hear it. Tell me please, what does it sound like? Is it as elegant as the humans' ballets, or as harmonious as an Angels' orchestra?"

Beck's face became serious. "Mataya, my words of description cannot do the song justice. Neither can I demonstrate it in a hum or a whistle."

Mataya's smile changed. Since her first dip in the brook, she pondered greatly the emotions that her essence absorbed. Almost envious of the gift bestowed upon Beck, she sighed. Human emotions had given her new insight into the human world that fused so quickly and strongly with their Leader. Her Guardian mind perceived the meaning of the emotions that often affected her, but her Guardian heart could never comprehend what human love was to be.

"My dear, Beck," she responded, "I do not believe that I am able to fully appreciate the miraculous gift the Creator granted the human entities. It burdens me, for this gift is not always received well by the humans. Many of them reject love by committing acts of violence and murder. I have witnessed what seems at times their hatred dominating the human emotions—destroying their humanity." Mataya became very quiet, looking back toward the brook.

After a long moment of silence, Beck spoke so softly it was almost a whisper. "Have I offended you, Mataya?"

"Ah what ... ah no," she said hesitantly. "I was just trying to listen for the song that plays in your ears; however, I cannot hear it. I feel that it is my loss."

"Perhaps, but do not dwell upon these things too much, Elder. With the song comes a curse."

"A curse? I do not understand. What do you mean by this?"

"Mataya, the song is the remnants of humanity's cries. I have told you the sorrow that enters from the other worlds flows into the brook each time the mist forms."

Mataya looked puzzled. "What do you mean each time the mist forms? I thought this was a rare encounter. You must tell me why this happens."

"My dear, Mataya. It is not for me to tell the secrets of this place. I am the keeper of this realm. The protection of this place rests in my hands."

"Tell me please ... Beck. If you hear the cries of humanity, then how is it that you can rejoice in the songs?"

"As I have told you many times before, I must keep the secrets of this place secure. Please do not ask me again." Beck stood up putting some distance between Mataya and himself. She must never know the power of suggestion that she held over him. His desire to answer her every question had made him expose the secrets to her once before.

"Beck," she broke into his thoughts, "do you trust no one—even I, a Great Elder?"

"Mataya, my dear. It is not a matter of trust. How can I make you see this? It is a matter of honor. I swore to myself to uphold the beauty of this place and its integrity. It is not trust that makes me keep the functions of this reality from you."

"Then may I ask what it is that binds you so tightly to this place forbidding even a Great Elder access to its inner workings?"

"It is...." Beck trailed off lost in thought. The fact was that he had already shared this place's beauty with her in a dream. The same dream he professed his love to her. It happened so fast. Sol's magnificent rays glistened off her dark auburn hair enhancing her glowing smile. The song in his heart played so powerfully that he swore she must have heard the song herself. There was no force on Earth, or in this realm of Beck's that could have stopped him from acting on the moment. The kiss transferred his emotions of love and admiration toward her. Mataya received them gladly taking comfort in hearing the thoughts of another in her mind.

It was then that Beck realized he had taken advantage of the moment and dishonored the Elder. The guilt seemed powerfully over bearing. He knew then that he must never allow such indiscretions to be witnessed from him again.

"Beck, please forgive me if I have upset you in any way."

"Mataya, what is it that has put this notion into your head? You could never upset me."

"It is your silence, my dear friend."

"Please, Mataya, do not think such thoughts. I often get lost in the surroundings here. This place has become a part of me and I allow it to consume me whenever possible. I am sorry I have given you a reason to misunderstand my intentions."

"No, Beck, do not be sorry. This conversation has ended. You do not have to explain this place's meaning. I should not have pried." Mataya looked at Beck for some time as her thoughts wondered. Briefly, a vision of her embraced in his arms flashed into her mind.

"Shall we?" He extended his hand toward her gesturing to the stone lined path that led into the forest.

Mataya smiled with a nod of her head accepting his assistance to stand. She gratefully grasped his hand into hers. As Mataya strolled toward the path, she disappeared into the mist that gently crept in. Beck's face lost its smile and his lips formed a grin. Quietly, he turned to face the brook and then Beck left the path to sift the stones. Someday, he would allow her visits to remain in her memory. Someday he would profess his love openly for all to know.

10.

SECOND ENCOUNTER

Earth—present-day

Josiah couldn't fight the urge to see his beloved again. If he could have just one look at her or perhaps stand secretly in her presence—then the burning in his Guardian heart may dissolve. He scanned the universe and found her on a California college campus. Ironically, his Esprit de corps has also brought him there on a daily occurrence. The lecture hall was only a few doors down from his Esprit de corps' lab. To think that they may have been in the same hallway once before and he never knew it. Could his essence have been that dim to her presence?

His chance meeting would be easy enough to arrange. If he was only to view her from a far then he could do it in his true form unseen. However, that would mean he was unseen by her, too. He knew a glance from a distance wouldn't be enough. His heart ached too much not to speak to her.

Against his better judgment, Josiah gave in to his human desires. One effortless minute in the student office and his registration to her Cellular Biology class would be complete. The lecture hall was large with more than a hundred students in an attendance at one time. The semester had just started three weeks ago; he could have easily blended in with the crowd until today. The Professor was not a concern, and none of the classmates would question his presence. He could stay near her for the length of the class without drawing attention to himself. Maybe he could attend more classes if this one meeting couldn't calm his desires.

"Raina," his voice quivered.

"Do I know you?" she asked, confused as to who this man before her was.

His breath returned and so the human heart beat. It was a deep regret for him. "We met once a long time ago in Silver Lake."

She looked at him puzzled trying to remember their last meeting. "Excuse me, but I don't remember when."

"As I recall, you had a broken bike," he added, trying to address her apparent confusion.

"My bike." Her eyes lit up forcing a smile to envelope her face. "Yes, I remember now. Your father fixed my bike chain. My pant leg was caught in the chain, and I crashed coasting down a hill. I can't believe you remember me. That was so long ago."

"I could never forget someone with your qualities."

Raina giggled nervously because Josiah had embarrassed her. "Well, thank you."

"Here, have a seat." Josiah shoved his book bag aside to allow Raina to sit at the desk next to his.

"Um, sure thank you," she said under her breath.

Professor Cutter cleared his throat. This was a warning to them to be quiet. Raina took the seat next to Josiah. She was the Professor's best student. Her disruption would be forgiven in time.

The moments he sat there next to Raina troubled him immensely. He knew this was wrong but he had to stay. Josiah had so many questions concerning her presence on Earth living the new life she led. Was the Sentinel playing a cruel trick upon him? Did he do something wrong, and this was his punishment? No conclusion Josiah came to added up in his philosophical mind. Raina was to be gone to him. He was told her life ended for the Sentinel's sake. It was as if she died a martyr, whose death meant nothing to anyone, except him. Then through the conclusion of the Sentinel's plan, she was given back her life. However, this life didn't include Josiah. Now here in this noisy lecture hall her presence went against every instruction he was given that sad day.

There on that steep hill in Silver Lake, he endured great torture to find she lived right where he left her. Raina was there and she could never be his. Now on this day, her presence was so close to him. He could reach out and grasp her cheek as he had done so many times before. He wanted so badly to hold her in his arms and whisper the words of his love in her ear. However, she was not the Raina he had loved so dearly. So once again, just as in his terror-filled visions she remained out of his reach.

Raina caught him staring at her from out of the corner of her eye. This was one time that she wished her peripheral vision wasn't so keen. She shifted her body to break his eye contact. Raina didn't know if it worked because she never looked back at him.

Impatience was an old human trait that seemed to have

resurfaced. For Josiah's sake, class was lasting too long. He entertained the idea of manipulating time, but the offense was so severe it would warrant his exile. Josiah fought to contain himself in his seat, as his eagerness grew disrupting his concentration. His thoughts shifted too rapidly for his human brain to assimilate. Josiah had to get a hold of himself, but it proved to be too difficult to do so. He spent his whole life honoring his people's customs and obeying their laws. Then one day, a power beyond his comprehension changed his priorities. Now next to him sat the reason for his existence, and she didn't even know. The urge to tell her, to wrap her in his arms grew wildly out of control. Yet, he knew there was nothing he could rightfully say without risks to either one of them. So now, he faced once again the sadness of a broken heart and unanswered hope.

Mysteriously, he felt the intensity of the stranger from behind him. Like him, she had never been in this class before. He wondered what made her appearance acceptable to his professor and to his new classmates. Did she know what war raged inside of him? Would she dare to come this day to add to his misgivings? Even if she had, he almost felt a comfort to know the stranger was in the room. He recognized the energy, but its magnitude presented itself in a different manner. The energy reminded him of who he was and what he was. The entity was the only reason Josiah didn't flee the room or pull Raina from her chair and whisk her away with him. Surely, his fellow students would think he was insane for leaving too abruptly or acting so irrational.

When Professor Cutter dismissed his class, Josiah followed Raina at a close pace out of the lecture hall. His human body couldn't move fast enough to set his impatient mind at ease. At this moment, the entity meant nothing to him. Being with Raina was all that mattered. Once he was outside of the classroom, he could approach Raina unseen and speak to her.

When he finally made it outside, the sunlight shined brightly glistening off her blond curls. Though much shorter than in her youth, they still waved in the wind. Her features hadn't changed, and the years didn't blemish her complexion. Josiah caught himself staring into her softly lined eyes as his memories of Raina charged through his mind.

"What? Why are looking at me like that?" Raina asked annoyed, interrupting his thoughts.

"Like what?" he asked embarrassed, breaking eye contact with her by tucking his book into his backpack. Josiah needed a moment to clear his mind, so that he could be reminded further of his duties to his people and his parents. That moment didn't come.

"Like a child on Christmas morning," she said, staring at him oddly.

With no hesitation, he spoke boldly, a boldness he should have controlled. "Because honestly, Raina ... I cannot breathe when I look at you."

Raina's face turned pale, and her expression went blank. She stared at Josiah not moving. He had said too much, and now he feared that she was afraid of him.

"Are you all right?" he asked, concerned for her well-being.

"Yes," she spoke in a low tone, "this conversation just seems so familiar it is almost freaky. Talk about déjà vu."

Josiah forced a laugh, and Raina smiled in return. Before he could say anything more, he became alerted to Jaleel's presence. Had his good friend come to rescue him or chastise him?

"I must go now or I'll be late for my next class. I will see you around," she said. Then turning away from him, she strolled off across the courtyard. As she got a few feet away, she glanced back and shouted to him. "Hey, maybe I'll see you in the Library later."

"Sure," he answered back nearly breathless. He doubted it would happen. Even his hope knew their meeting shouldn't be.

Josiah instantly blended his shell's molecules with his essence to absorb his shell. Then he dematerialized without regard to any one witnessing his disappearance. When he returned to his study, he found Jaleel was there ahead of him speechless. He didn't need to ask why, because he had seen their meeting through the eyes of another. He gestured a welcoming greeting to his dear friend.

Josiah knew he shouldn't entertain the idea of seeing her again. Raina's life was on a course without him. The course as the Sentinel stated was one that her life was meant to follow. Josiah barely tolerated knowing she was somewhere out there in an undisclosed universe untouchable by his essence. This thought gave him no joy or peace. Her absence from his life only brought him pain and confusion. Emotions his fellow Guardians were spared from knowing.

Josiah measured time unlike other Guardians. Time afflicted him and toyed with his Guardian rationality. It moved too slowly and served as only a plagued reminder of his lonely eternity. A destiny he hadn't seen for himself or desired.

Some days he functioned as a true Guardian lost in the customs and practices of his people. He lived immersed in the many tasks, and responsibilities required of a Head Elder. Josiah was chosen by the Sentinel to be the leader of the Guardian world. An endowed leadership he felt trapped him within the enormous walls of many chambers.

They created a prison he hated and offered him a sentence he bore out of duty for the Sentinel.

Yet, sometimes he examined the similarities of his people and that of humans on Earth. As he considered the vast requirements needed to allow the human body to survive, Josiah analyzed the material items of each culture. All enjoyed large rooms beautifully furnished with elegant pictures and furniture. Both sought recreation in the fantasy and knowledge of books. Humor brightened their days, even if laughter meant something else to their cultures. Music brought them joy and strength, giving them security to face the unknown. Music gave humans peace to shun their disappointments. Yes, similarities that Josiah noticed, and his people didn't. Even adapting emotions to kindle the unity of Guardians and humans left most Guardians blinded.

Their existence seemed very similar on the outside, but their realms functioned much differently. Humans can't see Guardians. They wouldn't be able to acknowledge the tokens that filled their chambers or read the languages within their books. Humans can't grasp the sound of their music or know with certainty the companionship Guardians experienced. The love each entity felt existed much differently and was experienced on a unique level.

Josiah found that nature and recreation of his world didn't entertain him or satisfy his aching heart. The life he led in Raina's world fulfilled him. He found great enjoyment breathing in her air and socializing with the humans considered less superior than his own people. But most of all, he loved listening to her perform her specially written piano pieces.

To a Guardian, nothing seemed magnificent about her world. Guardians believed the beauty of their world was not there on Earth. Josiah believed differently than his fellow Guardians. His world held nothing for him as Raina's world was everything. This he believed with all of his essence.

He sat at his desk numb to his surroundings. His essence didn't feel the smooth mahogany wood—just as his eyes didn't need the light that shined from his desk lamp. He didn't need to use the pens in the holder off to his right—but they fit so comfortably in his celestial hands. Materials Guardians didn't need and humans couldn't function without. He created these human materials, but they were as real to him as his Raina.

Jaleel spoke trying to be sympathetic to Josiah's human thoughts. "I am sorry, Josiah. I know how difficult that was for you."

Josiah shouted bitterly, feeling his pain escalating. "I cannot do this anymore. I cannot sit here and pretend. I have to leave. I have had enough of these treacherous dealings."

"Leave to where, Josiah? The Guardians need you here. This is your place and where your responsibilities lie."

"No—my place is with Raina. My responsibilities are to her—they always have been."

"Josiah, do not be misguided. You know that your destinies are not meant to cross paths. If it were so, then you would have been created as a human or she as a true Guardian. Do not do this to yourself again."

"Do what?" he asked annoyed. "Live and exist in a state of happiness. I have to be the most depressed Guardian ever willed into existence. These human emotions are destroying me. Other Guardians are not plagued with the troubles that I am. They have adjusted. It is my job to rescue those in my condition. I do not understand why my life has to be written to exist so miserably. Tell me, Jaleel, where is the humanity in all of this? And do not tell me that this is a sacrifice the *Chosen One* must make. You have no idea what torment I am living through."

"You are right, Josiah. I do not know why this has to be. I do not know the human emotions as you do. Even now I am also playing with love I cannot answer."

"Jaleel, you can act if you choose to do so. Do you not think that your existence is too short not to act? It would be a shame and a dishonor to stand idly by, and allow love to pass you by."

"Josiah, you know very well it is a dishonor for me to act upon my feelings. Just as it is for you to follow that human and give up everything you have worked for."

"Follow that human. You sound as if she is an awful entity. Do you not understand what she means to me, Jaleel?"

"Josiah, do you forget what means your father and I went through to keep her safe? Do not stand there and take your pity out on me. Even though we had different parents, to me you are my brother, and you always will be. I feel for you. Please understand that?"

Josiah winced trying to remain composed. Jaleel stepped closer to his dear friend. He had to say the words once more as difficult as he knew they would be for him to hear.

"Josiah, why are you doing this to yourself? I thought you agreed to remain distant from her when you discovered her in Silver Lake two human years ago"

"I did, however, now she is in California. How can I ignore her?"

"You must, Josiah. You both are not meant to be. Do you dare defile the wishes of the Sentinel?"

Josiah opened his mouth to speak, except he found himself to be at a loss for words. He was even more dumbfounded when he realized his parents stood before him.

"Josiah," Jon called to him from the doorway.

His wife was at his side with a worried look thick upon her face. Josiah responded, speaking rudely with regret at their appearance. He had already lost his case to Jaleel's logic. To lose more of a foothold worried him.

"What do you want, Father?"

Jon dismissed his behavior. His unwarranted outbursts had become familiar to Jon and Kiersten. Their son had lost his grip, and they stood by helpless to intervene.

"Josiah, please come with us. We need to talk."

He shook his head no. "Perhaps ... later, Father. I have business to attend to."

"I think now would be a wise time," his mother commanded, in a tone Josiah couldn't refuse to listen to respectfully.

This was the last discussion he wanted to have. He knew his grieving essence deeply affected his parents. He could see the persistence in his mother's eyes—the same eyes that shed tears the day he was sentenced to Deimos.

Josiah turned away from Jaleel to face his father, and then headed impatiently toward the door. In one simple command, Jon had whisked Josiah and his mother away to a snow-capped mountaintop in the Alps.

"What is going on, Josiah?" Jon demanded, already knowing the words Josiah spoke in his study. His son's newfound erratic behaviors never ceased to amaze him.

"I am leaving this place, Father."

"To where?" his mother asked, with concern building in her thoughts. Her heart grieved for her son.

"I am going to Earth. I am leaving my seat on the Council."

"You cannot do that. It would be forbidden. You are our Leader. We need you to stand for our cause. Think about this. Do not act so irrationally."

"Existing like I have been should be forbidden. Father, this is not fair. Even humans have a reprieve from this loneliness I face each day."

Kiersten's voice squeaked. "Son, let us help. We can seek the advice of—"

Josiah silenced his mother waving his hands in the air. "No Elder can help this. I have found Raina again, and I am going to her. I will not miss this chance like I had before."

His father's voice softened. "You cannot, Son."

"Why not, Father? Do you think I fear the Deimos Universe? If I cannot have Raina, then I welcome it."

"Do not be so foolish, Josiah. This will pass in time. You must be patient and remember that your cause is for you and our people."

"Pass—pass! Father, it has been two human years. My essence is strangling me without her. I beg for non-existence."

Kiersten sighed. "Josiah, no Guardian has ever killed themselves. Non-existence comes only when one's time is fulfilled. You are in your prime. Please reconsider this, Josiah."

"No! I will seek the Council for exile to Earth. I must see if ... I must have Raina back."

"And if the Council says no, then what will you do?"

"Then I am sorry, Mother. I will go to Earth anyway. If they seek me out to punish me, then my torment will end in the Deimos Universe."

Anger brewed deep within Josiah again. This emotion clouded his thoughts daily disrupting his duties. Kiersten worked to continue presenting a calm atmosphere despite the sorrow in her heart. She didn't want Josiah's uncertain emotions to charge the situation. If Guardians cried, then she would have no end to her tears. No mother ever wants to say goodbye to her son.

Josiah had made it clear that his life ... as she knew it ... was over. With the intention of approaching the council for dismissal of his seat—Josiah embraced them both—and then he was gone. Kiersten remained rigid where she stood. She knew the pain that her son suffered from. It haunted her daily.

"Oh, Jon, what do you think will happen to him?"

"I do not know. We can only hope he comes to his senses."

"Jon, do you think he is right in his judgment?"

"Kiersten, it pains me as well to see our son like this. However, he has an obligation to our people. It is with high honors that he was chosen. He needs to accept what has been written in the Scroll of Deuel."

Kiersten crossed her arms scolding her husband. "Really, Jon? Do you mean to tell me that if our existences were switched you would so eagerly let me go? Do you not recall what we went through to save Raina just to lose her anyway? Now I will lose my son, too."

Jon stood quietly observing his wife. The answer was already in his heart. "No, I could not."

"Then, Jon, we must try to help him."

"Kiersten, I do not know if there is anything we can do."

"Jon, you have been a Keeper of the Courts for over five-hundred years. The Council respects your word. Can you not persuade them to make exceptions?"

"Kiersten, Josiah is our Leader. It would be his decision in the end, and he cannot choose to vote himself off. You know that, my dear."

"Can he retire then?"

Jon laughed, humor seemed appropriate at this time to one that didn't understand human etiquette. "You have been hanging around old humans too long, my love. No, I am sorry. Josiah cannot retire."

"Then what would help him to vacate his seat? We must come together and think of a way."

"Kiersten, please understand. There are two ways Josiah can end his role for the Council to release him from duty. He has to either cease to exist, or be removed for ill actions."

"And ill actions will put him in Deimos, would it not?"

"Yes ... it would."

"Oh, Jon, how could we have allowed our rules to consume us to such a state? This does not make sense. He cannot vote himself off, and he cannot retire. This is barbaric. I thought our people had evolved past primitive rules and principles. Even humans can change the laws of their government."

11.

THE COUNCIL

Guardian Realm—present-day

The Council of the Twelve had gathered to discuss the issues pertaining to the entities in the Neptune Universe. Josiah's attendance as Head Elder was required for such proceedings. His appearance was deemed necessary for the judgment of the entities in question.

The Council meeting had begun by the order of Brielle, the fifth Elder of the Council. As Josiah entered the chamber, he could hear their voices echoing out into the hall. Each Council member had immediately stopped talking and stood when Josiah entered the chamber. In unison, each Councilmember bowed their heads as a sign of respect and then took their seats.

The room remained quiet as Josiah walked to the center podium to take charge of the proceedings. He could feel each of their eyes following him across the room in a reserved manner. He felt as if their stares were burning into his essence. Josiah had not yet presented his request to the Council in person, however, he already felt judged. He knew the sins against his people that he was willing to commit. To Josiah the punishment was never an issue.

"Your Honor," Brielle said, with a smug overtone, "we have begun in your absence. Our first discussion has been regarding the Triton people."

Josiah cleared his throat. A certain habit the Elders had become familiar with witnessing. "And what is the issue at hand, Elder Brielle?"

"Your Honor," she answered. Brielle was stunned that Josiah seemed void of the current situation. The news of the pending invasion had become public knowledge against the Council's wishes. "The Triton people have been secretly plotting to overthrow the Nereidians. Our Watchers have discovered tunnels burrowed deep into the eastern side of the mountains. Hundreds of soldiers have taken up camp within the tunnels—waiting for the command to attack and take siege of the Nereidians."

"Brielle, what are their motives?" Josiah asked, in a demanding tone unbefitting of a Guardian's behavior.

"Excuse me, Head Elder," Brielle spoke surprised. "Their motives are not relevant. In fact, their actions and motives are irrelevant to this preceding. They must be stopped for the sake of the Nereidan people."

"I agree," Kadeem the ninth Elder spoke up. "If they are allowed to continue, then their actions will be devastating. They must be stopped, and this conflict ended. There is no question about that."

Josiah grew uneasy waiting for his chance to make his request. Gripping the podium tightly with his fingers, he tried to hide his impatience. The discussion of the facts of this case hindered him from making his desires known.

"Elders Brielle and Kadeem, there have to be a cause as to why they act as wrongfully as this Council has pointed out. I want to know what their motives are. Please tell me—what makes them so eager to take control of the Nereidians?"

Elder Uriah tapped his fingers on the table before him. "Head Elder, as Elder Brielle has stated, their reasoning is not the issue here. The Tritons' actions violate our laws, and they must be punished."

"Elders of the Council of the Twelve, do you sit before me and believe that their reasoning is not in question? We cannot damn these people to Deimos without further knowing the facts of their actions."

Uriah didn't dare to glance around the room. He had a purpose to fulfill today, and maintaining his concentration proved difficult. If he allowed the intentions of any who sided with Josiah to affect him it would ruin his plan.

"Head Elder ... please," Uriah insisted impatiently. "This case you propose is neither here nor there. The motives of the Triton are not our concern."

Josiah loosened his grip from the podium and let out a muffled sigh. "Elder Uriah, are you telling me that we neither care nor respect their reasoning?"

Torrey, the second Elder, looked up from the stack of papers he was rifling through at that moment. Surprised by the Head Elder's hesitance to act upon the recommendations of Brielle and Uriah, he interrupted Josiah.

"Head Elder, I do not understand what you mean by your statement. These entities are plotting to commit murder against the people of Nereid. We cannot allow ourselves to become victims as well. We are not here to judge why these entities chose to act, but to judge their immoral intent."

"Are you sure, Elder Torrey, that the Tritons plot any misgivings toward the Nereidians at all?"

"Excuse me, Head Elder Josiah," Kahlil, the tenth Elder interrupted. "I am just as confused as Elder Torrey. Why are you so intent on knowing their cause? Torrey has brought before us a valid point."

"Because, Elder Kahlil, if one breaks a law they have a reason for doing so. If their reasons are so important to them that they will risk bringing damnation down upon themselves, then we must consider the importance of their cause."

"Head Elder," Torrey continued. He felt as perplexed as the rest of the Council members. "Again, I must agree with Uriah. Their motives are irrelevant to—"

Just then, Aryanna, the third Elder spoke raising her voice. "Head Elder, I will not consider any such thing. Their sin should not be glorified or entertained by the innocent members of this Council."

"Why not, Aryanna?" Josiah demanded, gripping the podium once more. He could feel the last bit of his sane demeanor slipping away.

"Surely, Elder Josiah, you do not expect me to answer that question?"

"Yes, I do, Elder."

"Head Elder, this is preposterous," Dasia, the fourth Elder, mocked. Her weakness for controlling her newly acquired human emotions showed.

Josiah closed his eyes and sucked in a ragged breathe. "Council, I want you to understand both sides of this conflict. The Nereidians do not deserve to have destruction brought upon them—just as the Tritons do not deserve to be judged—and condemned before their actions have been brought forth."

Jovan, the eighth Elder screamed, with a snarl in his

chest. "Head Elder, you are straying from the issue at hand. The Tritons are committing a crime with the intention to occupy the people of Nereid. The Tritons' actions will result in the termination of their race. Their motives are of no concern to us. Elder, you must give the order to stop this heinous attempt."

"Fellow Council members, do you forget that I was once sentenced to the realm of Deimos? I felt the burning soil beneath my feet and the heat scorching my essence. My life was taken from me on that barren planet."

Josiah looked around the room with stern eyes. These people had become cold and unsympathetic. Josiah suffered a cause, whether he liked it or not. These Council members had no cause, yet they judged over the actions of others. Right or wrong, the Elders decided the fate of many. Josiah wondered how many were *innocent* and acting for a cause just as he had.

"I was sentenced," Josiah said, forming each word so it sounded precise. He wanted to make sure his point was clear. He would be heard here today no matter what it cost him. "Because, good Guardians, I broke the law. The reasons of my actions were of no concern to anyone in this room. My intentions were deemed blasphemous. My essence vanished without a second thought by any of you here in this room. You have learned now what intentions were behind my actions.

"Thus, here I sit redeemed in this Council. I knew what I faced and felt my cause was worthy enough for me to trade my life for another. She is the one who came as the voice of the Creator and made it possible for me to sit on this Council. Therefore, had the Council not been so judgmental—the essence of the Sentinel would not have been jeopardized. I tell you, Council members—all entities are of value and importance. Do not forget this,

Guardians."

Each Council member remained silent as their eyes skimmed the room for one another's response. Their Head Elder had just made a plea before the Council to consider the actions of the Triton people. Truly, their intentions alone warranted prosecution. However, this fact now seemed overlooked by the Head Elder.

From out of disbelief for what he was hearing, Rashaad, the sixth Elder, now found the strength to speak out against their Leader. "Head Elder, excuse me. Please allow me to ask for confirmation of what lesson you have desired to teach those of us in this room. I indeed, believe all who are charged have the right to present their case. All are innocent until proven guilty. However, you forget that the Tritons threaten the lives of another race of beings. You broke our laws of touching a human. Your actions offended no one, except yourself. Redeemed or not ... you stand before us. The Nereidian people will not, if we do not stop this atrocity from happening."

Josiah felt the human emotion of anger surfacing. The Guardians before him were naïve existing without the tenderness of human compassion. A trait he found at times to make more sense than that of the intellect of a Guardian's essence.

"Elder Rashaad, I am not instructing this Council to sit idly by. On the contrary, we must end this conflict. However, my plan as we pass judgment is to consider what their motives are. We must consider what has brought them to this state. We must evaluate the missed warning signs and be conscious that a situation, like this matter at hand, does not repeat itself. I am simply saying that understanding their intentions is of great importance—"

"Elder," Brielle interrupted, "yes, we will take their motives into account. Now may we please move forward with this session?"

Josiah gritted his teeth at their ignorance. "Very well then. Guardians of this Council, please tell me what you believe is the best solution to this issue."

"Simple," Uriah voiced, "we must stop them. Send the Watchers to secure the Triton army in an orb and take them to the Phobos Universe for holding. We shall try their case as with any other entity that has entered through our doors—with the same diligence to right the wrongs and bring justice. After their trial we will deal with them accordingly."

"All right ... carry on, Uriah." Josiah turned his head to face those who assembled before him. "As Head Elder, I will send the Watchers to subdue the Triton people as Elder Uriah has indicated. Send word to the Watchers to bind the people of Triton and proclaim to the Nereidian people the looming destruction."

Those in the room nodded in agreement. Elder Torrey remained cautious of Josiah's behavior. He sensed Josiah's dismay. It was a feeling Torrey remembered experiencing quite strongly in a dimly lit chamber two human years ago. Even to this day, the unexplainable blue light haunted his thoughts. The Sentinel wanted and needed something from him. His understanding of her was void. Torrey was just an ordinary Elder. He had nothing to offer the Sentinel. Yet, the look in her eyes told him what his mind couldn't comprehend.

For one moment in the universe, his mind heard the thoughts of another. Those thoughts warped with his own brought confusion upon him. Even his retreat to Adrastea to seek solace had not helped. Daily Torrey pushed the undecipherable visions from his mind. The vision may have been lost in the darkness he created, but the soothing creaking noise of a rocking chair always stayed with him.

The Head Elder looked around the room at each Council member before him. As his eyes met Torrey's, he found them to be enchanting as he locked his thoughts upon him. From inside of the darkness that Josiah created in his own mind, he recalled a memory he once saw from the human Tori's thoughts. It was from the day Josiah found Tori dying in a hospital bed. Her husband had perished in an automobile accident that was claiming her life as well. At that moment, Josiah envisioned a striking green pair of eyes too bright to belong to a human. They contained a grace and beauty found only on Callisto in the Garden of Love. He had recognized those eyes, but from where he couldn't recall. Josiah felt he should know this, or that he had once before. Then unable hold the vision, it slipped away. When he realized his attention had drifted from the proceedings, he looked away from Torrey in embarrassment.

Those assembled had begun to leave their seats. Josiah's desires to be with Raina took on a new edge. Boldly he pulled strength from within, to state his cause.

"Fellow Guardians, I propose a question to you this day."

Each Guardian stopped, and then tuned to face Josiah. Before them, stood their Leader still firmly planted at the podium. His expression oddly called out to them gaining their full attention.

"It is clear that my motives are not equal to those of you who sit on this Council. My time here has not been without many challenges for each of you. My appearance ... my role has brought about numerous changes for our kind. Many of you have remained quite compliant out of respect for their chair on the Council. Today, I remind you all of the triumph and mysteries my role has created. I call you to order to assemble and to hear my request. I, Josiah, Head

Elder of the Council of the Twelve, respectfully request your agreement in my desire to step down as Head Elder."

Instantly the room broke out in gasps as each Council member stared at one another in disbelief. Torrey rushed to Josiah's side to stop him from saying anything further. Josiah must not be allowed to step down from his position.

"Elder, what are you attempting to do here?"

"I am doing just as I have stated to each of you, Elder Torrey."

"Josiah, this is preposterous. You cannot say this openly," he barked. Then forcing a loud bellowing laugh, he slapped Josiah on the back. "Elder—you never cease to amaze me with your human tendencies to enlighten us with their humor. I believe you have just accomplished, as the humans say, 'a rise' from every Guardian in this room. Surely, their stunned looks have brought you the satisfaction all humans desire when they tease one another.

"I have always enjoyed the human characteristic you bring to this courtroom. I shall laugh many days at your words and from the expressions of my brothers and sisters. Come with me please and show me more of the human amusement."

Torrey smiled at his fellow Guardians as he latched onto Josiah's arm. He ushered him through the stain glass doors exiting into the courtyard. Torrey didn't let go of Josiah's arm until he had led him into the heart of the garden positioned in the center of the courtyard.

"Elder, what are you doing?" he demanded, appalled at Josiah's conduct in the chamber.

"I have already told you, Elder Torrey. I did as I intended. I have made a request to be removed from my seat on the Council."

"And what are your reasons? They had better be important to bring such discord down upon you and those present in the chamber."

"Torrey ... do I need to remind you of what has come to pass. You of all entities know the sacrifices we have suffered for the cause of the Sentinel."

"I do not know what you are speaking of," Torrey said hesitantly.

"Then do you dare tell me the blue light that haunts your memory and the tingle, which scorches your finger tips, means nothing to you?"

"Elder Josiah, you know nothing about what I experienced that day."

"Do you really believe that, Elder? I too, have felt its sting upon my hands. Its power courses through me. This light affected both of us for a reason. A reason, you have chosen not to investigate. I on the other hand cannot look the other way. The light and the powers the Sentinel imposed upon me—I do not know how to control, nor do I want to. I have one true desire that dwells deeply within my essence. It is to be with Raina."

"The human girl?" he asked bewildered. "Josiah ... have you gone mad? She was a vessel for the Sentinel and nothing more. Her human life meant nothing, and she perished on Earth."

"No, Elder Torrey. She is alive, and I have found her."

"That is impossible, Head Elder."

"No more impossible than the blue light affecting just you in a room with other Guardians. It is no more impossible then the Sentinel sparing her life and secretly sending Raina elsewhere to live. She is alive, and I intend on being with her. It was always meant to be ... this I am sure of."

"Josiah, you cannot abandon your people for the soul of a human. Our laws have not completely changed. You know it is still forbidden to touch a human. Your cause this time will not be found worthy. No Guardian has ever shed their existence for another way of life. You will be a rogue and when found sentenced to Deimos."

"I am counting on that, my friend. It is a place I have been sentenced to before with the expectation of remaining there for all eternity. It is a place I am not afraid to return to."

"You are being foolish, Head Elder."

"No, Elder. I believe I am being adventurous," he said, then laughed to himself.

Then Josiah turned and dematerialized from the courtyard. Vowing to take back his human form, he fled to Earth. He didn't care anymore about what was written in the Scroll of Deuel. He would leave it all behind. His seat on the Council, his leadership over his kind, and the family he loved.

This time Josiah didn't take such precautions in creating the human façade to live by. His true purpose was to see Raina. His shabby college dorm he created months ago in Pasadena would be sufficient. He was already a student because of his assignment with Professor Russell—therefore he fit right in. Determined to be with Raina he scanned Earth and found her in the Hemet Library.

She had not changed. She was still a proficient studier keeping her notes and outlines written in detail and highlighted in order of importance. Raina indeed had matured as Josiah once envisioned.

Raina wasn't as engrossed in her books as she looked. She noticed Josiah sitting across from her. She smiled to be friendly, but it was nothing more than that. Josiah longed to get her attention. He didn't realize he already had it.

She removed her headphones, and Josiah froze when he heard the music playing. The song was a breathtaking piano composition he remembered well. The title was soothing as it matched the moment. Espérer means to hope. That is what Raina titled the song when she wrote it for him. It symbolized their love and their hope to never part. That is what Josiah was full of this moment. That is how he lived these last two human years.

Raina stared at the odd boy in front of her. His expression was almost amusing, but to anyone else it may have been creepy. She spoke with a humorous edge to her tone. "Hello, is anyone home?"

He blinked finding reality in front of him. "That is beautiful ..." His voice trailed off angelically, into a soft hum.

"You can hear that?" she asked surprised.

He nodded calling his attention to the grin he had loved so well. "Can you not?"

"Yes, but I know how the song goes. I hear it in my head every day." What she didn't know was that Josiah had as well.

"It sounds familiar to me. Who is the composer?"

"I doubt you have ever heard it before. I wrote it many years ago. My mother had me take piano lessons. I had to show something for all of the money she spent on lessons as a child. I think it makes me well-rounded or cultured ... or something."

"May I listen some more?" he asked, holding out an overly willing hand.

Embarrassed by his request, she granted him his wish. As Raina handed him the music player, she wasn't prepared for what she had seen next. Josiah fastened the headphones around his ears, and instantly he began waving his arms into the air. His movements matched the beat of her song. He looked almost angelic as his eyes fixed upon her.

Then all of a sudden, the darkness crept up on him. The pull was too strong, and Josiah found himself sucked up into another daydream. The dark cave seemed more intense this time, and the dreadful end came much sooner than usual. His fears seemed twice as bad, as a weakened cry came from the shadows off to his right. His eyes adjusted quickly, and a sense of horror washed over him. There in the corner, Raina crouched against the wall of the cave. Blood spewed from her hands and face as her torn camisole flapped in the chilling breeze. A natural instinct for protecting her urged Josiah to attend to her. Consumed by fear his heart forgot to beat. After he extended his hand to grab hold of hers, a shrilling laugh came from behind him. Josiah turned facing a mass darker than the fallen ones on Deimos.

"Well, if you thought it was that bad," Raina shouted loudly, with no regards to the rules of the Library, "all you had to do was turn it off!"

"What?" he questioned, feeling the drops of sweat bounce against his skin.

"I said if you didn't like the song—then all you had to do was turn it off."

Her tone didn't mask her anger. She reached forward grabbing the player from his hands roughly, showing her displeasure for the reaction to her music. Raina moved so fast, that he did not have a chance to remove the headphones before she yanked them off his head.

"No," he shouted, realizing he sounded too mean. "Please ... you have misunderstood me." His voice softened, but his breath still panted deeply. "I believe it is the most elegant piece I have ever heard. I have very much enjoyed it."

"Well," Raina interjected sarcastically, "you could've fooled me. You looked like you were going to die."

"I am sorry. I have been faulted for intense facial expressions. Please believe me. Your song is wonderful."

"Well, if your expression was one of pleasure—I would sure hate to see it when you're dying."

"That is not pretty either." He pretended to smile. He had to get a hold of himself and smooth this over. "Please, if I have not offended you too much, perhaps we can go to the coffee shop on State and Stetson. I can give you an overview of the musical choices loaded in the old jukebox. They have some pretty good '80s tunes to pick from."

"Hey, how did you know I like listening to hair bands?"

Josiah froze, he offered too much again. He smiled to cover his slip-up. "Your player, I read your playlist."

"Oh," she said, not sounding convinced.

Josiah stood up reaching for Raina's bag. "May I?"

She smiled with a slight nod of her head and then stood up.

The wind blew gently, but Raina tucked her coat tighter around her neck, sighing. The February weather in California was warm by most people's standards, but still after all of these years—she detested any cool weather.

Josiah felt an odd sensation of energy flow between them as they walked briskly down the sidewalk. The strange energy nearly incapacitated Josiah making him more conscious of every move she made. He became sensitive to every beat of her heart and her rapid breathing.

"Am I walking too fast for you?" he questioned, not taking his eyes off her.

"No, your pace is fine. So, tell me, do they really have good coffee at the cafe?"

"I guess so. I have not tried any myself; although I have heard many people rave about it."

"Fine, coffee it is."

Josiah nodded and then opened the door for her. The coffee shop was crowded and noisy. This certainly wasn't a good place for this Guardian to investigate her presence.

After ordering their coffees, Raina and he found a set of empty seats toward the back of the shop. Raina said nothing at first to him clearly being uncomfortable from the way Josiah stared at her.

"So, where is the jukebox you were talking about?" she asked, trying to make conversation.

"It is in the corner over there." Josiah pointed, jumping to his feet. He hurriedly removed some change from his pocket and counted out the amount needed to play a song for her.

Raina watched him stroll across the room. She could see his expression seemed so serious. It was apparent to her that he was intent on finding the best tunes to play for them. She watched him stroll back with a large grin on his face. Immediately, her favorite love song had begun to play.

"Hey, I haven't heard that song in years. It used to be my favorite." Raina paused and then her eyes closed. Josiah could hear her taking deep breaths.

"Is there something wrong?"

"Ah no, I just thought the song was something else ... that's all."

"Do you not like it then?"

"No, it is a great song. Thank you for picking it."

Josiah smiled. "Wait until you hear the next one. I particularly chose that one just for you."

"Tell me what it is, please?"

"Shhh, I am not telling. You will just have to see what song I have chosen when it begins to play."

"Oh, come on. Just give me a little hint?"

"No way. You will just have to learn to have a little patience."

"Gee, thanks for nothing," she added sarcastically.

"Yeah ... let us just wait and see if you say that in a few minutes."

Josiah smiled and then took a sip of his coffee. It had been years since he indulged in human food. When Raina was taken from him, he found no reason to create a shell strictly for recreational purposes. Now that he had the only one he would ever love before him, life seemed a little different for him. He had found a reason to indulge once again.

"So, tell me what brings you here to California anyway?" Josiah asked, with more curiosity than Raina could ever know.

"The observatory is why I came here."

"What?" he asked her, somewhat surprised by Raina's answer. "The observatory is almost two hours away from here."

"I know. And the university is almost two hours north of here, too."

"I do not understand why you live here in Hemet when you attend classes in Pasadena."

"The observatory at Palomar Mountain is the reason I came. I visited there as a child with my parents. There was something about the observatory that totally fascinated me. I couldn't get enough of it. My parents practically had to drag me out of there one day. We were to be in Southern California for two weeks touring all the hottest spots. I was so hung up on the observatory that my parents had to change our plans.

"We stayed a whole week here picnicking in the state park and gazing up at the stars. I have been drawn here every year since then. So, when I got older, I made up my mind that I wanted to be close enough to visit this place every day if I could.

"My dad thought I was nuts when I chose Astronomy as a career. He protested even more at my decision to travel back and forth from Palomar to Pasadena as much as I do.

Although for some reason, he did approve of me living in Hemet. That is after some convincing, of course. My dad felt it was a safe little town for his 'baby girl' to live in." She chuckled to herself. "Don't you see how amazing it is to look up at the stars and wonder if there are really other forms of life out there? Beings we never knew existed. It is just amazing to think about what outer space really holds. Someday I will be out there among the stars. I can just feel it." Raina paused, staring up through the sky light in the ceiling. When she looked back at him, Josiah could see the magic behind her eyes. The same magic he saw each time he held her in his essence showing her through his mind the wonders of his world.

"And what brings you here to Hemet anyway, Josiah?"

"Actually, I do not live here in Hemet. I stay at a dorm in Pasadena. I guess I attend the institute because I like to study molecular and cellular biology," Josiah replied weakly.

Raina laughed. "Yuck, you must be desperate to live a life of loneliness."

"Why do you say that?"

"Just think about it. You will be stuck in a lab all day doing what, playing with test tubes, and petri dishes. You will become a hermit like Professor Cutter. No ... I know— you will turn out demented and all exocentric like Professor Russell."

"Well, actually ... he is why I came. His research is incredible. I do not want to be in a lab all day. I want to be free out in the open world. I want to go to the places he has been and see the things he has seen. Yes, that is what I want. You will not catch me in a lab all day. I want to do field research just like him."

"Okay ... so I live in Hemet–'Daddy's little safe haven' for his daughter, because of the Astrophysics course at the institute. I sacrifice hours on the road making the long drive to the institute every other day for my classes. What is your excuse for making the ... four hour drive back and forth from Pasadena to be in the spot light at the observatory?"

"I am working on getting an internship with Professor Russell. He keeps an eye on the students who participate in the volunteer programs at the observatory. If I get just one semester as his aide, it will all be worthwhile."

"Then I guess you can justify the travel. So, I was thinking about our schedules. We should see if our schedules would coordinate with one another. We could car pool and save the environment. That will give you more of a chance to read up on your *hero*."

"Very funny." He chuckled. "I am here because of Professor Russell. Why did you not just stay in Silver Lake and attend the University of Chicago? They have an excellent astrophysics program there, and the observatory in William's Bay is an affiliation of it. And of course what about the observatory in Whitewater? That is certainly a lot closer to your home than here."

"I don't know. I have been to the University of Chicago and to the observatory in William's Bay. I guess that I just like it here much better. Maybe it is the mountains, or the warm weather. I dislike the cold and the thought of everything winter brings with it. Here, I always know what I am getting. The weather never gets too cold to keep me from walking in the trails in the mountains. At night, I'll toss a blanket on the ground and look up at the stars. You can't do that all year around in Wisconsin." Raina smiled uncomfortably. This conversation was the same as the one she had with her parents. Like them, Josiah didn't seem to understand the attraction she had for California.

"So, tell me?" Josiah asked, trying to make her feel more

comfortable. He could tell by the change in the color of her cheeks that she was embarrassed. "What makes you stray from your academic courses to sit in on Cutter's Cellular Biology course? I did not know that his class was a prerequisite for Astronomy."

"It's not. The idea of cellular change and the conversion of molecules in one's body are intriguing to me. Just think about the possibility of a human body converted into another form by subjecting it to energy and even surviving the energy consumption. The whole process is impossible I know, but what if it actually did happen and someone survived this transformation?"

Josiah became startled. Her speculation was clearly bizarre for any normal human being. However, in Raina's case, during her previous life she did survive this transformation when he joined with her. He couldn't fathom what thoughts or memories lingered in her mind for Raina to believe it possible.

"I wonder what she wants." Raina's voice broke through Josiah's thoughts.

He snapped his head in the direction Raina was looking. When his eyes found the target, he gasped.

"What is she an ex-girl friend or something?"

"No, an old friend." He smiled falsely, taking in another deep breath. "Will you please excuse me for a moment?"

Raina nodded, taking another sip of her coffee. At that moment, another song selected by Josiah rang out from the jukebox. Josiah stood up and walked toward the door. Grabbing the woman's arm, he led her from the coffeehouse to the parking lot.

"Brielle, may I ask why you are here?"

"You look right at home with her, Head Elder. Even with your ties severed, you two make a nice pair."

"Excuse me?" Josiah asked, trying to hide his surprise at her appearance.

"I have come to tell you something, however, you must swear that you will never reveal what I am about to say."

Josiah stared at her a moment wondering what her words would mean to him. "I will not speak of our conversation to anyone. Now tell me please, what do you want?"

"Head Elder, openly, I must side with the Council regarding the previous matters of the Nereidian people. This includes the damnation you are bringing upon yourself by congregating with your past Esprit de corps. Even though the Council owns my judgment to rule in Guardian affairs, it does not own my conscience. I have always believed that you and the human girl deserved to be together. My point of view on this matter will not change."

"Why are you telling me this, Brielle?"

"Head Elder, my behavior in session today will remain my public stand. I just wanted you to know of my personal view. I say this, because when it comes time to prosecute you for your current actions, I want you to know that whatever the Council decides, I will remain as neutral as possible."

"Why do you care about what becomes of me?"

"Because, Head Elder. I cannot stand by any longer and watch you self-destruct. The line has to be drawn, and your current actions have no place on either side. I do not envy you or the predicament you have found yourself experiencing. No, all I have is pity." Then looking away from him, she left as fast as she appeared.

12.

CAN TIME HEAL?

Guardian Realm—return to Earth's timeline 1926

Sariel glided into Malachi's chamber. The look of confusion lay branded heavily on his face.

"Malachi, come quickly, I have terrible news!"

"What is it, Sariel?" Malachi asked, withholding any sign of emotion.

Sariel's olive colored face turned pale. He couldn't hide the human emotions he trained himself to feel.

"The Watcher, Guardian Talib, has ceased to exist!"

"How is that possible, Sariel?"

"I am not sure, Malachi. He was carrying out his orders when the human image he fashioned succumbed to a supposed accident. He was crushed by a moving train."

"His orders? What were those orders? I did not give instructions for the Watchers to take any forms."

"Sir, it was Great Elder Mataya who gave the order."

"When did she do that?"

"Three Earth weeks ago."

"Why did she give you orders without consulting me first, Sariel?"

"I am not sure, Malachi. The human Clement fell from a cliff three weeks ago while cutting down a tree for firewood."

"What are you talking about? I was not informed of any such event."

"Malachi, Elder Mataya said that I must remain silent about the accident."

Malachi moaned in disapproval. "Go on, what happened next?"

"Sir, Talib was guarding the human female, Naomi, and did not see the danger until it was too late. He felt very concerned that the future of the human did not warn him. When she approached Enoch and me, we agreed with Elder Mataya that this was an extremely severe situation. I do not know why she did not mention this to you. I thought you had been informed." Sariel paused at the expression on Malachi's face. It contained both a look of horror and of shock. "Sir," he persisted, "Clement's death seemed too coincidental considering our cause. Elder Mataya instructed Talib to hide the body and produce a form of Clement's image. She believed we needed to carry on as planned. If we allowed the human Naomi to grieve, it would create unnecessary complications. No one could know of his death for it might have changed the outcome of our plan. Therefore, together Elder Mataya and Talib created a duplicate of Clement. Talib acted as he was instructed to and returned to Clement's home posing as a human."

"What right did you to have to play God?" Malachi managed to say in a raspy voice. It was difficult to keep his composure when he learned of such illegal actions from those who pledge to uphold their plan. He sighed as his words sunk in; reminding him of the affliction, his people were subjected to experiencing.

"Malachi, the Elder must have been correct in her reasoning. An unknown force attacked Talib's human form. Enoch was there when the attack occurred. Malachi, I must inform you that Enoch sensed no danger. When he realized Talib was combating a supernatural force, he ran to remove the human woman from the area. He arrived too late to assist Talib."

Malachi paced back and forth restlessly. The words he heard from Sariel seemed too incredible to believe. "I do not understand how the evil remained cloaked."

"Sir, this apparition proved to be very strong. Talib could not subdue it or convert back to his natural state in time. It is as if the apparition planned for the train to strike him down."

"And the woman and the child—how are they now, Sariel?"

"Not well, Malachi."

"What do you mean, Sariel?"

"The woman ... she is missing, and the child is gone as well."

Malachi refused to indulge in human emotions, but now fear made its appearance in his voice replacing the raspy tone it carried earlier. "Missing—that is impossible. What do mean by this?"

"Sir, the woman and the child disappeared from the cabin. We are looking for the two of them now."

"Who is searching for them?"

"Sir, Observers, Zafirah and Askari, are searching diligently as we speak."

"Have we heard any news from the town's people? Do they know a situation has occurred?"

"No, Elder. The town is oblivious to the spiritual assault. They do not know at this moment that the woman and child are missing," Sariel said, desiring not to answer the question that pressed in his mind. "Surely they will sense the disruption, Malachi."

"We must keep the humans from discovering what has happened, Sariel."

"I know this, Malachi. However, the woman and the entity are not in this current realm. Of this, I am sure. I have the Watchers, Isaiah, and Benaiah, scanning the solar system for them at this moment, sir."

"How are you so sure, Sariel, that they are not currently in this realm? What gives you this impression, my friend?"

Sariel lowered his eyes to break contact. Guilt burned deep inside of his essence. "We do not sense them, sir." It troubled him to admit as an Observer, he failed to protect an Esprit de corps. "Enoch believes the same as I, Malachi. The evil has struck in secret. Perhaps it is cloaked by more powers than we are familiar with or have seen. None of the Observers report sensing other life forms. Malachi, the evil moves undetected."

"This is extremely out of the ordinary. Our essences are superior. I cannot believe within myself or accept the fact that a power stronger than the one bestowed upon us by the Creator exist."

"Sir, we must admit that the entity is not within our reach. I do not want to believe it myself, that there is a force greater than ours is. However, the child has been removed if not destroyed from our realm." Sariel felt anger and regret brewing in the pit of his essence. "I just knew this was a mistake!"

Malachi jerked his head in surprise of Sariel's sudden statement. Sariel had been a huge supporter of Mataya's plan. This change in belief for their cause concerned Malachi.

"How so, Sariel? What is it that makes you question our efforts? You know what good we have done and what lengths we have gone to make this plan work."

Sariel's tone didn't hold the angelic hum it had normally displayed. This was very alarming to the wise Guardian. "Malachi, did we learn nothing from Ladarius and Lexis? Did our people not suffer enough from the intermingling of Guardians and humans?"

"Sariel, please consider what you are saying? We have learned through the Great Elder that we need each other to function. This is evident more now than ever, young Sarial."

"I do not believe this to be true, Malachi. We should stay on the path that we were created to walk. The fabrications of human forms are too dangerous, as we have just seen. Giving up on our own is wrong!"

"No, Sariel. We made the right decision. Apparently Enoch and Talib had a situation we did not predict."

"A situation, Malachi?" Sariel questioned, exhausted from the emotions interrupting the even balance of his essence. "Who do you think you are you fooling? A Guardian does not disappear unless there is some evil force at work. It must be great if I have not felt it myself."

"We will find the entity and make things right."

"Malachi, you speak of foolishness and half truths. Why do we extend ourselves to the boundaries we have crossed? Why does He just stand idly by and do nothing? Surely, if He just intervened, snapped His fingers, or spoke the word He could change this. We would not be lost to the entity."

"Sariel, you know the purpose behind his actions. Yes—He could just snap His fingers or wave His hands, or whatever hocus pocus the humans believe in and end this now. Although, why would He do that? He loves His children and wants them to know His love by having free will. He wants them to understand His love while enduring hard times. So that when it is fulfilled, they would be right back into His safe arms. To what benefit would it be if He treated us like puppets or china dolls? We would be created and denied all that we have before ourselves today, my friend?"

"I just do not understand, Malachi, why this evil has to reign. Why do we have to extend such great effort for her survival? He has the power in His hands to keep her safe and take her from harm's way before it arrives?"

"Sariel, if the evil is not allowed to happen and the good to prevail, then no one would know that good does exist. With the good comes the bad. A cycle our Creator has finely fashioned. Do you not believe in His omnipotence?"

"I believe in His wondrous works. Do I not stand here before you? I do not understand or fathom why death is allowed to riddle humans or that terror befalls them. Why do their illnesses run wild and their children suffer from hunger, disease, and violence? What reasoning is there? How cruel this is."

"Sariel, has He not said if one cannot understand the mysteries of this world—then they cannot understand the mysteries of Heaven. Have faith and do not lose sight. He has a far bigger plan than any man can comprehend. He knows what He is doing."

"Yes, and what is the rest, Malachi?"

"Sariel, my dear brother. Just live as He has taught you. A kind heart built upon faith in His word and His miracles. The rest will take care of itself."

"So, then we play this out with no petition before the Creator? We search and pray the entity lives."

"Yes, young Sariel."

"This is ridiculous. He has the power to turn time back and stop this. Why does He not do something?"

"He already has. He gave us all that he had ... you know the sacrifice."

Sariel's expression went blank. Here in the few words spoken by Malachi, he realized what greatness the Creator really contained.

"I know ... I am sorry. I do not understand much about the new world we are subjected to participate in daily. Life was once so simple until Elder Mataya charged us to assist the humans. I live on what the humans call an emotional roller coaster. It tries my patience and my faith. I do not know how much longer I can endure."

Malachi laughed taking compassion upon his dear friend. "Young Sariel, you face the same tribulations and trials as the humans have since the beginning of their time. How better to appreciate the mental workings God had when He created them ... and loved them. Do as He has instructed them. Have faith, my friend."

Just then the Watcher Isaiah, materialized in the room. He cradled in his arms an ashen colored baby that was barely alive. Isaiah fell to his knees in grief as strange tears seeped from his eyes.

"Malachi, the baby—look!"

Before them in Isaiah's arms was a baby whose life force was diminishing. Isaiah's distraught appearance alarmed Sariel.

"Isaiah, what has happened to her?"

Isaiah wept as his tall thin frame shuttered with each sob. "I felt it, but I could not discern it. Something dark held the woman and the baby under the ice. I could not rescue the woman in time. I felt the baby's heart grow weak, so I pulled her from their realm."

Malachi rushed to Isaiah's side. "Hurry, Sariel! Summon the Great Elder Mataya—we need her to help the child." He grasped the dying baby relieving Isaiah of his burden. Fear of failure flashed through his mind. "Isaiah," he ordered, "quickly—go now! Summon the Watcher Enoch and bring him back here. Do not tell him the reason for the urgency, and keep your thoughts to yourself."

Isaiah nodded fighting to regain his composure. "Yes, sir." Then he disappeared from the chamber.

Malachi held the child tightly in his arms waiting for Mataya to arrive. Her healing powers and guidance would direct them further. Her objectives for the Sentinel's protection had been followed to the letter. Even when there were reasons to doubt her plan ... he complied. Malachi didn't understand the total workings or the ramifications of what the past, or Mataya's new future held. He only knew the wise Elder was adamant, and their actions were for the protection of Earth.

The Council banned time manipulation after a series of events drove rogue Guardians to selfish acts of destruction. Mataya risked much to act as she had. A future she lived through went terribly wrong. She devised a plan in her mind to change the past and make the wrongs right for a brighter future. It was a plan that could cost Mataya her very existence. She believed it was small price to pay for humanity if she failed.

No other Guardian in Malachi's era knew the details of the disaster that occurred from Markian's mind control. Although the temptation was great for each member of the Secret Council to seek out the details, none had. Honesty kept those involved waiting for the truth. They knew only of Mataya's arrival in the past and honored the silence of the future facts.

Immediately, Enoch arrived with Isaiah. Fear showed thick on his face. Isaiah found him this wintery evening held up in the boarding house where he had stationed himself. He was keeping careful watch over the other Esprit de corps whose life ran a course very close to the Chosen One. The boarding house gave him careful view over his Esprit de corps and assistance to the others on the Secret Council.

The young Miss Netamae Burrows, who is an aristocrat's daughter, was destined to open an orphanage. She would care for many children fighting for their survival during the upcoming economical depression.

"Oh, my!" Enoch screamed. "The baby—will she live?"

"I do not know, Enoch. We wait for Elder Mataya as I speak."

Enoch grasped his face and screamed falling to the floor. "Then I have failed." He wept, filled with regret and shame.

At that moment, an Angel's song soothed his discontent. Mataya appeared behind him placing her hand on his shoulder.

"Do not be so quick to give up, Enoch. The child will live ... there is another plan. She took the child from Malachi and hummed a beautiful melody. The heartbeat strengthened, and the child cried tears of joy.

The members of the Secret Council stood silently observing Mataya. She held her poise as confident at that moment as she had been during their first meeting. Little did Malachi and Sariel know what they were to face when she appeared to them that day so long ago.

It was just as any other perfect day. The Creator's ambiance filled the meeting hall as the orchestra performed off in the distance. Sariel and Malachi were playing a game of chess, reminiscing about their past missions. Each well advanced in their essences looked forward to life relaxing on the grounds of Prometheus.

Malachi told more of his earth-learned jokes, and Sariel quoted lines from plays written by the people of Calypso. Their visits as always felt refreshing and graced them with the knowledge of the Creator's supremacy.

Mataya appeared to them with tales of unchartered universes that ran consecutive to their own. At first comprehending her seriousness was not easy. When she had made her plan clear, neither one could refuse her their aid. The prestigious group of Guardians who pledged their eternal friendship to Sariel and Malachi followed without hesitation. Their essences were at risk; however, each knew the need for a greater outcome. One that would make most Guardians shudder and flee from the dangers of Deimos had encouraged the newly found Council to press onward.

"Isaiah," Mataya instructed, "retrieve the Watcher Talib's form from Earth. We must be sure no evil inhabits it in the future."

Enoch stared at the Great Elder. "What about me? Will I take leave from Earth as well, Elder?"

Her expression fixed brightly on the child. "No, Enoch, a new plan has been formed. You will remain on Earth to see it out."

"Elder Mataya, what about the entity and the child?"

"Enoch, you and your Esprit de corps will care for her."

"How—Elder? What do you have planned? My service is about completed. My Esprit de corps' choices are made, and she will begin the first steps needed to carry out her destiny. Her life is ready to move on without my service. How do you propose I proceed?"

"Enoch, the one whom I spoke of, his fate relies on our actions. We must do this for him."

"What do you ask of me, Elder?"

"We must continue to keep the entity safe in this new path to keep the evil from finding the Sentinel as before. When the time is right, I will guide Josiah toward the child who will be the vessel, and he will relieve you all from your duties. After Raina's course on Earth is complete, we can rest. Until that point, do what you must to secure a future for this child."

"What do you want me to do?"

"Go to your Esprit de corps, Enoch. Follow the human love you have finely fashioned within your essence for her."

"Elder Mataya, do you not know that she is in love with someone ... else?"

"Enoch, what I know is what you feel. I have seen the admiration in your eyes for the human. You are not faulted for those emotions. Those emotions will guide this situation. Do what you must—however, I ask you to do what you know is right."

"What is right and what I must do is not clear to me, Elder. Please, will you not offer me some guidance in this matter?"

My trusted friend, Enoch. I know what you hide deep inside of your essence. I have seen the love surface in your smile. The way you look at her is indiscernible."

"I am ashamed, Elder."

"What have you done to bring shame upon you?"

"I have broken our rules, Elder Mataya. I indeed have loved the human."

"Is this love strong, Enoch?"

"Yes, Elder. It is very strong."

"Is it strong enough to risk your very existence to be with her?"

Enoch looked down at his feet. Shame had visited his essence, but love reigned greater than his guilt. "My existence is nothing without her."

Mataya looked down at the child she held. "There is another way."

"What plan is it that you will carry forth, Mataya?"

"Enoch, go to Earth and make Miss Burrows yours. I will follow after shortly. When I arrive we will put our new plan into action."

13.

WHEN THE LOSS IS LESS THAN THE WIN

Guardian Realm—Earth's timeline 1926

The evening star had begun to rise in the Guardian world. What the humans called nightfall steadily approached. It opened Heaven's window to a miraculous shower of bright lights and falling stars. Tonight Tahir and Evi wouldn't enjoy the beautiful display, as they had done since the moment they joined. An unexpected visitor interrupted the tradition they started over two thousand years ago. If it were not for the high honor of receiving one as grand as Elder Mataya into their chamber—any other request would have been denied. The belief that the Great Elder arrived because of the birth of Evi's children soon took a new direction in its meaning. She was here not because of the children, but one, the girl. Mataya had not come to bring her blessing; she brought a plan of misery and pain.

"What do you propose, Mataya?" Evi glanced back and forth from her husband to Elder Mataya hesitantly.

"Your twins have not yet been announced. We can use this to our advantage."

Evi tilted her head to one side. She didn't like the sound of Mataya's words. Tahir stiffened, calculating where Mataya's conversation would take them.

"What does that mean?" Evi asked.

"Are you aware of the legend behind the Guardian named Lexis?"

Tahir nodded. He knew the story well. He had met Lexis once in his youth. It was a random meeting. They barely greeted one another in the shuffle of Lexis' surveillance concerning his Esprit de corps. Tahir's mission of exploration brought him to the Larissa Universe. Larissa was a small planet with enormous beauty. Tahir went there to acquire rare plant extracts to build Evi a magnificent garden. Lexis was there over-seeing his Esprit de corps, a traveler from a distant realm beyond Earth's solar system.

"I am familiar with him. Why do you ask, Elder Mataya?" Tahir questioned, still leery of the Guardian's visit.

"Then you know, Tahir, what actions he performed and the outcome affecting our people?"

Evi shook her head and smiled. "Elder, we are indeed familiar with his claims. What does that have to do with Tahir and myself?"

"As the two of you know from our current recordings in the history books, nineteen human years ago, Lexis placed the Sentinel in the human vessel, Raina. Before her birth, Markian and his daughter discovered that she harbored the Sentinel. They attacked the vessel wanting to destroy them both. As the two of them searched to locate the Sentinel, Dinah acquired the Scroll of Sychar. She used it to open the Abyss. The Demons of the Abyss were unleashed upon Earth nearly destroying the planet. Our Head Elder, with the assistance of Councilmen Jon and Jaleel, stopped the commander of the army of Demons. The Sentinel restored Earth to its prior course and enlisted Josiah as our Head Elder."

"Great Elder Mataya, I do not need a history lesson," Tahir retorted.

Mataya ignored him and proceeded to explain her story. "What you do not know is that I have created another realm. There I have gone back in time and assisted Lexis to place his daughter's essence in the great-grandmother of Raina. The human female's name is Naomi and—"

"You did what?" Tahir interrupted her completely shocked by her actions.

"Please, Tahir, allow me to explain further before you get so irate."

Tahir clenched his fist demonstrating the human anger he witnessed many times before. An action he had never preformed, but now seemed so natural.

"I am not acting irate. I cannot believe—"

"Tahir, please, let her finish," Evi begged, in a compassionate tone as she patted the back of his hand. "I want to hear what she has to say."

"Thank you, Evi," Mataya interjected. "As I was saying, the human child is named Rebekah. I did this in hopes of covering the essence of Rayna's aura from discovery by Markian and his daughter. I believed that this would allow the original timeline to continue as it was meant to."

Tahir grinned in distaste for the Elder's casual behavior over such a serious issue. "Mataya, you have changed the past thus changing the future. How do you expect the result to be the same? And tell me, Elder, what is the original timeline if you take Markian and his daughter out of the equation?"

"Tahir, I cannot explain my actions as in depth as you would like. Trust me; I knew what I was doing in that timeline. However, somehow an evil entity that I am unable to identify found the new vessel and her parents in the Earth timeline of 1926. This entity is strong and cunning. I believe he was brought to Earth in secret by a supernatural being at the hands of Markian and Dinah."

"Those malefactors were punished along with your brother, Elder. Do you now create stories to lessen their guilt?"

"No, Tahir, I do not. Please allow me to continue," she insisted eagerly.

Tahir grinned moaning for his dislike of Mataya's actions.

"After it attacked the vessel's parents, my Watchers retrieved the human baby and the Sentinel's essence. He saved them before the evil one drowned her in Silver Lake. As we speak, she is in a safe location under great protection. The Sentinel has not been harmed."

"Just a minute, Mataya. How can you take charge over one as the Sentinel? She is all-powerful. I do not believe you could contain one such as her in any form that is not predestined by the Creator."

"Trust me, Tahir. I can do with her essence, as I need to. My realm continues in a different parallel universe than this one. The Sentinel has not yet emerged. This universe is still controlled by Lexis. It is only after he ceased to exist did she become independent. Her time has not been fulfilled in my realm; therefore she is subject to my desires."

"I understand what you are hypothesizing, Mataya. However, please tell me how you will be able to bring the many timelines together. At what point in your plan will her supremacy reign?"

"I am thankful for your concern, Tahir. However, what I desire will come to pass with no regards to her supremacy. No ill effects will hinder her arrival at the appointed time."

"Elder Mataya, forgive me for seeming so callus, but what does this have to do with us?" Evi questioned, interrupting Mataya. "Your stories seem too incredible to have anything to do with my children. I cannot fathom your philosophies or reasoning for control over the Sentinel. If the Creator has designed her life, then no one else can have control over her. Do not be fooled by your desires."

"I do not stand in the way of the Creator. I do not intend to defile what He has designed. I just want to make the wrongs right and put back all that was changed."

Evi frowned. Mataya's words had as many flaws in them as her supposed plan. "Mataya, you are playing with fire. It is not our right to change or question the Creator. What makes you think my husband or I will assist you in what you suggest?"

Anxious, she groaned forgetting her need to remain calm. "I need my brother back. I cannot stand the darkness that fills my mind. The loneliness taunts me daily. Sister ... our Head Elder needs his life back. The life that has been taken from him unjustly by my brother. He is a great ruler who is destined to die alone because Markian stole Mateo's mind. We have the chance to change the outcome of Markian's and Dinah's actions. We can give back all that was lost."

Tahir became impatient with Mataya's avoidance of answering his mate's question. "Elder Mataya, you ramble on with nonsense of time travels and evil entities. You still have not answered my wife's question. What does this human woman, the child, and the Head Elder; have to do with my family?"

Mataya cleared her throat annoyed. She rebuked the couple before her for their misunderstanding of her plan. "The evil tracked Lexis to Earth and attempted to kill the human infant that I had placed the essence of Lexis' daughter, Rayna, within after Naomi's conception. The entity believes Lexis' daughter perished when the human baby, Rebekah, supposedly died. It does not know that a Watcher retrieved the child and the essence of Rayna, before the human child could take her last breath. Rayna's essence waits in a secret location to continue her destiny, and the human child Rebekah is safe." Mataya closed her eyes drawing upon her eternal strength to go on with her plan's information. "My intention is to place your child's essence in Raina's grandmother Rebekah. Your daughter's essence will disguise Rebekah's existence until the conception of Raina. At that time, I will return your daughter to you. I believe once this is done, the evil duo, Markian and Dinah, will not be able detect Raina on Earth. Thus, everything that has come to pass will not. Earth will not be in danger, and my brother will not have been manipulated. The Sentinel's coming would be postponed until the appointed time written in the Scroll of Deuel."

Tahir buried his face in his hands praying his thoughts were not true. "Mataya, your words make no sense. Raina was never an Esprit de corps. You changed the timeline, if the Sentinel is not harbored by her, how would the two meet?"

"I believe fate will take care of that," she said sternly, to the two Guardians before her. The only two who could make a path of repentance for her brother. "As far as the entity is concerned, the events of the vessel's death have already occurred. It does not know that I have the power to change the past—let alone to bring the future into it with me. The evil will not sense your Guardian child's essence, just as we do not, even though she lies before us. When I am finished, then the Sentinel can continue on her original course. This will guarantee that Raina and Josiah can be together. The evil will not know that she lives and will not come back for Rayna—it has no reason, too. Our plan will work, and all will be restored—"

"Our plan?" Evi interrupted. "What plan are you talking about, Mataya?"

"See, I believe Josiah and Raina's love was always meant to be. The early arrival of the Sentinel stopped that. The events of the scroll unfolded prematurely, because the outer realms of Heaven became unstable—due to the actions of Markian and Dinah. This is why I propose using your daughter to conceal the bloodline from them."

"Mataya, you tire me with your dodging. Do you have a set plan of action?" Evi questioned regretfully, as she began to process exactly what Mataya was conveying.

"Mataya, you are demented," Tahir spoke sternly.

"Tahir, I assure you that all will conclude as in the original timeline. I will travel to each era myself at the proper moment to ensure our success." This was a promise she knew better than to make.

Evi sighed in disbelief of Mataya's claims of time travel. The thought of Mataya being able to manipulate the Guardian world scared her.

"How is this possible? No Elder has had this power in mine or your existences."

"Do not be alarmed, Evi. I have this gift bestowed upon me. I have kept it hidden for the sake of all. I intend to use my powers to change the past and the future, to continue with the original course the Creator designed. The entity will never look for the Sentinel in the future."

Evi turned to look out her chamber window. The glow of the evening stars cast their grace upon the golden streets of Callisto.

"If you expect me to believe your story, then you must show me the town this plan of yours will unfold in."

Mataya became alarmed by her request. "Evi, please, it is not necessary."

"Yes, it is. If I am to comply with your plan, then I must go to the place that will consume part of my life."

"Evi ... if you are not careful, it will consume all of you."

"Then let it be so. Do you not realize what you are asking of me?"

"Yes—you must show us," Tahir insisted. He was just as eager to see the place their child would dwell.

Mataya lowered her eyes in shame. Yes, she knew what request she had made of Evi and Tahir. She knew the sacrifice that she begged Evi to make. She requested a sacrifice to clear her brother's name and to save the love of a human and a Guardian.

"Yes ... I do know the sacrifice, Evi. And if I could make it myself I would."

"You say it—but do you mean it, Mataya?"

"Evi, if I was bound to another ... if I had the power to will my own into existence than believe me ... I would. I chose you because of the rare circumstances within you."

"Do you believe that our actions could be part of the Creator's plan, Mataya?"

"If not His plan completely, then that of His representative. Face it, Evi; this is more than a consequence. It has to be."

Evi looked at her sternly assessing the many possibilities. "If one believed in such acts of randomness, then I am not convinced you are correct in this thought, Mataya."

"This morning you held in your hands two essences, Evi, and only one ... was announced to the world in His song. The other remains quiet. Her birth has not been recorded. No one knows she dwells before us."

"And you believe my child is our only hope, because her essence does not proclaim its existence?"

"Yes, I do, Evi."

"Then you must show me more to make me believe your story, Mataya."

"Very well, come with me if you feel the need to. I will show you both all that you need to see to have faith in me this day," Mataya said, motioning Evi and Tahir to follow her.

With a wave of her hand, a white mist developed by the chamber window. The particles in the mist glistened from the glow of Mars through the balcony door. Within the glow, musical notes formed that danced in the air. Tahir recognized the song to be a child's lullaby from his youth. For Evi it was the song of joy when she bonded with Tahir.

Instantly, they were walking along the quiet street of North Cogswell Drive. The beach lay ahead, and the smell of fish lingered thick in the air. They stepped to one side to allow the few cars that passed this early in the morning to proceed. The automobiles wouldn't have harmed them—they moved simply because of human-acquired instincts to flee danger. These instincts were not natural for them, but seemed appropriate now for some unknown reason.

Mataya and Tahir thought nothing about the passing automobiles, but Evi found them to be strange.

"How primitive. Their mode of transportation destroys their main source of life. Even I can taste the pollutants in the air and see the haze it has brought."

Mataya grinned. "Please, do not judge them too unkindly. They do not understand the severity of their actions. Had you been of service in the outer realms of Heaven—none of this would surprise you."

Mataya took a few more steps; stopping in front of a faded fence made of wooden beams. The fence outlined a small beach surrounded by homes and trees on both sides. The water gently washed up on the beach making rippling patterns in the sand that filled with white foam. The branches of the willow tree swished in the water, as the sound of the loons called in the distance.

Her eyes cast forward to the edge of the sand. It was there she saw the vision in the refection glimmering off the lake. Mataya saw a gallant dark-haired hero—who lay slain on the burning rock littered ground. His twisted expression sent a chill through her essence. His screams reminded her of the torment her mind experienced with the emptiness of her brother's thoughts.

"Mataya, are you well?"

She looked up pulling her eyes from the vision. "Yes, thank you, Evi."

Evi saw the anxious look upon her face. "Was it here?"

Mataya looked back toward the calm water. "Yes ... it began here."

Evi bent down and ran her tiny fingers through the dry sand. The crystals glimmered like a thousand sparkling diamonds. She scooped up a handful of sand and turned her palm over examining them much closer.

"I can feel it. The intensity of what exists here is almost overpowering."

Mataya and Tahir nodded. They too had felt the echoes in the sand. Evi froze examining the few crystals remaining in her palm.

"I feel her sadness and his ache to take her pain away. I can also sense the rage of evil ... that has followed," Evi said discouragingly.

Mataya looked up with an unchanged expression. "I too, have felt the emotions of the humans. Look now—here they come," Mataya said, gesturing toward the road with a thrusting motion of her hand.

Evi turned her head to watch a young couple walking hand-in-hand. Their faces were hidden in the shadows, but their postures presented confidence and contentment. They stopped at the edge of the water standing in the same place Mataya had envisioned the fallen hero lying seconds before.

Evi folded her arms across her chest. She mimicked the embrace of the early morning lovers. "Their feelings for one another are very ... strong. It is incredibly captivating, Mataya."

"Yes, as I have warned ... you."

Evi's eyes widened as she watched the boy grasp the face of the young girl in his hands. She recalled how the touch of her husband felt against her celestial body. She smiled, comparing the similarities of the love each man held for their mate.

"He handles her like a porcelain doll. Is she that fragile?" Evi asked.

Mataya laughed. "No, Evi, it is human nature for a male to touch his mate like that. The Creator commands this of them."

Tahir tilted his head evaluating the couple's touches. "Do all obey ... this command, Mataya?"

"No, Tahir. Many do not and harm the one they claim to love."

"Why ... how could they? Look at his embrace. I feel the warmth and the sincerity. Who would not want that?" Tahir asked, feeling confused by their actions.

Evi glanced toward her husband and then back to the strangers kissing in the early morning sunrise. "Yes, tell me why one would forsake such an intimate action for violence."

"Evi, Earth is a different realm than those you are used to visiting. The Creator gave humans free will, and still, after all of these years many struggle with it. The dark one has crept into their lives, and brought the spirit of confusion. He has turned their human hearts cold. Because of this, many are not capable of experiencing the emotions you see here. They have lost hope and respect for the Creator."

"I am amazed, for he looks so much like their kind. How does he do it? How does he mimic the humans so perfectly?" Tahir asked curiously. He realized the answers to his observation relied solely on the Great Elder.

Mataya smiled bringing her cheeks high up to meet her eyes. "It is human love that allows him to act this way. It is the same love that I am asking you to help me save."

Evi looked down at the grains of sand in her palm. She watched intently as she rubbed her fingers together. Then the few remaining grains of sand slipped through them, blowing fluidly in the wind.

"Show me more," Evi requested eagerly. "Please, show me the land that cries."

"Very well ... come with me," Mataya said softly. She would honor Evi's request.

Soon, they were strolling down a winding country road. Mataya had stopped walking when they reached the place where the two roads met by the railroad tracks. The three Guardians stood still in the middle of the road surveying the land.

Evi smelled the scent of more water surrounding them. "I smell the salt in the air."

"Yes, it is strong."

"Even after all of this time, how can that be?"

"Since when do you mark the passing of time, my sister?" Mataya asked inquisitively.

"From the moment you joined me in my chamber. Did you not think I could be subjected to such an environment and mission not to acknowledge the passing of time?" Evi brushed her blond curls from her face, catching a loving smile of her husband.

"Do they know where the water comes from?" Tahir asked inquisitively, evaluating the world, he came to visit at his wife's urging.

Mataya answered him sadly. "No, they do not, Tahir. The humans have no comprehension. Their life span does not exceed a hundred years. None in this place were alive at that point in time."

"It is a shame that they cannot appreciate the water they drink or bathe in. Look around at the flowers and the trees." Evi pointed, turning in a circle, absorbing the environment around her. "I can taste the blood of the righteous feeding the trees and the plant life. How could our Head Elder stand before this place and not be subjected to its meaning?"

"Josiah did not know at the time, Evi, of the events that came before him. Like you, he thought them to be a fable or a children's story. And when he learned the meaning of Camp Lake's existence, it was too late to change anything."

Evi left her husband standing with Mataya and strolled further down the road in silence. Her ears rang with the cries of the murdered Angels. Her mind saw the deadly battle bringing a sense of sorrow and loss to her heart. Tahir and Mataya joined her by the side of the road. With a blank look, she stared at the small field that grew flowers next to the train tracks.

"Tell me, my sister, will no one—no human ever know the secret?"

"In time when those who were faithful walk the golden streets, they will know the sacrifices of the Son."

"Show me the place where she died?"

"Who do you speak of, Evi?"

"You know the one. The visions fill my mind. I do not know how ... nor do I understand them. However, I see the child. It was near here. I can feel it. Show me where my child's human future would begin."

"Yes, you must show us," Tahir said. He also shared his wife's fascination of the surrounding area and for what this place meant to them.

"I will take you there ... but remember—you have been warned."

Mataya led Evi and Tahir back down the windy road to the other side of Silver Lake. The wind had begun to blow and snow flurries developed dancing in the breeze. It accumulated at a quick rate covering the ground in an elegant white blanket. Although the cold weather didn't bother the three Guardians, Evi pulled her cape tighter around her neck and shivered. When the three of them reached the center of Silver Lake Park, they stopped at an area where a wooden structure once existed. Evi could see the ghosts of many humans from a time long ago. They were dressed in coats and gloves made of animal skins. She watched them move about shivering as they loaded the large chunks of ice into the boxcars.

Evi knelt next to the edge of the frozen lake. As her hand touched the crystals of ice and snow, the ice melted revealing the beauty of the blue waters beneath. She stood there silently for a long time just staring into the water. Then she swirled her hand in the water watching as it dripped from her fingers. Looking up at Mataya, she broke her silence speaking with trembling lips.

"I see the flesh of the one who perished in this lake. Her death calls to me."

"Yes ... I know. She calls to me as well."

"Who is she? Who would take this precious human's life?" Tahir asked sadly.

"It was the evil one, the one I need your help to stop."

Evi reached out and touched the body of the decaying woman. Immediately her eyes opened, and Evi fell backward. Human instinct would have made her scream; except her Guardian composure absorbed the woman's pain.

"Mataya," she said softly, "is this the mother of the child you want us to save?"

"Yes, Evi ... she is."

"How is it possible, that her soul has not yet entered Heaven?"

"Evi, you do not understand. What you see before you is greater than the souls of humans."

"How is this possible? This is an innocent woman. She is due her rest in the Holy Gardens."

"Evi ... we do not always understand the Creator's plan, however, we must act as He wishes. You see the remnants of the woman's life force. She is not in this lake. I assure you, my sister, she has passed."

Evi looked down at the ghost before her. The woman's eyes were still fixed firmly upon her. This time they were tender and reassuring. Evi looked up with tears in her eyes. Her husband's expression gave her the strength she needed.

"Yes ... Mataya. I will assist you."

—————————

The echo of the empty room was deafening. No laughter filled the hallways of the mansion this morning. Sol's rays shone brightly into her chamber, but its warm rays brought no joy. Evi sighed deeply. Sometime in the course of the night, she made a decision, a drastic one. Evi made a great sacrifice that both haunted her and astounded her.

The liquid in her eyes didn't cease throughout the night. Tears, the humans called them. They were drops of salty water that fell during times of pain, joy, and sadness. Drops of water that didn't develop in the eyes of a Guardian, now streamed forcefully down her cheeks. The dawn's light wouldn't dry them ... only time would. And time was something she had too much of and didn't need. Time would create a barrier to mend the broken dam, but the pain that endured until then would be indescribable to her. Evi's existence changed last night, and there was nothing in all of her Guardian powers that she could do to stop the transformation.

Evi crossed her arms seeking comfort. Painfully she recalled the warmth she held in her arms the night before. She desired once more, to hear the soft exchange of air moving through a set of tiny human lungs. A sound that temporarily soothed her apprehensiveness and gave her the courage she needed. Even the coos forming from the other room of their chamber gave Evi no solace. She had a son who she would now raise alone, separated from his sister.

He was to become a son who would grow tall and stand in his father's shoes.

Even though her decision had not left her childless, her heart wouldn't move on soon enough. The human emotions she acquired while visiting Earth with Elder Mataya, would confirm this. Mataya warned her about the visit, but Evi was sure she was strong enough to handle the human emotions. She wasn't, or perhaps the love of the Creator for the humans ran deeper than any Guardian could fathom.

Tahir entered Evi's chamber removing his cloak. He had intended to greet his wife in the same manner as he always had until he caught the sorrowful expression on her face. Her appearance troubled him greatly. He did not care for the Sentinel's commands to experience human emotions. For Tahir, they simply got in the way, hindering the even balance that the Guardians lived their existences by daily. The despicable human traits caused more damage than good. This was evident in the distraught eyes his wife displayed.

He questioned how their perfect world could even consider subjecting themselves to a defiled race bent on destruction. The Creator granted humans free will and allowed them to walk on a separate plain of existence than that of the other entities He designed. Humans were His children set aside for His glory. They had all that, and still humans ignored their own and wasted the resources given to them. The thought of modeling a Guardian's life after them seemed incomprehensible, even to the intellectual mind of one as wise as he is.

Tahir chose to accept the Sentinel's command as a faithful Guardian would have; however, he refused to participate in the human emotions of fear and joy. He took pity instead upon a race he knew would never truly understand their place.

"Evi?"

"Is it done, my husband? Is it almost over?"

"Yes—all will be complete soon. Are you well, Evi?"

She didn't answer him at first. Her thoughts were several years away. She was busy scanning the future of a young Guardian's essence. She found her four human years in the future. The creaking noise of a small rocking chair possessed her. She would have to go to the place that she saw in her mind.

She responded to the Guardian who joined her in the dimly lit study. "Will they think me wrong for my decision?"

"It is true that some will not understand, however—"

"Do you understand?" Evi interrupted, turning to face her companion. "Do you really know what this means?"

"I know very well, Evi, what sacrifice you have made this day. It will be for the best. This I promise you."

"I do not believe that you can keep such promises."

"I would not say the words, my love, if I did not mean them."

"You could mean them, Tahir, but you cannot control time or the fate of my daughter."

"She is our daughter, and the risks outweigh your human desires."

"Human desires, how strange to hear you say that. If I had human desires then I would feel greater remorse for what I have done."

"You are a Guardian. You do not experience remorse as you would propose to."

"Do not stand there and tell me what is expected of me. I have lost my child today. I will not be led from the feelings of loss. Until you have waited as long as I have to birth a child, you cannot understand what it means to lose one.

"I do not care if grief is a human flaw. For Guardians to live without emotions is wrong. Without them, how can we truly aid our Esprit de corps? They need more help than any Guardian has ever comprehended. If it were not so, I would not have sacrificed my child for any human."

Tahir spoke the words of reassurance with the same harmonious stone that stole her heart. "Evi, do you ignore the fact that I have waited just as long as you. The planets have revolved around one another the same amount of times for me as well. From the moment we joined, I knew of your desire to have a child. I too, felt your need for our essences to create enough energy to will our child into existence. Your thoughts constantly sang in my mind. I shared your concerns of our compatibility and the lack of our energy levels to produce a child. Evi, you forget that the sacrifice is also made by me this day."

"I do not forget that, my husband. I know you are at a loss, too. I truly meant that you do not share my fondness for the fragility of humans. It is a luxury you do not have, Tahir."

"My dear, that is not a luxury, it is a curse."

"I do not consider this a curse. I would gladly experience the human emotions of regret and sorrow—knowing that her memory will truly be honored in my mind. Do not let me sway you and your Guardian beliefs."

"You have not persuaded me in this matter. I will honor our child in the same customs as our people have always practiced. You should know that the only time you ever had the power to sway me was the day I saw you in the Great Hall." He smiled with a low chuckle. "I have never taken my eyes off you since. These three thousand years have changed my existence forever and for the better. You can believe that, my dear."

"Tahir, I have never doubted you. I have had complete faith in your choice to bond with me and the existence we created together."

"Then tell me; what is it that brings this unnatural character about you?"

"I am sorry, Tahir. Please, forgive me."

"There is nothing to forgive, Evi. I understand what you are going through at this moment. I truly know that you do not contain your emotions as I or any other Guardian does."

Tahir reached out and grabbed Evi around her waist, pulling her into his embrace. All eternity could cease to exist, and it wouldn't matter to them. The bond they shared had no human words to describe the utter serenity of their essences becoming one.

14.

IT IS DONE

Guardian Realm—parallel time shifts between universes

The mist formed by the window at her command. Mataya glided up the transparent staircase entering into Beck's world. He waited for her by the brook this evening oblivious to the late hour he summoned her to visit. It was his favorite place to meet Mataya in the daylight. Beck preferred standing here, because of the way the light shone through her lustrous hair. The sparkles of the mist always enhanced the auburn eyes that twinkled every time they gazed upon Beck. He felt the attraction, too. From the first moment in time that he saw her, his essence chose her. It was then when he placed a wish for love within the brook.

He often left a token of thoughts behind when he sifted through the tears. Beck did this hoping that a little of the love he couldn't share with Mataya—might filter back through the mist, and bond upon a broken heart. If her forbidden embrace could never satisfy the love he felt for her, then perhaps, another could use the wasted love.

Of the many Guardians who attempted to experience human emotions, Mataya was one Guardian that couldn't handle them. Beck often wondered if it was because of the superior mind of a Great Elder, or the lack of her brother's thoughts that made them so difficult.

"Mataya, why are you so upset?" he questioned, before she reached him.

"Beck—Beck, it has happened—" her voice broke, showing her unnecessary fear.

"Calm yourself, Mataya. Tell me what has happened?

"The evil found the child. It took the lives of the Watcher and killed Naomi."

"What, are you sure of this?"

"Yes, Beck, I am certain."

"How do you know this to be true, Mataya?"

"The Secret Council summoned me. Sariel and Malachi had the human baby with them. Isaiah had just rescued her from drowning. Beck, the entities essence was failing, and I had to revive her."

"Is she well now?"

"Yes, however, her life is no longer safe. Now the essence of Rayna is in danger once more. Do you not see how this changes everything?"

Beck looked away to the brook. Indeed the plan had changed, and this new turn of events was very unsettling. "Where is the child who carries Rayna's essence now, Mataya?"

"She is tended to, please do not worry. She is under the protection of Malachi and Enoch. You should know something, Beck," she said in a worried tone.

He turned concerned by her words. "What?"

"I made a decision concerning the child's welfare and our plan without consulting you."

"What is it, Mataya?"

She didn't want to answer him. To tell him her plan would expose more than her mischievous actions.

"The evil one still looks. He moves swiftly. He is very cunning, Beck. I had to act. We could wait no longer. If we are not prepared, we will not prevail when he strikes."

"Then, I suspect that you have put your plan into motion, my sister."

"Yes, Evi will give her child for our cause."

"And Tahir is in support of this plan?"

"Yes ... he understands its significance."

"His compliance surprises me. I had not known that he stood for a cause other than his own."

"Yes, Beck, I am surprised as well. I believe it is because he does not share in the human attachments as we do."

"If that is so, then why does he conform to the plan?"

"I am not sure. Evi is very persistent."

"And you believe she understands fully the sacrifice she may be making?"

"I do. Human love has touched her Guardian heart. She has felt the tears of salt in the waters of Trevor."

"You took her to Earth," he said, alarmed at this new turn of events.

"Of course I did. I had to."

"That may have been a mistake."

"What choice did I have? Did you expect her to give up her child without an explanation?"

"No ... I just thought your plea would be enough."

"My dear, Beck, you underestimate maternal love whether human or Guardian."

"What was her reaction to the place our people despise?"

"I am not sure how to answer that. She saw them."

"Mataya, that was very careless of you."

"Beck, do not lecture me. She had a right to see them. After all, you know what place Raina will hold in her life. She had a right to see whose life she was trading for her daughter."

"Yes, I suppose you are correct. I am being too overly cautious."

"I do not blame you. You have protected this place well. I understand your concerns. I know you profit nothing in your exposure, Beck."

15.

THE TRACKER

Guardian Realm—present-day

Tarik jumped out from behind the bushes. His glaring crimson eyes pierced through Uriah's supernatural body. He immediately recognized the entity before him. He was a Tracker from the Hyperion Universe. Uriah knew that pure annihilation was his sole purpose in life. The goal that kept this entity motivated was to pursue death.

Like all Trackers, death gives them a rush of enjoyment. The horrid screams of their victims enrich their wretched demeanor and tendencies of violent behavior. Hostility and fear encourage the evil within them to seek out their enemies. Life is of no value to their kind, and they are no friend to the human race.

Humans are their greatest rivals. Trackers despise the affection the Creator displays toward them. In their eyes, humans are unworthy of such devotion and adoration. The sacrifices made by the Creator to save the human race disgusts the Trackers. The Hyperion race believes the Creator has become misguided, allowing humans to flourish while destroying their world.

Trackers, as revolting as they are to their adversaries, treat their own kind with reverence. It is a code of ethics burned into their genetic makeup. Their cultural beliefs forbid aggression toward one another. No Hyperion entity has ever taken the life of another member of his or her race.

"What more do you want of me? I have already done all that you ask," the fallen Guardian, pleaded.

"Hardly, Uriah. You have been a fool and careless."

"You are wrong, Master Tarik. I have followed his plan thoroughly."

Tarik laughed, and Uriah felt the vibration of his evil shake the ground he stood on. The loose dirt bounced, interjecting small pebbles and dirt into the air. The small contents of soil fell across Uriah's translucent feet, outlining them in the shadow of the Moon.

"Do not insult me," he spoke boldly. "You have erred, and it will be very costly for your kind, Uriah."

"Erred—how, Master?"

"Are you so naïve, Uriah, that you know not what you do? Your actions are a prime example of why your race is less superior to my people."

"Please, Tarik," Uriah begged, feeling his essence shudder. "I do not know what it is you speak of. Perhaps if you enlighten me, I may know what you accuse me of— Master."

"Come now, Uriah. Are you so moronic that you cannot account for your actions?"

"No, Master ... forgive me, please. I am just confused as to what I have done to warrant such anger from you."

"Very well, Uriah. Allow me to make the situation clearer to you. When you assisted Markian with his time travels and with destroying the plane—you left a trail of your essence inside. That meddling Keeper of the Courts discovered remnants of your essence on board the plane. Jon has known since that day, it was not Markian or Mateo who killed those occupants of the plane. He will search for you one day, and he will find you. When he subdues you, Uriah, your mind will not be strong enough to survive Deimos.

"Regrettably, my interaction with you will also be discovered. This, my friend ... I cannot allow. Too much is at stake to lose now. I am very close to destroying the human girl you let live. I sent you into the past, and your worthless essence still cannot fulfill the task you were assigned. Your instructions clearly indicated in what realm you were to go to Silver Lake. You arrived too late the first time, and the Guardian twin saw you. Do you have any idea, Uriah, who it was? Can you even comprehend what this means? Now, I will have to strike him down as well. His diminished essence will be noticed. I cannot make this go away as quietly as I had made the human Clement's death that you blundered as well."

"Master, send me to correct my mistake. I will not let you down this time. I promise to conclude my assignment."

"Toah relies on my expertise. You, Uriah, have damaged my credibility. Should he doubt me for one minute, then I truly will lose as well. Do you understand how difficult it is to cover your three time travel visits to that vile planet Earth?"

Uriah fell to his knees. He knew this mistake had indeed cost him dearly. If he attempted to flee now, maybe he could make it to another realm. He could hide out there until the Tracker grew weary of his little game and ventured elsewhere for a more suitable opponent.

"I do not understand how. I carried out Markian's orders to the letter. He guided my thoughts and impregnated the instructions in my head so that the Great Elders could not read my mind."

The Tracker chuckled, amused at the cowardly behaviors of the Guardian bowing at his feet.

Uriah glanced around absorbing the scenery. The tranquil view of the Promethean Mountains gave him one moment of solace. Uriah this time was not of dim mind. There was no escape from his transgressions. Uriah's failures had caught up to him, and the Tracker's punishment would prevail.

"I understand, Master, what I have done. I acted carelessly, and I deserve your punishment. Do as you may for my failures, Master."

Uriah closed his eyes releasing his essence. His energy shouldn't go to waste but prosper within the beauty of his world. The act of commending his essence before his death would create a portal to end his sins. This action granted redemption for those who were slain by his hand. Those he unjustly killed would feel his energy release and know the one who was responsible for their death had met his fate cruelly.

Tarik smiled and then extended his hands outward holding them over Uriah's head. Tightly clinching his fingers, he chanted words unfamiliar to his doomed servant. The same words Raina had heard many times in her dreams. A red glow emanated from his hands surrounding Uriah. His celestial body began to convulse as he screamed in pain. A torture technique he developed for a race that had no pain receptors built into their genetic make-up. Uriah's screams ended as quickly as they began. His body exploded from the current of Tarik's power integrating with his own.

Tarik rejoiced with satisfaction in his accomplishment. Just one more inferior entity to destroy and he would reign forever victorious.

16.

THE PETITION

Sentinel, is it not love that we cherish? What we want the Creator's children to feel? Anani asked, with the most delicate thoughts a Guardian could have.

It is, my sister, she replied, with the same gentleness.

Then, Sentinel, why does He deny this love?

Anani, all are welcomed to receive His love and wisdom. He has not denied His love to anyone.

No one—Sentinel?

I see ... no one, but the Chosen One. Is that what you are asking of me, Anani?

Anani smiled, as always the Sentinel carried herself supreme yet humble. *Yes, it is, Sentinel.*

You know, my sister ... why this had to happen, what purpose was needed to be fulfilled? You know what the Son endured. The atrocities I cringed to think of, it disgusts me to know the evil that the fallen ones were allowed to create.

Sentinel—we all have free will. Anani interrupted the Sentinel's thoughts. *He gave us a mind to choose. He has not erred. The Creator offers more than any spirit can comprehend. It was the only way. The Son knew that ... and gladly ... accepted His fate.*

You are wise beyond your years, Anani.

Then if you think me wise, Sentinel, please, hear me out. Oh—how we owe Him so much and He, like the Father, asks for so little. Yet, this day ... the Son has His reward, eternally blessed to dwell with the Creator in this Holy City. I have seen it, Sentinel. I have seen the twinkle in the Father's eyes when one of His children comes home. That is the greatest reward one could ever ask for.

So, tell me, my sister. What do you ask for this day? the Sentinel asked softly.

Anani's smile grew wider. *Sentinel, you already know my request.*

Anani, has not the Creator said to ask whenever you have need?

Yes, Sentinel, He has instructed His children to state their request.

Then, I will also request that you tell me what your need is?

I come not asking for myself, but for another.

The Sentinel laughed, and the room shook with her low chuckle. *Who do you come petitioning for then, my sister?*

I petition for our Head Elder Josiah, the Chosen One, Sentinel.

The Sentinel returned her reassuring smile to reinforce the glad thoughts she heard in Anani's mind. *And why has he placed such a burden upon your heart, Anani?*

Because, do you not see, Sentinel, his heart is broken. He guides his people instructing them in the laws and encouraging love. Yet—he cannot even feel it for himself.

The Son was betrayed and His heart broke. Who petitioned for Him? the Sentinel asked very sternly.

The twelve … and His mother, father, and God petitioned. The Chosen One has none other than me to petition on his behalf.

Sister, speak your petition freely and let me decide if there is anything I may be able to do.

Sentinel, I ask you to give the Chosen One back his reason to live. His life will expand a great era of time lonely. I fear the one you appoint to profess the Father's love will lose himself. Grant him, I pray ye, what the Creator grants each of us. Grant him my prayer and give him back his Raina.

Sister, do you think she is enough to fulfill the Chosen One? Do you believe her life alone can encourage Josiah to live out the life he was destined to in the harmony of all Guardians?

Yes, I believe this with all my essence, Sentinel.

Anani, Father will want to know if he is worthy of such a petition. What you ask may not come to pass. God makes His decisions for reasons that we cannot understand. There is so much involved with manipulating the outer realms of Heaven. Do you have any idea what it is you are really asking for?

Sentinel, I understand what I am asking. You did this task once and restored Earth to its original course. Even though no one on Earth remembers—this day forever marks the essence of a kindhearted creature with an unbearable burden.

Not everyone receives what he or she prays for, nor believes they need, she reminded Anani.

I know this, though any soul the Father creates—is worthy of love's petition. Did you not change time once already, Sentinel, to return Earth to what it was before Dinah opened the Abyss?

Yes, I did, Anani. Please, do not forget why that was necessary. Had the humans destroyed their world, I would not have intervened. However, it was not the humans' fault that a spiritual war flowed over from another realm into their realm. I restored the Earth's natural balance, to what it existed upon before the attack. No human knew what he or she had suffered, or what was lost.

Not even the human girl? Anani thought boldly. *Yet, her life was not restored to your finely fashioned balance. Why did she have to lose her first life? All other humans' lives suffered no interruption in their timelines. All things remained for them. However, Raina's life and the lives of her parents were changed.*

Anani ... as wise as you are, you still allow the human theologies in that classroom of yours to cloud your mind.

Sentinel, I do not understand what you mean.

Raina's life was meant to secretly harbor my essence until the appointed time the Creator deemed fit. Her life was never meant to be threatened or changed unnaturally. However, once Markian and Dinah opened the Abyss commanding the Demons, we could not proceed with her as we did with the others on Earth. Too many events affected her. The evil should never have located her on Earth killing her father. She should have never known the essence of a Guardian. Yet, once Josiah joined with her, there were too many artificial circumstances.

The logical choice was to place her soul on the path it was originally destined to walk. Do not think that the Creator or I are blind to the sufferings of your Leader. However, He must act spiritually for the benefit of His children. I will plead your cause before the Creator, she grinned, bowing her head. *Ultimately, His divine wisdom will make the final ruling.*

Thank you, Sentinel. My request is for a good cause.

Most requests are, my sister. Although, I believe yours has a more valuable meaning behind it.

Why do you say that, Sentinel?

Well ... one would think the earthy cultures you have exposed yourself to, being void of your own Esprit de corps, would shed some light upon the matters of your newfound human heart.

Anani's face lost all expression. *Then you know what I have been doing?*

Of course, we do, the Sentinel replied, placing her hand on Anani's head. *If I had not observed your actions myself, then surely you know that your thoughts are not hidden from me.*

When you say we ... do you mean the Creator as well? Anani asked hesitantly.

Your presence on Earth and other locations has attracted much attention.

Other locations? Anani said timidly.

Yes, Anani. I know the place you have visited. It is good that you have somewhere to think in your moments of loneliness.

Then, am I to be judged unworthy, Sentinel? Anani asked, fearful that she would face punishment for acting on her own.

No, Sister, you are not. Sometimes we make decisions that are not entirely our own. Perhaps your reason to watch over Josiah in the lecture hall is a good thing.

I do not understand what you mean by this, Sentinel, she questioned.

It is not important, my sister. Now go, I do believe you have a lecture to take notes from for your Molecular Biophysics class.

Thank you, Sentinel. I will not forget your generosity.

Before you go, tell me, Anani, have you ever acquired any of the customs of the humans?

Excuse me, please, Sentinel, but I do not understand what you are asking of me.

Anani, the humans enjoy many activities. Some are strenuous like their sports and others soothing like collecting pretty objects.

Yes, I have seen this behavior, except I have not adopted any of those customs. I pretend to collect purses for my human façade, but they mean nothing to me.

So, you practice their human behaviors, yet you do not indulge in them?

No, Sentinel. Acting and indulging in human activities do not need to be practiced together to accomplish what I have set out to do.

I understand that, Anani. I just want to know why you do not live as the humans do.

Because, I watch over Josiah, so that I can pray for his well-being. I do not go to Earth to benefit myself.

What a shame, Anani, that the Creator has offered the humans so many interesting luxuries, and you do not sample any of them. Truly, there must be one luxury that has intrigued you?

No, not one of the human luxuries has intrigued me. Even as I see how they affect the humans around me.

Why do you think this, my sister?

Because, Sentinel, their luxuries are not my cause. I have an objective that I need to fulfill. In the human fashion, I have a few worthless materials for the sake of my mission, but their value means nothing to me.

This is true, although you can serve your cause and experience the true human nature.

Forgive me, Sentinel. Please do not think of me as being unlearned, except I do not understand why I would need to practice their cultures? I do not need any distractions to lessen my desires for helping Josiah. Did not other Guardians fall into human snares and meet their destruction? Even as you have instructed our Leader to encourage our race to experience emotions, you have never suggested indulging in their lifestyles.

Young Anani, some have fallen, as they were careless and became self-absorbed. I challenge you to accept human indulgence and take up a hobby. You are wise beyond your years, and I do not believe that a human hobby will interfere in your mission in any way. On the contrary, you may benefit from it more than your celestial mind can calculate.

Forgive me, Sentinel, except Josiah is very strong, and now he suffers from his indulgence of love. I can never surpass the powers he contains in his essence.

You are strong, Anani. Do not dismiss your strengths.

Fine, Sentinel. I will take your challenge. What do you propose? She thought, uncertain of the Sentinel's motives.

I believe your time on Earth will be most benefited by a special hobby that offers serenity.

Then I will begin one immediately, Sentinel.

Very well, my sister. Although, will you permit me to suggest the one I have in mind?

Yes, of course, Sentinel. What hobby would you like me to take up?

I think a rock collection is very admirable. When you collect the right one, the rock becomes a most valued treasure. Many would offer money and some their soul for the perfect stone.

Thank you very much, Sentinel. I will start a rock collection then.

Perfect, my sister. You will see the riches in profitable treasures. Allow me to help you begin this collection.

I would be honored if you did. Thank you, Sentinel.

Then the Sentinel waved her hand in the air forming her delicately proportioned fingers into a fist. When she unfolded her hand, she presented to Anani a uniquely shaped stone with blends of earth tone and turquoise colors that glittered like crystals. She rolled it around in the palm of her hand, marveling at its exquisitely blended colors and polished finish.

Anani smiled brightly. *This is very beautiful, Sentinel. I will cherish this as the humans do with their many treasures.*

I am pleased, Anani. Perhaps, you will learn to cherish this stone much more than a human could ever comprehend.

How so? she asked curiously.

This stone is known by many names. It is as rare as it is unique.

Anani gasped nervously. *Sentinel, are you sure that I am worthy of such a magnificent stone?*

Of course, my sister, or else I would not have given it to you.

Please, Sentinel, tell me what makes this stone so unique? she asked, holding the stone carefully in her hand—as if it were as fragile as a china doll.

As I said, many would give their lives to get their hands on one such as this stone. The rarity of it is just part of the stones magnificence. What action the stone performs outweighs any comprehendible value one places on it.

Please, tell me. What this stone does to deserve such a reputation?

If I were to tell you the stone's secrets, then you may not understand its true value, Anani.

Do you not agree that knowing its value will help me appreciate it more, Sentinel?

And do you not agree that finding out the value on your own is more esteemed than just being told? Time holds no meaning and the song in your heart is always close when you keep the stone with you.

Do you desire for me to learn the meaning on my own, Sentinel?

I desire many things for you and for those under my protection. It pleases me to watch you comprehend the stone in your mind. Consider the human worth this stone can have on you as you complete your preordained mission.

My mission, Sentinel?

Yes, Anani. I charge you with using this stone to assist those in need.

Forgive me, Sentinel, but how will a stone assist me to help others?

Fine, I will tell you one secret. The stone holds the past and the future. Guard the stone. When the time is right, cast it into the waters of pain and sorrow.

What do you mean?

That, my sister, you will have to discover on your own.

I will, Sentinel, this I promise you. Anani nodded, feeling the Sentinel releasing her thoughts.

Then quietly Anani left the chamber. She channeled the enormous amount of excitement she felt, attempting to remain calm. The humans called the emotion yearning to escape from her essence love—while this emotion guiding her consciousness the Guardians called infatuation. Anani had never felt love in a humans' aspect, although she had seen the effects on her truest friends, Jaleel and Josiah.

Orphaned at a young age, Anani never experienced the wonders a sentient life could hold. Her mother and father were prestigious Guardians serving in a universe located in the outer realm of Heaven. A war erupted between the inhabitants of the planet they were stationed on, and many occupants lives were terminated in an explosion. The useless battles raged on for days as her parents watched, waiting for the moment to break protocol and assist.

Guardian rules forbid their interference if the war didn't directly affect their chosen Esprit de corps. But

Anani's father believed that all entities needed their help and he acted without instructions. Her mother left the planet to petition the Council for permission. Per Guardian customs—her request was denied, and she returned to her husband's side.

The fighting increased, and so did the need for the two of them to act. Her parents lost their essences trying to usher as many souls as they could to the Prometheus Universe. Their unselfishness for the duty each swore to fulfill in their roles as Guardians—took their lives and left their daughter an orphan.

Anani found herself in the care of her maternal grandparents with Jon and Kiersten's guiding assistance. Her grandparents were wise Elders set in their ways and didn't fully accept the new laws of the Guardian world since Josiah's reign. Anani was truly fortunate to be exposed to the various cultures of her race, as well as those of other entities her parents introduced her to in her youth. These cultures unknowingly helped her develop the compassion she needed to save her dear friend. In her strength, Anani also acted against Guardian customs as she followed her parents' example. The same compassion that drew them to fight for a cause which wasn't theirs, also guided Anani to Josiah's side secretly.

Although willed into existence many years after them, she gained immense wisdom and insight from her friendship with Jaleel and Josiah. Anani grew boldly, having no hesitance about making her passions and desires for humans known. Her overwhelming passion is what allowed her to go, so determined for her cause, into the Sentinel's chamber to petition for Josiah's benefit.

Anani's boldness had prepared the path she was to walk since her youth. A path unbeknownst to her was one that only the Sentinel could mold. Anani believed her kinship with Josiah had placed his burden upon her Guardian heart. She had no idea her actions were merely the result of another's desires.

Josiah's life became a lock securing the wineskins that contained the good and evil of the world. He traded much for the protection of Earth. His sacrifice had cost Josiah much more than he had comprehended. In his mind that horrid day when he had lost Raina—Josiah knew the trade-off as painful as it felt, was the only way. In this, his essence bound the cares of the world into a power so great it cast out the evil. Since God does not close one door before he opens another, Anani became a finely fashioned key. When the time comes for Anani to understand her role—she will be able to unlock the burdens Josiah accepted on behalf of Earth and destroy them—so that order would remain in the realms of Heaven.

Anani was eager to return to Earth and continue the façade she had created—living as a human woman attending a California college. As soon as the Council received Josiah's instructions to dwell with other entities in a more personal setting, she hurried to Earth. Her wisdom gave her a clearer mind than many Guardians had at her age to deal with extreme situations. She lived her newest life very reserved and quiet. Anani attended many classes, utilizing these as watching posts for looking after Josiah.

Anani was surprised when she stumbled upon Raina in Hemet several weeks before the semester had started. With her essence, it was no problem to arrange to be Raina's roommate. This coincidently assisted her in her self-proclaimed mission. The new turn of events, helped her to blend in with the other students, taking care in being discreet. Those who knew her simply called her Ann.

Her life on Earth was of no less importance than any other assignment a Guardian would take. Anani had no Esprit de corps, but she didn't need one.

The professor cleared his throat rocking back onto his heels. "Miss Liam, do you intend to participate in my lecture today or have I just provided you with a personal nap time? One that I am sure will please your accountant when I charge you for a class you will fail."

"No, sir, please excuse me." Anani sat up straight in her chair. She focused on the many drawings on Professor Preston Cutter's blackboard. Einstein's equations were most impressive to many, too difficult to grasp for some and too boring for Anani.

Situations just as this classroom experience were one of the most tedious sides to pledging one's life as a Guardian—although the rewards surpass the negatives. To help cultures advance or to save a soul from despair, allows them to perform in complete reverence without complaint and the need for self-worth. It is this form of service that covers a Guardian's pride.

The position of a Guardian is a most difficult task to hold. In the end, it is fulfilling to see the smiles of a child when his or her father has come home from war—or to hear the music that would have been silenced too early. For this reason, Guardians endure the rash, inconsistent, and uneducated judgments of humans, and other entities.

Anani repositioned herself once more allowing access to her pocket. She removed the rock she had received from the Sentinel and rolled it around in her palm. The classroom lights reflected off the stone producing as much intensity as it had in the Sentinel's chamber. For a brief moment, she swore that the stone played a musical note. Just as she was about to examine the rock more carefully her thoughts were interrupted once more.

"Ms. Liam, we are waiting for the answer," Professor Cutter insisted.

17.

STONE OF FAYRUZ

Earth Realm—present-day

"Are you joining me for lunch today, Ann?" Raina asked, without looking at Anani. She continued to fumble through the small silverware drawer looking for a spoon to stir her tea.

Anani's answer didn't come. Her attention was diverted to the colored stone in her purse. A faint melody called to her, pulling her thoughts from the clanging noise Raina was making. As she reached into the floral embossed handbag, her fingers brushed against the stone and her body felt a cold chill rush through her. The sulfur stench that filled the air burned her nose, but it didn't pain her as much as the vision before her did.

She stood in a dark room with echoing footsteps growing closer to her. The worried voice coming from the other room was her mother's voice. Her tone didn't hold the tenderness Anani grew to know in her youth. She crept forward resting her hands on the doorframe. Her heart pounded hard at seeing her parents in the room in front of her. Anani's mind told her that they were dead, yet they seemed so real now.

"Mom?" she whispered. Her mother didn't look at her, nor did she respond. It was hard for Anani to stand there knowing her mother was within reach, yet she was not real. Anani watched her mother's frantic actions, feeling her fear. An emotion she shouldn't know, although it seemed too real to ignore.

"He is guilty, Offie," Kryssa insisted, whirling around in circles and pacing back and forth.

"We must inform the Council."

"Kryssa, you know they will not believe us. Markian has them fooled. They have denied us assistance once already. The Council warned us to depart from here. We face persecution for staying."

"It is not his doing alone, is it, Offie?"

"No, my love. There appears to be another who controls Markian like a puppet."

"It has to be that Count from the Hyperion Universe. I have sensed his evil from the day the Council welcomed him. I knew it was a mistake to allow him to join us here. He has only made the situation worse. We had control until he took charge."

"I agree. Count Toah is not the upstanding entity he claims to be."

"You know, Offie, that he started this war. I can see it in his eyes. He takes joy from the suffering of the people of Cressida."

"Yes, Kryssa, I am sure he is the reason the Council will not support us."

"What do we do then? How can they stand by while the Biancian people plan to annihilate the planet of Cressida?"

"We stay and deliver these people and ours from his pending destruction."

"There are too many of them," Kryssa shouted, burying her face into her hands, "how will we defeat them all, Offie?"

His words burned deep into his heart. "We cannot. We will die trying."

"No!" Kryssa screamed, looking up to see the solemn expression on her husband's face.

"We have no other choice."

Kryssa lowered her eyes. "And what about our daughter, Offie? Who will provide for her?"

"She is safe, my love. If we fail, her life will be well protected. Jon and Kiersten will see to that. I promise you." Offie stood and then went to his wife's side. He embraced her tightly in his arms speaking in a confident tone. "We will encase as many citizens as we can and send them to Prometheus."

"That is too far away. We will never have enough power. We should send them to Portia."

"No, Kryssa, that planet is too close. Toah will just strike them down next."

Kryssa nodded in agreement and took her husband's hands into hers. The two of them concentrated on joining their powers together. Immediately an orb began to develop around their hands. It grew immensely consuming the room. Then as fast as it developed, the orb drifted out of the nearby window. As their minds linked, they envisioned the Cressida people continuing with their daily affairs completely unaware of the pending doom. The orb moved through the streets collecting the unsuspecting entities.

The distant footsteps Anani heard grew closer. Then off to Anani's right, two cloaked men passed by her. Before their footsteps were silenced, her mother's screams billowed through the chamber. Anani stood still as stone watching her parents fall to the ground. She realized that the scene playing out before her was the last few minutes of their lives.

She screamed wanting to help them. The two cloaked figures turned to face her. Their beady red eyes and ghastly grins stared at her piercing into her mind. Toah took a step toward her and then stopped when he felt her essence's energy. Her power was new and nothing like he had ever felt before. He sensed that this power was artificial and not born from within her. Toah concentrated harder on his thoughts in an attempt to penetrate the energy that forbade his approach. He needed to gain control of her mind as he had done to others.

She heard his voice rushing at her like a whirlwind. Toah could feel her endurance weaken and rejoiced in his pending victory. Just when he was sure that Anani's mind was open to him, he felt a pain shoot through his temple. Before Toah could react, the link to her mind was severed. What he didn't know was that the thoughts she heard were not his words of persuasion, but the memory of his last conversation with Tarik.

Sensing that something was wrong Tarik proceeded to intervene. He leapt forward oblivious to the energy that stopped Toah's earlier approach. Anani stood immobilized and unable to run away. She watched helpless as Tarik extended his arm pointing his finger at her. Suddenly the room grew dark and she felt the stone drop from her fingers. She closed her eyes clenching her teeth as Raina's voice pulled her back to Earth's realm.

"If you want to eat alone, that's fine with me. I checked a book out from the Library yesterday and it's really good. I'll just plow through a few more chapters."

The melody changed its tune once more, as Anani imagined her parents' fear and pain being absorbed by the stone. When it stopped, she opened her eyes to find Raina standing in front of her. As Raina's lips moved, Anani heard the words of the Sentinel.

What action the stone performs outweighs any comprehendible value one places on it. Guard the stone and when the time is right, cast it into the waters of pain and sorrow.

"Well, what are you going to do?" Raina asked, pulling Anani from her bemused state. Then she placed her spoon into the sink.

"I am going to lunch with you," she said, shaking off the previous sensation that overwhelmed her. "What do you have in mind?"

"Burgers, pizza, I don't know. I was hoping for something different."

"What about subs?"

"Sounds great to me, Ann," Raina replied. Then she smiled grabbing her car keys from off the end table.

Together they walked through the courtyard of their Hemet County apartment. The only sound booming in the air was that from the fountain in the center of the courtyard. The pattering of the water splashing onto the cement caught Anani's attention. She clutched her purse tightly, hearing the faint melody emanating from her purse. The urge to approach the fountain took a hold of her. Without hesitation, she walked up to the fountain then sat on the edge of the wall.

The desire to dip her hand into the synthetically colored water became too powerful to fight. Subconsciously, she reached into her purse removing the stone. In a swift move of her hand, she submerged the stone under water. Instantly, the music changed, and her grip on the stone began to loosen.

There in her mind she saw another who held a stone like hers. She could feel his curiosity about the token he grasped tightly in his hand. Anani knew then that she had to find this Guardian. She believed he might hold the answers to the questions that lingered strongly in her thoughts.

"Good evening, Mother," Torrey said, as he entered the hall.

The radiant Guardian smiled back at him, and gestured with a nod for him to sit next to her. Her son's visits were staggered because of his chair on the Council. Anytime spent with him was always cherished. Torrey complied with her wishes by sitting on the davenport beside her.

"You are a busy representative on the Council. What matters do you find so important to break you away from your duties, my son?"

"I need to speak to you about a memory I recall from my youth."

"You had many adventures, my son. Your father and I showed you numerous worlds and you experienced magnificent cultures. Which one in particular do you refer to?"

Torrey closed his eyes. He knew it was a bad idea to discuss this. Yet, how could he not? The burning room always lay in the back of his mind, reminding him of the child. His fingers still tingled, demonstrating what he experienced that day.

For a very long time, the same image flashed before him. The steadily creaking noise squeaked in his ears day and night. Impulsively, he found himself tapping on his thigh or at the edge of his desk in the same rhythm. This action almost became neurotic interrupting his thoughts. At times, he even found himself tapping on the Council table during court sessions. The subtle clearing of the members' throats often were not enough to reel him back to reality.

As he fell aimlessly into the strange vision again—Torrey watched as the dust particles danced in the air glistening in the moonlight's reflection. Her small frame rocked in the wooden chair engraved with her name. She swayed gracefully back and forth with the swishing motion of the chair, her feet never touching the cold worn floor.

Her smile welcomed the four-year-old Guardian encouraging him to approach her. Then, there was the voice that sung in his head. Its harmonious tune formed rhyming lyrics capturing Torrey's essence and forbidding him to think of anything else. The lyrics heard solely by Torrey were the soothing words of the toddler who resembled this now grown Elder.

She sat before him holding out an object in her hand. It was obvious she wanted him to take what she offered. Perhaps it was a kind thought or a trinket whose importance couldn't be measured by any standards known to man.

Torrey extended his open hands lightly making contact with hers. She loosened her grasp on the object and it fell gracefully into Torrey's palms. Gently touching his hands, she wrapped her hands around both of his and then closed them balling their hands up together into a fist. Softly speaking more words that he didn't understand as a child, her expression told him the story. She had so much to explain to him about her earthy encounters. He listened attentively, engrossed in the passion of human life. Her countenance flourished saturating him in her purity.

The energy Torrey felt from her body became intense forcing him to pull his hands away from hers. He examined his palms staring at the stone she had given him. Torrey was amazed by the colors admiring the unique blends of earth tones and blues. Something about this trinket captivated Torrey. There was a special kind of peace emanating from the multi-colored rock. It brought him contentment, assuring Torrey he needed to be mindful of the stone.

Now in his adulthood, the lyrics meant much more to Torrey than a peaceful song. Even today, their significance tugged at his superior intelligence demanding he decipher the conversation. The fire that burned out of control in the chamber on the second floor appeared to blaze hotter in his mind than he had previously recalled. His tingling fingertips were almost illuminated by a pale blue color that appeared as bright as that first moment he felt the odd power in the chamber.

Guard the Stone of Fayruz with your life, my brother. Tell no one you carry the secret.

Just when he was sure the vision would show him more, it ended abruptly. The vision always ended just before he saw the face of the woman standing in the doorway. This memory grew stronger every day taunting him as the stinging surged through his fingertips. It reminded him that he was somehow needed in the tiny cabin in Silver Lake.

Torrey reached into his robe feeling the urge to confirm that the rock was safe inside of his pocket. In the many years of his existence, he had always kept the rock safely in his desk drawer. But lately, the strong desire to keep it within his reach day and night consumed him.

The day the Sentinel emerged drawing him into her blue light had changed his perspective on Guardian life. Torrey didn't realize this, but his course of thinking and his rationality had been affected tremendously. The reality of this was becoming evident to Torrey throughout the last few weeks—a time frame he found not measured by his Guardian world—but time measured by Earth's standards. How perplexing for him to feel this odd need to be mindful about anything the wretched humans cared about acquiring.

Torrey was not a huge supporter of the Sentinel's orders or of Josiah's willingness to comply. Yet, he sat on the Council of the Twelve, and his duty to his people came before his own existence.

"Your question, my son?" Evi inquired. "What did you want to ask me about?"

Her voice pulled him from his thoughts. Now that the child's lyrics made sense to him, Torrey hesitated to say anything at all. He shoved the stone back into his pocket, and then walked to the open window. The floral smelling breeze diminished the pungent odor of smoldering wood from his memory.

"Torrey, dear. Are you well?"

"Yes, I am, Mother. Why do you ask?" he questioned nervously, looking out the window.

"Son, you seem so distant. Are you experiencing great difficulties?"

"No, Mother. I am sorry I was immersed in my work today and other situations. I apologize that I allowed those issues to interfere with my visit today."

"Torrey, you need not apologize to me. The Council is a very important matter. I am proud that you have chosen your path well."

"Thank you, Mother. I must give you and Father the credit for the education and encouragement you have bestowed upon me."

Evi got up from her seat and stood next to her son. She knew deep inside her essence that the distractions Torrey suffered from were far greater than he first tried to make her believe.

"The memory, my son?"

"Ah ... of what?" he questioned, looking away from the window to face his mother.

"I asked you about the memory," Evi said eagerly.

"Oh ... Mother that seems so unimportant now. Forgive me for interrupting your book."

"The memory, Torrey," she demanded this time.

Her demeanor changed denoting her son's vagueness. One thing Evi learned about her son was his dedication. Never in all of his years had he allowed issues with the Council to affect his personal life. His excuse was just that, an excuse.

"I told you, Mother, it is of no importance to me any longer," he insisted, confused by his mother's sudden change of tone.

Evi rested her hand against the satin curtain adjusting it slightly to stop it from blowing in the wind. She now turned her head to glance outside into the meadow.

"Tell me, my son. Do you still hear the song?"

"The song?" he pretended to be at a loss to her question. Somehow, he knew what she was really asking him. Deception was not a custom he practiced, however, at this moment the truth seemed too dangerous to visit.

"I hear it every night—" her voice broke, "if I could dream, my son ... I am sure I would hear the words to the song, too."

Evi turned back to face her son. The song had become so familiar to her that she heard its faint melody from his robe pocket. Torrey stood amazed at her proclamation. He thought he was the only one who heard the strange humming sound from his desk drawer since his youth.

"The stone, Torrey," she said. "You have it with you now, do you not?"

He answered, hesitant to admit to her that he indeed had the stone with him. "Yes, I do, Mother."

"What does the song tell you to do?"

"Nothing, Mother, I have never heard the lyrics to the song. I have just heard the humming noise that calms me day and night."

"Then, she did not tell you the secret?"

"Whom are you referring to, Mother?"

"You know who it is I speak of, my son."

"No, Mother, I do not. Please, tell me who she was."

"Be careful what you ask for, Torrey. Sometimes we do not want to really know what the answers are."

"Do you speak from knowledge, Mother?"

Evi closed her eyes wondering how she ever existed this long pretending. "I have asked the question and wished for the answer."

"Was it not what you wanted?"

"Son, there has been much I have done for the sake of others that I regret daily."

"Tell me, Mother, please. What are your regrets? Do our people not exist without regrets living in true harmony?"

"They are just that. My regrets are mine and not yours to share, Torrey. Do not trouble yourself over them."

"Mother, if you propose to live in an essence filled with regrets, and your regrets trouble you, then they trouble me as well."

Evi sunk down into the chair by the window and buried her face into her shawl. "Torrey, my son ... please do not ask what I cannot tell you. Just remember that the stone plays the music, which will in time, lead us to the place we must be."

"And where is the place I need to be?" he asked curiously.

Without answering him, she stood up and left the room. Torrey remained there quietly all alone. He closed his eyes and sighed. He knew that something had upset his mother and he didn't understand what it could be. Torrey understood that the stone called to both of them, but its reasoning for doing so remained a mystery in his mind.

Guard the Stone of Fayruz with your life, my brother, a voice spoke to him through the emptiness of the room.

"Who are you?" Torrey demanded. His eyes darted back and forth looking for anyone in the shadows.

Guard the Stone of Fayruz with your life, my brother. Tell no one you carry the secret.

"I demand that you tell me what you want," he ordered, still waiting for the voice to reveal itself. Uneasiness grew over him, a sensation that was new to this Guardian.

Tell no one that you carry the secret, the voice moved in the wind growing louder. The room began to dim as the squeaking noise increased in volume taunting him.

"What secret?" Torrey now remembered asking the little girl before him, a question he didn't commit to memory as a child. Then suddenly, he was in a cabin. The musty smell oddly welcomed him to the place he shouldn't call home.

It was dark outside, but the light from her aura lit up the room.

She spoke to him in open words as if she meant for others to hear. "One will come and steal all that is pure and full of love. He will take its substance and its heart far away from the place where you dwell."

"I do not understand what you are telling me," Torrey's child like voice responded. "What is this pure love you speak about?"

"It is the life of two entities whose love is stronger than the universe itself. The affection they feel for one another has neither barriers nor end. Their love must be allowed to reign again. Without this enduring love, the realms you know will suffer a sadness no Guardian has ever witnessed in the times past or to come."

"How do you know this to be true?"

"My brother, I have been to the future, and I have lived in the past. My eyes have seen much, and my essence has experienced birth and death."

"Tell me what I must do? What is it you ask of me this night?"

"Guard the Stone of Fayruz, and when the time is right, cast it into the waters of pain and sorrow."

"Where will I find this body of water?"

"Brother, you shall find it when you are not looking. It is then that the tears of desolation will fall."

"Answer me this, my sister. What sign shall you give me to know what you speak of is about to come?"

"Brother, the signs are all around you. Even now the wicked stalks the devoted." She turned her head to look out the dusty window.

A shadow that Torrey saw out of the corner of his eye pulled his attention from the tiny rock, forcing him to look across the room. Outside the window, he saw a man peering through at them. The stranger's spirit felt familiar and yet he was a stranger. He didn't belong there anymore than Torrey knew he did.

Torrey wondered what brought the strange entity to this same place. Did this stranger know the secrets, or had he come to steal them away?

"Be mindful of what has passed and what is to come," she instructed. "One who is void of understanding will inflict the universes and the thief will call righteousness in the name of his god."

"What must I do," he asked hesitantly, still unclear of the child's request.

The girl motioned back toward the window. "Stop that one," she ordered, pointing at the stranger.

At that moment, the candles blew out and the room went dim. Torrey focused on the figure watching as it disappeared. In the absence of the strange power Torrey felt, he once again assessed his surroundings. Beside them, their mother looked on pleased at their reunion and grateful for their eager acceptance. Completeness filled the mother's eyes with tears of joy. She knew at that moment without a doubt her sacrifice was not in vain.

"Excuse me, sir, would you like some nectar or a loaf perhaps?" the chamber aide asked, carrying a tray through the doorway.

He had been so consumed in the memory Torrey never heard her approach. "No, thank you, miss," he replied, annoyed by the interruption. Her appearance had not given him enough time to recover from the episode that left him confused. Torrey disliked the uncertainties these episodes brought and the pull they had affecting his outward appearance.

"My lady takes her nectar by the stream. Perhaps, sir, you shall do the same."

"No, I told you that I do not wish to consume refreshments at this time."

"I understand, sir, although you may find yourself more comfortable by the stream."

"What concern of it is yours regarding my comfort? You are my mother's assistant, not mine."

The young woman smiled. "I am not her assistant either, sir."

"Who are you then?" he asked, somewhat curious by her odd behavior.

"Is that not what you have been asking yourself?"

Then a wave of warm air rushed past Torrey. Instantly the creaking noise filled his ears. He looked out the window to glance at the stream and then back to the chamber aide. The woman was no longer standing in the doorway holding the tray. Torrey hurriedly turned back to face the stream, and he saw her kneeling at the edge swishing her hand around in the water. In an instant, he dematerialized from the room to join the stranger at the edge of the water.

"Do you desire your nectar now?" she asked.

"Who are you?" he demanded, grabbing a hold of her arm. Hastily, he pulled her to a standing position not caring about being gentle.

"Excuse me, Elder Torrey, but you seem to be a little distraught at the moment."

"I am not distraught by any means," he interjected rudely.

"I beg your pardon, but the grip you have on my arm tells me otherwise. You will please release me immediately," she voiced sternly.

He stared at her hesitating to comply with her request. It was only after he loosened his grip did Torrey realize how firmly he had held onto her. Embarrassed at his behavior he stepped backward and let his arms fall to his sides.

"Thank you," she said, rubbing her arm. "If I were human, I do believe this would have bruised. You must learn to restrain yourself in the future, Elder Torrey."

"Who are you and what do you want from me?"

"My name is Anani. I was passing by here and the music called to me."

"The music, what music are you talking about?"

"Why, the music coming from your robe."

Impulsively, Torrey brought his hand to his side. He could feel the smooth stone pressed against his hip.

"Do you understand the song?" she asked quietly.

"The song?" he asked, trying to lessen its own meaning to him. To admit he had the stone to this stranger seemed dangerous. After all the years of secretly hearing the music, he wasn't about to confirm her questions regarding the song.

"I hear the words, Elder, except they have no meaning to me. I thought perhaps that you could shed some light on the song for me. I only know that it is a beautiful sounding melody, which is disguised, and it must have a meaning behind it."

"Where did you come from? Why do you bring me here to this stream?"

"I have brought you nowhere. It is you, Elder, who has followed me."

"Why do you come to the stream?"

"It just seemed natural. Does the water not call to you when you are holding the stone?"

Torrey hesitated to answer her. It wasn't until now that he realized the stone did seem to draw him to water. *Guard the Stone of Fayruz and when the time is right, cast it into the waters of pain and sorrow,* he recalled, hearing the child's voice in his head. He didn't have to admit to Anani that he was void of this knowledge for she already knew this.

"Since I was given this stone, I have found myself attracted to many places with streams created in splendor and rivers forged by Mother Nature. Yet, none has brought me the sensation of knowing that I have been to the right place. Have you found the water that soothes the yearning within you?"

"No," he had to admit. Her words truly related with some urge that brewed inside of him. For just now, he too, desired to dip his hand into the stream. Kneeling down, he inserted his hand into the water and gently swirled it around in a circular motion.

"The cool water is refreshing against your body; however, it does not soothe the urge, does it, Torrey?"

"No," he said. Then he rocked back onto his heels and stood up.

"It does not sooth my desires either. Not any stream or river that I have dipped my hand into has calmed the urge. Since the day I acquired the rock I have searched with no avail."

"Tell me, please," he asked, now looking at her with his complete attention, "how did you acquire your stone?"

"It was a gift, however, I can say no more."

"Tell no one that you carry the secret," Torrey spoke softly.

The girl said nothing as the words, too, echoed in her head.

"It would seem that we have defied our instructions, child," Torrey said, hoping the young girl would reveal more to him. As he examined her features, he tried to compare her to the child in the cabin. It didn't take long to know she was not the one.

"What do you make of this, Elder Torrey?"

"I am not sure. Do you have any ideas?"

Anani looked away, cautious of what she should share with him. *This rock is known by many names. It is as rare as it is unique,* the Sentinel's voice sang through her head. *Many would give their lives to get their hands on one such as this stone.*

"Do you not agree, that finding out the value of this stone on our own is more esteemed than being told?" she finally said, responding to his question.

"I have neither time nor patience to continue this conversation with you. If you cannot tell me, then I must search this out without further delay from you."

"What now makes you so eager and impatient? Time holds no meaning, and the song in your heart is always close when you keep the stone with you."

"If you are void of the rock's understanding as you have said, then where do you come up with these riddles, child?" It occurred to Torrey then that she just might have a clearer understanding than he did.

"They are not riddles as you propose."

"Then what is the meaning behind the words you choose to recite to me?"

"I suppose I have just repeated what I have heard, and nothing more."

"Then you are hiding information from me." He snarled reclaiming the step he gave up earlier. He grabbed her arm once more demanding information. "Tell me, who gave you this stone."

"I beg your pardon, Elder, but forcing me to speak in such a manner as you have chosen will not profit you anything." Anani tugged her arm away and stepped aside to leave. "I believe I was wrong for coming. Please excuse me?"

"No, wait, miss please," he begged, coming to his senses. "I do not know what has come over me. All of my existence I have heard the stone's songs with no reason to its meaning. To know that someone else has heard the song confuses me. Please do not go. Let us discuss the stone further, for I can no longer hide the music in my mind."

"I believe we have said all there is to say. Neither one of us has the answers, either by choice or truth."

"Then what course are we to follow, child?"

"I believe all we can do is to allow the stone to guide us."

"You appear to have a better understanding of this stone. What do you suggest we do?" Torrey asked.

Without saying a word, Anani removed the stone from her pocket and lowered it into the water grasping it firmly as to not drop it.

He removed the stone from his own robe pocket whispering the words he heard in the cabin. "Guard the stone and when the time is right, then cast it into the waters of pain and sorrow."

A mist swirled above the stream then and Torrey and Anani disappeared. They found themselves standing next to a beautiful brook whose water overflowed with a sensation of compassion. Torrey looked down into the water amazed at what he saw. There before him and Anani were thousands of stones glimmering in the light's glow lying at the bottom of the brook. Torrey held out the stone he had submerged into the water. Those within the crystal-clear water mimicked the stone's beauty.

There was a strange draw that the submerged stones had on Torrey. He almost heard a voice instructing him to reach in and take a stone. The impulse to comply was overpowering. Torrey held his stone above water and dropped it in. As the stone splashed into the water, a melody played capturing Anani's attention. She, too, complied with the urge dropping her stone as well.

Together they knelt moving as if they were one unit. In unison, they reached in grasping another earth tone and turquoise shaded stone. As they did this, their swooshing moment within the water disturbed some of the stones, sending a glorious melody into the air. As Torrey and Anani examined their stones, the mist rolled back in. Torrey noticed that it looked dim and he felt abnormally restless in its presence.

Anani stood up and stepped backward, putting some distance between her and the grey colored mist. Her worried expression told him that, she too, felt the dismal effects of the mist. Then all at once, it disappeared into the water and the melody's tune had changed. The resonance spoke in words plainly heard by Anani and Torrey.

"When the world sees no end to the sorrow, then the evil will win. The people live on wishes hoping for dreams that never end pleasantly. It is they, who are lost and full of despair that is led away to their demise.

"In the river, there is hope. The river full of tears of the repentant brings hope for the others. For by faith in prayer, the sinners are forgiven, and their lives renewed. The *stone* that is cast aside and left unnoticed becomes the foundation of humanity. This *stone* will abolish the fear and sorrow consuming the darkness in the water of peace.

"In your darkest hour, renounce the evil through faith and call upon the *stone*. It shall withstand any storm projecting its strength into the lives of the forsaken."

Anani began recalling the thoughts she heard from the stranger. Until now, the foreign language meant nothing to her. The words were only sounds undecipherable by the gestures each man had made. Torrey sensed her shifting demeanor and responded by placing his hand on her shoulder. He only intended to give her some reassurance, but what happened next equally alarmed him. As strange as it was, Torrey could hear her thoughts and witnessed the conversation replaying in Anani's mind. He recognized the language putting the pieces together. Anani heard his mind evaluating the evil plan that was now exposed. She felt human fears consume her essence when she realized Raina might be in danger.

While she thought only of saving Raina, Torrey's thoughts considered much more. He now realized who the child in the rocking chair was. After all of these years of being lost to the meaning of the stone—he found the answers. In the mind of the young Guardian was the face of the shadowy figure peering through the window. He understood now what chain of events was unfolding. There was another way to defeat the evil intentions of the man he now knew as a Tracker from the Hyperion Universe. The plan was ingenious and well advanced.

Then too prompt for their Guardian eyes to see, a bright white mist shot out of the water. As it darted across the sky, Torrey noticed Anani's body began to fade. Holding his hand out in front of him, he was assured that she wouldn't leave him there.

18.

FORBIDDEN LOVE

Guardian Realm—present-day

Yakira knew Jaleel stood behind her. She didn't need Guardian powers to sense this. Just his very thoughts of her and the moments they shared—sang loudly in her mind—calling for her attention. He too, could hear traces of her desires that only encouraged the attraction they felt for each other. Somehow, their minds linked with one another when he searched her out in the Promethean Universe for assistance with the imprisoned Josiah. This link spiritually bound Jaleel and Yakira in a constant state of unity, unnoticed by those around them except for Yakir.

They may have parted ways that horrible day Jaleel fought for Josiah's existence, however, a part of each of them remained joined in one thought. Yakira needed her brother to guide her thoughts back from the transparent depths of Jaleel's mind. She was sure, when he left her chamber that day, she wouldn't suffer any more moments of weakness. Yakira was wrong.

She had invited Jaleel back to their home for lessons on enhancing his powers. She wanted to absorb the mysterious workings of Jaleel's mind—to feel what it was that allowed him to be entangled up in the mind of a Great Elder. Yakira's research began a chain of events neither one of them imagined possible.

She came into existence born to be a Great Elder and destined to remain apart from other Guardians. Her mind, just as with her twin brother, Yakir, is to remain superior and unaffected by the sins and weakness of other entities. Isolation from the outside influences assures intellectual purity. This enhances their senses and divine wisdom that they use to direct their kind in a steady course. In return, they have become the peacemakers of the Guardian world.

Once maturity has been reached—they use their skills to unite the outer realms of Heaven benefiting all entities. Therefore, the companionship of her brother's mind would be all she knew until she joined with another twin. Since the willing of twins is rare among their kind—and only the most reserved and intelligent, Guardian twin would be allowed to court her—she may remain at her brother's side for years.

Human love is a strange concept to a Guardian, practiced now under the advice of the Sentinel and the Head Elder Josiah. While Guardians researched the actions and the meaning of human love—few cared enough to attempt to experiment with this emotion. Since Guardians view emotions differently than humans, many don't comprehend love as a human does. The practices of joining and bonding develop on a level no human could understand—yet a few humans felt the embrace of a Guardian, and two bore their children.

Deception is another flaw that binds humans and other entities to loneliness and despair. A Guardian never practices deceit; for truth is what compels Guardians to live as the Creator commands. Should one act wrongfully and indulge in questionable behaviors, that malefactor wouldn't survive to tell the story. Some Guardians argued if Josiah's previous actions were deceitful, or if his actions were truly required to save the Sentinel. In any case, that one Guardian paid a price more severe than exile. His punishment was life without love.

"Come, Jaleel, and sit with me, please." Yakira motioned to him from the balcony. The sound of her voice flowed elegantly in the wind performing a song of beauty that sounded more majestic within Jaleel's mind. The floral breeze gently made her hair dance in the glistening rays of Sol. Yakira truly was one to be placed upon a pedestal.

Her eyes commanded Jaleel's attention. This was nothing new. The look in her eyes had possessed Jaleel like this since the first time he gazed upon her. She too, shared a similar attraction. His mind consisted of a clarity Yakira had never known and never grasped until that day. If the two of them were human, then lust would have won them over.

To avoid the troublesome matters of their Guardian hearts—they played useless games pushing themselves to hide their deepest feelings. It was not easy for these two intellectual beings to hide the emotions that they were forbidden to act upon—for the cause of their race. Even with the separation of planets miles apart from one another, the distance didn't break the link that connected them.

Jaleel approached slowly, admiring every detail of the vision before him. He unwillingly reached for her cheek as he cautiously surveyed her auburn eyes.

"Yakira," he whispered. Then delicately he traced her cheekbone with his fingers. The tender touch of his hand sent a pulsating wave of energy through her body. She closed her eyes in response, but it didn't cut off her mesmerized view of his face.

Jaleel's mind told him to leave for her honor and safety's sake, although his essence called for him to stay. Neither of them had ever imagined such an experience could exist, and yet be forbidden. Jaleel wanted nothing more in the Guardian world than to bond with Yakira. Her presence utterly stole his rationality, allowing him to forget his cause on the Council. Yakira fell unequivocally in love with Jaleel on more levels than he could comprehend. The mystical sensation he experienced when joined with Yakira consumed him at every thought and deed. In her presence, there was no escape or desire to leave.

Against her better judgment, she grasped his hand in hers finding it easily. Their essences tingled through them—overwhelming their senses, and drawing them together. Then it all happened too fast, and neither one could break the hold on the other. Jaleel's essence released, swirling around the two Guardians. The current grew stronger consuming her essence's molecules, binding them with his by pulling her into his cocoon. She tried to jerk away and protest because of her conscience for her duty to their people. At that moment, the tingling sensation jolted them again—much stronger this time than it had before— and their minds linked becoming one. Only then, did they control the passion long enough to remember their duties.

No, Jaleel, her mind begged.

He loosened his embrace, barely aware of her desire to leave. *Yakira, my love,* his mind whispered. *I am sorry, Yakira I know better than this,* he whispered once more into her mind.

And I as well, Jaleel. She thought, not really wanting him to let go of her.

Jaleel withdrew his essence releasing Yakira from his embrace. He looked away lowering his head in shame.

"This gets harder every day."

"I know. I feel your uncertainty ... and your desires. They overwhelm me as well driving me from myself." She raised her petite hand to his cheek. As she brushed her fingers along his face, a tiny surge of energy jolted from her fingertips. Immediately she lowered her hand, looking into his eyes.

"I wish I had your strength, my dear," Jaleel spoke softly. His tone reminded her of his weakness.

"And I wish ..." Yakira hesitated.

He couldn't hear her hidden thoughts, and she knew her words were safe. To speak them in his presence was dangerous. They risked so much to be in the same room together, and she would risk more.

"What is it, Yakira?"

"I dare not say it, Jaleel. You know the path we both walk must not be."

He lowered his eyes once more, assuring any connection between them was broken. He honored her virtue and didn't want to allow his weakness to shame her in any way.

"What are we to do then, my love?"

"Jaleel, you know the answer to that."

"It is only if you say the words that I will have the strength to act upon them. I am not strong enough to leave you, Yakira." Jaleel embraced her in his arms, once more fighting the urges growing within his essence.

"I cannot say the words. You give me too much credit. I choose to burn in the desert soil before my lips will utter those words."

"Then I will burn with you, my dear."

"No one will burn today," a voice from the back of the room spoke.

Jaleel turned around quickly, positioning himself between the stranger's voice and Yakira. "Who are you and what are you doing here?"

"Jaleel, you are a hard Guardian to locate," the stranger said, with a snicker in his tone. "I see that Council concerns are not enough to keep you from engaging in activities considered damned. And you, Elder Yakira. How have you persuaded your brother, Yakir to look the other way? I am sure the trivial thoughts in your head of one as minute as the counselor here—must drive your brother insane."

"What do you want?" Yakira raised her voice showing her authority. "I am a Great Elder. Your presence here was not requested nor is it welcomed. The matters of my life and that of Yakir are of no concern to you."

"I beg your pardon, Elder, except my presence here is much needed, regardless of what actions you perform. Your misguided love affair with the Counselor means nothing to me. Yet, I wonder, if your fling is the reason Yakir has taken leave of Callisto for the mountain terrain of Prometheus. Can you still hear his thoughts, or has the distance given him the reprieve he seems to be seeking?" The stranger laughed smugly. "However, your social status is not relevant at this moment. I am here for the sake of our Head Elder."

"Josiah," Jaleel whispered alarmed. He vowed never to allow misfortune to visit his dear friend again.

"I order you to explain yourself and your reasoning. How did you get in here? This place is forbidden," Yakira said boldly. Then she moved swiftly to stand next to Jaleel.

"Yes—it is my intent to explain everything to you, Your Excellency. However, please permit me to continue with a brief explanation at this time."

"I demand that you thoroughly answer my questions," she ordered in an authoritative tone of voice.

"I beg your pardon, Elder. You must trust me when I tell you that there are things I cannot speak of at this time. Do you not withhold information yourself, for the benefit of others—until all reasoning has been met for the safety of your race?"

"Very well," Yakira said, glancing from the intruder to Jaleel.

The stranger indeed knew that the role of a Great Elder was to maintain order among their kind. Even if keeping the order means not making other Guardians aware of issues that arose—until it became pertinent to do so.

Yakira tried to hide her concern that she had not sensed his presence. Through special powers that were created in the Prometheus Universe—no one was permitted to enter the Promethean Palace without invitation. This power was a form of protection to ensure that the Great Elders were not defiled by the minds of others. Clearly, this entity found no resistance.

"My name is of no importance to you," he insisted, moving a few feet closer to the surprised Guardians. "All you need to know is that where I am from, I am an Elder. I come to you today with disturbing news."

Jaleel watched the intruder closely, observing his hand gestures as he spoke. It occurred to Jaleel that humans often used hand gestures during dialog when nervous or excited about their conversation. He wondered what cause inspired this Guardian to be so animated.

"Our Head Elder is not himself, as I know Councilman, you have witnessed with your travels to Earth quite recently."

"What do you know about my travels? Are you a spy acting deceitfully?" Jaleel challenged, even more greatly suspicious of their unwanted visitor. "I do not know you, nor have I seen you at any of our Council meetings."

"It is true that you do not know me, Jaleel. However, please understand that my actions are no more deceptive—than the ones I witnessed from you two just now."

Jaleel shifted his weight to approach the intruder. Yakira grabbed his arm instructing him to remain by her side.

"No, Jaleel—wait."

"Please, Councilman Jaleel, do not act rashly. I am not your enemy."

"Then what is it that you want? Present yourself, and end this nonsense that you have brought with you."

"Jaleel, you know the human Raina resides on Earth, and that *our* Leader has found her."

"Yes—it was a chance meeting," he answered reluctantly. "What does that have to do with you?"

"Perhaps Councilman, it was not a chance meeting after all," the stranger said suggestively.

"What do mean by that, Elder?" Jaleel demanded, putting off his passive demeanor. "It will do you well to speak of what you know. For now, I see you as no more than a rogue hiding in the shadows."

"I cannot speak freely; therefore I offer you merely a warning. An evil seeks out the Head Elder in revenge. It will act at great lengths to accomplish its goal. It is vengeance that guides the evil entity. Trust me when I tell you that this vengeance is great."

"If you want me to trust you, then you should tell me at least how you know this," Yakira said. Showing her confidence, she moved closer to the secretive Elder. "You have not explained to me who you are or where you come from."

"Again," the stranger said correcting Yakira, "I cannot tell you. Please, just heed my warning. Keep a close eye on your Head Elder." Then instantly he was gone as quietly as he came.

"Yakira, how did he get in here?"

"I do not know, Jaleel. I could sense his essence, which is strange, for he is indeed a Guardian. However, he is no one I am familiar with."

"Are you sure about him, Yakira?"

"I have no doubt he is what he says, and that he does not belong in this place."

"Of course he does not. He is an intruder," Jaleel interjected, annoyed at the Guardian's intrusion on them. He remained motionless, surveying the room as if he believed the self-proclaimed Guardian would return.

"Jaleel ... he is more than an intruder with an unbelievable message."

"How so, my love?"

"Jaleel, when I say he is not from this place, I do not mean Prometheus. He does not belong here in this time period at all."

"That is impossible. Yakira, are you certain of this?"

"I am most certain."

"His visit troubles me, my dear. In my weakness, I have just exposed our behaviors. I am sorry, my love. I have just put us both at risk."

Yakira raised her hand to touch his lips. "Hush, my dear. We have acted jointly in our decisions. We have exposed one another, and our shame will be upon us."

"What shall we do about this, Yakira?"

"There is nothing we can do, except bear our guilt and shame. I do not believe that he will reveal the secret we hide."

"How can you be so sure of that, Yakira?"

"I am not. However, think about it, dear. What would he have to gain? He has admittedly broken our people's rules himself by his time travel. He came here for a purpose that appears to be our Head Elder."

"Yes, Yakira, how could I be so consumed in myself to forget about him?"

"Jaleel, you, and I have created a very distracting situation. We have not learned to adapt to our emotions, and this has occupied much of our thoughts and energy."

"I know ... except he is my dearest friend. I consider him my brother, and I will fight for him ... for any cause necessary to protect him. I should have seen he was having difficulties. Yakira, I should have sensed the dangers that plagued him."

"You must go to him now, Jaleel, and tell him of the intruders warning. If something truly is about to strike against the Head Elder, he needs to be prepared."

"Yes, my love, you are correct. I shall go to him and tell him what we have learned. Together Josiah and I will investigate the intruder's claims and search out the evil. I will inform you of our every move so you may be prepared as well. What will you do until I return?"

"I am going to search out the intruder's essence and see if I can locate him."

"No, Yakira," Jaleel spoke, concerned for his mate. "That is far too dangerous."

Amused, Yakira laughed. "Jaleel, just who do you think you are dealing with? Is my essence not stronger than yours is? Do I not have powers that you can only imagine to be possible? Please do not insult me, love."

Jaleel stepped closer pulling her into his forbidden embrace. "No, my love, I do not intend to insult you. Yakira, you know why I worry for you. Is that not enough to make you see I desire no evil to befall you?"

"Yes, Jaleel, however, there comes a time when the love of someone you hold dear—cannot stop the forces that must be dealt with. My existence alone far surpasses yours in strength and in wisdom. You must not forget that. While I cannot take a life in self-defense or otherwise, I still have a duty and a role I must perform within. Please do not stand in my way."

Jaleel's face lost its smile. The strengths he admired in her had now become an obstacle. Yakira was correct in her reasoning. She indeed far surpassed Jaleel's wisdom and powers in any measure and quality of Guardian life. Her reasoning reminded him of how much they should never be together, except Jaleel couldn't help himself. He stared deep into the emotions projecting from her eyes and leaned in to kiss her. The passion of before didn't rekindle the flame in this kiss.

"I will keep you in my thoughts, Yakira, praying always for your safety."

She smiled wide, but it became evident that the flame in her eyes, too, was dim. "And you know where mine will be also."

Jaleel's wasn't sure if it was his Guardian heart or his mind that processed the quiet emptiness, but he knew what it would mean in the end. He swallowed hard, hoping his thoughts were wrong.

"Yakira, when we have abolished the nature of the intruder, please go away with me."

"To where?" she asked, already knowing that their escape planned in Jaleel's mind couldn't be.

"To Luna or one of Jupiter's smaller moons, or anywhere you desire. I do not care, just so we will be together." Jaleel reached to take her hand, and cringed as Yakira pulled it away.

"No," she whispered. "My love, I have realized just how far I have allowed myself to drift. We should not be. I will not be the cause of your sentence to Deimos."

"You will not be. We have broken no actual laws, just customs that have become old and stiff."

"Customs, my dear Jaleel, that are the foundation of our existences."

"What are you saying, Yakira?"

"Goodbye, Jaleel," she said softly. Then she disappeared from the chamber.

19.

OBSERVATORY

Dream World—present-day

The peaceful breeze enhanced the aroma of the Garden of Love. The flowers danced in harmony to the lullaby that played Raina's song. Each petal glowing in Sol's rays magnified the atmosphere of tranquility. This garden always brought Josiah peace in the turbulent storm that surrounded his life. Here in this garden, he knew right from wrong. He could see unmistakably the path his Guardian life should follow ... and the chosen path of his human heart.

Off in the distance, he studied the magnificent sundogs playing their games over the western mountaintops. Each one performed a brilliant show for Josiah's benefit—displaying unique patterns of bright colors and shooting streaks of light. The sundogs played tag with Sol remaining evenly balanced in distance and proportion. It is in their beauty Josiah found solace from the pain that filled his heart. Before long, the heavens would open pouring its purifying rains above the land. As the sundogs retreated, the sign of God's promise would replace their presence. No two people have ever seen the same rainbow at the same time. None, until Josiah and Raina found themselves connected.

The wind shifted, changing the garden's song. The lullaby became softer and slower making the moment more intense. For it was during this song, Josiah had picked the most vital sunflower ever grown within the walls of the garden. The sunflower's beauty surpasses any other flower of its kind. The significance and meaning of a sunflower go unnoticed by most and forgotten by many. Like all flowers, they grow with tender care into a splendid blooming pallet of beauty and strength. With time, the life's circle concludes, and the sunflower withers away. Then in their death emerges a new life with seeds of hope that bring about the tender love it needs to blossom.

With one thought, this extraordinary flower ended its dance wilting by Josiah's command. Instantly, its life force began to fall aimlessly to the ground. He reached out his hand cupping it beneath the sunflower's head, catching the velvety predestined seeds of love, and then he closed his hand gently.

As Josiah hummed the song, Raina loved so well, he willed the seeds to life. When he opened his hand, he stared at a gold locket lying in his palm. Delicately engraved onto the front was a sunflower. Each line detailed and etched with precision. Josiah slid his thumb smoothly over the image. He closed his eyes imaging the steps that bring a sunflower to life.

While examining this token of adoration, he recalled his first kiss. How shaky his hand was as he traced Raina's cheek, and the smile that encompassed her rose tinted lips. He remembered the tenderness that called to him from her eyes, and how the incredible indigo color mesmerized his essence.

He gladly allowed his Guardian rationality to diminish and float away over the cascade of remarkable terrain common to the garden. This was a fair trade-off in Josiah's standard ... no matter what the consequences would be for him.

With that thought, he willed into existence a tiny picture of himself and Raina posed in an embrace. Grasping it between his fingers, he brought the picture to his lips. His energy bound the love he felt and determination for her safety deep in the fibers of the paper. After sliding the picture into the tiny flawless frame, he closed the locket. With his essence, he sealed the core of his passion securely within the shiny trinket. In awe of what he created, Josiah placed the locket into a golden box wrapping it neatly in foil paper.

As Josiah turned to approach the doorway to her world, he heard a scream. He recognized it immediately to be Raina's voice. He reached out into the universe to find her. There in a dark cavern she leaned against a wall. Blood trickled down her face staining her torn camisole.

He screamed rushing to aid her. "Raina!"

She stared at him trying to process the moment. Who was this stranger? How did he know her name?

"Raina, are you all right?" he begged.

Raina didn't respond to him, she just stared seemingly to look right through him.

The howling wind whipped against the cavern wall dislodging rocks and dirt that flew through the air pelting

Raina and Josiah. His shell jerked as each rock found a new target. Raina didn't appear to be fazed by any of the pain Josiah imagined this beaten girl should feel. It was then when he realized this was another dream. The dream began as Josiah's fondest memory. The day he created the sunflower etched locket for Raina's seventeenth birthday gift. Always, just before he was to materialize on Earth and give her the gift, he found himself enduring the terrifying echoes in the darkness. He knew somehow, that he had already given Raina the beautiful locket and her life as he knew was gone from him. The distraught beauty in front of him was not truly there.

Josiah couldn't comprehend why these episodes were happening to him. He had indeed witness Raina looking as tormented as she appeared now, but it was not in a cave. The day her swollen eyes pierced his being so drastically was in the woods near her home. An evil entity had kidnapped her from her home under a deceptive allusion. Josiah found her dazed and broken. His compassion for her state brought him to a dangerous decision. Looking deep into her eyes, he commanded her to forget. With one simple command, she was healed and had no memory of the attack in the woods.

"Raina—it is me, Josiah. Let me help you, please," he urged. He knew he had to play along with the episode that consumed him now. Josiah bent down to scoop her up into his arms. Her pleading eyes met his, affirming the fear that swallowed her up into the night. Just as his warm skin brushed against her chilled flesh, she vanished before his eyes.

"No," he begged. His voice echoed in the cave answered by a horrid laugh.

Sweat poured down his face, as he stood ready to fight the owner of the wretched noise. Its footsteps beat hard against the crumbling soil. Each scrape of the aggressors step pierced sharply into Josiah's ears—magnifying the tension brewing in his body. Josiah searched the dark looking for the route his foe would take—ready to engage the one who dared to harm his Raina. The steps became stronger amplifying the twisted laugh. Off in the shadow to his right, Josiah saw the cloaked figure appearing.

The pounding of his footsteps ricocheted between the rock-lined walls. Josiah's steps were much tighter, quieter than the cloaked figures. Josiah increased his pace, but his human shell began to tire. Left with no other options—he shed his shell and pressed on in his celestial form. As he watched his shell collapse to the ground, the footsteps stopped. Josiah's essence began to scan for the offender in the stillness of his dark horror-filled dream. A dream that he found himself lost within and no answers as to why.

"Not again?" Anani mumbled, arriving back to her earthly fashioned façade. "Raina, wake up your dreaming!"

Anani launched a pillow at her through the dark. A loud crash shortly followed. She presumed it was Raina's bedside lamp.

"Great! Now she will never wake up."

Anani crossed the room and turned on the overhead light. There in the bed opposite of hers was her roommate propped against the headboard. Her hair lay flattened against her head matted from sweat. She sat very stiff grasping something in her clinched fist.

"Raina ... are you all right?" Anani asked alarmed.

"Yes." She let out a loud sigh.

"What was happening to you?"

"Nothing—it's just a dream, okay?"

"I do—"

"Don't okay, Ann? Please ... I am sorry I woke you. Why don't you try and go back to sleep?"

"Too late ... I'm up. I think I will go make some coffee," she implied. Anani really wanted to stay close to Raina for her protection, but how she didn't know.

"What time is it, Ann?"

Anani looked at her watch, then continuing in the charade, she sighed louder than Raina had moments before. "Ugh."

"That early? I am sorry. I didn't mean to wake you."

"No sweat ... at least for me." Anani laughed in a low tone. "I got finals to study for."

"What are you doing?" Raina questioned, as her roommate turned to leave the room. "Finals are months away. What is the hurry?"

"There is no hurry; I just want to be prepared. I am going to make some coffee. I think we are going to need it."

"You may, 'Miss Over Achiever', but I don't seem to have any trouble waking up."

Raina glanced at her lamp on the floor and then she bent over to pick it up. The red digits on her clock clearly explained Anani's annoyance with be awakened so early on a Saturday morning.

"I am sorry," she whispered. Then grabbing her robe, she followed Anani into the next room. The kitchenette already smelled of coffee arousing Raina's curiosity about its taste.

"Do you want some, too?" she asked, holding a mug out toward Raina

"Sure ... please."

Raina took the mug, and began to put her customary amounts of cream and sugar into the black liquid. She questioned why she even bothered to add the sugar as she stirred the coffee intently. Over the last few months, Raina realized her sensation to taste was fading. Along with that went her appetite.

"So ... have you decided yet?" Anani asked, curiously with a snicker.

"About?"

"You know what I am talking about. Please do not avoid my question."

"Oh, that. I don't know. I think that it is a mistake for me to go."

"Why do you think that? He seems like a very nice guy."

"That's it. He seems almost too nice. I think something is up with him."

"Well, I thought you had a great time with him at the coffee shop?"

"I did. He's funny and all, but he ... I don't know. There is just something about him."

"Well, he is not my type, Raina, but I think it is a mistake to let him get away."

"I didn't think you felt that way."

"Why not? He clearly likes you. Get to know him better and see if you still have the same opinion. I think he is going to be a nice guy."

"I don't know. You never seemed to comment on any of the other guys who noticed me."

"Well, let us see here." She smirked. "I will count them. Oh, yeah ... the number is one. I do not know what it was like back in Silver Lake, Raina, but the guys certainly are not lining up at the door now. Anyone who had intentions of sweeping you off your feet gave up weeks ago."

"All right then I'll try it. I'll go with him to the observatory this morning. Why don't you and Vincent come with us? We'll have a great time."

"No way—are you stupid or what?" Anani scowled, topping off her coffee.

"Excuse me?"

"Raina, he wants to go with you not with us. You need a chance to hang with him alone."

"I don't think I need anything at all. I seem to be doing just fine the way I am."

"You are wrong. Yes, you do need to be alone with him. You need to spend real time with people. You are just too stubborn to admit it. Listen to me, Raina. Life is not just about school. There is so much more out there to be experienced and enjoyed then what you are seeing now."

"Don't be silly, Ann, I know that."

"Do you really? Look, Raina ... all you do is go to the observatory, and if you are not in Pasadena, then stare out into the stars. Have a little fun once in a while."

"I do have fun. I have told you before, Ann, that I absolutely love being there. I feel so at home. It's a great place to be."

"Well, that is another one of your weird hang ups."

"It's not weird. My infatuation for the stars is no different from yours for that silly purse collection in the closet. Just how many purses does one person need anyway? All they do is just sit there collecting dust."

"Fine—you win," Anani said. Then taking a sip of her coffee, she smacked her lips at the taste. She smiled, recalling how those human items meant nothing to her. "But just go alone and have a nice time, okay. Then you can really see if he is as creepy as you thought he was at first. I bet you will see things differently. Trust me on this one, all right?"

With that, Anani got up and went over to fire up the computer so she could begin her studying. Raina followed her from the kitchenette into the small living room. There she sank into the black leather chair resting her feet on the ottoman. Then recalling her last dream she sat quietly until she drifted off to sleep. For so many years, her dreams were predictable, except now something had changed. The dark-haired boy from her class continued to pop up randomly. Her dreams were always just about her and the cloaked figure who hunted her.

Then a few years ago, the plane crash dreams began surfacing much more. She shivered to think about the cold water stealing her breath and her life. But that thought wasn't as scary as the unknown woman who was floating next to her inside of the sinking plane. The blond curly hair and petite fingers seemed familiar to Raina, except the blue tint of the woman's skin obscured her memory as to who this stranger really was to Raina.

"So, did you change your mind after all?" Anani questioned, shaking her shoulder.

"What? Ah no ... wait ... what time is it?"

"It is eight o'clock. You must have fallen back to sleep. I am glad you could," Anani added to be sarcastic. "Here is your brush. You had better hurry, or you will be late."

Raina reached for the brush gratefully. "You're such a wonderful friend, Ann. How can I ever repay you?"

Anani laughed, leaning her head backward. "Just let me get some sleep sometime—okay?"

Raina just nodded, and then darted off to the bathroom to get ready.

As she showered, she thought about what she would say to Josiah. He was very quiet and seemingly reserved ... that is until he listened to her playlist. An expression that became offensive to her at the Library now seemed somewhat amusing as soap bubbles ran into her mouth. After rinsing off, she dressed in a hurry then brushed out her wet curls pulling them into a ponytail. She took one last look in the mirror and decided she looked presentable. Then grabbing her car keys, she waved goodbye to Anani and left for the observatory to meet Josiah.

The car ride passed swiftly as Raina's mind was preoccupied with so many issues. She felt an attraction to Josiah that she couldn't clearly identify. His voice and some of his actions had a familiarity about them. This was too strong to be a memory of their meeting from years before, when his father assisted her with her broken bike chain. Even the brief moments she noticed him in class were not enough to bring about the feelings she felt now.

When she arrived, Josiah was waiting for her near the parking lot entrance in the visitor's lot. He looked content even with the rain drizzling down upon him. He held the umbrella in an awkward position, not protecting him from the rain at all. He greeted Raina with a smile as he opened her car door. Only then, did he adjust the umbrella to offer her a reprieve from the rain.

"Hello, Raina. How was your drive this morning?"

"Fine, thank you. I guess I have driven it so much that I could do it in my sleep. There was nothing particular about it at all. In fact, there never is."

"I see," he mumbled, closing her door. "I bought our tickets already. The tour starts at eleven thirty. I was thinking," he added, in the same breath. "If you come here as often as you say, then you should have a special frequent attendee pass. No wait," he blurted out, amused with himself, "they should have the Raina plan."

"Great and what's that?" She grinned.

"Researching Astrology in New Areas. All Funded by Raina Mae Stone's generosity."

Raina stared at him not responding to his joke. He had said too much, and she heard it.

"What?" he asked surprised at her sudden quietness.

"What made you think that my middle name was Mae?" she questioned curiously. "I don't remember telling you it was. And don't say it was on my playlist—because it wasn't."

"You said that Mae was your middle name when we were in the Library. I am sorry, did I remember it incorrectly?"

"No, it's just that I don't remember telling you."

"Well, I am sorry that I offended you by saying that."

"No, you didn't offend me. I was just surprised that you knew it. That's all."

"Shall we?" He motioned, pointing to the large white dome. Then holding out his arm, he motioned for Raina to go in with him as he started up the long sidewalk.

The rain had picked up with the sudden change in the wind. Unexpectedly, it began raining very hard and they had to run to keep from getting drenched. Josiah broke out laughing, knowing secretly how being cold would displease her. He didn't want Raina to be uncomfortable; it was just that this was something familiar about her. It made knowing how out of reach she was a little easier for him to be with her.

When they entered through the large door of the Visitor's Center, the cool building made Raina shiver just as Josiah had predicted. Removing his jean jacket, he offered it to her for warmth.

"Here ... why not take this. I think it will help a little."

"Oh, I can't take your coat. You must be chilled from the rain, too. Besides, you will need it in the observatory."

"No, I am fine. Please just take it ... at least until you warm up, okay?"

"Thank you." Raina reached out to take the coat, but he held it back.

"No, please allow me to assist you. My mother would be very upset with me for not minding my manners."

"Okay." She chuckled. "But it is just because I see how much my mother gets after my father. I rather feel sorry for you guys. There is always so much pressure to be all prim and proper."

"Thank you for noticing. Believe me, I appreciate it."

Raina held out her arms, permitting Josiah to slip his coat over her body. He nodded and then proceeded to be the gentleman he claimed to be.

"See, it makes me well-rounded, or cultured, or something ... I believe you would say."

Inside the Visitor's Center, Josiah followed closely behind Raina, watching her move about from one display case to another. He had been in this center many times before himself while observing Professor Russell, except he had no desire to examine the special exhibits as Raina had demonstrated this morning. These exhibits were temporarily on location as part of a new Astrological Program.

Her behaviors and actions as she viewed each new exhibit brought a sweet familiarity Josiah had long since believed he would never feel again. Each time they viewed the case containing moon rocks and space debris, Josiah swore her smile got wider. It was good to see her eyes light up, for his memory didn't do them justice.

"Aren't these amazing? Just think about it, Josiah. This rock came from another planet somewhere out there in the universe. Can you imagine what undiscovered life could have touched it? Think about it. A whole race of super people patrolling the universe, and their only purpose in life is helping those in need."

"What?" Josiah snapped his head to look at her. She had just described the existence of his people. "Where did you ever get that analogy?" he asked cautiously, and somewhat concerned.

"I don't know. But imagine the possibility of those lives being true. There could be a race of people just like that watching us."

"Well, it seems a bit farfetched to me," Josiah said, immediately recalling Raina's description of a white lie.

"Well, I think I would sleep much better believing in Guardians of the world, instead of creepy aliens wanting to probe me the first chance they get."

Josiah laughed half heartedly as he looked closely into the case. He had to hide his astonishment for her nearly accurate assessment of the outer realms of Heaven. The dull-white jagged rock did indeed come from another universe. He recognized the rock from his many visits to Adrastea. Three hundred earth years ago, Adrastea found itself on a collision course with a large meteor. When the meteor struck the eastern side of the planet, it sheared off a chunk of the planet's crust hurling it into space. The debris scattered into the planet's orbit and then floated off into the moon's orbit where obviously, it was collected on one of the humans' space expeditions.

Raina tapped Josiah's hand excitedly. "Well, just think about it. Can you imagine what life may have touched this rock?"

"No, I cannot begin to imply what type of life may have touched it. Does the sign say where it came from?"

"No, it just classifies it as space debris."

Josiah smiled and then walked over to the next presentational kiosk. There were so many charts and graphs, Josiah wondered if anyone ever felt overwhelmed by them. For Josiah this was information he subconsciously acquired and dismissed like much of his Earth's intellect, that is until he met Raina. Then, and only then, did Earth and the humans who occupied it, begin to mean something to him.

He found himself particularly fond of the planet Jupiter. In his world, it contained a wondrous realm of planets and life unimaginable to a human. There in its orbit was the Callisto. To humans it was just the eighth satellite positioned as an outer Galilean moon. For Josiah's people this planet contained a mysterious realm where the Great Elders Mataya and Mateo dwelled. It's there where the Garden of Love existed, growing flowers of harmony and spiritual love.

"What are you looking at there?" Raina questioned, moving to stand next to him.

"Apparently, more of your Martian people's planet," he answered, trying to downplay Raina's earlier statements.

"No, not Martian people, Josiah. I am talking about a race that's beautiful, whose world represents goodness."

"Who is to say that your green guys are bad? Just because they are alien like does not mean they have to be different than us."

"You're absolutely right. I guess the television shows have ruined my perception of space aliens."

"And that is the problem with this world, Raina. People allow themselves to pass judgment of a few bad people, and no one takes the time to get to know everyone else."

"What—are you saying I am prejudice against the green guys?"

He grinned. "No, not you."

"And what makes you so sure of this?"

"Because, Raina, everyone is the same in your eyes. You always look for the beauty and forget the rest."

"So, then are you saying that you're somewhat prejudice?"

Josiah looked back toward the case. He hated to admit to himself that he once had a dislike for the world that produced such a beautiful entity.

"Yes ... once, a long time ago. However, things are different now."

"Different how?" she asked surprised.

"I guess you could say I grew up and got much wiser. I do not live with blinders on anymore."

Raina laughed. "Wiser ... right? Then why were you standing out in the rain and gave me your coat? You have to be cold right now, I just know it."

Josiah smiled back. "I think it is the whole gentleman issue."

The morning moved along too fast for Josiah. He enjoyed being with Raina finding it minimally difficult not to reach out and touch her delicate face or grasp her soft hand into his. They continued to move about the large room exploring the valuable information.

Then standing in front of the second to last kiosk, Raina froze. She had viewed this astrological chart many times before, but today something about the planet's satellites struck her in a peculiar way. Josiah noticed the rapid blinking of her eyelids that didn't mask her enlarged pupils. Her beautiful smile had faded giving way to a set of quivering lips. He watched concerned as her complexion instantly became pale. Even her rose tinted lips lost their glow.

Then glancing from Raina to the space chart on the screen next to her, he soon realized what she was staring at so intently. There in front of her glowing bright red, as if it were a beacon beckoning them from the planet Mars—was the tiny satellite orbiting the seventh largest planet in the solar system. Staring back at them was Deimos ... the wasteland Josiah found himself sentenced to for the crime of loving Raina. The beautifully innocent girl he claimed as his Esprit de corps—whose plea reached him deep inside of the depths of torment and chaos.

"Raina?" He waved his hand in front of her face trying to make her focus on him. "Raina, are you all right?"

Then breaking into a sweat her knees buckled, and she began to fall into an ocean of darkness. Josiah caught her, bracing her body against his, before she collapsed to the floor.

"Raina—can you hear me?" he shouted, feeling alarmed and a hundred more emotions he didn't understand.

She barely heard his voice as the scorching void began to swallow her up. Before she knew it, Raina was standing in what appeared to be a desert. The hot sand burned her feet through her shoes—boiling the drops of sweat developing upon her body. The whipping wind brought no relief from the heat as it scattered the planet's crusted soil, tossing its particles wildly in the air. The sandy debris scratched her skin, leaving its bloody mark by branding her body with scars of fear. Her mind began to fade, consumed by the torment that carried out each violator's sentence.

Frantically, Raina turned in circles looking around her. There seemed to be no shelter from the fierce air that stole her breath. The moans and cries of the planet's inhabitants squealed in her ears. Distraught and giving into the moment, Raina fell to the ground covering her ears and screamed for relief.

"Help me ... help me!"

Her desire to call for help faded as her childhood memories rushed through her mind. Sometimes she saw visions that didn't seem to be hers. At certain intervals, the visions became more familiar than the memories she clearly identified.

When Raina was ready to give up her memories to the planet's commands, refreshing water splashed against her wounds. The cooling brook soothed her body with peace and healing powers, washing away the dismal feeling of failure and sorrow. The aroma of sunflowers filled the air as they pointed upward to a brilliant blue sky.

"Raina, are you all right?" Josiah questioned worriedly, embracing her supine body tightly against his.

"What happened?" she asked, opening her eyes slowly. She was disoriented and confused. The air was no longer hot, and her skin didn't burn. Then just faintly, she thought she smelled the aroma of flowers that danced to the music of flowing water. Embarrassment swarmed over her as Raina realized she was lying on the cool floor and not a flower meadow. The warmth she felt on her wrist was an older man checking her pulse.

"Bev," the older man said to his wife, who had gathered with the assembling crowd around the unconscious girl. "Please get her some water."

"Yes," she replied. Then she left the group abruptly. Her absence wouldn't be enough to dissolve the humiliation Raina wished she would die from at this moment.

"Miss, my name is Ruben Osori. I am a doctor in San Diego. I was standing next to you when you fainted. Can you tell me how are you feeling?"

"I am fine." She moaned, disgusted that her episodes chose this moment to incapacitate her.

"Do we need an ambulance?" Bev questioned, returning with the water.

"Hold on," he replied, not taking his eyes off Raina. "Can you tell me your name, miss?"

"It's ... Raina Stone."

"Well, Raina, have you been ill lately? Are you experiencing any pain?"

"No—please, I am fine."

"When was the last time you have eaten or drunk any fluids?"

"This morning. Please, just let me get up, okay?"

"Sure, but I would like you to sit up for a few minute first, please? Ah no, Bev," he added, responding to his wife's question. "I think she will be fine."

"Are you sure, Raina," Josiah questioned, feeling helpless and afraid for her.

"Yes, please, let's just get out of here. I seem to be the freak show at the moment."

"Fine," he said, helping Raina to sit up. The separation of her body from his made him more uncomfortable. He felt a strong urging to protect her, but from what, he didn't know.

Dr. Osori had intended for her to sit for a few minutes, but Raina wasn't stopping in the sitting position. As if Josiah knew her body's wishes, he took her hand into his, gracefully bringing her to a standing position. Raina swayed slightly before catching her balance and bracing herself against Josiah.

"Please, drink some water," Dr. Osori instructed, pushing the glass toward her. "It will help your symptoms to pass. You must keep yourself hydrated in the high desert temperatures."

Raina took the water, refusing to make eye contact with the man in front of her. With every minute she remained, the gathering crowd grew larger. Again, knowing her desire, Josiah took the glass from her handing it back to Dr. Osori. He gently nudged Raina forward not letting go of her waist. She followed alongside gratefully.

"If your symptoms persist, then I recommend that you see a doctor right away. Do you understand?" Dr. Osori called after them.

"Are you sure you are okay?" Josiah asked, opening the Visitor's Center door.

"Yes ... I am sorry about that. I don't know what happened. I didn't mean to make it a circus show in there."

"You have nothing to be sorry about. I just want to make sure that you are well."

"Yes, I am. Really ... I'm fine," she confirmed, not letting go of his hand.

"Do you want to leave and see the observatory another day?"

"Please ... do you mind?" she asked, still embarrassed.

"Of course we can. I do not mind, Raina. We can go anywhere you want."

"I am sorry. I didn't mean to ruin this for you."

"No, do not think like that. You did not ruin anything. Actually, I think it would be nice to see a change of scenery. After all, we do spend so much time at the observatory already with classes anyway."

"So then, Josiah, what do you want to do now?"

"Honestly, we do not have to do anything at all. I do not want you to push yourself."

"I'm not," she said, almost annoyed. "You're just like her."

"What ... who are you talking about?"

"Ann, she is my roommate. She's always after me about these episodes."

"Always?" Josiah said, as he stopped walking and tugged on her hand.

She looked at him, hesitating to respond. "Yes," her voice was soft, but loud enough for Josiah to hear her.

Josiah grew concerned. "What happens to cause this?" he asked, with distress in his eyes.

"Ah ... I don't really know. They just kind of happen."

"Have you seen a doctor?"

"No, it's nothing. Don't worry—I'm a big girl and I can take care of myself."

"Raina, passing out does not happen without a reason. You need to see a doctor."

"My father is a doctor. Don't you remember me telling you this? He thinks that I am fine."

"Well, I am not so sure of that. You should get checked out at the hospital."

"Maybe." Raina teased, pulling her hand free from Josiah's and walking toward her car. "But I'm walking ... talking ... and breathing. My assessment tells me that I'm pretty much alive and well."

"Hey, where are you going?" he called after her.

"I'm going to Hemet to get some lunch."

"Oh ... is it a private engagement then?"

"No, you can join me, if you like," she said, as she looked back at him smiling. "I'll race you up Interstate 76."

"Okay," he said, running to catch up with her. "But where is lunch going to be?"

"You're not supposed to ask me." She laughed. "See you at the California Palms Restaurant on East Florida Avenue." Then she opened her car door and climbed into the driver's seat.

Josiah shook his head then got into his car too. The warm temperature had heated up Raina's vehicle. She wiped the sweat from her forehead and then turned the key to start the engine. As promised, after reaching the on ramp to Interstate 76, Raina accelerated with Josiah far behind. After an hour and twenty minutes, Raina pulled up outside of the restaurant.

She leaned against her car anxiously waiting for Josiah to arrive. Raina much enjoyed her lead foot. The high speeds gave her sense of soaring free and weightlessly as the wind blew in through the open windows. She had beaten Josiah by more than five minutes. Her impatience grew as she watched the traffic pass her. When he finally arrived, Josiah could see the look of irritation on her face as he parked behind her car.

"Man you drive slow. What held you up?" she asked, as the tone of her voice interjected her edginess.

"Nothing ... I have been stopped once before for speeding. I was lucky to get off that time. I do not want to push my luck."

"So, you think life is all about luck then?" she asked with a smirk, while shoving her car keys into her purse.

"No, Raina. It is about being careful."

"Well being careful never got me anywhere."

"Hey ... how can you say that?"

Raina's face went blank as she stopped speaking. After a moment of silence, she answered Josiah uncertain as to why she said that to him at all.

"I'm not sure. Come on let's just eat, I am famished."

Josiah nodded and then held the door of the restaurant open for her. The smell of food gushed passed them in a puff of blowing air. Josiah inhaled deeply through his nose and chuckled softly.

"What's so funny?" she asked, glancing from Josiah to the hostess.

"I was just wondering if they sell cheeseburgers and how good they taste. I had an awesome cheeseburger with barbecue sauce once at Scully's Silver Lake Grill before my father and I moved away."

"Oh, I know the one you're talking about. It is very good, but I don't think you'll get a burger like that here, sorry. The Scully's have cornered the market on that one."

"No, that is fine. Steak sounds great right about now."

"Hey, do you like tortellini?"

"Yes, I do."

"Well, if my parents come to visit I will get my mom to make her famous tortelli alla zucca. She serves it with steaks fresh from the grill."

"That would be perfect—" he began to say, then stopped speaking as the hostess greeted them at the door.

"Good afternoon. Would you like a table or a booth?" she asked, grabbing two menus from off the counter.

"A table please," Raina answered.

"Fine, this way please," the hostess replied. Then she led them to a table in the center of the room.

Josiah pulled out Raina's chair for her allowing his hand to brush against her shoulder. A touch that was forbidden to experience, but so welcomed to be felt.

"Here are your menus. The specials are on the back pull out. What can I get you two to drink before your server arrives?"

"Two root beers, please," Josiah responded, forgetting to wait for Raina to order. Thinking about her episode at the observatory, Raina overlooked his knowledge of her favorite soda.

A few minutes later, their server retuned with their beverages and then took their food orders. Raina was quiet for a while twirling her straw around in the glass of soda. The awkwardness in their silence was deafening. Josiah was relieved when their food arrived. Raina began to eat her potatoes, twirling them around her plate as she had done with her straw in her soda. Every now and then, he would catch her staring at him. She would blush at being caught and then divert her eyes back to her plate. Josiah also toyed with his tortellini noticing that she played with her food more than she ate. After an awkward length of silence, Josiah tried to break the ice.

"Is everything well with you, Raina?"

"Yes, why do you ask?"

"Because you have been so quiet since we got here."

"I'm just thinking ... that's all."

"Thinking about what, can I ask?"

"Well, I was thinking in the observatory that you seem so familiar, but that's impossible. I didn't know you when we lived in Silver Lake, yet the way you look at me seem so natural. The way you walk and the sound of your laugh is very familiar too. Why do you suppose that is?"

"Déjà vu?" he said. Then forcing a laugh he thought over the day to see if he slipped in anyway.

Raina laughed too and then got very quiet. Before Josiah could ask her what was wrong, she looked up at him with sorry eyes.

"I am sorry about what happened at the observatory, Josiah."

"Please, do not be."

"But?"

"But ... what?"

"I heard it, Josiah. There was something else you wanted to say."

"No ... well, I am concerned for your health."

"And I told you don't be. I am fine ... really. Remember my father's a doctor."

"Are you sure?"

"That my father's a doctor?"

"No. Are you sure that you are well."

She laughed. "Yes, and to prove it to you I think we should do something together after lunch."

"Like what?" he asked, taking another sip of his root beer, thrilled at spending more time with her.

"Well, there's the Historic Hemet Theater we passed a few blocks from here. There was a fire and the theater received some damage, but it's open now. It's a pretty cool place inside. How about we go and catch a movie?"

"Yes, I would like that very much, Raina."

"Perfect, let's go," she insisted. She dropped her napkin onto the table pleased.

"But you hardly ate any food."

"I ate enough. What about you?"

"Yes, I am full," he replied, and then he stood up smiling.

Raina got up from her chair and grabbed her purse. Josiah waved the server down for the bill and left a hefty tip on the table. The silence once again followed them to their cars, but her smile encouraged him to believe she was well.

"Okay, just follow me and I will have us there before for you know it."

"Right and how quick will that be, 'Miss Lead Foot'?"

"Fine, I will drive slowly."

Josiah smiled holding her car door open. "Perfect ... after you."

As promised Raina drove slow. Once inside the movie theater, they had their tickets and headed for their seats. In the back of his mind, Josiah couldn't help, but to recall their first date. He found the same serene atmosphere with the lights down low and the background music of the movie. Raina also seemed to be content. He missed her laugh and enjoyed it when she did. Even in the dim light, he could make out her smile and the twinkle in her eyes.

"You know," she whispered, "you're not so weird after all."

"What?" he asked, much louder then he should have.

"Shhh, I'll tell you later."

It was getting dark by the time movie had ended. They shuffled along with the crowd of people into the sunset. The California air felt good blowing on Josiah's face, but he enjoyed the time spent sitting next to Raina much better.

"Isn't that beautiful?" Raina asked, pointing up into the sky above the mountains.

"Yes, it is."

"Hey, Josiah, do you have to be home right away?"

"No, why?"

"Cool. I have blanket and a telescope in my car. Let's go star gazing."

"Great. It sounds like fun."

"It will be, I promise."

"Perfect," he said. Then he grinned with a wiry smile that brightened his eyes.

"Good, we'll take my car."

"Maybe I should drive."

"Why, what's wrong with my driving?"

"Do I really have to say anything at all?"

Raina laughed. "Fine, I'll drive slowly."

Raina did drive slow as promised, but Josiah could see the smirk growing as she accidently drove over the roughest parts of the roads that lead to Diamond Valley Lake.

When they arrived at the west dam, the gate was closed.

"Great. Now what?" Raina moaned.

Josiah looked around surveying the area. This did seem like a beautiful place to watch the stars and Raina appeared very disappointed.

"Hey, I have an idea."

"What?"

"The fence is not too high. Let me help you and we can scale it."

"No, we can't. We'll get into trouble."

He smirked. "Only if we get caught. I think we will be fine. We are not really trespassing to cause trouble. We just want to view the stars from the dam. I am sure it will be fine," Josiah said. In the back of his mind, he thought about persuading anyone who found them with essence, not to press charges against them for their actions.

With that, Raina agreed, and he lifted her up to start her climb. When she was on the other side standing on the ground, he tossed the blanket over the fence. Then he swung the telescope over his shoulder and began to climb upward. In just a few seconds, he was on the ground next to Raina who seemed amazed by his appearance.

They spent hours under the moonlit night looking at the stars. Josiah and Raina took turns pointing at the images in the night sky. As Raina tried to apply her astrophysics knowledge to educate Josiah, he told her not so "tall tales" about the planets and their origins. Raina noticed his eyes light up as he told his make-believe stories about inter galactic wars and celestial beings inhabiting planets that didn't exist.

As false as they were supposed to be, Josiah had Raina hooked with every word. His details were so vivid that Raina could clearly imagine the planets and the civilizations they harbored. One story he told her about Jupiter's moon, Calisto and its gardens, reminded Raina of a dream she once had. It was then when she realized that the dark-haired stranger from her dream, who strolled through the mystical rose garden, reminded her of Josiah.

They stayed late into the evening until the security broke up the event and sent them on their way. As Josiah predicted, the security guard unlocked the gate and let them go with just a warning. Raina drove Josiah back to his car and then headed back to her apartment. She tried to be quiet, but Anani heard her come in.

"You are home late," Anani said, flipping on the light.

"I am sorry, did I wake you?"

"No, I just turned out the lights. Did you have a good time?"

"Most definitely," Raina answered, heading for the bathroom.

Anani jumped out of bed to head her off by the door. "Wait, what does that mean?" she asked curiously.

Raina laughed, and then pushed her way passed her roommate. "It means he was great."

"So, he is not as creepy as you thought?"

"No. In fact, we're going to the Hemet Museum and the Science Center tomorrow. We want to have picnic. Do you want to come along?"

"No way!"

"Why not?"

"Do not be so dense, Raina. I told you before that you should spend time with him alone before I tag along."

"All right, have it your away, but you don't know what you're missing. He's funny and very interesting."

"That is ok. I think I have the general idea of his character." Anani laughed, recalling her friendship with Josiah and then she crawled back into bed. "Good night," she hollered, turning off the light.

20.
DEMON FOE

Guardian Realm—present-day

Beck came to his senses feeling cold and damp. The sand beneath him was soggy, and the strong wind chilled his essence. Guardians didn't normally react to the temperatures of their surroundings when it wasn't beneficial for them to do so.

He found himself still afflicted by the Demon's mind control. The dream he had entered held onto him, refusing to let his mind free. Beck couldn't discern immediately between the dream world and his reality. One minute he was at the Brook of Tears admiring the beauty of the world he created. Then suddenly, the garden was gone, and he was running through the dark cave in a human form.

Beck jumped to his feet surveying the area around him. He had been here before. This place was far from his shelter and his reprieve. He searched for clarity as to what could have happened to him, to allow the darkness to pull him into the cave. This time the dream came on unannounced, taking him from the brook before he even sensed his mind fading. He didn't intend on viewing anyone's dreams today. Therefore, the correlation between how he entered the dream and whose dream this actually was, remained unclear to him.

He had been to this cave before, and each journey there got darker and colder. At first, it was always only him wandering through the musty caverns. The only sounds he heard were his footsteps. If the occurrence wasn't strange enough, he always seemed to end up there in a human's form. Beck always appeared in the form of the entity whose dreams he entered. He was never sure if it was because that is how their mind would have perceived him, or if it was from his doing. The fact that the cave always seemed empty, and he took the form of a human brought him great curiosity.

After several trips to the desolate cave, he finally heard another's voice. It was a soft female's cry followed by a male's plea offering her assistance. The urgency in their voices was answered by a hideous laugh. The very sound of its bitterness sent a wave of mixed emotions into Beck's essence. Emotions were new to him, and if he had his choice, fear wouldn't be the one he experienced the most.

He continued to search through the cave for the girl and the one whose laugh troubled him greatly. Like today, he found her crouched in a corner shivering from the cold. Her clothes were torn, and her hair mated with streaks of dirt that lay caked against her cheeks.

It became clear to him instantly on his first visit what was happening in the cave. When he realized who the girl was he felt his essence quiver. One look at the girl huddled in the corner and he knew this was not a normal dream.

No human could harbor enough fear or disappointment to create a dream such as this. There was another reason the girl found herself there. That reason was the doing of one more evil than Beck had ever imagined. He had seen this kind of entity before who came from a distant planet. They were a violent civilization whose inhabitants were band from many planets throughout the expanse of space.

The Council of the Twelve had tried several of the entities from the Hyperion Universe and banished them to Deimos. They practiced wickedness and mind control, using the elements from the victim's environment to destroy their minds. These entities were referred to as Demons because of their horrific actions. Many were cunning and wormed their way into the lives of innocent entities that provided protection for them. Their blind actions and misguided trust allowed the Demons to escape capture.

The dream world this Demon created containing the cave was well advanced. Beck knew the Demon was close to executing his plan. Soon he would destroy the one who would unknowingly save Beck's realm in another lifetime. In an attempt to save her, Beck risked everything, including his life, and brought the Redeemer to the brook for a brief moment. It was just long enough to distract the Demon and free her from his hold. However, it was long enough to show Beck the vision of his brook perishing by the hand of the Demon. He couldn't be sure if the vision was true, but he believed that good would only prevail in his place of mystical beauty.

On his journey today, he lost his balance tripping on an exposed tree root and plunged helplessly into a pool of murky water. Beck knew he had not really fallen into the bleak waters in the cave. In fact, he knew the cave never really existed. It was knowledge he wished the Head Elder and his Esprit de corps could acquire. For too long the Demon tormented them both in his sinister realm. Beck knew that the brook contained peace and would bring them safety. However, the consequences would be too numerous if the Demon found Beck's retreat. For the mystical powers that illuminated from the brook were too great for the evil one to secure. If he found a way to reverse the power of the stones, he could return the sorrow they filtered from the universe into Earth's realm. Then the evil one would be able to unleash the misery within the stones, forcing many humans to self-destruct from their despair.

Beck and Mataya reviewed many possibilities for Josiah and Raina's rescue. Not every conclusion they came to provided enough details to ensure victory in Mataya's mind. There was a supernatural power over the realm that their Head Elder and Raina were brought to. Mataya's mind had no control over the Demon's realm. It was humanly frustrating to have to stand by waiting for a weak link in the Demon's realm.

A familiar voice broke his concentration. He looked up pleased to see a new honored guest approaching. With a smile, Beck tried to collect himself and recompose his demeanor.

"It is so majestic here. I hear the birds' songs so clearly by the brook," she said.

"Yes, they do have a way of magnifying their song. I believe the valley assists with their actions."

"Of course, Beck, you must be correct."

"Tell me, have you been on your walk today?"

"No," she replied, "will you join me, Beck?"

He extended his arm toward his honored guest, so that she could take a hold of it. "Most certainly ... please allow me."

Beck escorted her down the hill to the berry path. Its entrance stood adorned by a steel-forged archway with hand casted swirls positioned decoratively in alternating directions. Each swirl displayed roses, sunflowers, and lilies that represented the beautiful meadow. She recognized the decorations etched deeply into the steel layers of pressed minerals. The carvings on the archway matched that of the bench set off to the side. Their appearance enhanced the beauty of the magnificent bronze stepping-stones that lay lining the walkway.

Together they walked to the outer side of the path, oblivious of the trees that cast cooling shadows upon them. She inhaled strongly, taking in the sense of pleasant odors around her. The garden bloomed with angel face roses, rich in purple colors. They blended harmoniously with the pink shades of the heavenly-scented stargazer lilies. The tall golden sunflowers guarded the garden with their seeds of hope and love. They were willing to spill upon the ground when the season called for the cycle of life to end and begin again.

"You were dreaming again, were you not?"

"Yes, I was," Beck admitted hesitantly.

"It reaches you here as well now?"

"If I cannot fight through the vision, then yes, it will." He smiled waiting for the courage to tell her what was on his mind. It was no use. He had to say the words. "I have kept the scroll safe. I did what I promised. Nevertheless, I cannot keep this charade up any longer. My friends are suffering from the secret."

"Beck, you must remain silent for the sake of all that is involved."

"This is too much to ask of me?"

"If there was another way ... then you and Mataya would have found it."

"Do you not think that too many have suffered enough?"

"You mean the Chosen One?"

"Yes ... you know of whom I mean. And even you have suffered, child."

"Beck, please show some restraint. I have not lived a Guardian life; however, my intelligence tells me that the Scroll of Espérer's existence here must remain a secret. The knowledge of its power would change the course of humanity."

"Child, is that not what we are attempting to do?"

"Beck, we are attempting to save humanity, not change it."

"What is the difference? Their hearts have grown cold and heavy. The humans need the light to shine upon them. The scroll will make this happen."

"That is not your mission. You must remember that humans have free will. They can find the joy if they choose to. The scroll will give only false hope. You know yourself that it just fulfills the bearer's wishes, and those wishes are not of the Creator. It is His divine intervention that guides His people, not the magic of the scroll."

"Except, you forget. Most humans do not know how to find the joy. Josiah is our Leader, and even he does not know."

"I am sorry, Beck. We did not make the rules. The humans did that two milleniums ago. Now we must continue on with what we have to work with and nothing more."

"This is barbaric, and you know it. You saw the future; she held the scroll bearing its secrets. If the redeemer has not broken the rules, then truly others will have the strength to continue on in that manner?"

"Beck, please contain yourself. She has no idea she held the scroll, and therefore, she has no secret to tell. Your mind merely sees the outward elements. Open your mind and begin to understand the true matters here. What we do now will also affect the future."

"I understand the true matters, all right. My agenda is to bring them both here, and yours is to stop me."

"What you propose is a mistake. She must remain on Earth."

"No, it does not have to be a mistake. Look around you. This place offers protection. The redeemer will keep the secret just as I have. I am sure of it."

"It is too risky."

"You keep saying that, but you have not expressed a clear reason for your concerns. We should bring them here. Josiah, can win this."

"No, Beck. They must fight this on Earth. Do you really want the Demon to discover this place?"

"Of course not. However, she has a fighting chance here. On Earth, the evil consumes her dreams. Do you have any idea how difficult it is for me to break through? I almost did not survive the last time."

"Beck, to assist you with bringing her here for the brief moment I did was very risky. If the Demon had followed you or sensed who I truly am, then this place would be destroyed. The lives of more than your friends depend upon this place. The humans' tears regenerate here. Without this place, they will find no comfort. Please, just remain true to the course. He will make it."

"How can you be so sure?

She stopped walking. "Beck," she said sternly, "you know very well what I know." She looked away, saddened by the truth in the moment.

"Are you not happy living here in the brook with me?"

"Yes, I am. You know this place brings me peace and solitude in this foreign realm. If I must be in a state of limbo waiting for the right timeline to appear for Mataya to switch Rayna's essence to the body of Raina, then this is a good place to be." She looked down at her feet quietly. When she spoke again, her words were strong. "I will remain observant in silence, for there is nothing else I can do at this moment. I am not lead by the Creator or instructed by His will. My actions are my own. I am trapped here in this time portal by Mataya and the workings of her mind. When this is finished, you can complete your life and profess your love for her. Then I can go home to my brother and my parents. There is a life waiting there for me, and I know nothing of it."

"I know that this has been difficult for you. If there was a way I could have changed Mataya's workings and left you out of this, I would have."

"I know. Regrets are for humans."

"You are very wise."

"No, I lived among them, remember. That is the only reason I know this."

"You will find life on the Guardian world much more different than in this brook."

"And Beck, you will find the Guardian world much more different when the mission is complete."

21.
HEMET

Earth Realm—present-day

Morning came faster than Raina believed possible. The fact that she just got home six hours ago made no difference. She felt well rested and somewhat relieved. For the first time in years, she had not dreamed about the cloaked figure who hunted her. Instead, she could only remember faint traces of a dream that brought her back home to Silver Lake.

She was sixteen, and school had just started for the semester. The dark-haired boy who had been in several of her nightmares sat at a desk across from hers. His wavy hair and deep emerald-green eyes seemed very bold and warming. Like the rest of the cheerleaders, she wore her uniform in anticipation of the Home Coming game. The star running back was promised to give a great performance and Union was guaranteed their victory.

The smell of coffee lingered in the tiny apartment and Anani's rustling in the kitchen was no surprise. Somehow, she managed to turn the efficiency-style kitchen into a gourmet diner.

Raina stretched trying to hold onto the last few memories of the dream before climbing out of bed. The dream was a new one but she could remember the boy asking her out on a date. It all seemed too familiar, envisioning the coach tugging on the running back's jersey and forcing him back toward the field.

"Raina, are you awake?" Anani asked, turning over the chocolate chip pancakes.

"Yes, I'm coming."

Raina walked from the bedroom and pulled her chair away from the table. Anani already had juice and coffee poured. Before Raina scooted her chair in, the pile of pancakes had multiplied on the platter.

"Eat up," Anani encouraged. "You must be famished from your late night."

"Kinda," Raina said. She reached over taking a pancake with her fork. She had no real desire to eat, but she couldn't hurt Anani's feelings.

"Well, you never filled me in last night on how things went."

Raina smiled, laughing softly. "At first I thought it was going to be dreadful. When I pulled up to the observatory, he looked so corny standing there in the rain. I almost got back into the car and left. Then there was ... well, I rather made a fool of myself. But he just overlooked it, and everything went great."

"So, are you glad you went after all?"

"Yes, you were right. He isn't as bad as I thought he was going to be."

"You were out late." She snickered. "Mind telling where else you went last night?"

"It isn't what you're thinking, Ann."

"I do not think you know what crossed my mind. So just tell me, please."

"Well, we went up to Diamond Valley to star gaze."

Anani shook her head. "Of course you did. Was he board?"

"No, as a matter of fact, he had a good time."

"Really?"

"I am serious. He is very funny and creative."

"How so?"

"Well, every time I told him something about the astrology charts he ad-libbed some amazing stories about outer space."

Anani leaned back in her chair curious as to what the Head Elder could have said, not intentionally braking any rules.

"Like what kind of stories?"

"Now don't get sucked in like I did," Raina warned her. "They're just fairy tales that he was very good at making up."

"I promise I will not get sucked in. Please, tell one of his stories."

"It is very funny actually. I pointed toward Jupiter and began discussing its moons. Before I knew it, Josiah was telling about life on the satellite Callisto. He had it down pat, as if he had told the story many times before. Josiah said that the life forms lived there in harmony, and everyone cared about one another. He spoke of a beautiful garden called the 'Garden of Love'. Ann, his words were so descriptive. I could imagine it just as if I was there. Then before I could even get enough of that story, he started a new one."

"A new one, what was that one about?"

"The Sun. Can you believe it? According to him, a near five billion year old cloud of gas and dust could form a planet that sustains a race of people created to guide others."

"That is impossible. The Sun is too hot."

"That's what I said. He was cleaver. If I came up with a proven fact to discredit his story, he came back with another dreamt up excuse as to how there is a grand civilization living there right now."

"The Sun cannot support life. What is his hypothesis to allow life to exits on the Sun?"

"Ann." Raina chuckled. "I told you not to get caught-up in the story. But if you must know, according to his fairy tale, the universe and its solar systems as we know them are nothing compared to what is really out there. The universe is more vast and dimensional than our minds can comprehend. There are parallel universes to ours where life can dwell on planets and satellites uninhabitable by humans. He said that we aren't the only life forms in existence."

Anani stared at Raina in disbelief. The fairy tales she heard from the Head Elder were indeed true. It would seem that discretion was far from his current capabilities.

"Now you are meeting him today?"

She looked at her watch in anticipation. "Yes, in a little while. I am waiting for him to call and confirm the time."

"I do believe you said something about a picnic last night."

"So, you really were awake when I got home."

Anani chuckled. What Raina didn't know was that she never slept. At night when Raina lay snuggled under her blankets, fighting off the demons of the night, Anani left her human façade and traveled to her home.

"I told you, I had just gone to bed."

"I know, but I thought you were being nice."

"No, being nice is what you will find in the basket over there," Anani said, pointing to a wicker basket with a red checker lining that sat on the counter top.

Raina immediately got up to look inside the basket. Anani's smile grew wide as Raina rummaged through the mound of sandwiches and desserts.

"I don't believe this and you even have a blanket and ... bug spray, too."

"No picnic is complete without the luxuries of comfort."

"Thank you, Ann. This is so sweet."

"Please, do not thank me yet. Who knows what today will bring. Just promise me you will have a good time, okay?"

"I'm sure I will."

"And promise me you will not be tempted to fly off to one of his imaginary planets."

"Okay, I promise to have a good time and remain on Earth."

"So, where is this picnic going to be?"

"I'm not sure. We talked about Diamond Valley or driving up to Buena Vista Park in Corona. Josiah and I have never been to the Hemet Museum, and we wanted to check it out."

"Too bad the aquatic center was not open. That is a nice place to spend the day."

Raina frowned. "Ann, can you imagine this," she asked, pointing to her body, "parading around a water park? No thank you."

"I think you look nice in a swimming suite."

"Maybe, but let's spare Josiah from witnessing such an atrocity. But really, Ann. Thank you so much for everything. You are such a terrific friend."

"I told you, do not thank me now. The day has just begun. It could rain, you could get a flat tire, or food poisoning from my sandwiches."

"Ann, you're such an optimistic person," Raina interjected. Then she strolled off to her room to get dressed.

Josiah called by nine o'clock as promised. They made plans for him to pick her up at her apartment, and they would ride together in his car. Josiah was there promptly at eleven o'clock, greeting her with a large smile and the peculiar green eyes that seemed to have caught Raina's attention. Anani made an excuse to slip out before he arrived. She risked too much already acting as his fellow student. Coming to his aid again was a mistake, and she needed to avoid him now. She knew he sensed her essence hidden within the human image she created. To expose her mission prematurely was dangerous.

"Are you ready?"

"Yes, I am. Just let me get the picnic basket first."

"Picnic basket?"

"Yes, my roommate, Ann, packed us a lunch."

"That was very nice of her."

"If you would have eaten anything I cooked, then you would really know how nice she was being."

"I am sure your cooking is not all that bad."

"Don't be too sure. You haven't tried my cooking yet."

"Is that an invitation?" Josiah chuckled.

"Maybe," she answered hesitantly.

Josiah drove cautiously the few miles down busy Florida Avenue. Traffic was heavy and the cars were bumper to bumper. He nearly was rear ended as he turned onto a side road to circle the block. Before Josiah could say anything negative about the less than courteous driver, he pulled into the small parking lot in front of the museum. Raina's face immediately lit up as she stared at the teal and red trimmed 1898 fright house of the historic Santa Fe Depot.

Josiah got out of the car and walked to the passenger side to open Raina's door. She got out at a slow pace, still staring at the building. Josiah wondered if she could see what he saw—remnants of the people from past lives scurrying through the depot in a hurry to reach their destinations.

Once inside, Raina found herself intrigued by the record book that belonged to the local hotel dating back to 1903 and the 1906 newspapers preserved inside glass cases.

"Look at all of this," she said amazed. "Think about it. Here in this one place is the rich history of this town and its people."

"It is amazing to look at," Josiah agreed, absorbed by the girl who stood before him. He had missed the twinkle in her eyes and the sound of her voice. Everyday her memories followed him, but it was only now that he realized his superior mind had not remembered her exactly. "Come look at this," he insisted, tugging on her elbow.

He brought her to a section where pictures and stories were displayed explaining the history of Hemet and its important residents. It was then that the lovely Museum Curator introduced herself. She spoke with Josiah and Raina for a long time about the history of Hemet and the acquired artifacts.

Josiah also found himself amazed at the origins behind each display. As he ran his fingers across the old piano—he could hear the songs of the family who owned it and saw them gathered around in unity enjoying the music. His mind faded away immersed in the song until he found himself sitting in the same room with the large family. The only thing that could pull him away was the sound of Raina's voice.

"Do you play the piano?"

"Ah ... kind of, but I do not think I am very good at it."

"I can teach you sometime, if you like."

"Yes, I would," he answered, looking up from the piano toward Raina. "I do not know if I am a quick learner though."

"That's okay, we'll take all the time you need."

"Thanks."

"Here, let me show you something," Raina said, pointing to the other end of the depot.

They spent another hour walking through the museum engrossed in its antiques. Each thrilled at being able to touch the old army issued uniforms and stoves. Raina admired the Indian pottery and farming equipment, while Josiah paid special attention to the old switchboard and model trains.

As they left, the Museum Curator bid them farewell, and she escorted them to the door. After Raina got into the car, she put her seat belt on and began viewing the pictures she took.

"Did you get some nice ones?"

"Yes, I did. But my favorite one is this," she said, positioning the camera for Josiah to view the image. It was one of Josiah standing next to the piano. Even lost in thought, his expression was angelic.

"I do not think that is a very good picture of me."

"Yes it is. You're just biased."

"Biased?"

"Yes, I think so. This is a very nice picture, and you know it."

"If you say so," he finally agreed. "Where do you want to have lunch at?"

"Well, it's later then I thought. Let's go to Diamond Valley and eat there. Then we can go to the Western Science Center afterward."

"Great," he said. He laughed with excitement as he turned on the car.

It only took a few minutes to reach Diamond Valley. Josiah pulled into the parking stall and popped the trunk before turning the car off. Raina got out and went to the trunk for the picnic basket. Before she could even remove it, Josiah had it firmly in his hand.

"There is a set of picnic tables over there between the buildings. Shall we?" he asked.

"Sure, lead the way."

They walked to the entrance of the building. As they reached the picnic area, Josiah found a table that was shaded from the sunshine.

"This looks like a nice spot," Josiah said. He set the basket down on the table admiring the view.

"Fine with me."

Raina opened the lid removing the tablecloth from the basket. She spread it out, fighting the breeze that tried to steal it from her. Josiah laughed as he watched her struggle. Raina glared at him for laughing at her misfortune. Then remembering his manners he grabbed two of the corners, holding the tablecloth in place until she secured it with the weight of the food.

Raina ate quickly, eager to see the displays in the Western Science Center. Josiah saw her eagerness and matched Raina's pace. When they finished he helped pack up the food and then took the basket to the car. When he got back, Raina was in the gift shop looking around. He approached the counter and bought their tickets, then he joined Raina by the door, and they left for the museum entrance.

As soon as they entered the center, a volunteer greeted them. Raina admired the man for how polite he was and his willingness to answer their questions. He gave them a tour of the exhibits, explaining the facts involved in the Diamond Valley Lake dig site.

Raina stood for several minutes looking down at the re-created quarry site that held the actual bones of a discovered mastodon.

"This is impressive. Can you believe this, Josiah?"

"It is magnificent," he said. Then he knelt down to get a closer look at the bones placed beneath the glass in the floor.

Raina knelt down next to him. "It is hard to comprehend that an animal like this once walked on Earth."

Josiah smiled to himself. He looked around the large room at the replicas and actual bones of the mammoth and ground sloth. He had walked beside the same animals in other parts of the world. Josiah admired the archeologist accurate replications of the prehistoric beast, remembering what they looked like in their natural environment.

"What?" Raina asked, looking at Josiah's glazed over expression.

"Nothing," he insisted, turning from the exhibit to look at Raina. He didn't expect her face to be so close to his. The moment became intense as he gazed into her eyes. Their blueness was deep, and captivating. A flood of memoires washed through his mind as he recalled each time he looked into her eyes from a lifetime before. He almost felt as if his shell couldn't breathe, and he would suffocate at the very appearance of the goddess before him. He had to break the connection that was forming between them before his essence released. He took in a deep unnecessary breath and closed his eyes. Then he felt his control stabilizing, and his essence calmed. When he opened his eyes, Raina was still there. Her expression seemed to be full of embarrassment, and Josiah wondered if his was the same.

Lost in the moment neither one of them could speak. Nothing around them mattered. Then he felt his essence whelping inside of him again, and he knew this was too dangerous. He stood up offering Raina his hand for assistance. When she took it, he felt the same energy building that once encased Raina in his cocoon. He jerked his hand away and moaned.

"Sorry, I didn't mean to shock you. This carpet is full of static."

Josiah rubbed his fingers together waiting for the energy to fade. "It is not your fault. Did you get shocked too badly?"

"No, I am fine. Let's go look at the fossils. They have clay and molds to make our own fossils. That might be fun."

"Okay," he agreed. He followed Raina to the fossil exhibit, avoiding being close enough to touch her. He kept some distance between them the rest of the afternoon, hoping Raina wouldn't feel his hesitance.

22.
NIGHTMARES

Earth Realm—present-day

She staggered fearfully screaming through the park. Raina's terrified voice echoed back at her through the canyon walls, taunting her with its dismal façade. The darkness enveloped the path she was walking on, blocking the shimmering light of the once bright sun. Nightfall had come quickly, too quickly. Only moments ago, the afternoon sunshine lit her way to the lookout point on Boucher Hill. As she had entered the overgrown path, Raina could see without a doubt what lay ahead of her, but now the night swept in blinding her.

She squinted attempting to see in the dark. Her cobalt-blue eyes could almost see her breath in the air swirling like a white mist. When she was a child, she saw that the same mist formed unique musical notes swaying in the calm breeze. She read each note humming the melody in her head. This became Raina's reprieve to keep her sanity until the dreams finally ended, except tonight no song played for her. The music's silence clearly demonstrated once more her human fragility. Without the music, Raina couldn't measure the length of time she must endure and hold out before the path's end welcomed her. The intense situation brought more panic and fear to her mind. Her natural instinct told her to scream for someone to help her find the way—except Raina knew with certainty that Scott's Trail was a day trail, and now she was all alone in the darkness.

Raina pressed forward concentrating on each step she took, sorting out the terror that enveloped her mind and her senses. She tried hard to push the terror aside. Raina knew that remaining calm would be the only way she would be able to think clearly. She had eluded the dark one once before. She must again elude him, this time to survive. Raina knew if he caught her, then her life would end at that very moment.

Her breath became more visible as the chill in the air engrossed her. Raina examined the mist looking once more for one musical note. That note was all she needed. She was an accomplished piano player and her mind would fill in the rest making a beautiful song of escape. Nevertheless, even her skills wouldn't help her tonight. No song played and Raina knew that she was truly alone this time.

Then the wind began to blow fiercely around her. She wasn't sure if it was the howling wind or the evil one's moans that pulsated loudly in her ears. The sound had become familiar to her over the years—always growing stronger with each walk along this rugged mountain path. She tempted fate on these nightly strolls, but she had to. The one that followed her day and night turned her world upside down. Raina had to know whom ... or what it was that tormented her constantly.

Her pace increased as her anxiety grew wildly out of control. There was something different about this stroll tonight. Its edge ... its intensity, took on a new sense of dread. The atmosphere around her changed somehow. The dim moonlight that forced its way through the shadows the evil used to cover the day light—made it too difficult for Raina to find her way. She stumbled aimlessly in the dark to keep her balance. Raina's foot caught on the uneven terrain and it caused her to trip and fall. She tumbled to the ground skinning her exposed knees. Raina's skin stung from the abrasions caused by the jagged rocks. Instantaneously, her skin reddened across the palms of her hands accenting the abrasions. Raina realized as she winced from the pain that it was much sharper tonight, and the pain traveled faster than it had the other times before.

She shook off the pain, pulling her gold locket out from under her shirt. She held it high up in the air in front of her hoping that the locket would guide her way. The long chain twirled in the air catching the stray beams of light that shone in the darkness. Then the gold from the locket began to reflect the light around her illuminating the path. She had learned several months ago by accident, how much light reflected from off her locket. Since the day her great-grandparents had given her the locket, Raina used it to light her way. This had worked many times before, and she was counting on it working again.

To her relief, the locket would once again help her to endure this path in the darkness. Raina didn't understand how the shiny gold sunflower directed the moonlight—she simply knew how much easier the locket made her journey. Then brushing as much of the dirt from her hands as she could, she wiped the blood on her shorts—cursing herself for not using the gift sooner.

Raina's head started to tingle, and her vision blurred distorting her view. Each vein along her neck began to pulsate while her temples throbbed from her pounding heart. This was all happening too fast. She should be further down the path by now, and the meadow should be closer. Raina became conscious of the fact that it was ... winning. As she looked back, she barely made out the dark figure emerging into view. Who was the cloaked man whose evil nature radiated from within? Why did he hunt her tonight ... like so many nights before?

As Raina scurried to her feet, she managed to get her balance and sprinted through the mountainside. She felt the rocks and loose dirt shift beneath her weight. The swishing sound of the weeds and tall grass snapping against her legs announced her presence. The thorns of the cactuses tore her flesh adding to the intensity of the moment. Raina knew there was no way to hide from her hunter with the locket's glowing light, but without it, she couldn't run away from him.

A large screeching eagle flew overhead. As it passed, it extended it wings with a deafening cracking sound. The eagle's flapping wings stole the light that illuminated from her beacon of hope. The dark was now closing in on her at a rapid pace. She fumbled franticly with her locket, she held it out in front of her like before, but this time nothing happened. She couldn't reflect the light off her locket to guide her way. This terrified Raina more than she admitted to herself. As dangerous as it was, she was going to have to finish this in the dark.

She continued running aimlessly, feeling her way with extended arms. She made it a few feet further down the trail when the large eagle returned, swooping down on her location. Raina jumped out of the way and slid uncontrollably down the steep hill. In the tossing movement, she could make out a set of two horrid red eyes among the darkness.

Raina's heart beat harder and her lungs hurt as each gasp of air escaped. She felt the cold growing tighter around her like revolting claws choking the life out of her. She knew from the temperature change the fiendish figure was closer than before. The air's temperature always got very cold when it was near. The cloaked figure had gotten closer this time ... closer than ever before. Raina had moved too slowly, and now her sense of direction was gone.

The cloaked evil grabbed a hold of her, pulling her body into his clutches. He sunk his repulsive sharp nails into her left shoulder and tossed her into the air. As she fell, Raina plunged head first into the pond. The chilling waters splashed against her face, and she inhaled aspirating some of the murky water.

Her body began to tremble from the chilling temperatures. Raina tried to scream for help, except she couldn't stop coughing long enough to speak the words. More water splashed onto her face prohibiting her from taking another breath. The cloaked figured laughed forcing a wild current to develop around her. The turbulent water smashed her body into the pond's embankment. Raina fought to get her head above the water to breathe. As she swallowed more water, Raina became dizzy and her head bobbed sideways. Just as she had sucked in a ragged breath, the dark one grabbed a hold of her in a violent jerking motion. Then without mercy, he dunked her head under the water, holding her with his powerful hands. Raina struggled to get free, thrashing her arms and kicking her legs in attempts to break away.

As her right hand emerged from the bitter waters, she clutched onto something warm that brushed against her fingers. Her mind told her it was someone's hand. A helpful stranger perhaps, who had heard her distress and now, came to her rescue from the terrifying predator. She felt the helpful stranger's arm wrap around her, forcibly pulling her from the attacker. She attempted to help her rescuer guide her to safety by wading through the water.

Her mind questioned who her liberator could be, and how he came to find her. Then her fear increased, as the thought occurred to her of the cloaked figure hurting this innocent rescuer. She had to warn this person and make him leave before her demon hurt him, too. Raina's eyes searched through the dark until they met his. The emotions of fear and relief rushed through her as she looked into the face of her great-grandfather. His touch brought her a comfort she was missing since his death, but the peace he offered diminished as horror washed over her. She realized that this was not the first time he came to rescue her from the cloaked figure. Then just as every time before, he faded away and she found herself at the head of his coffin.

"Raina, wake up. You are dreaming gain." Anani grabbed her arm to wake her from her frightful state. "Come on—wake up," she insisted. Anani shook her arm again as she watched the beads of sweat roll down Raina's forehead.

Raina let out a loud moan as reality crashed into her thoughts. She knew it was a dream, but it fought hard to keep her in that terrifying sate. The nightmares had become increasingly worse and chased after her every move.

"I'm awake." She sighed, rolling over onto her back clutching her Black Hills gold locket in her hand.

It was a beautiful gift from her great-grandparents. The two of them gave it to her the day they died the past fall. That dreadful event became a memory Raina never forgot. It was a memory that dwelled deeply within her heart.

At times, she pondered their last visit together wiping her tears of sorrow away ... and pulling happiness from her great-grandfather Enoch's last words. When she did this, the loneliness and the thought of never seeing them again faded. However, the reality of their absence always managed to crush her hopes.

Raina scooted herself up onto her elbows resting her back against the headboard. The cold wetness of her sweat lay across her face matting her hair against her cheek. The ache in her head throbbed as the blood pulsated though her veins. She breathed in and out through her nose trying to concentrate on relaxing. Sometimes it dulled the throbbing, helping her to recover from the episodes much quicker.

"Was that thing chasing you again?" Anani asked, in a serious tone of voice.

Raina wiped the sweat from her brow, feeling the sticky dampness on her fingers. "Yes—he got me this time—although, this dream did have a weird twist to it. Someone came to my rescue and saved me just before I drowned."

"Listen, Raina. You should see a doctor about those crazy dreams. The nightmares are getting worse." Anani moved to sit on the bed next to Raina. "You know ... I think that there is some type of medication you can be prescribed. It will—"

"No way, Ann," Raina interrupted angrily, sitting up straight, "I am not crazy."

Anani sighed, rolling her eyes. "I never said you were crazy. It is just that your dreams are not normal. If it is not the cloaked figure chasing you"—she paused, feeling her human heart skip a beat—"then it is that terrible plane crash. It is almost as if you are projecting some fear of death into your dreams."

Her mind recalculated the episode by the brook. She knew Raina's life might have been in danger, now she was sure of it. How could she have missed it before? Raina's description of the cloaked figure was too vivid to be just a nightmare. Could it be possible that the dreams were of the evil one's doing? If it were true then she had to be on her guard.

Raina sat motionless pondering Anani's words. The plane crashes ... they were the worst of her nightmares. That dream began to haunt her when she was sixteen. The horrid wide eyes of an unknown stranger screaming at her went unidentified. She could feel the woman's warm grasp through the chilly water. Even in the dark, she made out her terrifying expression clearly.

With the dreams in the park, Raina knew that there was an escape. In the plane, there was nowhere to go. When she tried to pull free, the woman's pale face moved closer ... taunting her with eyes of uncertainty. Raina swore her lips moved, but the words they formed were never heard in the depths of the water.

"You're over exaggerating, Ann. Maybe you should re-evaluate your psych classes."

"Raina, my classes have nothing to do with this. Ask anyone. What you go through during your sleeping hours is abnormal."

"Enough—all right. Ann, I am fine. Please, let's go get some breakfast."

Anani giggled, attempting to lighten the mood. "Are you buying?"

"Sure, Ann ... anything to change the subject."

Raina grinned and slid out of her bed. With a quick glance toward the clock, she headed off to the bathroom.

"Where do you want to go, Raina?"

"It doesn't make a difference where we go," Raina shouted through the door, "it's not like I can taste anything anyway. But hey, I feel like doing some shopping. Let's go somewhere near the mall."

Raina leaned against the sink and took in a deep breath trying to shed her dream. He had gotten closer this time than ever before. Raina could still feel his withered fingers touching the back of her neck. She shivered to think of his touch. Closing her eyes, she tried hard to push his scaly face from her mind. When the dreams first started, he was barely a black mass following her, now this Demon's crimson eyes hunted her even in her wakened hours.

"Are you all right in there, Raina?" Anani called out to her interrupting Raina's thoughts.

"Yes ... I'm coming. Please, just give me a minute?" she said, removing a washcloth from the linen closet.

After she washed her face, she laid the damp cloth in the sink and turned from the mirror. Her instinct to jump away took hold as her peripheral vision registered something moving toward her. Turning her head back toward the shadow, Raina saw the dark looking object exiting the mirror. A scaly hand appeared from the mass and grabbed a hold of her hair. It started tugging her body back toward the sink. Raina screamed, punching, and slapping her hands at the figure, trying to pull herself away.

"Ahh ... Ann, help me! Ann, please," Raina pleaded, as she punched the figure harder. When her fist made contact with his hideous form, she heard a crunching noise. It confirmed that her wrist had just been fractured. "Leave me alone," she demanded, grabbing her wrist in agony.

"All right," the evil replied, thrusting his hand in front of him. Instantaneously, her body flew backward into the bathroom wall with a loud thud. Her head slammed into the plaster before she tumbled to the floor. The impact sent a stabbing pain shooting through her head that traveled down her neck. The force of her body smashing into the wall had knocked the wind out of her making Raina dizzy. She gasped trying to catch her breath. Raina kicked her feet outward into the air still fighting the evil of her dreams.

Terrified, she looked around for a way to escape. The monster from her dreams clutched onto her again and began to pull her into its darkness. During the scuffle, Raina grabbed a hold of the towel rack trying to gain the advantage. The towel rack snapped in two, making a popping sound as it tore away from the wall. Chunks of crumbling plaster broke loose and fell across her face then collapsed downward onto the tile floor. The clunking noise boomed throughout the tiny room but was unheard by Anani from where she was standing.

Raina continued struggling with the evil intruder, screaming for Anani to come and help her. The intruder had a mysterious power and silenced her voice, so that her screams were not heard outside of the bathroom. Unaware of his trickery, Raina kept screaming and begging for help.

"Ann—Ann!"

He laughed callously, at her weakness knowing she had no way to escape. "Yes." He hissed, with a revolting odor seeping from his mouth. "Scream for help and see just who comes to rescue you."

Raina punched at the figure before her and then without any warning, her hands disappeared within the form becoming invisible. The coldness burned her fingers and she felt its chill radiate through her body. At that moment, her radiant blue eyes grew heavy and the night overtook her.

She wouldn't have known that morning had come, if it were not for the faint ray of light peeking in through the crack in the ceiling. The caverns stench smelled of sulfur, stinging her nose. Raina followed along the walls with her hands scratching and pounding against cold clay and stone, searching for a way out. The damp clay and tiny pebbles caked deep under her nails, drying her skin. Her hands felt tight and her skin pulled when she tried to open her fists and close them again. Sweat streamed down her face soaking her torn camisole. The silk strap hung across her chest tattered. Her hair clung to her moistened shoulders, tricking her with the allusion of bugs crawling on her. She swatted the make believe insects becoming more freaked-out as the clay tumbled down her arms. She swore she heard the buzzing of tiny insect wings in her ears taunting her.

Raina called out for help again, alarmed by the husky tone of her voice. It sounded rough from the many screams she uttered in the night, helplessly trying to free herself.

"Help me, please! Can someone hear me? Ann, are you there? Someone help me—please!"

Then just as she had heard throughout the night, she made out another vindictive laugh off into the distance. She shivered to think of her dark hunter watching her and feeding off her fear. Why was he doing this to her? What did this Demon want from her?

"Please," she pleaded, sliding down the jagged wall in despair. The rocks scratched her back snagging her already torn camisole. "What do you want from me?" The anger grew deeper inside of Raina forcing an odd boldness to surface. She shouted, wanting to hide the fear that still seeped through her newfound boldness. "Answer me, you coward!"

The only response from the Demon was a wicked chuckle from somewhere in the darkness. She forced her eyes shut, willing for this dream to end and return to her apartment in Hemet.

Then in the darkness, a soft glow appeared before her. The light began to form into the shape of a human. She scrutinized the man whose form developed before her eyes. She had seen this person before, except Raina couldn't remember if he was in the cave to help her, or if he was the one behind the wretched snort.

An incredible urge for her to runaway swelled up inside of her, but something called to Raina telling her to remain where she sat. She opened her mouth to speak, but she couldn't. Her mind formed the words, only her mouth didn't move.

The man's face seemed gentle and reassuring. He extended his hand as if to help her ignoring Raina's hesitation to take his hand.

"Who are you?" she questioned, focusing on his facial features. "Why are you here?" Her voice cracked from fear, and her trembling body shook causing her teeth to chatter. "Please just leave me alone," she begged.

Her fear ate at the man, and he could sense her mind going into shock. Helplessness to comfort her swarmed over him. He had to find a way to save her from the evil. If she could just absorb his essence now, then her fear could subside.

The echoing laugh grew closer, and the stranger knew that time was running out for the two of them. Raina scurried to her feet trying to escape, only to lose her balance. She fell hard and fast into the wall striking her head on the right temple. Her vision became blurry making her dizzy and nauseated.

"Go away! Leave me alone!"

"Raina ...Raina, listen to me. Are you all right? Do you not recognize me?"

Raina stared at him trying to focus on the man. The sound of his voice didn't match the laugh and seemed familiar.

"No, go away—please," Raina screamed. Then her walls of resistance fell and she began to cry. Her chest felt hollow as she inhaled and exhaled while trying to stop from crying. The man leaned in closer still extending his hands to help her.

"Raina, it is me, Josiah. Raina, can you hear me?"

Josiah panicked. What kept her from responding to him? Was she hurt? Was he too late? He stiffened, afraid for her well-being. "Raina, answer me, please," he pleaded, with urgency in his voice. "Are you all right?"

All of a sudden, a wicked laugh echoed into the cavern. Josiah crouched, spinning his body around slamming his weight into the coarse rocks. His essence twisted at the evil that radiated in the cave. The air began to grow cool, and the mildewing stench thickened.

"What do you want from her?" he demanded. "Leave her alone—she is of no use to you!"

A hoarse voice answered his plea. "What do you know of her usefulness? How dare you trespass into my realm? I reign here and will take what I please!"

Josiah moved to stand in front of Raina. This was an action that he saw himself performing many times before while trying to help her. This was not the first time he found himself here. This cave had pulled him here from his study and the lecture hall many times before. Each time it played-out the same, and he knew that this was the moment when Raina had always disappeared.

"Leave her alone," Josiah ordered, appalled at what this despicable entity was making his Raina live through.

"Do you really think you are a match for me? Have you not realized what you are up against, boy?" he snarled.

"It is you who should question what you are up against. Leave this place now, I command you," Josiah ordered, charging his essence's energy preparing to fight the entity. "I am taking her with me."

"You are in no situation to command anything." The entity laughed so hard that the sound of his shriek boomed through the cave. Raina screamed once more and then covered her face. Her cry squealed in Josiah's ears, forcing him to lose his firm concentration on the entity. He turned his head just in time to see Raina's presence fade.

"Raina, no," he cried, and then he felt his essence twist in pain. He clinched his eyes shut trying to fight off the negative energy that had surrounded him. The coldness increased, consuming his essence's power. Josiah tried again to project his energy forward, except he failed. Josiah found himself trembling just as Raina had. It was a great struggle for him to maintain his composure and fight the invisible force that held him against his will.

Josiah somehow found strength from within him, and then projected his essence's energy outward flinging the energy toward the owner of the cave. A bright light shot across the darkness, and something hard slammed against Josiah's chest. He felt himself being whirled through the air as his body began to sting. It was difficult for Josiah to distinguish between the sensation of being in his shell or in his true celestial form. When he opened his eyes, the bright light vanished turning the cave pitch black. All of a sudden, the coldness disappeared and Josiah felt an intense amount of heat touching his body. It took him a second to process that he no longer stood in the cave.

Josiah realized he was sitting at his desk holding his book. "Raina ..." he whispered as his fingers automatically rubbed across the title of the book. He sighed confused, blinking the sweat out of his eyes. "I am sorry, Raina."

The many sensations affecting his essence at this moment were human characteristics. In his true form, he shouldn't suffer from any of these ill effects. Only now, as he leaned his head back against the chair a single tear escaped from his eye. This was too real. His essence was becoming more human with each terrifying vision of Raina. He knew then that his Guardian mind was having difficulty sorting out his reality from his dreams. It became a daily occurrence to find the terrified eyes of Raina looking back at him. Each time he was unsuccessful at rescuing her from the cave. When he hoped to be able to dream of her, this was not the dreams he wanted to experience. No, his dreams of her should be pleasant and happy. They were supposed to be together living a life unaffected by the true past. A life where they were never separated and her smile never faded. A life where his existence on Sol was obsolete and Raina was his only obligation.

With a deep sigh, he flipped open the book and began to read the preface. It was a poem that he had found among Raina's belongings. He copied it to his book on that dreary day Earth was destroyed and rejuvenated. After the Sentinel left him on the train tracks, Josiah went to Raina's home in secret. It was a risk for him to go there, but what punishment could be imposed on him that would be worse than what he was facing without his Raina?

Josiah's human tears flowed so heavily from his eyes that he was barely able to read the writing. Nothing could help him now, not even all of the celestial powers in the universe. His tears soaked the paper, so that the corners curled up. With a shaky hand, he laid it back down on her bed next to his yearbook. Then he flipped through the pages trying hard to swallow the lump that formed in his throat.

Without a warning, Josiah's knees buckled beneath him, and then he fell forward onto her bed. The aroma of Raina's floral shampoo lingered on her pillowcase, filling his mind with sweet thoughts. He recalled the memory of their second kiss and the songs she performed for him that day. Her laugh filled the breeze, and her smile enhanced Sol's rays.

Then the joyous moment faded with reality, and he knew it was over. What they once shared was gone, and he could never be with her again. Earth no longer held a beauty for him. The seeds of life that fell from the sunflower would be wasted, the chorus of flowers in Raina's garden ceased.

In his despair, he began to hum his favorite tune and then got up from the bed wiping his eyes. He sucked in a deep human breath and then dematerialized from her room, vowing never to return to Earth, and never to feel the human pain of love again. Had he seen into the future, then Josiah would have known that his service to Esprit de corps to come, would indeed take him back to Earth. Back to the place that would make love's pain hold him captive by more than the memories of Raina.

The bird's song played outside the window of Josiah's study. As he held the book gently in his hands, Josiah's last thoughts of that day weighed heavily on his mind. Somewhere, lost in the pages of his love story, Josiah knew he would find his hope. If not physically, then through the ink that lay so carefully scrawled out on the parchment in his handwriting.

———————————

"Raina, can you hear me? My name is Dr. Melvin Bailey." He patted her forearm again in hopes of reviving her. He looked at Anani searching for answers and then began to question her. "How long has she been unconscious?"

"About an hour now," she answered with uncertainty. "I found her on the bathroom floor. I heard a loud crash and ran into the bathroom. She was lying on a pile of plaster from the wall."

Dr. Bailey examined her scalp again feeling for injuries. "Plaster, do you know if she hit her head?"

"No, Doctor, I do not." She could only imagine what happened to her in the few moments she left her alone.

He tested her pupils, flashing a penlight into her eyes. After a few quick passes of the penlight, he mumbled something under his breath. Anani was not sure if she had made out his words clearly. Then he began testing her reflexes moving from her elbows to her knees. With a tongue depressor he pulled from his lab coat pocket, he ran it across the bottom of her feet. Anani watched as her toes and feet jerked in response. He examined her wrist paying careful attention to the unexplained bruising. Then he turned her arms over looking for needle marks along her forearms.

"Well, all of her responses to my neurological exam are normal," he mumbled again to himself and then looked at Anani determined to get the answer he wanted. "Does she have a dealer? Do you know how to contact him?"

"What—no! She does not use drugs."

"Are you sure of this?"

"Yes, of course I am sure. She is not a drug user."

"Can you recall if she has she been ill lately?"

"Ah no—I do not think so."

"Does she have a history of any medical problems that you know?"

"No—yeah."

"Is that a yes or a no?" he scowled.

"Yes ... I guess. See, she has been having a lot of nightmares. I mean really bad ones. She does not eat anymore because she says she cannot taste the flavor of her food. And her mood swings, she has been like really edgy and just says off the wall comments."

"Are you saying that you believe she's been demonstrating abnormal behaviors?"

"Yes ... it is really messing her up."

"When do you think she began to display these abnormal behaviors?"

"I am not sure ... maybe a couple of months ago. I do not know. She says she always had bad dreams as a child, but lately ... they have been increasingly worse. We have been roommates for only about seven months now. I am not sure how she was before. I just know that she is different now somehow."

"Her mood swings, can you explain how she reacts?"

"Well ... she like ... will be happy one minute, then sad the next. Sometimes, when we are in the greenhouse she will just stare off into nowhere. It is somewhat freaky. I would shake her to get her attention. When I asked her what she was looking at, she just smiles and says the followers."

"And, miss, you are positive she isn't a user?"

"Yes, I am," Anani snapped back. "Raina is against that stuff. She enjoys life too much to screw it up."

"Do you know if she has received any head injuries or ... has she been in a recent car accident?"

"What ... no, at least I do not think so. What does that have to do with her now anyway?"

"Well, you said you found her unconscious. Something affected her in such a way to make her lose consciousness. With the other symptoms you have mentioned, it suggests that there is a good chance her current condition is either from drugs or from a head injury. It would make her diagnosis much quicker if we had a definite cause."

Anani bit her lip from frustration. "I am sorry, I just do not know."

"That's fine. I'll order a head CT as a precaution. Have you notified her family?"

"I tried, but I cannot reach them. They do not live around here," she mumbled, focusing her attention on Raina.

"Where are they from, miss?"

"Her parents live in Wisconsin. Raina is out here for college. Her father is a doctor at one of the city's hospitals. I am not sure how to contact them apart from their home number. But I do not understand. If she was ill and her father is a doctor, he would have known ... right?"

"Perhaps," Dr. Bailey said. Then he looked away taking in a deep breath.

Anani looked at him puzzled by the change in his demeanor.

"Nurse," the doctor said, trying to get her attention.

"Yes, Dr. Bailey," the nurse replied, adjusting Raina's monitor leads.

"Please take this young lady's information and start calling the local hospitals in her hometown. I need to get a hold of her medical records."

"Yes, Doctor, I'll also order that CT for you."

The doctor nodded, and then turned leaving Raina's bedside. The nurse grabbed Raina's patient chart and then left the room briskly to obtain Raina's medical information. Once she was at the Nurse's Station, she would begin the task of calling Wisconsin to locate her parents.

"Come on kid, just wake up, okay?" Anani sunk into the chair next to Raina and closed her eyes. She would give anything for her newfound friend's health, anything that was in her power to perform. This was not the first time her roommate disrupted their daily routine or left Anani feeling human helplessness. But this time, Anani feared something greater was happening to Raina. If the men she saw in her episode were taunting her—how could she fight them off when they were in Raina's mind?

"Excuse me," a man's voice broke into her thoughts. "I am from Radiology. I'm here to take Miss Stone for her test."

"Sure," Anani answered. Then getting up from the chair she moved out of his way.

The young red-haired man smiled, and then pressed the call light requesting the assistance of Raina's nurse for lifting help. She watched as he lined up the gurney with Raina's bed and then carefully adjusted her IV line.

"We'll be back shortly. You may wait here or go to the cafeteria if you like. They're serving meatloaf for dinner."

"Oh, yum," she said under her breath. "Thank you, but I think I will go with her for the test."

Just then, two nurses arrived to assist the man from Radiology to transfer her to the gurney. Anani watched fascinated at how smoothly their actions slid Raina's body onto the gurney.

With precision, the man steered the gurney through the doorway and began pushing Raina down the hall. Anani followed closely watching Raina's unresponsive body until they reached the elevator. She hadn't moved or made a sound until the wheels jerked over the elevator track. Then a soft moan flowed past her lips calling Anani's attention to her face. It was then when she noticed the blood seeping onto the pillow from her left ear.

"Oh, my!" She grabbed a hold of the bed rail alarmed.

"What's wrong?" the attendant demanded of her, staring at Anani concerned.

"Her ear—it is bleeding!"

"What?" he shouted, pushing past Anani to see what she was describing to him? Shocked at his findings he screamed for the nurse who was charting in the computer. "Nurse! Something's wrong—we need help!"

He hit the stop button on the elevator to hold open the doors and then pulled the bed out of the elevator. Another nurse, hearing his command also came to assist. She began checking Raina's vitals.

Anani stood still, watching the commotion unfold around her friend. "Will she be all right?"

Her question went unanswered as Raina's doctor arrived with the Emergency Response Team following closely behind him. Each member medically trained to react under intense situations, to treat the emergent condition of the patient. One doctor assessed her vitals paying careful attention to both ears. Another physician performed a new neuro assessment examining her eyes. The examination showed no pupillary reaction in response to the penlight. Nor did she show any superficial pain sensation when the neurologist ran a broken wooden cotton-tipped swab along her feet. Her condition proved to be grave when Raina didn't respond to pain stimuli.

"Let's get her to CT—STAT!" Dr. Bailey ordered. "Nurse, have you located this patient's parents yet?"

"No, Doctor, I haven't. There is no answer at her Wisconsin residence. I have called the three hospitals in the nearby city and none of them has contacted me back so far. I keep running into dead ends, Doctor."

"What about you?" he questioned Anani again. "Do you have any more information to offer?"

"No, Doctor, I am sorry. I do not know any of her family. But I can go back to the apartment and look for an address book or something."

"Yes, please. That will be very helpful."

The elevator door closed, leaving Anani standing there in shock. She leaned back against the wall. This was not supposed to be happening. It was herself-proclaimed job to watch over her. Somewhere in the plan, things went wrong. She needed to find away to help her. There was only one Guardian she knew of who was strong enough.

Matters seemed to get worse when Dr. Bailey checked in with the CT technologist moments after her scan was completed.

"Roy, what do we know?"

"Your patient is a mess. I'm surprised that she's breathing at all."

Dr. Bailey became alarmed. "What do you mean?" he asked, pulling a chair over to sit in front of the scanner.

"Well, look at her cerebral cortex. The gyri are effaced indicating swelling. Normally they should be wavy and look like the surface of a sponge."

"Are you sure, Roy, that the scan is accurate?"

"Yes, the scan doesn't lie." Roy tapped his finger on the screen. "Look here at her frontal lobes. Do you see the dark areas here and here?" he said, continuing to slide his finger along the monitor. "She has definite signs of brain trauma, but there are no visible facial or skull injuries detected on the scan. Did you do a neurological examination, Melvin?"

"Yes, Roy, she was unconscious when she arrived in the ER. My tests were inconclusive. Nothing about her condition warranted me to suspect any of this. Frankly, I was waiting for the toxicology screening to come back. I would have bet you a steak dinner in Vegas that she was a user. Now I'm even more concerned that she has not regained consciousness yet."

"I'm not surprised she hasn't. Here ... look at these images from the limbic system. The hypothalamus and the amygadala both show abnormalities."

"Roy, I have been told that the patient is experiencing nightmares and abnormal personality behaviors. She was found unconscious this morning after suffering from some form of an episode."

"The condition of the hypothalamus and amygdala would explain her unconsciousness and the dreams. Are there any reports of hallucinations from her family?"

"I haven't been able to reach them. Nurse Merrill has been trying constantly since her admit. The patient's roommate did indicate behaviors resembling hallucinations. Why do you ask?"

"Well, look at the occipital lobe." Roy tapped on the monitor again. "It has the same mass or dark areas, as her frontal lobe and her temporal lobes are the same.

"Have you seen this before, Roy?"

"No, Doc, but check with the Radiologist. Last time I saw him, he was gathered with several others speculating her diagnosis."

"Speculating?" Dr. Bailey questioned, surprised that his colleagues were speculating anything at all.

"Yes ... it would appear they are as intrigued about her condition as we are. I heard them discussing treatment plans. It sounds like they are leaning toward doing an

MRI. Doctor Gev Yannick wants to rule out a tumor, except Doctor Cong Anming, overruled him."

"Why did he do that, Roy?"

Roy shook his head. "Because Anming believes the abnormalities are congenital and not tumors at all. Although I heard Anming suggest a biopsy, but Yannick felt her condition was too grave to perform such an invasive procedure."

Dr. Bailey shook his head. "I'm no Neurosurgeon, but I think I agree with Yannik. Any treatment, Roy, would be simply exploratory and very dangerous." Dr. Bailey sighed, losing his enthusiasm for his patient's diagnosis.

"I am just a Technologist, but if you want my opinion, I believe Anming is correct with the congenital disorder." Roy manipulated the dials, changing the imaging windows. "Her entire brain is abnormal. Do you have any idea of what causes this condition?"

"No, but I have seen enough scans and read enough patient presented symptoms to know the difference. You know that tumors develop rapidly showing obvious symptoms. If her case is congenital, she could've displayed these behavioral symptoms for years, and her family chalked them up to her personality. Thanks, Roy, I am going to find Dr. Yannick and his colleagues."

"Catch you later, Melvin."

Dr. Bailey wandered into the Radiology reading room with no optimism of Raina's recovery. The voices of Doctors Anming and Yannick carried loudly through the hall. Bailey could hear their heated discussion about Raina's treatment. Her prognosis sounded no better now than it had looked on the images in CT.

"Doctors." He cleared his throat to shed the lump that appeared. In the back of his mind, he pitied Raina. She seemed to be such a nice girl from her roommate's description. What a waste that no one discovered her medical condition earlier. Perhaps, if a friend or family member would have noticed her behavioral changes and reported it—she wouldn't be in critical condition now.

Melvin shook his head. This case hit too close to home. Experience told him that it is always doctors who tend to overlook their family member's medical history. He thought this every time he remembered the face of his six-year-old daughter lying dead in her silk-lined coffin.

"Do you have a set treatment for my patient yet?"

Anming sat upright in his chair. Running his fingers through his midnight-black hair, he shook his head in disgust. He frowned in anger forcing a crease to form above his eyebrows.

"No, Melvin. Her condition is extremely advanced. We're not even sure of what we are dealing with. We have to go in. It's our only chance."

Yannick slammed his fist down on the counter. "No—no—no! It is too dangerous. We cannot subject her to such an invasive procedure."

"Dr. Yannick, I am the Neurosurgeon here. I say we go in."

"You don't even know if she can handle the anesthetic," Dr. Yannick interjected loudly. "You could kill her before you begin."

"Yes, that's a possibility; however, she will die without surgery."

"Perhaps, Dr. Anming, but at least if we wait her family can see her before we hack up her skull. We must wait for custodial permission."

"Didn't you read her history, Yannick? She's an adult, and no family can be reached. We must go in. It would be unethical to wait any longer," Anming insisted, persistent to proceed.

"Yes, I read her history. That's why we must wait."

"Doctors, please," Melvin shouted. "I'm still her attending. I think the decision is up to me."

"Nonsense, Dr. Bailey. You're not a surgeon. You don't have any idea as to what we face with this patient. We must go in if we have any hopes of saving her."

"Dr. Anming, I agree with Dr. Yannick. If she's dead anyway, then we should wait. There is no sense in her family seeing her with a cracked skull and tubes spewing from her head."

"Dr. Bailey," Anming said, shaking his finger at him. "You don't belong here. I say we operate and that's final."

"Well, I'm telling you no," Bailey said boldly. "Let's preserve whatever dignity this patient has, and let her go in peace. Her father is a doctor. I think he would agree."

Doctor Anming grew restless at being placed in the situation of embarrassment, more than the compassion of saving a dying patient. "If he's a physician, then he can appreciate the value of honoring our Hippocratic Oath to heal. We must operate."

Yannik said nothing, listening to the two doctor's argue over her care. He agreed with Melvin. Her dignity should be preserved for the comfort of her family.

"Dr. Bailey, you're killing your patient with this delay. I cannot and will not stand here while you play God."

Melvin laughed, rolling his eyes. "Playing God—is that what you think I am doing?"

"Yes, and I won't allow it. I'm going to the Chief of Staff. Sanderson will side with me." Anming turned and strolled out of the room. Dr. Yannick waited tensely for Melvin to address him.

Doctor Bailey moaned as he glanced once more at Raina's CT scan. "Tell me, Gev, do you think I'm doing what is right with my patient?"

"Melvin, I agree with you. I am a Radiologist, and I see the facts. Cong lives for the outcome even if it isn't what he wants."

"So, what do I do then?"

"Stand your ground. Let him spout off to Sanderson. The last I heard, our Chief of Staff wasn't too impressed with him anyway."

Melvin laughed. "Oh, yeah—what did he do, spit in the water?"

"Cong is quick to react, and his rash decisions have cost patients' their lives. The last I heard he was already up for review on a malpractice suit."

Melvin didn't comment on the bit of information. He simply smiled and left the reading room.

After the scan was completed, Raina was taken to a room in the ICU to await Dr. Sanderson's decision. Dr. Bailey made his own visit to Sanderson, to plea her case of dignity versus medical science. He left convinced that Sanderson would wait for the family to decide. However, Melvin was not too confident that Anming would lose the fight.

Bailey checked in again on Raina to reassess her vitals. Outside of the ear bleeding that had stopped during her scan, there was no change in her condition.

"Dr. Bailey," Nurse Merrill said.

"Yes?"

"Doctor, I have reached her family. Dr. Stone will be on a plane here tonight. I took the liberty of reading her chart. I saw that Dr. Anming wanted to perform surgery."

"Did you get consent from her father?"

"No, sir. He refused any aggressive treatment until he could review her chart himself."

Bailey sighed, but he wasn't sure if it was from relief or exhaustion. "What time did you speak to them?"

Nurse Merrill looked at her watch. "About an hour ago. If they could arrange an immediate flight, it shouldn't be too much longer. You figure four hours in the air and two more for packing and travel, they should arrive just after the end of your shift."

"I want to speak to him when he arrives. I'll crash in the doctor's lounge. Please leave a note at the desk to get me as soon as he arrives."

"I will," she replied, and then left the room.

"Come on, kid. What's going on in that head of yours?" Bailey put her chart down and left to finish his rounds.

He had been asleep for an hour when Nolan and Tori arrived. Before the night nurse could offer Nolan a chance to speak to Raina's attending doctor, he was already demanding a consultation with him.

"Nurse, I am Dr. Nolan Stone. You have my daughter admitted here. I want to speak with her attending immediately," he demanded, with no regard to the late hour.

"Please Dr. Stone, just calm down, and I'll get him for you."

"Don't tell me—"

"Nolan," Tori said, "yelling at the nurse isn't going to help our daughter. Now please calm down."

He sighed. "You're right. I'm sorry ... please, forgive me."

"Your daughter's room is across from this desk," she said, pointing at the door. "Please, why don't you two go and see her. I'll get Dr. Bailey for you. He has been waiting in the lounge for your arrival."

"Waiting for us?" Nolan asked surprised.

"Yes, he hasn't left your daughter's bedside all day."

"Thank you," he said softly, feeling great remorse for his behavior.

The whole plane trip Nolan and Tori were on the edge of their seat anxiously worried for their daughter's health. Even with all of his medical training, nothing could prepare him for the state that he found his daughter.

The sounds of her heart monitor were the first indication of her condition. He didn't have to look at the strip to know her heart rate was too low and weak.

"My God—Nolan. Look at her. Oh, my baby."

Nolan began taking her vitals himself. He had the chart in front of him, but for some reason, Nolan would take assurance only in his own assessment.

"Nolan, what is it?"

"I don't know, Tori."

Dr. Bailey entered the room extending his hand to shake their hands. "Good morning, Doctor and Mrs. Stone. I am Dr. Melvin Bailey. I have been your daughter's attending since her admittance this morning."

"What is wrong with my daughter?" Tori pleaded. "What has happened to her?"

"Mrs. Stone, that's what we are trying to determine."

"What is her treatment plan, Dr. Bailey?" Nolan interrupted eagerly.

"Well, her toxicology reports have all come back negative. There appears to be no outward appearance of head trauma, but let me show you her CT scan."

"How have her vitals been?"

"As you can see, Dr. and Mrs. Stone, from the monitor her heart rate is abnormal and her labs are not conclusive at this time."

"Dad," Raina said with a raspy sounding voice. "What's wrong with me?"

"Oh, honey." Tori rushed to her side with Nolan and Bailey close behind. "Oh, sweetie, you're awake."

"Have I been sleeping for a long time?" Raina asked still groggy.

"Raina, my name is Dr. Bailey. Do you remember what happened to you this morning?"

Raina stared blankly at the three of them trying to recall anything significant. "No."

"Do you know what day it is?" he asked, flashing the pen light in her eyes repeating for the hundredth time a pupillary test.

"Friday, I think," she said hesitantly.

"Actually, it is now Saturday. You have been unconscious since about seven Friday morning."

"What time is it now?"

"It is two in the morning," Bailey informed her, "you've been unconscious for about nineteen hours now."

"Man ... that's a long time," she whispered, more confused than before.

"Honey," Nolan said, trying to get her attention. "Were you involved in an accident of any kind?"

"No, Dad."

"Have you hit your head, maybe in some sporting activity?"

"No, why do you keep asking me if I hit my head?"

"Because, honey, you have been unconscious a very long time. Some of the tests Dr. Bailey ran after you were admitted indicated a possible head injury. We just want to make sure you get the proper treatment and get better soon."

"Mom ... Dad, I'm sorry," she said apologizing needlessly.

"Sorry?" Tori asked confused. "For what, Raina?"

"I'm sorry that I have scared the two of you."

"No, don't think that, honey." Tori grabbed her hand wanting to comfort her daughter. She sighed at the unusual bruising. "You just concentrate on getting well, okay?"

"Please, Dr. Bailey, let me see the CT scan?" Nolan insisted, still uncertain of his daughter's condition.

"Of course," he said, walking over to the computer. Bailey brought the electronic CT scan image up on the computer. He gave Nolan a moment to review the scan himself. "As you can see the—"

"Run them again!"

"What?" Bailey asked surprised.

"Something isn't right here. There is no way she could be conscious if her scan was that bad."

"Dr. Stone, I promise you we have been very careful in her diagnosis."

"I am sure you have. However, her scan and her condition don't match up. Her slow heartbeat as you have witnessed has increased since she awoke. Her labs and toxicology reports as I can see from her medical chart haven't changed all day."

"Doctor, I assure you we have followed every rule to the letter. Indeed her condition is a bit perplexing; however, clearly you can see that her state is critical?"

"Critical?" Raina shouted, freaked-out by her father's persistence and her doctor's choice of words.

"Hush, Raina, just relax," her father ordered. "Maybe so, Dr. Bailey," he continued, "but I must insist that you run them again. Look at my daughter. She's conscious and the neurological exam I performed is normal. This CT indicates that not only should she not be breathing on her own, she shouldn't be breathing at all. Now run them again!"

Before Dr. Bailey could give his rebuttal, Tori screamed. Bailey and Nolan looked at her alarmed to see Raina having a seizure.

23.
IN THE DARKNESS

Earth Realm—present-day

Jaleel immediately found Josiah on Earth at the college campus in Pasadena. Josiah's dorm room that he had created as an illusion appeared adequately decorated by Jaleel's primitive earthly standards. There was a desk near the door and a refrigerator by the bathroom. Next to the bed was a dresser with a lamp perfectly centered and a television. Josiah had not improved the room's quality even after he decided to pursue Raina. This room was intended to be part of his façade as one of Professor Russell's students and nothing more.

"My friend," Josiah said, without looking up from the picture he held in his hand. "What brings you here today?"

"Josiah, do I need an excuse to visit the one I swore in my youth to always protect?"

"Normally, I would say no, except lately, my friend, you have been preoccupied with other matters. To have you visit me here on Earth must bring with it a reason other than socializing."

"You know me well, Josiah."

"Tell me then what separates you from the other life you have been leading to come here?"

"Josiah, you surprise me. You say that with a tone which suggests something. Will you not share with me what it is?"

"I suggest nothing, Jaleel. Is there another cause that makes you think otherwise?"

Jaleel walked across the room and sat in the desk chair. His confident posture that Josiah knew so well from their visits in Jaleel's chamber, didn't accompany him here. Josiah noticed how his celestial body, invisible to humans, slumped in the old wooden chair. Even his essence, Josiah sensed, didn't present itself in a calming matter.

"Josiah ... I come with a matter far greater then I would ever desire to bear."

"Speak your mind, Jaleel. You have my attention," Josiah said, waving his right hand in the air with a swishing motion.

"Josiah," Jaleel began, hesitant of where to start. Josiah again found himself amazed at the insecure way Jaleel carried his essence.

"I have had the unpleasant opportunity to meet with an entity whom I would have chosen not to."

"Unpleasant? That term seems to be a bit too rash and reserved for those such as the vile Guardians I cast out. Perhaps you should choose another form of speech, Jaleel."

"Josiah, my words are correct."

Josiah sat straight up in his chair displaying the posture he missed from his friend. "What do you mean, Jaleel?"

"My visitor came to us announced, Josiah."

"When you say ... us, do you mean—?"

"Yes." Jaleel cut him off. "Please do not say her name for others may be listening now. Do you have any idea how hard it is to keep my thoughts to myself in fear we will be discovered?"

A smile formed slightly on Josiah's face. It was more from annoyance for Jaleel's lack of memory than from humor. "Do you ever think before you speak these days, Jaleel?"

Instantly Josiah's meaning became clear to him. "I am sorry, Josiah. Trust me; I do understand what you have been going through. There was a time when your actions were blind to me by my own choice. A time when I did not understand what emotions existed in your mind. And I did not understand how those emotions had forced you to make the random decisions that you did in her name. However, now I know very well what you faced with your human companion."

"Then, shall I give you the lecture that you gave me, Jaleel?"

"No ... you should not. For we both know that the same determination runs through our essences. You cannot say enough words or point out enough dangers to make me leave her now."

"Maybe, Jaleel. However, you two have been discovered. Was it not in a compromising way?"

Jaleel sighed, changing his position in the chair. The uneasiness that projected from Jaleel grew more intense. He felt confident to tell Josiah, except his words refused to obey.

"Jaleel, how compromising was the situation?"

"Please, just respect that there could have been no worse time in my existence to be discovered than at that moment."

"Who was the one that walked in on you?" As soon as Josiah asked the question, the supremacy of a Great Elder's mind had occurred to him. His expression of awe showed on his face. "Jaleel, how did anyone walk in on you two unannounced? I can think of no situation that could hinder her mind from assessing the presence of another."

"That is why I am here. The intruder, who so cleverly escaped her knowledge, appears to be from another timeline. He came with a message of warning."

"Do you believe he speaks the truth?"

"We are not sure. It was difficult for ... her to discern his true motives or even his actual existence in this realm. However, he spoke of things with the knowledge he should not have. Josiah, he knew that you recently crossed paths with Raina."

Josiah bolted upright from his chair. "How is that possible?"

"We do not know. His warning was clear, Josiah. He says there is an evil that seeks revenge upon you."

"Revenge upon me?" he questioned. "I have not created any enemies who I have left free from punishment of their crimes. I can think of no entity who desires revenge upon me."

"I am sure you are correct, Josiah. Perhaps you should take this warning with more direction."

"There is no direction that I need to follow. I do not believe that my essence is at risk of any dangers befalling me."

"Josiah, it may not fall upon you at all. He stated that your meeting with Raina may not have been a chance meeting."

Josiah immediately felt his human rage swell within him. Any thought of harm finding his Raina tortured him.

Her life, whether entangled with his or not, was too greatly valued to hear of such distressing news.

"What did he say about her?" Josiah yelled jumping to his feet.

"Easy, Josiah. You must calm yourself. Your anger will not serve as any form of protection for her or anyone else. You must remain in charge of your faculties. We have no proof that she is in any form of danger."

"Then why did he mention her at all?"

"Josiah, he was very vague in his words. As I have said, we are not entirely sure of his motives. I have come to you with his warning. All we can do is watch and ..."

"And what, Jaleel?"

"Well, I think it wise to keep your distance from Raina."

"Jaleel, you know I cannot do that."

"Well, for the sake of all involved right now you must."

"No, please, Jaleel. Do not ask this of me."

"Josiah, you must listen to reason. Even if the intruder was wrong about your meeting, you know what the consequences will be if you continue to pursue Raina."

Josiah sat down on the bed and rested his face in his hands. He sighed deeply as he fought to control his sporadic thoughts.

"If I could only see into her future and know that she is well. I would give anything for just one small glance, Jaleel."

"And what would that accomplish for you, Josiah?"

"I ... I would feel some peace knowing she is safe."

"Josiah, you must believe that she is safe. The Sentinel restored her life to the plane she was to live before Lexis sought her out. Do you really believe a misguided Guardian would have information on a subject controlled by the Sentinel?"

"I am not sure, Jaleel. I would like very much to believe what you say, except you know how I feel about her. You know what we mean to each other."

"What you meant to each other, Josiah. Remember, she is not the one you once knew. Dwelling on the past is so humanistic. Move on, Josiah. Can you not understand, my brother, that I am tired of seeing you so distraught?"

"I cannot, Jaleel ... you know that Raina is my life."

"Was your life, Josiah. The existence of the Sentinel changed that for you. Besides, it was a life you never should have entertained in the first place."

"Entertained ... Jaleel, she is not some humanoid movie that I watched to pass the time. I did not entertain my feelings for her. I loved her. Can you get this straight in that over-enhanced philosophical mind of yours?"

"Josiah, I have that same over-enhanced philosophical mind as yours. You need to get that straight. Raina was never to be part of your life. You were her self-proclaimed Guardian and nothing more. Giving in to those underdeveloped inferior human emotions cost you dearly. The relationship you shared with her was never intended to be."

Again, his conversation with Jaleel peaked into one of accusations and disappointments. To contain his annoyance for Jaleel's blindness for his emotions proved more difficult with each passing conversation.

"Just look who is swimming with the sharks now, my friend. Do you forget that your relationship with her is as welcomed as mine was with Raina? Have you also cast your life vest aside?" he asked, speaking the words before he thought. Josiah's spoken reference was remnants from the emotions he felt when his love for Raina controlled his life and his rationality.

"No," Jaleel nearly shouted. "The issue at hand is different."

"Is it, Jaleel? Tell me how you believe your relationship is different from that of Raina and me? We face damnation for our erring ways. No Council will care about our motives."

"Do you forget that my relationship with her is not as lawfully forbidden as yours is? I simply face the immoral implications of my actions. You, Josiah ... face Deimos."

"Yes—and what does Raina face?" Josiah asked sarcastically.

"Josiah, I heard a rumor that you made a request of the Council. Was it a horrible, humorous attempt at being human, or did you really petition for dismissal?"

"Jaleel, I did ask for dismissal. However, Elder Torrey took my moment of weakness as he called it and smoothed it over. He made my words seem worthless and untrue."

"How did he know you were serious?"

"I am not sure. He gained control of the Council meeting and had every Elder in attendance laughing at my failed human motives."

"What happened after that, Josiah?"

"Elder Torrey ushered me out into the courtyard and lectured me on my behavior."

"Well, he had full right too. You are not acting rationally, Josiah."

"Rationality has no place here, Jaleel. You have not seen the things I have. There is something terribly wrong, and I do not know what it is."

"Then how do you know anything is wrong at all?"

Josiah got off the bed and walked over to his desk. He opened the drawer and pulled out an earth tone colored stone that was thickly crusted with green ooze.

"This, my friend, is how I know."

Jaleel reached out his hand to take the stone from Josiah. After hesitating, he handed the stone to Jaleel.

"Where did you get this?" Jaleel inquired suspiciously.

"I do not know. In a cave, I guess."

"You guess? Do you not know where you have been?"

"In this case no, I do not."

"How is that possible, Josiah?"

"That is what I have been trying to figure out. There is something wrong with me. I have found myself dreaming."

Jaleel let out a slight laugh that he immediately muffled when he realized Josiah was serious. "Tell me how you know they have been dreams?" he questioned, surprised and unbelieving of Josiah's statement.

"It does not matter," Josiah said in a low tone, "where I am, or the time of day. It seems whatever has plagued me knows no time frame. Against my will, odd visions surface, and they completely incapacitate my human shell."

"Then perhaps you should take a leave of absence from your Earth bound Esprit de corps."

"It is not easy, Jaleel. The visions also consume my essence."

Jaleel bolted out of his chair, humanly alarmed. "Josiah—tell me more about these episodes and how they affect you."

"It is odd, really. I have no control or notion of when they will strike me. The episodes have left me in a few embarrassing dilemmas myself. The visions always seem to happen in a dark musty cavern. I hear a loud horrid breathing and a laugh that pierces my essence. Always, to my left, I find Raina huddled in a corner terrified and crying. There is an evil entity that holds her captive, and she pleads for her life."

Josiah's essence began to weep. This was unusual for a Guardian, for they didn't cry. However, this was not the first time Josiah had shed tears. This abnormal behavior surfaced the day his Raina emerged as the Sentinel. The tears that day were excused as an effect of the Sentinel's presence. This time Josiah knew they were enhanced by the mysterious rock he acquired during his last vision.

"Are you well, Josiah?"

"I do not know. Strange things have been happening to me. I do not know why I have been cursed or what deed will stop them."

"What happens in the cavern?"

"Jaleel, it is awful. In the darkness, Raina screams for help. Her body is bloody and mangled. Her state is wretched, and it twists my essence to see her like that. And when I try to assist her, she cowers away from me. I believe she does not know who I am in these dreams, even though I address her by her name.

"The look in her eyes is very alien to me, and it afflicts me to see the pain looking back at me. In any event, as I reach to pull her from the evil one's view, she disappears without warning. As always I remain there staring at the empty spot, hearing his vile laugh."

"Josiah, do you recognize the evil entity? Do you think that it is possible your dreams are what the stranger was referring to during his visit with me?"

"No. I do not really see the face of her captor. If your visitor were referring to the dreams, then he would have to see them as I do. You might have an interesting theory, Jaleel. When the evil one challenges me to a duel with his threatening words and actions, sometimes it feels as if there is another's presence in the shadows lurking around silently. I do not know his motives, but clearly, he is not the one harming Raina. I feel as if he is there to help me somehow, but either chooses not to or is waiting for a particular moment to spring from the shadows.

"If I accept the evil one's challenge, I feel myself hurdling through the air and then I awake to find myself surrendering to the moment in terror. A few earth days ago, the unnamed girl came to my aid. I could not shed my shell and was completely useless to make my shell function at all—"

"The unnamed girl," Jaleel interrupted forcibly. "Who are you talking about here?"

"I do not know who she is. Her life force is not familiar to me."

"Josiah—are you saying that you have discovered another entity and have not searched out her identity?"

"Yes, I am."

"How could you exist with such risks? Clearly, your first objective is to communicate with her."

"I have ... at least somewhat. She sought me out during one of my episodes. I could sense her spirit, except I could not discern its value. I just know that she was helpful."

"Helpful. Josiah, she could have been your demise."

"Yes, except she was not. This girl kept me from being discovered. When I could not function, she escorted me back to this place and left with no further interaction. It was almost as if her sole intent was just to see me to safety."

"Where is she now?"

"I am not sure. I have not gone to class in a few days. I suppose when I do, I will find her where I always have."

"Where you always have? You are that close to her and have done nothing to identify who she is? Do you think she is connected to this in any way?"

"I do not know. We barely spoke when she found me. Her human behaviors were well endowed. She carried herself in a manner I do not believe I am capable of achieving even after all of my training with Raina and her human friends."

"Is it possible that she is the one who lurks in the shadows?"

"No, I am certain it is not she. The energy of her spirit is different."

"Josiah, if you are affected by the dreams then it is likely that you do not have a clear perception of her spirit's energy in the first place."

"Yes, I have considered that."

"Tell me about the sensation you experience during these episodes."

"As I have said, my essence and my shell are rendered useless. I can only wait for the episodes to pass and hope that I will not find myself in a compromising position when they do."

"Please, Josiah," Jaleel said. He was becoming impatient with Josiah's lack of information. "Why do you hesitate so much in your explanations? Just tell me plainly what you mean to say."

"I cannot for there is no easy explanation. I am conscious of my surroundings, and then suddenly they change. It is as if I came into the middle of a book. I am at a loss as to how it began, except it holds my curiosity, and I cannot put it down. When the episodes arise, I am just not myself. Sometimes I bring objects from the cavern back with me. I think that is how I acquired the stone. I am not sure where it came from. I do not know its purpose or usefulness."

"Objects, what type of objects have you acquired?"

Josiah didn't answer him. The items he hid in his desk must have some significance. To announce their existence before he knew seemed irrational.

"Could she have been the one who gave it to you secretly?" Jaleel asked, growing tired of waiting for Josiah's response.

"I suppose, I cannot rule that out, but I do not believe so."

"Then the stone has no meaning to you at all at this point?"

"No, it does not." Josiah sighed, attempting to sooth his weeping essence. He knew there was a secret behind the stone that he believed might carry dangers to the bearer. Josiah wanted to protect Jaleel from unnecessary harm. Vagueness about its existence and possibly the other objects would surely keep Jaleel safe. He didn't lie when he explained to Jaleel his uncertainty on how he obtained the stone. He didn't sense his unnamed classmate's energy around the stone and he ruled out her physically touching the stone. That didn't mean too much to Josiah, for he never cared to discern her spirit in the first place.

Jaleel also felt a sense of power from the stone. He was sure that it meant him no harm, and Josiah was keeping something from him as well. He grasped the stone tighter within his grip and gently shook it in his hand. The gurgling sound beside him caught his attention. As he looked up from the rock, Josiah's celestial body began to convulse. Jaleel dropped the stone, alarmed by what he saw, and reached for Josiah to steady him. Just then, Josiah's body dimmed and began to fade away.

"Josiah! Josiah, where are you?"

In that moment the rock rolled across the floor, vibrating as musical notes exploded from it. Jaleel walked over to where the green stained rock lay jiggling on the floor. He bent over to pick it up, but the stone faded as quickly as Josiah had, taking the strange song with it.

"Josiah, where are you?" he hollered again. "Josiah, come back here, now!"

Jaleel was not sure, if Josiah was playing a trick on him, or if he should be concerned about his disappearance.

"Josiah, I grow tired of this game of yours. Expose yourself now," he ordered, waiting for Josiah's return.

What Jaleel didn't know is that Josiah was pulled into another dream and he dwelled in a realm beyond Jaleel's comprehension.

"Josiah, I demand that you come back here—"

Before he finished speaking, Josiah appeared in front of him. The look on his face was indescribable. Jaleel stepped forward to grab a hold of Josiah's arm. His celestial body felt cold and damp to Jaleel's touch.

"Josiah, are you well? Where did you go?"

"What?" Josiah questioned, feeling perplexed by his good friend's expression.

"I asked you where you went."

"What do you mean? I have gone nowhere."

"Josiah, you were standing right there and then you disappeared."

Josiah sighed despondently. He had not seen the cave or heard its vileness, yet he felt the cold temporally swarm over him. He wondered if the vision had just begun to consume him and he had not yet become aware of his state.

"Jaleel, I do not know what happened to me."

"You say that you do not recall anything strange?"

"No, I do not," he said, reaching up to touch his moist forehead.

"I am telling you, that you disappeared. You were gone a briefly and then you came back. Do you feel all right?"

"I feel the same way when the episodes over take me, however, this time I did not see the cave or hear the evil one."

"You should be concerned, my friend. What if this is what the intruder was speaking about?"

"Perhaps," Josiah whispered.

"You need to report this to the Council immediately."

"No, not until I am sure."

"Sure of what?"

"Sure if I am in any danger. I need to be careful."

"That is an understatement, Josiah. At least inform your father about the episodes."

"No," he scowled.

"Why not?"

"And worry him and my mother when I do not even know if there is anything wrong at all."

"I think your disappearance has proved that there is something strange happening."

"No, Jaleel. Say nothing to them until I am sure."

"Josiah, someone needs to know what has happened."

"Someone does."

"Then what do you want me to do?"

"Do nothing."

"Josiah, I cannot just stand by and—"

"Please, Jaleel," he interrupted him, "do not act unless you are certain that I am in danger."

Against his better judgment, Jaleel complied. "Fine, but if I sense any danger I will go to your father immediately and inform the Council. Do you understand?"

"Agreed. So are you up to a game of chess?" Josiah asked, trying to divert Jaleel away from his own uncertainties. He questioned now if the intruder was aware of the visions of Raina and knew something he had not.

24.
CONSEQUENCES

Guardian Realm—present-day

Beck hollered through the garden. "Mataya, come quickly!"

"What it is, Beck? What is wrong?"

"The evil one has struck. He found Raina on Earth in the current reality."

"How do you know this to be true?" she responded alarmed. "We were very careful with our plan."

"We were not careful enough. As we thought, it is the one who Offie and Kryssa warned the Council about."

"The Count? Are you sure, it is he? It was only a speculation that he was responsible for the events on Cressida. I thought we ruled him out as being the one Dinah brought back from Adrestea."

"Yes, unfortunately I am not mistaken. I saw him with another in a vision. The evil surrounding the mysterious entity was great. I suspect he is Dinah's companion."

"Do you know how he found her, Beck?"

"Yes, I do. Indeed, we were very careful, except another's weakness brought this about. Someone else had played a card in the game of ours."

"Who was it?"

"Mataya, it was Evi who led him to her. I saw it a dream."

"No! How could she? Did you not have any visions of what she was about to do?"

"No, I did not."

"Why did she act so foolishly?"

"She could not resist those cursed maternal instincts you speak about and went to Silver Lake. As you have said, maternal love is very powerful. Her essence left a link to the realm, and he followed it right to her. The Count associates himself with Trackers from Hyperion. His henchman uses that maternal love and attempts to destroy the child again. The same love that caused Evi to expose our plan can very well put Evi in a compromising situation."

"I do not understand. What do you mean, Beck?"

"I saw him rejoice as he learned what had transpired. I could see his eyes burn with evil as he contemplated his plan. I regret that it is a plan I cannot completely decipher. I do know that instead of attacking the baby again, he went into the future. Mataya, he seeks to destroy the adult Raina."

"What?" Mataya gasped.

"I have seen her dreams. It is there where he holds her prisoner while her body suffers. He has taken her to another realm."

"Then the timeline—is all wrong. It has been interrupted again. I swear to you that I did not create this scenario in my mind. I have been careful. I am not the reason as to why things have changed."

"Relax, Mataya. You are allowing those human emotions to bring about an unnatural side of your essence. Now, please calm yourself."

"I am calm. Why did we not see this as a possibility?"

"Why should we have thought of this? Despite your uncontrollable time shifts, there was never an indication to believe that he could follow a Guardian into the past or the future. He must have been waiting for the right moment to strike. He has chosen not to touch her human body. He is wise and mighty. The evil one knows the true point of attack needs to be within her mind."

"What do we do now?" she asked weakly, feeling her hope begin to diminish.

"We must go to her in her dreams and fight."

"Beck, you are the only one with the power to do that."

"I am not so sure that I can."

"Then let us go now and together we can save her."

"No, Mataya. I am trying to tell you that it cannot be either one of us."

"Why not? We are her only hope."

"No, we are not. Mataya, we have to recruit another who can enter dreams. Her mind will search out the things she knows. We are no one to her. Our efforts will not be answered by our appearances. Even if we reach her, she will not recognize the signs of our help, and she will cast us a side."

"Then what shall we do, Beck?"

"She has called to the Head Elder, this I know, for I have seen it. However, he does not understand at this moment what he hears or the visions he sees. Even Raina does not understand whom she sees in her dreams. It appears that the Head Elder believes the episodes he experiences are dreams brought about because of his loneliness. Perhaps even by his guilt for not being able to save her. He has not comprehended that it is she who calls to him and not dreams at all."

"Then who do we send?"

"We will send Enoch. Raina and he have formed a strong bond during their earthly ties."

"Enoch is a Watcher. He has not been trained—"

He interrupted her. "You underestimate him, Mataya. He has already retrieved the locket from the other realm and hears the song within it."

"He did what?"

"He went through the portals of time and took the locket after the crash during Raina's first timeline. He can use that to locate her. I believe by the same actions that I have used to bring you to this brook."

"Beck, I do not understand. How can he use the locket to locate her?"

"He was very clever. He has placed the scroll of hope within the locket and given it to Raina. He knew he could use it if necessary."

"The scroll—how, Beck? I thought you had the scroll secured safely away in the brook."

"Enoch works for his own cause. He has discovered much more than you intended for the Secret Council to learn."

"That is impossible. I forbid the members of the Council to search out their own clues. They were warned to follow my plan without questions."

"Mataya," Beck scolded, "look what you asked him to do? Did you expect him to give up his existence without securing the safety of all involved?"

"What about the scroll's power?" she finally asked, still seeming confused. "Does he know its true purpose?"

"I am not sure of what he knows. His intentions are pure. Perhaps good will come from any wishes made upon the scroll. He must have a clear assumption of its power, or else I do not believe he would have risked time travel."

"Beck, too much is happening for us to have to deal with a rogue Guardian on the loose."

"Rogue, you say. Since when did he fall from your grace?"

"He has not fallen from my grace. However, the fact that he has something as dangerous as you have portrayed in his possession when he now appears to work against our cause concerns me."

"If you doubted his skills, then why did you include him in this at all?"

"I do not doubt him, Beck, except we are the only ones who know the true course."

"You sent him to Earth to live as her Watcher away from all he has known. Did you think he would give up part of his essence to raise the child and remain human all of these years—not to be concerned for her well-being or that of her offspring? He has spent his entire time on Earth planning ... anticipating any errors in our mission.

"You do not measure your existence in human time, Mataya, so let me confirm to you how tedious eighty-four human years can be to a Guardian. Enoch trained himself to be leery of failure. When he tied himself to the human Netamae at your instructions, he took on a cause as great as our own. One cannot condemn him for his efforts. He has acted the only way he knew how to, considering the circumstances of those involved in ..."

The lightning flashed across the sky and a stream of cold air blew over Mataya pulling her thoughts from Beck's conversation. His confirmation of her secret plan startled her. As she searched her mind for all of the reasons she chose to act as she had, Mataya faced darkness. In the mist of it shouted Beck's voice.

"Mataya, are you well?"

Mataya remained silent looking off into nowhere. Beck shook her gently; trying to pull her from the bemused state, she appeared to be in.

"Mataya, can you hear me?"

She blinked feeling the warmth remove the chill that had consumed her. "Ah ... yes."

"Are you okay?" he questioned again. Beck's face went blank as he caught the look in Mataya's eyes. There was something in her eyes he couldn't decipher; something that gave him the sense Mataya was hiding information from him.

"Yes, I am fine. Are you sure he will find her in time?"

"Yes, I am. The Scroll of Espérer will guide him just as he had planned. Enoch will make his wish through the determination found within his heart at that moment. Since we have chosen to proceed without the guidance of the Creator for our own benefit, and we seek the outcome our hearts desire, we must wait, anticipating what our next move should be. Enoch and Josiah each have their own course of action set, whether lead by God or by carnal instincts."

"Then, Beck ... let it be so." Mataya's smile faded, and she knew that Beck sensed her concern. "Beck, tell me please. Do you regret all that we have done?"

"I, just as the others, have made choices for my own reasons. Wrong or right, I acted to provide the answers I needed for my existence. My actions will be questioned, and I shall be made accountable for them. If life was fair, then none of what has come to pass would have done so, and in my eyes, no one would have suffered.

"If I understood completely, that the mysteries of Heaven remain void to us—then I would have remained in faith—waiting to see what the ultimate plan was. Because I am afflicted by carnal thoughts, I did not wait on God. I shall have to live with that decision and accept the consequences."

"You had your reasons, Beck."

"Yes, and God has His. My reasons may not have been good enough. Look what we have lost. Have we really gained anything at all, Mataya? We fight to maintain the proper realm, and with each attempt, we sacrifice a bit of who we were created to be. We may lose this, Mataya. We must be resigned to that fact. All may have been for nothing."

It was then as she pondered Beck's words of warning when an uncontrollable rage swelled consuming her rationality. In Mataya's anger, her judgment became clouded and the need to find justification grew more intense. Then turning to face the mist forming at the edge of the berry path, she ran toward it leaving Beck by the brook.

"Mataya—no!"

His essence felt her intent and he had to stop her. He ran after her but she reached the mist before him and then disappeared. Beck stopped at the edge of it knowing he was too late. He could only pray that Mataya came to her senses and didn't react too harshly with Evi.

Mataya materialized on Callisto outside of Evi's home. In her fiery, she rushed through the mansion searching for Evi's chamber. Because of her anger, Evi's protection seemed less important and vengeance became Mataya's primary goal. Evi was relaxing on her davenport reading a book. The loud shouts of Mataya concerned her pulling her attention from the story.

Mataya hollered through the corridors of Evi's home. "Evi—come here! Evi, where are you? We have a situation that is critical."

Evi got up from her seat to meet her. "Mataya, I am in here."

Mataya entered the room standing a few feet away from the Guardian who may have cost her everything. "Evi, a Tracker has found your daughter in the past and the vessel in the future."

Evi dropped the book barely aware of the crashing sound it made as the book shattered the crystal vase on the table in front of her.

"My daughter ... how did it find her, Mataya? Your plan was supposed to be fool proof."

Mataya slammed her fist down on the table missing the chunks of broken crystal, cracking the table's glass surface.

"How could you, Evi? We had an agreement. You knew the importance."

"What are you talking about, Mataya?"

"Just tell me why, Evi?" she shouted, losing control. "What possessed you to risk everything?"

"I do not understand what you are talking about."

"Oh, Evi—why?" She moved closer to her plan's traitor. "We discussed the ramifications of seeking her out. You promised that you would not go to Earth and visit her. You left a trail of your essence. He found her, Evi. The evil one sent a Tracker who followed your essence to Silver Lake in the past."

"Oh, no—I was so careful." Evi bowed her head in despair. Her human love led her blindly one night to act against her promise.

"Not careful enough. He has manipulated everything we worked for."

"Is my daughter safe, Mataya?"

"No, I do not believe so. The vessel is under attack in the future. If she perishes—so does your daughter."

"Oh, my." Evi felt her essence begin to weaken and then she collapsed onto the davenport. "But how? I was just there a few earth minutes. She was so happy. I just had to see her. Do you not understand what it is like not knowing? Not feeling my daughter's essence with me."

"You forget, Evi—that I do. Have we not started this adventure because of the absence of my brother, Mateo?"

"Yes ... I believed I was—careful."

"As you can see, Evi—not careful enough."

"No, Mataya, I am so sorry."

"This is important, Evi. What did you tell her?"

"Everything ... I told her everything about her birth and why she was on Earth."

"How could you be so careless? Our mission was a secret."

"I do not know. I did not think my actions would put her in danger. Please, Mataya, tell me. What do we do now?" Evi asked, wiping away the tears that began to form in her eyes.

"Nothing—we wait for a sign from Beck. Pray, Evi, that he has the power to undo your mistake."

"And if he does not have the power?"

"Then I must act. My only option brings me great discontent. It will change what I have started out to do."

"Will it save my daughter?"

Mataya didn't answer her.

Evi buried her face into her hands. The night seemed so right. Her human emotions tore at her endurance daily. The Guardian life she lived began to diminish, and nothing made sense anymore. Just one look at her daughter's face or the sound of her voice, would surely calm the storm that engulfed Evi's life. That is what brought her there against Beck and Mataya's orders. Evi risked everything, believing her cause wouldn't suffer. The compassion of motherly love stole her rationality. An act that now endangered so many lives.

25.
THE PLAN

Hyperion Universe—present-day

"How do you plan on taking care of the human? Her existence has caused me great trouble. She is the reason my adversary patrols the universe with his fellow Guardians, taking what rightfully belongs to me. When she is gone once and for all, he will lose his desire and my life will flourish."

"Do not worry, Master. You have other things to concern yourself with."

"Despite your beliefs, Tarik, she is my greatest concern. How do you plan on dealing with her?"

"I have not physically touched her, if that is what you mean. I do not need to stain my hands with her inferior blood. Her own kind will end her life for me."

"How will they do this? What is it that makes you so positive her fate is near?"

"Master, I have tampered with the child's health and medical diagnosis. As we speak, she lays in a hospital bed unconscious. This of course is my doing. I have held her in the darkness of the Hyperion Universe. To the humans she appears unresponsive. Even now, she screams from within the walls of the Acheron Cavern. The river flows over her feet, burning her with its vile contents. I have left her helpless against its woes ... just the way I like it." He laughed wickedly. "She hit her head when she fell in the cavern, and I have allowed her blood to spill over into the human world. The blood appears to be coming from her brain. I simulated a brain defect with their ancient medical equipment. The humans love to play God. The doctors will cut her skull open to relieve a mass that is not there. Of course, it will not be visible at first, so like all humans trapped by their curiosity, the doctor will do exploratory surgery. The end result ... is he will destroy her brain and she will die. Thus, her death will be upon his soul. You and I, Master—will be blameless in her demise."

"You are very clever, Tarik. Tell me more about your desired plan."

"This will indeed explain the effects of my mind control. Unlike most humans' brains that are weak and vulnerable, hers is strong and fights me. It is not without great difficulty that I can pull her into our world. My tampering has left her with some ill effects. As temporary as they seem, they have been observed by her human kind. My attempts to track and capture her appear to be what the humans call night terrors—and her dizziness, and odd behavior ... well, as I said. They will be passed off as defect in her brain."

Toah's wicked cackle filled the chamber. "You, Tarik, are well endowed with brilliance. I could not ask for a better plan."

"Thank you, Master. I am ecstatic with your approval."

"How long, Tarik, before what you speak of comes to pass?"

"Not long, Master. The doctors will move promptly believing their actions will save her life. I have arranged for her parents not to be reached immediately. Therefore, it will not hinder their treatment plan ... or mine. They will proceed without family consent acting as medical advocates."

"What about the self-proclaimed Watcher? Her appearance on Cressida could have cost us dearly. Had she realized it was not a dream and warned her parents, the moment we passed her in the hall our plan would have been over."

"Anani has no clue of my meddling. Her celestial mind is young and easily influenced. One thought from me, and you saw how fast she faded from the room."

"Yes, you do have some magnificent skills, Tarik. That is why you are so valuable to me."

"Thank you, Master. Trust assured, Raina's dreams have caused Anani some concern, but she does not realize it is my doing. Her thoughts are preoccupied with that foolish Guardian."

"Perfect, my young Tarik. You have thought of everything."

"No, Master ... I will not pride myself. There is still room for errors. I do not want to be distracted by my own pride. This way I will remain attentive to the situation. I will not rest until the events have passed and our problem is gone."

"I admire your commitment to my cause, Tarik." Toah snickered. His tone more wicked than that of the cloaked Tracker. "And what of my adversary? When will he perish? His very existence tarnishes my own. He has crossed my path too many times foiling my plans. He is the reason I lost two very good assistants to the wretched planet Deimos." Toah felt the anger brewing deep in his body. He clinched his fist angrily, imaging that he held Josiah in his grip twisting his essence until it faded. "He must be stopped. Do you hear me, Tarik?"

"Master, his time will come soon. We have already begun to beat down his defenses with the assault on the human's mind. He will perish, this I promise you, but I believe he has much to offer us, and his life at this moment is very valuable."

"Tell me, Tarik. What value do you speak of?"

"He has many undiscovered powers that could benefit you, Master. Allow me to toy with him a little longer. His self-proclaimed righteousness could be the human's down fall."

"How so?"

"He has the power to enter her dreams. I think it is possible to control his mind and discover the powers he has been given. If we can secretly steal his knowledge, that eternal power will be yours. When we are finished, I will simply end his life in a chosen manner."

"You are very clever, Tarik, however, what power can he offer that I do not already have?"

"His essence has been blessed. He is full of security and honor. If you steal the blessing and send them to Earth, then you will fool the humans and control them with a false sense of happiness. You know how much the humans value happiness and love. You can take it all from them. They will be in a wasteland of despair. In time, their joy will turn to sorrow and grief. In their anguish, they will rise up against one another. They will take their own lives and that of their children. The inhabitants of Earth will cease to exist, and you will rule their realm spotless of the blood they shed."

"You have a most interesting plan, Tarik. I suppose I could tolerate his existence a little longer."

Toah laughed in unison with Tarik. The game he played brought him enjoyment and a sense of fulfillment that was indescribable by mere human words.

Lost in the feelings of pride he arrogantly dismissed for his master's benefit, Tarik glorified his disgusting behavior. As he envisioned his victory—he allowed himself to be caught-up in the moment—letting his defenses dwindle. Tarik was unaware of a looming intruder in his domain. This one would challenge every fiber of his being, for his objective was as great as Josiah's was.

Enoch moved slowly, surveying the dim surroundings of the cave, sensing its discord and darkness. He attempted to mask his steps with the power of his essence, as he continued cautiously through Tarik's mysterious realm.

Enoch's essence couldn't penetrate the Demon's power nor discern the spells Tarik cast to trick unwanted visitors. With the aid of the locket his great-granddaughter wore to guide him, he knew that she was there somewhere trapped in this evil dimension. Enoch's sole desire was to find her before it became too late.

The spells Tarik used to protect his realm allowed very little of Enoch's powers to surface. The substrate of the cave was charged with some sort of magnetic pull that seemed to draw off Enoch's essence. It took great physical exertion for Enoch to find the strength to remain in a physical form Raina would recognize and not become frightened at his appearance.

While Mataya gathered with the Secret Council to put her plan into action, Enoch created his own as a precaution. With no regard to the rules of time travel,

Enoch sought out Raina in the future. He found an item belonging to her of great value. He removed it from around Raina's neck when she lay unconscious on Jon and Kiersten's fabricated boat.

On a hot Saturday afternoon, he set his plan into motion. Enoch blessed the object, sealing inside of it a reason to hope. He gave this secret gift to Raina, knowing he could use it to locate her if ever necessary.

This day the secret gift was needed. The murmuring sound of the locket called to him, directing Enoch through the dense universe. He was close to her ... he could sense it, hearing her terrified pants as her heart pounded erratically. It sickened Enoch to imagine what he would find when he reached her. Could he dare live with himself if he was too late? Enoch couldn't find the words to tell his Leader of his failures, nor could he accept the thought of losing his great-granddaughter.

In the distance, he heard noise of shifting rocks. Enoch stopped to assess where the noise had come from. A flash of light flickered down a long tunnel. Raising the glowing orb he materialized, Enoch started down the tunnel. In a few earth seconds, he stood at the entrance of a catacomb. He felt the warmth of the room inviting him to enter. When he entered the room, he saw Raina huddled in a corner. Her face didn't carry the look of fear he had seen before. This time there were no tears streaming from the eyes that focused on a shadowy figure standing a few feet away from her. He took no chances with this illusion. Holding the orb high into the air, Enoch called out Raina's name, claiming her mind from the cave.

Tarik continued in his self-worth behaviors of lying to himself. He became careless and less defensive of the realm he controlled, believing no other life form was superior to his. That was when he let his guard down.

Unexpectedly he sensed his intruder. The dark-master Toah noticed him tense.

"What is it, Tarik?" he questioned, unsure of how he should perceive Tarik's sudden stillness. "Answer me, Tarik. What is happening?"

"Nothing is happening, Master." He lied. "I must go now and make my rounds. I need to check on the girl. I feel a change in her state."

"What is wrong with her, Tarik?"

"It is nothing I am sure, Master. However, she is human and her life force is not strong like yours, Master. I want to make sure she survives until my plan is complete. With that, Tarik disappeared.

26.
LIFE IN DEATH

Guardian Realm—present-day

"I trust Evi has been secured, Mataya."

"Yes, Beck, she has been. I have assisted her to Prometheus where she will wait until I grant her permission to return. I believe she will be safe there. I have some rather persuasive friends from Dione who have invited her to be their guest. They will assure that she does not leave or receive any visitors."

"What about Elder Torrey? He will grow suspicious of her absence."

"I thought of that. Evi has spoken with him, and she is on a retreat as she called it."

"What about Tahir? What has he been told?"

"Tahir is away at the moment. He is not expected back immediately. When he does return he will join her on Prometheus. I believe once he understands the current situation, he will be obliged to keep Evi there until we send word."

"And Josiah ... is he ready to learn of the events that are to unfold?"

"I have been observing his behaviors and you must know that I am not alone."

"What do you mean, Mataya?"

"It appears that Josiah's little friend, Anani, has been watching over him in California. She has adopted a human façade, and she attends the same college as Josiah and Raina. Anani has witnessed his episodes and came to his aid undercover using her fabricated human image.

"Who is her Esprit de corps?"

"Apparently, it is Josiah."

"How strange that he does not sense her presence. Is it possible that if Anani can keep her essence from him, she may be aware of our plan?"

"Relax, Beck. No, she is not aware of what we are doing. Think about it. We have given no one an indication of what my thoughts have done."

"You say she is watching over him. What does she feel the need to observe?"

"They are friends. I am sure with the passing of her parents she has nothing to do. Josiah has been dreaming again, and made quite a spectacle of himself a few days ago."

"Then Raina still calls to him?"

"Yes, Raina does. However, Josiah still does not understand what is happening."

"He must for this new plan of ours to work, Mataya."

"I know. The episodes are very severe; I am concerned for both of their well-beings. Even now, Raina is in their hospital with a critical illness. Anani has been at her side and seems to be defenseless to assist her. "

"Josiah is strong. He will endure and we will prevail. Enoch will reach her and stop this."

"Are you saying this from experience, Beck?"

"If you are asking if I saw the outcome in a dream ... then no. It is my desire for our Leader's sanity and your brother's redemption that encourages me."

"I wish I had your courage, Beck. I fear we will fail."

"Do not fear the unknown."

"How can I not? Of all the human emotions I could experience, it is fear that consumes my mind."

"I can help you with that—if you like."

"No, I do not want to lose my only connection to the human realm. Beck, are you ready to proceed? Tell me, have you doubted our choice?"

"Doubt is for humans, Mataya."

"Then, Beck, who do you believe fear is for?"

Beck looked away. He didn't want to answer her. He knew she suffered enough without a constant reminder of her possible fate. He attempted to direct the conversation from her own disposition by reminding her of their mission.

Mataya bowed her head into her hands. She was asking much of this proud Guardian and offering him nothing in return. Beck sensed her disillusionment and pulled her into his embrace.

"I am here for you. You do know that?"

She looked up to meet his stare. As always, Beck's eyes gave her peace. She felt secure and sure of herself in his presence.

"I know you are. I can think of no one kinder than you."

Beck smiled, and gently kissed her cheek. She smiled back, wanting to tell him the thoughts she hid from him. The thoughts she was sure he had shared once and dismissed for her honor. He reached out to take her hand into his and urged her along. Sol was beginning to set marking their need to leave.

———————

The lightning shot across the sky, sending flashes of light dancing in the atmosphere. Josiah used to love listening to the sound of the rain and smelling the summer breeze. Mother Nature always had so much to offer with Raina at his side. Lately, the rain brought a renewed meaning to him. He got lost in the raindrops, imagining where his life would be if the Sentinel really was a children's fable and his life was back to *normal.*

"Your Excellency," a faint voice pulled him from his thoughts. "Excuse me; may I have a word with you?"

It took Josiah a second to realize that he was in his shell sitting in the Library in Hemet. The title of Excellency had no place for him here on Earth. Josiah spun around attempting to erase his face of any shock. The squeaking sounds of the chair ricocheted off the bookshelves adding to Josiah's dismay.

Before him stood the petite classmate who had helped him a few days ago. Josiah had dreaded this moment. The entity from the back of the class made her move. She too, had sensed Josiah's power. She also knew he was not just one of Professor Russell's students.

"You do not recognize me in this form, do you, Josiah?" she asked, acting as if this was a natural conversation between two friends.

"No ... yet I have felt your power. Why have you kept your true intentions from me?"

"I could ask you the same question, Head Elder."

"Who are you? What do you want from me?"

"Come, Your Excellency. There is no time to explain … please, just follow me."

"No—I will not until you tell me who you are? What need do you have to hide in the shadows?"

"Please, Elder Josiah … just come with me now. There is not much time," the stranger begged, trying to hide her urgency.

"Why should I listen to you or follow one who acts in secret?"

"Josiah—have you not also acted undercover for the security of your mission?"

Her words brought the memories of his discreet adventures with Raina flashing through his mind. "Yes … I have," he answered in a strong tone of voice. Josiah tried hard to hide his panic.

"Then please, no questions. You must come with me now. There is much at jeopardy as we speak," the stranger ordered. With great determination, she turned to escort Josiah to the hospital.

"Where are you going?"

"Josiah, I believe that the visions you have been having are not just random visions or daydreams. They are real and you must stop them before it is too late."

"Stop them—what are you talking about? Guardians do not dream. Are you not the same as I? Do you also dwell as part of my people? If so, then you know what you speak of is in error."

"Josiah," she insisted. The stranger demonstrated the same manner of character as she had the day she came to his aid in the corridor. "I believe those visions are a reality that your Raina pulls you into for her protection. The evil one is winning. As we speak she is losing her strength."

"Come with me!"

Josiah quickly got up from his chair looking around them for any witnesses. He grabbed her arm and began escorting through the aisles of books. When they reached the doors, he glanced around them once more, and then led her from the Library out into the parking lot. Josiah didn't stop until he had forced her around to the back of the building. When he was sure they were alone, Josiah roughly shuffled her body, so that she stood facing him.

"Who are you? What do you mean by this?" he shouted alarmed, as his human heart raced. His essence twisted within him at the news of his Raina being in danger.

She opened her mouth to speak, but in his haste, he didn't give her a chance. His words flowed so angrily, that Anani was shocked by the odd behavior of the one she considered her brother.

"What are you talking about ... Raina is gone to me," he insisted, jerking her arms within his grip. "She cannot possibly be calling for me. She does not even remember who I am. The Sentinel gave her a new life."

"I understand that. However, her old life runs a course parallel to this new one. Her mind recalls certain events from her previous life. You, Head Elder, remain an important icon in her mind."

"That is impossible. The Sentinel made it clear that my Raina is gone to me. Her life served its purpose."

"If that were true, Elder, then why do you pursue her attention?"

"I pursue nothing. Are you so arrogant to believe that you know of what I do?"

"I know, Elder, that you were with her yesterday. Is that not why you are here today? Do you not wait here hoping to glance into her eyes?"

Josiah felt his human hear skip a beat. Nearly panicking, he tried to contain his composure. It was clear that this entity had done her homework. While Josiah chose to ignore her presence, she investigated his.

"You are confused," he said, weighing his options to avoid further discovery. "Yes, I was with one who resembles the human I once knew, although the woman I was with yesterday is not the same person."

"Tell me, Elder. Do you truly believe what you say just because her memory is gone? Have you not sensed her soul? You know that it is her alive in the flesh. Can you so easily bury the emotions that sent you to Deimos?"

"You speak in riddles. Tell me plainly what you desire of me," Josiah demanded.

"Release me now, or I will say no more," Anani insisted, trying to tug her arms free from his grip. Josiah complied, loosening his hold on her. She thrust her arms away from him showing her displeasure with his behavior. Then she rubbed her biceps where Josiah held her. "Raina is in a hospital as we speak. Her condition is grave."

"In the hospital? You must be mistaken."

"No, Josiah, I wish I were. She took ill yesterday."

"From what?" he asked, thinking of all the illnesses he protected her from as a child.

"The humans do not understand her condition. Their primitive methods will kill her in the end."

"Kill her, what is wrong with her? Where is she? What must I do?"

"Josiah ... you must find Raina in her dreams and pull her back to this reality. That is what she has been trying to do. She has been looking for you, although Raina does not know it is you who she searches for to assist her. Raina's will to find the shelter of your protection calls to you. It is a remnant of the Sentinel's power that she uses to pull you into her sleeping world. She believes they are just nightmares haunting her since her youth, however, they are far more dangerous than a wild imagination."

"In her dreams ... what do you mean? Of course, she had dreamed of me once—all humans dream. She never had nightmares as a child. I saw to that."

"The evil that hunted her in your lifetime still travels the universe in search of her now. It did not cease to exist when you sent Dinah to Deimos."

"What evil do you speak of? Dinah and her father are no longer a threat to us."

"Do you believe that they acted alone? You must think clearly about this. Allowing your dull human mind and emotions to get in the way will be detrimental to our cause."

Josiah shifted his weight, ready to react to the stranger if need be. "Our cause? You elude my questions. What is her illness? I am a Guardian. Tell me where she is, so that I may go to her and heal her."

"Josiah, for reasons beyond what I can tell you, an evil Demon continues to find ways to destroy our universe. It searches for weakness in our kind, waiting to pounce when our defenses are down. He has manipulated many entities to acquire the powers he practices now. The evil one has found Raina in the new life that the Sentinel gave her. It is possible he believes she still harbors the Sentinel or poses some other threat to his existence. Because of this, he is trying to destroy her.

"He has found a way to take her mind from Earth. I do not understand why he just does not take her life openly. Instead, he resorts to destroying her mind. Since her mind is controlling her bodily functions and she is not ill by true human standards—your powers cannot heal her until you have accessed her mind and destroyed the connection the Demon has with her."

This information was too much for Josiah to absorb. His body began to tremble as he recalled the horrid visions he had experienced. This new information explained what he was seeing in his visions. His Raina was really being tortured, and there was nothing he could do to help her. His essence whelped up from within him, and blue sparks began to discharge from his fingertips. Anani stepped backward cautiously, in response to the surge of Josiah's powers.

"Josiah," she begged in a human manner. Anani wanted to divert Josiah's attention back to the matter at hand. "You must control yourself. If the news alone affects you this way ... I cannot begin to comprehend how the Demon's presence will torment you."

Josiah said nothing. He continued to stare at the blue flashes dancing on the tips of his fingers. He hadn't experienced such a discharge of power since the day he fought Azazel. Sadly, the memories associated with that battle flooded his mind. It was on that day in Silver Lake, Wisconsin; Josiah accepted his destiny as the Chosen One and Head Elder of all Guardians. Only, this occasion didn't bring happiness, as it was no celebration for Josiah. Instead, it was a curse. He had to admit to himself that he was destined to live a life without the only soul he ever loved.

Out of this love, which no human words could describe, he joined in his mind with Raina, his self-proclaimed Esprit de corps. When he came into power, there was a trade-off of lives and her existence, as he knew it perished. The Sentinel, the Creator's designed protector, emerged from the body of Raina. From that day forward, Josiah struggled with loneliness. His assigned duties gave him no contentment, and he didn't find pleasure in the life he now functioned within for the benefit of his Esprit de corps.

The female Guardian reached out, grabbing hold of Josiah's shoulders to shake him from his bemused state. She was careful to position her hands in such a way as to remain clear of the dancing blue light.

"Head Elder—can you hear me?"

Josiah didn't respond immediately, the blue light consumed his every thought. The urge to fight swarmed over him. The reality that he didn't know who the evil was choked him.

"Elder—please," the stranger before him pleaded. She was beginning to grow impatient knowing they were running out of time. "Elder, we must go!"

Josiah faintly heard the words of this stranger before him. His mind focused intently on the painful memories of his Raina. Regret for his actions of letting Raina go mingled with his human-acquired anger. Humans spend their lives analyzing the "should haves" and "what ifs" of their actions. Josiah realized he also inherited that trait during his human excursions.

"How could I have allowed this?"

"Elder please," she urged. "We must go now. Get a hold of yourself—she needs your help."

Josiah acknowledged the stranger's urging, and pulled himself from his memories and regrets. "What must I do?"

"We need to go to the hospital here in Hemet. There lies your Raina in an apparent coma. Her mind has been consumed by a Demon from the Hyperion Universe. When we arrive there, you must open your mind and allow your Guardian thoughts to diminish the human ones.

"When this happens the moment in time, which remains hidden from you now, will guide you to the light that controls the realm's portal. It is in that reality he has taken your Raina to. If you do not succeed using the portal as a guide, you will be forced to wait for her to find you and pull you into her dream's realm. We cannot afford any delays. He moves swiftly, and her mental status is diminishing."

"What if we do not connect in any of the dream realms?"

She lowered her head in sadness. "I am sorry, Josiah. I fear the evil will win." Anani had come to know all too well the harsh reality of human emotions. Sadness was the first emotion to strike down this entity's endurance.

"Are you well?" Josiah questioned, sensing the change in her.

"Yes ... thank you." Anani closed her eyes diverting her attention to their needed location.

Josiah followed the female entity's lead and shed his shell dematerializing from the Library grounds. Instantly they arrived at the hospital appearing in their celestial form within the room. Josiah was stunned when he realized whom he had materialized next to and gasped.

"Anani?"

She placed her fingers over her mouth and pointed across the room. Josiah moaned when he saw who it was huddled over Raina's body weeping. The sight of Tori made him gasp. His Raina always stayed with his mind night and day. Her appearance was acceptable, but Tori died and he believed her soul entered Heaven. No amount of the Sentinel's powers or compassion could prepare him for seeing her in the room alive. Raina's father stood across the room intent on studying images on a computer screen. Josiah recognized them to the results of human medicine. The look on Nolan's face was cold and weak, far from the strong loving face of Tori's memories.

The sterile environment of the hospital room gnawed at Josiah forcing more memories of his human life to surface. They clouded his mind, obstructing the connection Anani tried to assist him with forming. His cause seemed worthless as he remembered the dangers he brought upon those he called friends. The ones he nearly killed fighting-off the rancid powers of their fallen Head Elder Markian in a burning barn.

"Elder ... Elder Josiah—can you hear me?"

Josiah looked at Anani oddly. His essence responded to the sound of her voice, but her words meant nothing. She slapped his celestial face quickly stepping away from any fury Josiah would retaliate upon her.

"Yes ... what do we do next?" he asked, staring blankly at Raina's new savior.

"Concentrate, Elder. Search for her soul in this universe. Find the energy of her spirit and then absorb it. You must concentrate. We cannot save her if you remain distracted."

"What do you mean search her out? She is right here before me."

"I did not say to look at her body. I know she is before us. Head Elder, you must search for her soul. It is only when you find it, can you absorb her energy."

Josiah closed his eyes. He tried to clear his thoughts acknowledging the he called sister and the girl he loved, except the state of Raina consumed him, shadowing his thoughts with fear and sadness.

"Elder—you must concentrate. Block the view of this room from your mind. You must hurry, Josiah. Please, search out her soul. "

"I am trying."

"Not hard enough," she voiced roughly. "You are the only one that can make this work. Now, please tell me. What is it in this room that troubles you the most?"

Josiah looked directly at Raina, lying near death, in the hospital bed. Her face was pale except for the dark circles under her sunken eyes. Raina's breathing seemed shallow and strained.

"Raina," he whispered, reaching his hand out as if she were close enough to touch. "I cannot bear to look at the wretched state of her parents. This should not be happening. They should not see her like this."

"Josiah—listen to me. I know her state is vile and consuming, however, you must trust that her outward appearance will mend when we save her. At this moment, that human body cannot even resemble the chaos she is experiencing in her mind."

"This is not easy. My sole purpose of existence was to protect her. I cannot fathom her in this condition."

"Well, you must put her out of your mind until we are ready. Your will is strong, you can fight this."

"I am sorry. You should realize it is not natural for me to allow such an occurrence to take place."

"Elder, do I need to remind you that there is nothing natural about this situation? We—"

Before she was finished speaking, Anani disappeared without any warning. Tarik had kept close watch over her. When he learned of Anani's actions, he removed her from the hospital just as he had done when they found her on Cressida. He erased all memory of her conversation with Josiah and of Raina's unexpected illness. He sent her back to her apartment where she found a need to indulge in a romance novel. Anani was completely unaware of her current actions or the danger that was brewing.

It would be a long time before his mind control faded and Anani came to her senses. To be assured of no further involvement by Anani, Tarik persuaded her to go home to the planet she missed dearly. His scheme included a hand written note to Raina explaining her abrupt need to return home. Tarik would have much enjoyed destroying Anani instead, except her disappearance couldn't easily be explained. It would attract far too much attention, and Tarik's plan didn't need any more interruptions.

Stunned by her disappearance, Josiah began turning in circles looking for the one who brought him there. "Anani ... hello? Where are you?" he called out, darting his head left-to-right, as he began to panic. Josiah's buried human emotions from a lifetime before rushed over him. His rationality faded into the bleakness of the moment.

The beeping sound that lingered in the distance since his arrival became louder and more forceful. Josiah turned toward the direction of the noise. There, in a bed too large for the blond-headed woman who occupied it, lay his hopes and his dreams. Josiah's essence drifted closer to her bedside. He watched the black LCD screen of the machine making the noise. Bright-white lines, moved across the screen. The speed and unique patterns they formed represented the core of her life force.

Her heart continued to beat slow and irregular. Regrettably, the machine's noise reminded him of this as the involuntary twitching of her muscles sickened him. Tremors are what the doctor called them. They controlled her lifeless body, turning her queen-like features dull and sickly. Raina's lips steadily changed various shades of blue that were enhanced by her snow-white completion.

She was dying and Josiah knew it. Now that the stranger was gone, Josiah knew he was helpless to aid her. He could only save Raina if she called out to him from her mind.

She would have to beckon him back into the reality that the evil created for his divine pleasure. His true hope of assistance disappeared when Anani left him. Josiah waited anxiously for her return, praying he wouldn't be too late.

Raina's state was too much for Josiah to look at. He had to comfort her, to feel her skin against his. He needed to be reassured himself, and only the softness of their love could help him. He moved across the room to the doorway, looking back at Raina and her parents once more. Then he left the room searching for a secluded place to transform. The ding of the elevator door caught his attention, proving to be an excellent place to hide. Once inside the moving elevator, Josiah closed his eyes, pulling the energy from the area around him into a solid mass. When the molecules and energy combined into one, Josiah King emerged.

He pushed the elevator button to take him back to the ICU unit. When the door opened, he hurried back down the hall to her room. Without knocking or announcing himself, he went to Raina's bedside. He took her hand in his and caressed it. It felt good to touch her, to remember what she felt like against his human shell. Her body temperature was abnormal, but her silky skin was still warm to him. Gently he touched her cheek with the tips of his fingers, just as he had many times before in another lifetime. A time when they were in love ... when he could guard the castle walls to keep her safe.

"Excuse me?" a voice broke into his thoughts. Josiah looked up to see Nolan standing next to him. "Who are you?"

A tear forced its way through his manufactured tear ducts. As it splashed onto his wrist, he swore the romance of a musical note branded deeply into his skin.

"My name is Josiah, Mr. Stone. I am a friend of Raina's. I am sorry; I came as soon as I heard. How is she?"

"How do you know my daughter?" Tori asked. She wiped the tears from her eyes trying to hide that she had been crying.

Josiah looked from Nolan to Tori. "We have classes together at the institute."

"Are you close friends?" Nolan asked, almost defensive for his daughter's sake.

"Yes, Mr. Stone ... we are."

"She has never mentioned you, Josiah. How long have you known her?"

"Nolan," Tori said. She got up from the chair and moved to her husband's side. Discretely she leaned over to whisper in his ear. "Can't you see that he is upset? Let's give him a moment, okay?"

Nolan said nothing as he allowed his wife to lead him from the room. "We will be back in a moment," Tori suggested. "Would you like something from the cafeteria, Josiah?"

"No, thank you. I am fine," he answered, not taking his eyes off Raina.

Quietly, she let out a moan, and Josiah's body flinched, becoming tense. If this were the moment, he would have to be ready. However, the seconds passed ... growing into hours, and there was no change.

Her parents returned resuming their previous vigil. Josiah could feel their questioning eyes watching him. He could almost hear their thoughts and most definitely felt their grief.

"Raina," he whispered tenderly, "can you hear me? Raina, it is I, Josiah. I am here—honey—" his voice broke. He noticed her heartbeat change its rhythm, and a chill trailed down his spine. The slower beat increased his fears.

Nolan got up from his chair to examine the cardiac monitor. Tori looked up at Nolan hopeful.

"Raina—wake up ... please ... for me," her father pleaded, with helplessness in his voice. "I am sorry that this is happening to you. I promise you that I am doing everything I can to assist you."

As Josiah felt Raina's body shiver, another vision swarmed over him. The dark cave he hated so much was once again his reality. Just as before, the grueling laugh of the evil entity echoed triumphantly. Its menacing laugh taunted Josiah as it rejoiced in his torment.

He had watched this unfold before, reacting differently each time. Every attempt to grab Raina and take her from there failed. In his supposed dream, Raina always seemed to disappear the moment he reached to take her hand. He didn't know where she went, or if she was truly gone. Now he knew this wasn't a dream. The cave was her reality. Josiah didn't dismiss the thought of her disappearance being a trick. It would be reasonable to think this if the evil entity felt that he was getting close to helping her.

Then acting on this theory, he reached for the frightened girl huddled in the corner. As his fingers touched her shoulder, she faded into the darkness.

"No," he cried, refusing to believe Raina was gone. Just then, a bright light shot across the cave, and a beeping sound rang in his ears. He felt a powerful force pushing against him, and his body hurled through the air. Pain was something Guardians didn't experience. Their essences didn't have pain receptors as humans did. Deimos could bring about the illusion of pain as one's essence burned out and submitted to their unforgivable sin. Pain was part of receiving your just punishment in a universe full of panic.

Josiah stood dazed, trying to comprehend if it was his vision or Raina calling to him, as Anani informed him. Outside the dream, Raina's body remained limp in the hospital bed, twitching as another tremor rippled through her withering body.

"Help me?" a voice moaned through the cave. Josiah turned, searching for the direction of the cry. In the shadows, he thought he saw a figuring moving. Josiah sprinted to chase after it. The figure led him into a small catacomb he had never been to before. Josiah looked around taking in his surroundings. The flicker of lit torches danced of the catacomb's walls and the room was not cold.

To his amazement, there in another desolate corner was Raina. Josiah sighed discouraged. At any moment, he feared she would disappear for the hundredth time with no chance of rescuing her. This time though, something was different besides the change of scenery. Josiah couldn't assess what appeared new in this dream, but his sense of fear for Raina was not heighten as it had always been before.

"Raina?" a man's voice gently spoke.

Josiah turned around to see who it was. The faint image of a man who Josiah didn't recognize stood by the entrance. He held a shinny object in the hand that he extended in front of him. The object dangled in the air reflecting off the torches, and it twirled around. Josiah moved to approach him, and then the man disappeared.

"Josiah?" Raina said disoriented.

He turned back around to face her and found that he wasn't in the cave anymore. Josiah realized that he stood next to Raina's hospital bed surrounded by her parents and a man in a white lab coat. Tori was crying, but it wasn't tears of sorrow. Nolan wore a huge smile that couldn't cover his tears of happiness.

"What are you doing here?" she asked, squeezing her hand around Josiah's hand. It was then that he realized he had never let go of it during his dream.

27.
GYPSE VANNER

Earth Realm—present-day

The plane landed in Milwaukee at seven o'clock in the morning. The flight took four hours and Raina felt every bit of it. She wasn't sure if it was from fatigue or knowing what she would find in Silver Lake. These last few months had been horrendous. The nightmares increased, taking a completely new direction. As Raina looked down at the bruises on her arms, she wondered where they came from. Then while rubbing them gently, Raina caught Josiah staring at her out of the corner of her eye.

He was always so watchful and protective of her. His loving looks and kindhearted behaviors weren't overlooked. Raina just didn't know how to respond to them. She lost so much the past fall. It wasn't fair to lose the both great-grandparents in one day. She never had a chance to tell them how grateful she was for their gift.

Instinctively clutching at her neck, she found the locket. It shook in her trembling hand. She supposed the trembling was from her uncertainties. Raina didn't really want to come back, but she did it for her parents' sake.

Her mother called her every day, sometimes twice, during the week since she was discharged from the hospital. Tori wanted to be sure that Raina was well. Her parents wanted her to fly back home with them immediately, except Raina made it clear that she had to catch up on her studies first. She assured them that she would be fine for a week, and spring break was more than enough time for her to visit with them. To convince her mother not to stay and to leave with her father was a difficult battle to win.

Her father was not so obvious when he called. He knew all of the right questions to ask of her and he knew how to ask them, so that the doctor in him would be satisfied. For Raina it felt like the Spanish Inquisition. A lab rat under a microscope having her whole world exposed and analyzed. She wasn't crazy, but how could she make them see that?

It didn't help matters that her good friend Ann had to leave so abruptly for her hometown. There was an issue with her family's business, and they needed Ann's help. Raina felt alone now that she was gone and couldn't wait to get back to Hemet. Ann's letter explained she would be back soon and that she would call her daily. The phone calls never came and that hurt Raina's feelings more than she let on.

"Are you all right, Raina?" Josiah asked, in a low tone knowing she grew tired of all the poking and prodding that her hospital stay had put her through.

"Yes ... I am fine. Thank you for your concern."

"No need for any thanks." He smiled slightly, feeling a bit awkward.

"Yeah ... I guess not."

Raina turned to look out the window. She could still feel Josiah's eyes fixed upon her. Why did he do that? Did he think she was crazy, too? He promised he understood her thoughts, although Raina doubted he really comprehended them. However, his concerns seemed much too genuine for him not to understand, even if his concern for her felt different from that of her parents.

Josiah laid his head back against the seat. The visions were coming more frequently with an alarming sensation during the last few days. Josiah had trouble discerning between the visions and his reality. He worried each day as he watched the toll the nightmares took on Raina. As much as he tried to recreate his actions the day he found Raina in the catacombs, Josiah could never enter her dreams when he needed to. The lit catacomb where she first found her reprieve didn't appear in his visions anymore. Neither did he see the shadowy figure who seemed to be a key player in Raina's freedom.

Josiah was a little surprised that after Anani alerted him to Raina's condition she had not appeared to him since. He foolishly believed she kept her distance as not to interfere with any plan he was forming. He didn't know that the evil Raina ran from was the reason for Anani's disappearance.

Jaleel had informed Josiah's father of the episodes against his wishes. This irritated Josiah because he could see how his parents grew as concerned as he was. They couldn't seek the Council for help because of the ramifications that would rest upon Josiah. The Head Elder indeed had rebuked all he swore to uphold on the Council, to aid one was who was not an Esprit de corps. To make matters worse, Jaleel was not himself. Yakira seemingly disappeared without word of her location. When

Jaleel approached Yakir for information, he was put off by him and denied the information he sought. The human emotions Jaleel learned only intensified his reaction to Yakira's absence.

Josiah wasn't there the day Raina's mother lost her life in another reality. Josiah couldn't possibly imagine what Raina felt remembering a life that wasn't suppose to exist. To see the haunting look of death in her mother's eyes and not understanding what it meant.

He wondered if knowing her life, too, was lost the day the Sentinel emerged would destroy what was left of her mind. Did she see a light, or hear the Creator's voice, or did she just slip away not knowing what her existence had meant to humanity ... or him.

Perhaps the Sentinel's thoughts merged with hers temporarily, and she had a glimpse into the chaos the Demons caused. He dismissed the thought that she felt pain, surely the Creator had seen to it. How could He not? Raina was a vessel chosen from the human love a wayward Guardian felt. A love that drove him to flee from his people for a cause the Creator charged him to keep secret.

The Creator desired to bring Guardians to a new plane of existence. He created a plan to bind Guardians and humanity together, while making the Guardians more susceptible to emotions. When a Guardian truly understood the workings of humans, then how much more capable they would be to guide them. Humanity needed this link of camaraderie after the fallen Angels brought so much devastation upon their own kind. God didn't intend for humans to suffer from anger, jealousy, or greed. They chose that when free will was bestowed upon them. The door of serenity was closed, so God did what He does best. He opened a new one.

"So, what do you think about that?"

"I am sorry ... what did you say?" Josiah asked confused. He had not heard Raina speaking to him. He felt foolish for allowing needless thoughts to consume him.

"I said I wanted to stop at the stable first. Is that okay with you?"

"The stable ... sure."

"Josiah, you didn't hear a word I said, did you?"

"I am sorry. I guess I did not."

Raina shook her head, somewhat annoyed. When she didn't want to talk, everyone tried to force her. Now that she had something to say, no one wanted to listen.

"Please, forgive me, Raina. I am sorry. I was lost in thought."

"You have that problem a lot lately. Are you sure that joining me here was not a mistake? I can help you get a ticket back to Pasadena."

"No, do not think that, please. I was being stupid. I guess I am just tired. Flying is a bit stressful. I allowed it to get the best of me," he lied, remembering Raina would have called that a white lie.

"Don't sweat it, Josiah. It's fine, okay?"

Josiah smiled, nodding his head slightly. Times like this, too many words were too dangerous. If he allowed himself to become too involved, he would risk more than just his existence ... he risked hers as well.

They didn't speak as the plane landed, and Raina remained silent during their walk to the baggage claim area. Her only form of communication was a slight jerk of her head toward her luggage as it rolled past her on the conveyer belt. She reached over to remove her suitcase refusing Josiah's assistance. Silently they walked toward the exit, fighting the crowd. He watched Raina skimming the faces of those passing by. He wondered what she thought of them ... what she thought of herself.

Nolan and Tori were just outside the double glass doors. They came to greet them with overly forced smiles. Raina knew their true motives were to see their crazy daughter home safely. She felt like a child lost in the night, while being judged for having a flashlight with no batteries.

They exchanged hugs and kisses while Nolan greeted Josiah pleasantly with a handshake. His grip was firm, giving Josiah the illusion that Nolan was serious when it came to his daughter's safety.

He wondered if this was how the first Nolan would have reacted toward him. Was he always this compassionate and determined to aid the helpless, or had the Creator fine-tuned Nolan, improving his characteristics for a greater cause?

"I suppose you'll want to be stopping at the stables first?" Nolan asked, already knowing his daughter's response.

"Yes, Father. How did you ever guess?"

"I just know how difficult it is for you to be away from the horses. Stargazer will be happy to see you, too. I know he misses you. Every time I pull up in the truck, he runs to the fence. When I'm the only one to get out, he snorts and then trots off. He's getting sassy in his old age."

"He's not that old, Dad."

"Well, he's old enough to be set in his ways."

"All right you two. I can already see where this is going." Tori butted in, once again being the peace officer of the family.

Nolan and Raina both stared at Tori. With surprised looks, they acted as if nothing was wrong. Tori of course, remembered how easily Nolan could get to Raina when he pointed out Stargazer's faults.

"Very subtle, dear," Nolan said. Then reaching to put his arm around his wife, he pulled her close laughing.

"Will you be going to the stable as well, Josiah?" Tori asked hopeful.

"Yes, Mrs. Stone, if that is all right with you?"

"Certainly it will be," Raina spouted out. "I wouldn't dream of letting you miss a chance to meet my old stubborn horse. However, please be careful how you act around him. He may become senile and bite you or something. If that happens, I'll have to send him to the glue factory where all the old stubborn horses go."

"All right, kid. I'm sorry," Nolan said, reaching out to ruffle Raina's curls.

She smiled back catching the look of disapproval in her mother's expression. "Sorry, Mom, but I had to top Dad. I couldn't let him win with the insults."

"I'm sorry, dear. I should know better, it is too soon for that."

A flash of anger shot through Raina. Did he have to remind her again? "What do you mean by that, Dad?"

"Nothing, Raina," he answered, evaluating her expression.

"Well, that's unlikely, Dad. Just tell me what's really on your mind."

"Excuse me, Raina, but you have lost me. What do you mean?"

"Dad, don't do this, okay?"

Nolan stopped walking, not taking his eyes off his daughter. "Raina, I don't know what you're referring to. Can you please clarify what you think I just said?"

Raina sighed loudly, losing her courage to fight for her dignity. "Nothing, Dad," she retorted.

Then angry with herself for giving in she turned away and continued walking to the truck. In her haste, she left Josiah standing there speechless next to her parents.

"We had better hurry, Nolan, if Raina wants to be at the stable for awhile. I'm starving and could really use some breakfast first."

Nolan nodded his head agreeing to a short visit at the stable. He didn't know that his daughter had other plans. "Of course we'll hurry, dear."

Raina was quiet the entire car ride to Silver Lake. She spent most of her time looking out the window; however, she didn't miss her father's glances through the rearview mirror.

Just as her father had said, the minute their truck turned down the driveway to the stable, Stargazer sprinted to the gate. Raina swore he could sense her by the way he pranced back and forth snorting.

She jumped out of the back seat, almost before Nolan even put the truck in park, running to the gate. Stargazer lowered his head and began nudging his nose into her face. For a few brief moments, Josiah saw the smile that stole his heart so many years before. The smile of another lifetime that existed before the evil, had found her.

"Good boy, Stargazer," Raina repeatedly said, rubbing his nose. "You're such a handsome fellow."

Josiah agreed, taking his place next to Raina by the fence. "He is most beautiful."

"Go head and pet him. He likes to have the top of his head rubbed."

Josiah reached out touching the top of Stargazer's head. Just as Raina had assured him, the horse definitely liked Josiah's attention. He snorted loudly, nudging his head against Josiah's hand.

"See ... he likes you. And look, there is no chance of being bitten by a stubborn horse."

"Do you ride him much, Raina?"

"Yes, I ride him all of the time. Well, at least when I'm not at school, of course."

"His coloring is so vibrant and rich. It is amazing to look at him. What color do you call his fur?"

"Well, he's a Gypsy Vanner, and he was bred in Ireland. My dad bought him for me a few years ago and had him imported here to the United States. Most of their breeds traditionally are piebald, skewbald, odd colored or blagdon, but he's a perlino color."

"Excuse me, but I do not speak horse. What are you telling me, Raina?" Josiah asked feeling a bit embarrassed.

"Sorry, those are names given for distinct color markings on their coat ... not fur. See, a piebald is black and white. A skewbald has the coloring of red and white, brown and white or a tri color. This means they have another color mixed into them. A blagdon is a solid color with a pattern of white splashed from underneath them, like the other horses over there." Raina pointed to the west end of the corral. "See, that mare's coat is black, but she has the white underbelly and the mare over there is a chestnut with a white underbelly, also. It's called a splash because of the unique patterns they form. Like white paint that's splashed onto them from the ground."

Josiah studied the horses, watching their movements and admiring their colors. He had many Esprit de corps whose cultures depended upon horses; however, he paid them no mind.

"And Stargazer is a perlino? What color is that?" he asked, sounding confused for Raina's benefit.

"It means that he's a cream color and not albino. He is rare and very valuable."

"Why is that?"

"Well, genetics are important when breeding a horse for color. Science can help you determine certain colors like bay, chestnut, buckskin, palomino, or even a sorrel. Sometimes you get a color you don't really want. Since a perlino has two cream color genes, you will never get a sorrel or bay foal."

"Well, what is the color that on his feet?"

"His feet and feathers are palomino."

"But is that not a breed of a horse?"

"Yes, it is. Some horses are named by their color or are called color breeds, like a Palomino. A Gypsy Vanner is named for their body type and not for their coat coloring."

"This is a lot to take in. How do you keep all of that straight?"

"It's easy, I like horses. Some people like to study foreign languages, becoming intrigued with people's names. I like to study horses and their genetics," she said absently, then briefly wondered to herself why she used the explanation of name research. "So," she encouraged, "shall we?"

"What?" he asked.

"I asked if you wanted to go for a ride. Do you want to take him for a spin?"

He responded sounding a bit hesitant. He found himself wishing he had seen this moment in her future. "Sure."

"You will be fine. Just hang onto me, and I promise we won't do any jumps."

"Jumps?"

"I'm just teasing. Come on chicken ... and follow me."

Josiah obediently followed Raina, staying closely behind her as they went through the gate. She led Stargazer into the barn, where he watched Raina tether him to a thick u-shaped bar that was bolted to the barn's floor. Josiah paid careful attention as she spread a blanket over his back and straightened out the wrinkles. Then she hoisted a dark leather saddle with oak leaves embossed onto it from off the wall. Josiah began to ask if she wanted some assistance, but Raina seemed to move with such ease that he chose not to. He watched her place the heavy saddle over the blanket on the horse's back. Josiah noticed her caring and smooth actions, while she fastened the straps to secure the saddle. The amount of effort she took in preparing Stargazer for their ride surprised him. He recalled the many times he observed riders in centuries past, and none used such perfection with blankets and saddles.

Raina spoke to Stargazer in a soft tone, continuously praising him for his temperament. The whole time the horse continued to look at Josiah, nodding his head. Josiah almost swore that the horse knew he was different because of the way Stargazer stared at him. Perhaps, Josiah thought, it was he who was doing all of the staring because he found the horse's crystal blue eyes as captivating as Raina's were.

"Well, are you ready?" she asked, in a teasing tone.

Swiftly untying Stargazer, Raina mounted him and guided the horse out of the barn and into the corral. Nolan and Tori were standing at the edge of the eastern fence line. Raina couldn't hear what they were saying, but she knew from their expressions they disagreed with her decision to go riding. She was already forming her battle plan to confirm why she was up to the ride. If her persuasion didn't work, she was prepared to gallop off ignoring them.

Nolan must have read the look on Raina's face, because he opened his mouth to speak and then closed it. Raina was sure he changed his mind, but she was wrong.

"Raina ... I'm not sure that a ride is such a good idea right now."

"Why, Dad?" she questioned, ready for an argument.

"Honey, it's too soon since your discharge. We are still waiting for some of the test results to come back. I think that—"

"So, what does that have to do with the ride?" she cut him off, showing her displeasure in her tone of voice.

"Well." Her father sighed. "I'm just concerned that the all of the bouncing may make you feel dizzy."

"I'll be fine," Raina insisted. "The doctor said I could return to normal activities."

"Raina, I don't think he meant horseback riding. It is hardly a normal activity."

"Dad, if this were a restriction, I think he should have said so."

"Raina, please," Tori interrupted. She had hoped to bring some order to their mounting tempers. "Your father is just concerned."

"And he needn't be," Raina said angrily. "We'll be fine. Besides, Josiah is riding with me. He will watch out for me. Won't you, Josiah?"

"Um ... sure," he said hesitantly. The animosity he felt from Raina was very peculiar. She definitely was not acting like the girl he had fallen in love with a lifetime ago.

Raina held her hand out to Josiah with determination in her expression. He reached grasping her hand into his, and then he climbed up onto Stargazer's back with ease. Stargazer shifted his body to the right, and then stepped back away from her parents at Raina's command.

"Mr. Stone, I promise I will take care of her."

Before her father could respond, Raina pulled on the reins and guided Stargazer through the gate. They trotted several feet before reaching the road. Carefully checking for traffic on Highway B, she rode the horse into the street. Within seconds, Stargazer was galloping along the highway. His beautiful long mane blew in the wind. His silky strands of hair covered Raina's hands, leaving the section that was braided flopping alongside his neck.

Raina didn't speak until they reached the intersection where Highway B and Highway C met. Gently, she pulled on the reins to let Stargazer know to go to the right.

"Are you all right, Raina?" Josiah asked, still sensing her abnormal mood.

"Not you, too?" she asked annoyed.

"No, I do not doubt your decision to ride. It is just ... that you are so quiet."

"There is nothing wrong. When I ride, I like to get lost in my thoughts. It's a great way to think through things more clearly. I believe I did better on tests in high school when I rode in the morning before school."

"You know, your father is really concerned about your health?"

"Yeah, I know. It's the doctor in him. He can't help it. It's just that I don't want to hear it. All of these years they never cared about the dreams, then, let one doctor suggest I have gone psychotic, and everyone worries. I'm not that fragile, and I'm not making things up. I don't know why I was unconscious for so long. I just know what I dreamt about when I was in the hospital."

"You had us all worried, Raina. If that nurse had not have found your parents in time, they were going to give you a lobotomy."

"That would have certainly messed up my hairdo a little, wouldn't it?" She laughed, soon realizing that Josiah was not amused.

"Yes, just a little. However, it would not change your looks. You would still be beautiful with a ten inch scar running across your cheek, with your eyeballs gouged out and no nose upon your face."

"Stop that." Raina laughed again, ignoring Josiah's demeanor. "You'd think differently if I really looked like that."

"No, I would not. Beauty is internal. What is inside of a person is what truly matters the most. What you think ... and how you feel."

"Well, from the sounds of the procedure, there would have been none of that left of me either."

Raina shuddered at the thought of being mindless and trapped in the dream she fought so hard to free herself from living through. She was sure that after a while, her great-grandfather would stop coming to aid her, and she would be lost in the dark cave forever. And the boy, who resembled her rider in back, would leave as well. Although, there could have been some solace in that. Raina would never have to relieve the memory of seeing her great-grandfather in his coffin.

"So, where are we going?" Josiah inquired, adjusting himself in the saddle.

"Well, not far if you keep that up."

"What do you mean?"

"You keep fidgeting in the saddle."

"Oh, well the saddle is a little hard on the backside."

"Yeah," she said then chuckled. "Let's hope you don't get hemorrhoids.

"What!"

"Relax, I'm just teasing."

"Oh, good."

"You would have to ride longer than what we are today."

Josiah sighed, adding to Raina's satisfaction. "So, where are we going anyway?"

"We're going to Chain O'Lakes State Park."

"Oh."

Raina could hear him moan as he switched positions again to relieve the pressure points forming on his backside.

"Don't worry it's not far from here. Actually, we're almost there now. It's just past the top of the hill. Do you see the prairie over there?" She asked, nodding her head forward.

"Yes."

"Well, that's part of the park. We'll be near there shortly."

"Do you ride there often?"

"As much as I can. In the summer when the stable is open, you get a lot of amateurs with the rental groups. They are somewhat difficult to work around on the trails. So, I find it best to ride there in the off-season."

"What do you mean by difficult to work around?"

"You see, when people rent from the stable they go out in large groups. They take up most of the trail. I like to get Stargazer up to a good speed. When there are many riders, it's too hard then. Besides, sometimes the new riders get nervous when people not in their group try to pass. So, I just like to avoid it all together. Anyway, it is just like cruising in your car. It's cool to have the open road ... path all to myself."

Just as Raina promised, the entrance came up quickly. She nodded as they passed the security gate and then headed deep into the park. Within minutes, Stargazer trotted along a well-worn path.

The tall grass blew in the wind as the morning sun began to beat down on them. Josiah took notice of the variety of birds that flew overhead. Their chirps and squawks faded in and out the closer they neared the tree line. Off to his right, Josiah saw a few deer scurry down an opposite path. He admired their grace as they took off running. Josiah must have verbalized how intrigued he was, because Raina broke her silence.

"So, do you like this?"

"Yes, it is very beautiful here."

"Good, I am glad that you like it, then." Raina seemed pleased with his fascination of their surroundings. She became more relaxed herself, changing her posture to a more comfortable one.

"It is getting warm now," Josiah noted.

"I know. We'll be to a cooler path in a moment. There are more trees over that way. It's not as open as it is now."

As Stargazer quickened his pace to jump the log blocking the new path's opening, Josiah lost his grip. Immediately Raina turned around feeling his tug at her shirt, just in time to watch him fall off. The loud thud rattled through Josiah's shell as he hit the ground hard. He saw stars, and his vision went dark when he banged his head on a rock. His shell became dizzy, and then Josiah began to lose consciousness.

"Josiah!" Raina screamed, as she pulled on the reins to turn her horse around. "Josiah ... Josiah!" she called out again, as she quickly jumped off Stargazer, and knelt down beside Josiah's limp body.

Barely conscious, he moaned trying to catch his bearings. The last time his shell ever suffered an injury was the day of the barn fire. Now, this sickened feeling inside of his gut reminded him of the moments just before he would find himself in the cave.

"Ouch!" he moaned again, grabbing the back of his head.

"Josiah, are you all right?"

"Oh," he mumbled, trying to roll onto his side.

"No, wait—don't move. You hit your head pretty hard. Are you okay?"

As she waited for his response, the memory of a dream Raina once had flashed into her mind. The steam and smoke filled the air, enhancing the Demon's stench. The boy resembling Josiah stood poised and ready to react. Raina noticed how he held his hands in a peculiar way. He seemed to move like a conductor directing his orchestra, and the dancing pebbles on the ground were his audience. The Demon lunged forward jabbing his sword into Josiah's side. A beam of light flared from the wound, illuminating his appearance. The impact stunned Josiah, knocking him off-balance. His body shook as the poison seared through the wound fiercely attacking his essence. Josiah fell hard to the ground screaming and thrashing in horrific pain. Raina screamed at Josiah's state feeling her heart ripped in two.

"Ugh! I think I just died," Josiah said, breaking into Raina's thoughts.

"No, I have seen that before ..."

Josiah opened his eyes. "What did you just say?"

Raina rocked back onto her heels to lean away from Josiah, grasping her mouth.

"Raina, what is it?"

She looked away and whispered, "Nothing."

"Raina, you are as white as ghost. What is wrong?"

"I said nothing—okay!"

"Raina—"

"Just forget it, okay," she said angrily.

Josiah rubbed his head some more. He felt the warm sticky goo accumulating on the back of his neck. He brought his hand in front of his face to exam the wetness.

"Josiah, you're bleeding!"

His words sounded garbled as he tried to sit up. "I ... am ... all right." It was more important now than ever to concentrate on assessing his shell's condition.

"Maybe you should lay still. I'll ride to the ranger's station for help."

"No, just wait. I ... I think that there are bugs crawling on me. Ouch ... ouch! I know they are. Help me up, please?"

Raina stood up, struggling to help Josiah to his feet. He swayed still dizzy making it all the harder for Raina to help him.

"Hey ... ouch! Something is biting me."

"They're ants, Josiah," she said, brushing them off his shirt.

"Ow! That stings ... yikes get them off me," he cried again, now swatting at his clothes.

"Hold still, I'm trying," Raina said.

"I cannot. They are down my shirt. Man—get them off me! They are biting my back."

"I'm trying. Quit moving. You're not helping jumping round like this."

"They sting really badly," he said, still swatting at his shirt.

"I know. Try to take your shirt off. I can shake them out and brush them off your back."

Josiah fumbled with the buttons on his shirt. They were difficult to unfasten with all of his moving around. He kept trying to swat at his body while tearing at the buttons.

"Here—let me help." Raina knocked his hands away and moved down the row with precision. In her haste, she tried to rip his shirt off his shoulders throwing Josiah off-balance. He swayed to the right slightly and then lost his stance falling forward into Raina's arms.

When his eyes met hers, they both froze. The ant bites and the gash on his head no longer mattered at this moment. His stare wasn't broken, even as a group of red ants crawled down his chest. This is where he was always meant to be—locked tightly in the arms of the only soul that could ever keep him on Earth. The starry night on her patio long ago proved this to him. In the shadows of Callisto, Josiah promised himself he would never live a life without her. If her body could survive, then he would take her there for all eternity. Yet, knowing the impossibility of this, he vowed to shed his existence and remain on Earth with her.

Raina was able to break the connection temporarily, at the sight of the ants crawling on Josiah's chest. She took her right hand and brushed off his chest, stopping just even with his breastbone. She glanced up again meeting his eyes once more. The look was so familiar. The shape of his cheeks, and the dark curl that lay across his brow couldn't be mistaken. This was the face from her dreams. Not from the musty dark cave, but the boy who sat next to her as she played their love song.

"Raina?" Josiah reached up and touched her chin. "Are you all right?"

She blinked gathering her thoughts. "Yes," she said in a low voice.

Josiah became distracted feeling a stinging sensation across his stomach again. He looked down to see more of the red devils biting him. He hurriedly brushed them off his stomach, removing his shirt the rest of the way. "Get off me," he moaned.

Raina took his shirt from him shaking it in the wind. "Are you sure that you're all right?"

"Yes, do not worry. Let us just get out of here, okay?"

"Sure." She nodded, and then handed him back his shirt.

Raina walked back to Stargazer. She didn't realize her hand was shaking until she reached to grab his halter. Her knees grew weak, and she leaned against the horse for support. Tears began to trickle from her eyes, and she tried to wipe them away without Josiah seeing. She knew it was a lost cause when she felt his hand on her shoulder. Raina turned around to face him, throwing her body into his chest and began to sob harder.

"Hey, hey now ... it is okay. I am the one who is hurt here."

Raina didn't answer him; she just closed her eyes and drew in a deep breath.

Josiah felt his heart melt and he pulled her into his embrace. He longed to hold her for so many years, but not like this.

"What is wrong?" he whispered, tenderly into her ear. He loosened his embrace moving his hand to caress her back. "Raina ... you can tell me. I want to help you."

"This is silly," she said, pulling herself free from his embrace. Raina shook her head and then turned to climb up onto Stargazer.

Josiah finished buttoning his shirt, quietly watching the troubled Raina sitting very still like a statue of a goddess. He rubbed his throbbing head once more, wiping the blood on his jeans. Then he climbed up behind her onto Stargazer, trying to adjust his position discreetly.

"Maybe you should hang on tighter this time?" she instructed.

Josiah mumbled something under his breath, and then placed his arms around her. She felt him lean closer into her, and she quivered drawing in another deep breath. The sensation of his body against hers felt oddly comforting in a strange familiar way. Josiah, also, felt her tremble, answering her body's impulses with his own.

"How is your head?"

"It stings a bit."

"Is it still bleeding?"

He reached back and touched his skull again. The moistness confirmed her question as he let out a moan.

"Are you still dizzy?"

"No, I am better now. Are you okay?"

"Yes," she mumbled, into the wind. "Sorry about that. I don't know what got into me."

"Believe me, I felt like crying, too." He laughed, regretting how the movement hurt his head.

"We'll be home soon and then we will get your head cleaned up."

"Actually, I am fine. Please, I would like to ride some more, that is, if you want to."

"Josiah, we should really get you home. You could be hurt bad."

"Do not worry about me. I like this."

"Are you sure?"

Josiah reached back round to check the gash on his head. It had seemingly stopped bleeding for the time being. "Yes. My head is not bleeding anymore."

Their short ride had blended into an a few hours, much longer than Nolan had hoped for Raina to ride. When they arrived back at the stable, it was clear her father was stressed-out with worry.

"How was the ride?"

"It was great, Dad. Man, I love just being on the back of a horse."

"You were gone a long time. Your mother and I were about to go looking for you two."

"Sorry about that," Raina mused, not sure if she really was sorry.

"Where did you ride to?" her father asked.

"Oh, we went up to Chain O' Lakes and rode through the trails. We even caught sight of a few deer."

"So, Josiah, was this your first time on a horse?" Tori asked, in a worried tone.

"Yes, it was, Mrs. Stone."

"Well, did you like it as much as Raina appears to have?" Tori asked.

"The whole thing was amazing. I have never seen such beauty in one place before apart from my home."

"Oh, a city boy," Nolan teased.

"A what?" Josiah questioned.

"Pay him no mind, Josiah. My father is just trying to get a rise out of you."

"All right the both of you. Let's take this to a different level, okay. So, what is the plan now?" Tori asked feeling famished.

"Well, I have to clean Stargazer up and brush him down. Why, are we in a hurry?"

"Kind of, dear. I missed breakfast this morning," Tori informed her. "My stomach is so famished; I think it is eating itself."

"Mom ... and after all the lectures you give me about the most important meal of the day."

"I know ... I know." Tori agreed laughing.

"Okay, I'll hurry, Mom."

When Josiah dismounted the horse, he staggered slightly while trying to keep his balance. He moaned, grabbing his throbbing head. "Ow!"

Tori gasped loudly at the sight of the blood. "What happened to you?"

"Oh, it is nothing. I just slid off the back."

"Slid." Raina giggled. "Crashed is more like it."

"Are you hurt badly?" Nolan questioned, moving to examine Josiah's head. "Man—that's a nasty gash. We need to get it cleaned up right away. You may need stitches."

Josiah moaned again jerking away from Nolan.

"Sorry, Josiah. I didn't mean to hurt you."

"No, it is fine, Mr. Stone. Please, I do not want to go the hospital."

"Well, we'll clean you up. But if you need stitches there is nothing we can do."

"Fine," he groaned. "It is just that I hate needles."

"Well, don't worry about that. You'll never see them coming." Nolan snickered. "Come on, there is a first-aid kit in the barn. Let's get a look at you."

Nolan tugged on Josiah's arm and ushered him to the barn. Josiah sighed in disgust at the sounds of Raina and Tori laughing.

"You think you have it rough, Josiah? Try living with a doctor." Raina called after him, laughing harder.

By the time Nolan had finished scrubbing Josiah's wound and assessing its severity, Raina had Stargazer brushed out and bedded down.

Tori couldn't help but laugh at the sorry state of Josiah. Nolan had him bandaged up like a war hero straight home from the front line. Raina buried her face into Stargazer to hide her smirk. Josiah just stood there trying to be a good sport. It wasn't working.

28.
PUZZLE PIECES

Earth Realm—present-day

The Sun shone brightly, as it should have. Right in the center of it was Josiah, except today, its rays were not as pleasing as usual to him. Today, this Guardian found himself consumed in his memories. Sometimes they were so vivid. The golden curls blowing in the wind. The cobalt-blue eyes gazing so intently upon him and the softness of her body wrapped tenderly in his human arms. Then there was the tingling sensation that encompassed his entire form as he held her in his essence. All of this added to the completeness he felt, as their thoughts became one.

However, these memories had a new edge to them. His beautiful memories of Raina became clouded as an unexplainable force pulled him from his study. It took him to a dark place full of terror that didn't compare to what he found on Deimos. To Josiah his memories of that desolate place were more pleasant than the dark cave that held him at bay. At least on Deimos he felt a few strands of hope. A hope that couldn't possibly exist on the barren planet, but a hope he knew was true. In the damp darkness that tormented his Raina, he found no hope for peace.

The look in her eyes pained him. He could feel her confusion and her doubt. How could he make her see? How could he be sure that she truly understood who he was and who he will be? His human heart burned intensely, sending flames of fire through his body. This brought a scorching lump to his throat, drawing the lump deeper, until he could no longer breathe.

Raina sensed his uneasiness with the situation. She knew something was wrong. She felt a fear in the pit of her stomach that begged for her attention. It was a fear from a lifetime ago gnawing at her memory. Its tumultuous force pushed her buried memories to the surface. They were memories that she passed off as dreams not knowing they were factual points in time.

"I feel like I have seen you before. That I knew you ... from some other time in my life. Who are you, Josiah? Where did you come from? I just know that I have met you before."

Josiah stood silent, examining the dilating pupils in her blue eyes. Somewhere in the dilation, the truth was surfacing. A truth he wasn't permitted to tell. A truth that screamed to be known.

His mind raced with human desires and loyalty to his Guardian world. Josiah faced this dilemma once before, many years ago, in a lifetime now foreign to his Raina. In his fear of losing her, he exposed his identity and his earthy secrets. This time nothing would be gained from exposure and everything could be lost. Lies were not part of his genetic makeup, except, this time, denial wouldn't cover his carelessness or strengthen his torn heart.

"Raina, I think it is your subconscious that is grateful for my father's actions that calls my presence to your mind. We did not attend the same school, so you could not have known me then."

"No, it isn't gratefulness at all. This all seems so familiar," she insisted perplexed. "I feel so comfortable to be around you. It's as if we are meant to be together. Like we are joined into one. I feel like my life is a big jigsaw puzzle and you're the final puzzle piece that makes me complete. It just seems too real to be my imagination. I even see you in my dreams, and there you're my hero."

He began to feel uncomfortable with the issue brewing between the two of them. "I am no one special."

"Don't say that. Every human being is special. Please don't forget that."

"I will not," he said softly, "I promise you this."

Raina turned her head away; his vision was almost too much to look at. He seemed much too real to her to be just an attraction in a dream. Their movements, their commonalities, were too great to be coincidence. She had to know more, so she pressed for the answers Josiah swore were not there. Answers Raina believed he was hiding from her for some unknown reason.

"I find it impossible that there isn't a connection between us, Josiah. We fit together better than puzzle pieces. We like the same songs and the same movies. You seem to know what I'm thinking or what moves I plan to make. It's almost as if we were destined to be together. Like soul mates."

The lump in his throat enlarged. With Raina, it was always suppose to be the truth.

"I fear I will drift away in the darkness; only you can bring the light," Raina mumbled softly.

"What did you say?"

"I'm not sure. It is a poem that I must have read from somewhere. It is rather pretty, except I don't know why or how I know it."

"Raina, it sounds beautiful. Will you finish it?"

"I'll try." She closed her eyes trying to concentrate. "I fear I will drift away in the darkness, only you can bring the light. I see you in the stars, your eyes shining bright. I feel you in the wind, your essence is near. I knew you before, it is all quite clear.

"I felt your breath; I have heard your sigh. Tell me the truth, from loneliness did I die? I know you are there, from me you cannot hide. I can feel your presence, your essence, and my soul are tied.

"It is all too familiar, the things I know. I can't hold out any longer, you are all I was meant to hold. Don't turn away from me; I must feel your caress. You complete my life, my soul, and all the rest.

"Your kiss still lingers on my lips, your hands upon my face. Your arms secured around my waist, hold me tightly in your embrace. My mind is never clear when you are gone; my heart, it fails to beat. I can't stand the emptiness when we are apart, I lay my dreams at your feet.

"Are you here with me forever now, within these castle walls to stay? Has Heaven answered my prayers, or will you leave me again, one day? Believe what you may, or call it what you must. I know what brings us together is fate; in this I put my trust.

"Like a flower that withers away, without you, nothing is right. Light the torches to point the way, our love is worth the fight. The realms of Heaven and its majestic Angels proclaim. He has made us one in unity, in His holiness God reigns."

Raina opened her eyes to find Josiah staring at her. The look of shock spread over his face, and Josiah's eyes were wide and dark from his enlarged pupils.

"Are you okay?" Raina asked, focusing on his trembling lips.

"Yes," he offered, much too quickly. His voice squeaked, and he sucked in a ragged breath.

"Are you sure?" she questioned again nervously.

Josiah forced a smile, trying to pretend nothing was wrong. She couldn't know the truth behind the poem. Her beautiful thoughts in another lifetime penned the lovely words. Words that were never truer than they were now.

"Puzzle pieces," Tarik murmured to himself, watching Josiah and Raina interact on her sun porch. "The realms of Heaven and its majestic Angels proclaim—how disgusting!"

"I missed that, Tarik. What were you saying just now?" Toah asked him as he entered the large chamber.

"Nothing important, Master. I was just about to toy with my little mouse. Although her frame of mind disgusts me her words do have a certain effect on the Chosen One."

"How so, Tarik? Please enlighten me."

"Master, her words hold a certain infatuation for him. His mind becomes obsessed by the prattle that flows from her mouth, and he lets his guard down. The words are weakness that I use against him for my benefit."

"That is very cleaver. However, remember he is not to survive the next phase of our plan. I want to be assured of his death," Toah instructed, reminding Tarik that he was still in charge.

"Do not worry, Master. He will not survive, and you shall have all you desire."

"Tell me, Tarik. What is your next point of attack?"

Tarik laughed demonstrating the pride he believed he didn't have. "Her night terrors have grown increasing worse. The Chosen One is so caught-up in her feelings that he does not see the warning signs." Tarik laughed again, more wickedly than before. "Although Anani paid him a visit and brought him to the hospital where Raina was, she was unsuccessful at revealing the secret of how to enter Raina's dreams. My realm is still safe from his essence."

"Where is she now?"

"That meddling pest is back on Sol. I felt it unwise to harm her so early in our plan, so I teleported her home and erased her memory of her visit with Josiah and her time spent on Earth. Others would become suspicious if she disappeared now. Josiah has covered his tracks well, and the Council of the Twelve does not know of his visits to Earth. Anani, on the other hand, has been witnessed and her presence there is known."

"Then you are wise for showing some restraint in this matter. How much longer, before you destroy them?"

"As I said, I was just about to toy with my little mouse. She has felt a small reprieve in the last few days. Just long enough for Josiah to let his guard down. I will strike him when he least expects it. The Chosen One has issues with his own mind when I am afflicting her. It is nearing the dark hours in her world and she will have to sleep. Tonight, I will begin a new stage in her dreams. She will face a terror she could never imagine to exist."

"Have you anticipated his response, Tarik?"

"Yes, Master. He is searching for a way into my realm. When the time is right, I will grant it. Of course, Josiah will believe it is of his own accord, and when his confidence becomes misguided—I will strike him down."

29.
WAITING

Earth Realm—dream-state

It was a day unmarked by any Guardian. A day that was too short for humans and a day too long for Josiah to get through. As usual, he sat in the lecture hall, hearing the mundane words of the professor. Josiah wished he could be able to dream of his Raina. Beautiful dreams of course about the tender moments and the happiness of having Raina at his side. Instead, he fought the visions that tried overtaking him by pulling Josiah from the lecture hall.

The night fell quickly, as it had many times before, except tonight, the path didn't start in the lighted clearing. It lay lost in the dark canyon, too deep into the rock formations to be seen by the road.

Josiah could make out the faint image of a small figure. He knew without a doubt that it was Raina. He began to run in his human form trying to catch up to her. The uneven terrain and deeply burled ruts in the ground hindered his movements. Josiah tried to ignore them because in actuality, they shouldn't affect him at all.

The coldness burned Raina's face as each exhale of air formed a cloud of fog in the chilly air. There was no sense in her running this time. The Tracker had found her. Before her stood the cloaked Demon ... tasting her fear with his slithering tongue. He grunted at his victory, raising his hand to her face. Then sliding his scaly fingers along her cheekbone, he brought his fingers to his mouth tasting the salt from her sweat.

Raina closed her eyes. She didn't like him touching her. His vile hands made her feel dirty. She pulled her head away slightly knowing there was no place to go. He would take her now—she prayed it would be quick. Death always hovered in her dreams, and this time it was more of a reality than ever before. Raina opened her eyes and stared intently at him. As if she could somehow absorb a bit of comfort from the moment, she cried out for deliverance from the pending death. Her body seized from the fear and she screamed waiting to feel the cold death swarm over her. Instead, she felt a comforting warmth as a low and even tone pulled her from the grip of her demon.

"Raina...."

The impulsive jerk of her body woke her. The startled expression of Josiah's face met Raina's stare. Confusion clouded his Guardian mind, just as easily as it had his human mind. He was with her in this dream. It was not her dream or his ... it was theirs. Josiah forced himself to concentrate knowing that she needed him. The mystery surrounding the vision, he felt for sure was real, would have to be investigated later. Right now, the only thing that mattered was the woman he loved, and he couldn't tell her.

"Are you okay? You were dreaming," Josiah asked, tenderly in a low voice.

"Yes," she said unconvincingly, brushing her hair away from her face. Raina stretched out her arms wiggling her fingers. She had fallen asleep watching the movie with her head propped against her hand and now her hand felt numb. "I'm sorry. I have made a spectacle of myself again."

"Raina, tell me why would you say that?"

"Because it's true—and you know it. Face it, Josiah, you have befriended a freak."

"You are wrong. You are not a freak, Raina."

"No—then what am I. I'm certainly not normal."

"Raina, what is going on here?"

"Nothing," she said sharply.

"I wish it was nothing. Please, do not talk about yourself like that."

"Why not, Josiah? It is true. Who else do you know ends up in the hospital with night terrors from an unexplainable brain condition?"

"That is irrelevant and you know it."

"Is it ... and do I?"

"Yes, it is."

"Josiah, I don't know why I dream the way I do. All my life there was always something that stuck out, something that held me in my dreams. When I was a child, there was always music blowing in the wind and the flowers dancing to its harmony. Even the crackling thunder seemed to play as an accompaniment to Mother Nature's melody.

"But when I got older, my dreams took on a new edge. They appeared to move at a faster pace, never seeming to be real, but not fake enough to forget when I awake in the morning." Raina let a soft sigh escape as she closed her eyes finding the strength to open her heart to Josiah.

"Some of the dreams frightened me. At first, I never saw what it was except a black hovering mass that used to chase me in my dreams. As I grew, the mass took on more of a figure; it looked like a hooded scaly creature whose breath smelled like rotting meat. I used to be able to out run it, but I became too slow, or it got faster. Now it nearly catches me every night. I hate to fall asleep, and I do anything I can to stay awake.

"Lately, the dream goes dark and I seem to wake up, except I'm not in my bed. I'm in a cold, musty cave. I hear a wicked laugh that vibrates inside my body making my skin crawl."

Josiah could feel Raina's body become tense. He knew it was because she was thinking about her nightmares. He also felt the chill that crept down her spine, stealing her words from her. The encouraging smile from Josiah pushed her to continue.

"Then all of a sudden, someone comes to my rescue. I can hear his voice and it sounds so sweet, so delicate like a song in itself. When the hero turns his body to face me, it is always you or my grandfather standing there. Before either one of you reaches me, I disappear. I hate these nightmares, and I just want them to stop."

"Come here." Josiah pulled her close, burying her chin into his shoulder. Her warm body tempted him to tell her, but obligation fastened his lips securely. "Please, do not dwell on the dreams. They are just dreams. Whatever is bothering you and causing them, we will figure it out and stop the dreams. I promise ... I am here for you."

Raina sighed. "I feel so safe when you're here. Please, stay with me until I fall back to sleep?"

Josiah nodded, vowing to stay with her, as a huge smile formed upon his lips. Then he leaned forward and pulled the throw pillow out from behind him. He placed it onto his lap then reaching for the remote, he clicked the black button turning off the television.

"Sleep now."

Raina said nothing to him as she unfolded the comforter from the back of the couch. She lay her head down on the pillow closing her eyes. Josiah tucked the blanket around her shoulders holding his torso perfectly still. Within minutes, her respiration slowed loosening her tensed muscles.

Hesitantly, Josiah lifted his hand to caress her forehead. He knew he shouldn't touch her; the Science Center was proof that he had trouble containing his essence when they touched, but the desire became too intense to ignore. The flawless completion of her youth was still as lovely and the fine out-line of her lips formed a soft smile. His fingers lingered over her cheek as he concentrated.

"I can do this," he whispered to himself. Then slowly he lowered his hand resting it on her forehead. He sighed feeling his essence begin to soothe her anxieties, allowing her to completely relax and drift off to sleep.

Hours passed slowly measured by Josiah's doubt. The war raging in him fought to consume him at every turn. Here in this life, was his Raina. She became a prayer of his come true ... and yet she wasn't his. She was not even whole and happy as the Sentinel promised. Sure, her parents were alive in the new life the Sentinel gave her, but she wasn't the same.

The nightmares marred her life. If his Guardian mind could feel the fear and anxieties, then how much stronger were they for her? Josiah knew of the mysteries of Earth and of Heaven. Raina was blind to them and her mind easily corrupted. To allow her to continue in this path of panic-stricken existence proved that the evil prevailed.

How could the infant who called to him that spring morning, end up in such a sorry state? She deserved more and all it seemed like to Josiah was that he just gave her pain. He broke the rules out of uncontrollable human urges. Yet, the essence of the Sentinel buried deep inside of her soul called to him. Was his love truly meant to be, or was she now suffering for his weakness and failures? Had he left Raina at his father's urging, her life would have continued forward happily with her mother. Yes, Raina was content with having one parent and a life before her sixteenth birthday.

Josiah moaned, cringing at the uncertainty of the moment. He loved her more than life itself. He needed her to fill the void her absence left. He needed her to heal his broken heart and give him the will to continue. And Raina ... needed him.

Tonight had proved that his desires and her dreams were linked beyond what he had believed was ever possible. Somehow, he found her in the wretched dream and pulled Raina from it before death took her. If he stayed with her, he could chase the dreams away forever. He sensed she knew this, too, even if her mind had not confirmed it.

However, did she still love him, or would he impose something so foreign upon her that Raina would never mentally recover. Perhaps he imagined her delicate touches and glassy stares. Raina was always very friendly and compassionate. Was Josiah fooling himself, and there was nothing there at all, or did she feel it, too?

He watched her breathing, feeling each breath of air pass through her lungs. Josiah counted the beats of her heart comparing them against the ones from his fabricated organ. As perfect as the simulation was ... it wasn't real. His body was not real, and neither was the boy who held the sleeping beauty.

Yet, how could he deny what he felt ... what they had before? If there was any chance of resurrecting the emotions that surfaced so uncontrollably three years ago, were they not owed this opportunity? Josiah closed his eyes imagining himself soaring through space looking for Raina. The planets and satellites were just blurry images lost in the darkness of space. Then hovering above the Earth, he found Raina in her dreams. She lay next to a stream in a beautiful garden on Callisto. The water flowed, singing their favorite song, as the soft rustling of the nearby flowers added to the serenity. The smile she wore and the glimmer in her eyes was from a time long ago.

"Josiah," she said softly, welcoming him to join her.

She patted the ground next to her where he was to sit. He complied, eager to be near her. The blossoming flowers smelled sweet, but not as sweet as the floral fragrance of her hair.

"This place is so beautiful."

"I know. I have never seen a place such as this. Do you come here often, Raina?"

"No. I found this place just today. The song of the birds attracted me. I saw them flying gallantly over the sunflowers. The roses seemed to dance with the beat of their flapping wings."

"I hear the rippling brook; it plays a song that I love to listen to."

"Yes, I hear it, too. What is it called, Josiah?"

"I am not sure. It sounds too magnificent for words to describe. This whole place is beyond anything I imagined possible."

"I know, I thought the same thing. There is nothing more perfect than this place is right now."

"You are wrong. I know of one thing that is more perfect than this place here," he whispered, and then slowly Josiah leaned in to kiss her.

This moment in the dream world wouldn't give Josiah what he desired in reality. He needed her ... really needed her. He knew when she awoke from this dream, where his real fate would lie. Raina was truly not his. She indeed lived a new life nonexistent of the seventeen human years that were branded into Josiah's mind. Both parents were alive, and she was an adult.

He held an attraction for Raina that she didn't seem to share anymore. In the real world, he and Raina had become friends, but her heart had not chosen him this time. Because of that, he would once again feel the loneliness of a life without her, life without the only soul he would ever love.

He had an obligation to his people, one that he avoided since he found Raina last winter. His brief appearances at council meetings began to raise questions. Surprisingly, Brielle became supportive of Josiah's actions. She was very good at making excuses for him, and she became a messenger delivering important news to Josiah when he was on Earth. His charade cost those around him much ... It needed to end.

30.
THE REUNION

Guardian Real—present-day

Benn found himself at home in the mystical garden. He lay his celestial body on the stone bench watching his *dreams* dance in the blue waters of the enormous fountain. He came here often to visit this serine place. Here, he could think clearly and understand what path he was to choose to walk. It was yesterday by Earth's normal rotation, when he came across the beautiful baby he found in his future. Her delicate auburn eyes told a story only he could decipher.

Benn didn't make his decision at that moment. The options were limited and he honored greatly his people's long-established cultures. To change the future and the past was punishable forever in the Deimos Universe. Benn shuddered at the thought of losing his essence and floating away into nothingness. What a horrid outcome to a humanly necessary mission.

Benn picked another rose from the Garden of Love. The very sensation of this rose in his hand made him tingle. Its impression was now magnified from the day before.

He whispered softly, to the strong Elder beside him, "I will protect her ... I promise."

"I know that you will. I have faith in your actions."

"I wish I had faith in myself. Lexis trusted me once and I let him down. If I had not been so weak ... we would not be here now."

"My sister will be safe because of you, Benn. What you are about to do will change everything that went wrong in my realm. My mother will not live ridden with the human guilt that drove her away from us. She pretended to be with us, except her mind was always somewhere else. She was always looking for her in the laughter of a human child. It has nearly destroyed me.

"And to think I had the answer with me the whole time. It sang from the Stone of Fayruz and I never understood its meaning, that is, until I saw you." Torrey grinned, trying to remain strong. "For that I cannot offer you enough of my gratitude. No words in the human or Guardian language can express this to you. The choice you are making now can never be undone, no matter what dreams or wishes a Guardian has. So, please, do not be so hard on yourself. You have done well thus far."

"Have I, Elder? You forget what my absence cost my Esprit de corps. What my lack of regard cost an innocent human."

"You mean what it cost the soul you hold dear to your essence. Benn, I knew from the moment the secrets of the stones were revealed to me, what choice I must make. It was perfectly clear that you were the one I needed to seek for help."

Benn nodded, fighting back the painful memories of his failures.

"You cannot blame the tragedy on yourself, Benn."

"Yes, Elder, I can, and I should. Had I been stronger, I would have stayed by his side. Instead, in a human rant I allowed jealousy to guide me and anger ... to overtake me and consume who I am."

"Trust yourself, Benn. You know it was not anger. You did what you should have. Even now as we make new choices, your strength from the past will overflow into the new path we are creating. The choices of old will hold no meaning now. We will no longer be bound by them."

"You are wrong, Torrey. They will always bind me. If I did what I should have—that vile Markian would not have won. Mataya's mind would be sound, and Raina would not be taunted by the evil."

"Son, Markian did not win. He is in Deimos serving his punishment."

"Yes ... I know. I will be reminded of his eternal damnation when I look him in the eyes."

"Benn—you knew your actions were questionable, and you responded the only way you possibly could. Your decision was correct."

"No ... you are wrong, Elder. If I would have been obedient ... been more faithful." Benn closed his eyes, recalling Tori's horrid screams. "If I was honorable, I would not have fallen in love with her. I would not have manipulated the situations, and I most certainly would have been at Nolan's side protecting them from the crash. That is where I needed to be—not held off in another universe, consumed by human self-pity. If I would have done my job by scanning the future and seen Markian's intent, we would not be dealing with this whole situation. So, doing well and doing what it is right are two different matters, Elder."

"Yes, you are correct, except you have brought together the most troublesome situations."

"They are troublesome only because I have brought them upon myself. If Nolan had lived through the car crash and Markian had not found them that day, then Josiah would be happy. We would not be contemplating our actions now. There are many Guardians who have suffered because of my lack of discretion."

"Benn, that is why we are here. This is why I sought you out. Any errors made in the past will be corrected by the future. I have told you, all things will be made right." Torrey's face lost its color as he spoke his next words. "The only one who will know the consequences is Nolan. However, his soul is safe. He walks the golden streets in song. I know this to be true, for I have seen him. His life was never meant to be on Earth. You changed that when you found his mother in labor. To heal them when they were not your assigned Esprit de corps had its consequences. Your self-proclaimed actions are what drove you to love Tori. This time, your decision will be different. You will make this right with your actions. Of this, I am certain."

"What made you so sure that I was the one, Torrey?"

"I saw you in the eyes of the child. I did not know it was you because we had not yet met. When I saw you in this garden, I realized there was a familiarity about you. The look in your eyes and the way she portrayed you in her memories held a very significant meaning." Torrey chuckled, wanting to put Benn at ease. "In the beginning, I did not understand why I saw you in her memories. I could not identify you in the midst of it all, or how your meeting with her could have been theoretically so. For you guarded the human Nolan, nonetheless, in her eyes you were clearly there. I pondered the memories she showed me and found them to be too complex for my understanding. All I had were her words of instruction to act upon."

Benn looked away from him to stare at the rose in his hand. Life seemed so much simpler to this Guardian before human love touched his essence.

Torrey continued, affirming he still had Benn's attention. "When I concentrated on them, her angelic words brought to my mind a theory. She told me she had been to the future and lived in the past. It was obvious she was talking about being conscious of Mataya's delusions. The child had literally been in both the future and the past, as Mataya pulled her through the realms."

Benn interrupted him callously. "You should have brought this to an end, Torrey. We should have stopped Mataya before she allowed Isaiah to marry Rebekah. It is against the Creator's plan to have underdeveloped essences dwelling in humans. Tori and her child would then be completely human. The repulsive Demon would have nothing to attack."

"Do not dwell on the past, Benn. We must accept that there are things we cannot change unless we act now. You knew Markian and Dinah were close destroying the vessel. Your essence called to the entity to prepare the human body for her birth. And you know that no one can control the motives of Mataya or the actions of her Secret Council."

"Yes, I may have alerted the entity, although, because I did not control myself, I made the situation worse. What Tori suffered to bring about the child was incredible. I cannot stop blaming myself for knowing what pain she endured. Watching Nolan die before her eyes must have been very traumatic. Nolan should not have died—he did not have too. I failed to protect my Esprit de corps. I am the reason the human Raina suffers so now."

"Benn, as I have said, do not blame yourself. We will make this work for the better of all who are involved."

"Then who is to blame, if it is not I?"

"You cannot look at it like this. You arrived in time to save the Sentinel. Your warning prepared the entity for the coming attack. The Sentinel fought Markian from within the womb and the vessel survived."

"Just barely and for what cause, Torrey? My selfishness could have cost them all their lives. Even though Raina survived that initial day, she was destined to suffer much because of me and my foolishness."

"Benn, you are not foolish and your selfishness cost no one. When the human Tori was near death, you followed the correct path, and helped the Sentinel call to Josiah to take your place as Watcher. You completed your mission and that is what truly matters. The future holds many new opportunities for you this time."

"You are doing it again, Elder."

Elder Torrey let a soft grin grow across his lips. "Yes, I suppose I am. I want you to know that I understand what you face. The sacrifice you will make is beyond any reasonable request. I do not forget that you make this choice for me as well."

"No, Elder ... it is not unreasonable. I love her ... I always have." He caressed the rose gently, in his hand. The aroma saturated the air around him. Its fragrance reminded him so much of her.

"I know, Benn ... it is evident in your actions. When the Creator changed Tori's course to restore all that was lost, I saw the look in your eyes. I did not know then why it was there or what the look meant for you. However, now I know that the thought of watching her again in another lifetime committed to Nolan and not you ... has been extremely difficult."

Benn glanced down at the purple rose he twirled between his fingers. The breeze blew through the courtyard, carrying the fallen petals across the grass. "Have you concluded your business, Elder?"

"Do not fear. I have been to the brook. All is well. We may proceed as decided without risk of our discovery."

"Yes, but what about the issue at hand on Prometheus, Elder?"

"Yes ... I visited them discreetly. I emulated another's appearance. I think you would be proud. I left the Councilman and the Great Elder a little startled."

Benn let out a nervous laugh. No simulated or true human emotions could comfort him now. "Do they know who you are?"

"Relax, Benn. I have kept the secret. They just heard my warning. My mind remained closed to the Great Elder. It is indeed a blessing for us. Just think about it. A genetic trait born only of twins can serve an even greater need than to maintain one's sanity. No one can read the mind of a Great Elder except another Great Elder. Nevertheless, the other mind must be willing. And mine, young Benn, was not."

"I bet that did not sit too well with her when she realized your mind remained dim to her?"

"Ahh, Yakira. Yes, she plays a good hand. I did not see any concern in her eyes. She covered her failure of not being able to read my mind perfectly. Although, young Jaleel is another matter that we need to be concerned for."

"What do you mean, Torrey?"

"He is very protective of her. It is a shame, really. All of that love wasted on a relationship which should not be."

"Excuse me, Elder Torrey, am I not acting upon a relationship that should not be? Are not my actions in this matter risky as well?"

"Yes, you are acting above the commandments, and the risk is great, except you, my young Guardian, have a worthy cause."

"Tell me what makes my actions worthy in your eyes and not theirs, Elder?"

"Because, Benn, you will risk your life to see your love through. That is not a commitment the two of them have made."

"Do you believe they will continue as we have planned?"

"Yes, I do, Benn. I know that Yakira is baffled as to how I came to be. I felt her essence testing mine with no prevail. Despite her outward appearance, I left the poor Elder quite nervous. That is of course, if she understands human emotions. Jaleel is a good friend of Josiah's. I have known this since Josiah's trial. Jaleel will stop at nothing if he believes Josiah's essence is in danger. He will not rest until he knows the Chosen One is safe."

"Are you sure, Elder, we have the right solution ourselves?"

"Yes, I am. Beck knows what lies within the brook, and what the Stones of Fayruz perform. He believes the stones only absorb the tears of the lost replacing the sorrow with joy. Yet, he has no idea what they are actually capable of doing. The stones are able to travel between the realms as they search for their appointed resting place. The one who holds the stone can use it to walk within the realms. That is how I found my way to the Brook of Tears. That is why I went to the brook. I took a stone trading it with the one I carried. This new stone has collected the tears of saddened Guardians, holding the magic of their essences within. You will draw on that power to revive the dead."

"It could fail, you know."

"Benn, you worry too much. You have a mission ... a cause, and that is what you must concentrate on and nothing more. When you have completed your tasks, nothing will come against our people again. You will not fail."

"I understand, Elder." Benn looked off into the distance. "The weather is changing, Elder Torrey. It is almost time for us to begin."

"I will go to Earth with you."

"I do not need your help, Elder."

"Of course not, Benn, allow me please to accompany you anyway. It will be my honor to stand in your presence."

Benn chuckled. "Elder ... I think the honor is mine."

Elder Torrey rested his hand on Benn's shoulder. This day the memories of a burning room would never consume him again. He understood the power of the blue light and the message hidden within the stone.

"On this issue you are wrong, my young friend. I found myself held captive by the fire of ignorance. I dared not to act and allowed the blue light to hold me captive. You, Benn, have allowed nothing to keep you back. It is because of your determination this is possible."

Benn closed his eyes. The moment was powerful. So many emotions whelped up inside of him. Tonight, he was a proud Guardian standing for truth and justice. Tomorrow, he would enter into the life of a fugitive. Much was at stake and the risks were worth it.

He crushed the rose of love he picked from the garden. After molding it in his palm, he opened his fingers, displaying a beautiful gold locket with a stunning rose engraved elegantly upon it.

"Your token of love ... Benn?"

"Yes, Elder. Nolan gave her a similar one many years before. It did not hold the same meaning as this one does to me. He pledged his love until death separated him. I, my brother ... have pledged it for all eternity."

"What you have created is most beautiful. She will adore it, Benn."

"I hope so ... she deserves this."

Torrey reached inside his robe and pulled out a light brown parchment. He unrolled it, reading from the scroll.

"And *he* will come to guide the lost. For the tears runneth over, and the waters grow bleak from sorrow. The dead cry for justice, and the broken hearts for comfort. It is then when the Stones of Fayruz will purify what dwells in the darkness, casting the evil from their path.

"The fire of righteousness will consume the vile remnants of shame and defeat bringing a song of triumph. Its melody sounds, chanting the song of victory. The tears of despair will vanish from their eyes. The dreams, void of all hope, will flourish from the blue power that feeds discouragement, and the torment will be put to ease.

"No man or being will know of anything less than the love that shifted from the brook. And lighting their way through the darkness stands a shimmering sapphire beam. It glows bright into the night as a beacon for peace."

The words gave Benn the encouragement he needed at that moment. Not for his own satisfaction, but confirmation that what he was about to do wouldn't be in vain. Humanity and the lost essences of the Guardians afflicted would prevail.

Torrey rolled the scroll back into its tubular shape and placed it into his robe pocket. Then removing a blue color stone with shades of brown and turquoise blends, he held it out toward Benn. With a grin, Benn took it and placed it on top of the locket. In barely audible words, Torrey spoke a prayer.

Musical notes from the mist drifted from the brook in Beck's realm appearing before them. The mist contained the music of life. A song so in-tuned with the Creator's miracles, no dread or human despair could tarnish the colors. Even in the roughest storms, the rock would stand firm as the foundation of hope and life. For buried deep within the Brook of Tears, this rock absorbed the hatred and failures of many entities. Then the mist swirled around the two Guardians.

"It is time, Benn."

"I know ... we should go," Benn agreed. Then he gently slid the locket into his pocket. He turned to take a step and then hesitated facing the tall admirable Elder. As he spoke, a tear formed in his eye. "I will never see you again—will I?"

Torrey bowed his head in sorrow pulling Benn into his embrace. "No, you will not, my son. I will face any consequences in this realm alone. Once you have reached your destination, do not cross back over no matter what appears to befall me. However, please know that I will always honor the choice you have made. As I have said ... your sacrifice will not be in vain. What you do this day, will not be easy, my son. What is to come will not pass quickly."

Benn sighed. "The first is not the easiest part of my mission. I still have to look her in the eye and tell her what she wants to know."

Elder Torrey grinned. "I envy you, if it is at all possible. You have known human love and felt love's embrace. Oh, how I long to be in your shoes."

"It is remarkable, Elder, indeed. I will not experience anything more powerful than this on Earth," he said lowering his head. "Protecting her will be easy. Leaving her forever now—is the hardest decision I will ever make. Pray that I do not waver when it is time."

"Benn ... you are strong. You will not waver ... of this I know."

"I can see myself considering it. I walked away once knowing I would see her again in Heaven's Court. This time I will not. Day after day, I watched her through Nolan's eyes, loved her with his heart ... and then to realize I loved her myself. She was forbidden then—and now the love I feel for her is still forbidden. To know that at last after all of these years, the void in my heart will be filled— just to have it empty ... it pains me so. I can pull no assurance from the path I am to follow."

"It will not be easy ... but you are strong."

"Perhaps, you have too much confidence in me, Elder?"

"No, Benn ... I do not have enough."

"You fool yourself, Elder."

Torrey laughed. "If I am fooling myself, then knowing you is the greatest most foolish thing I have ever been proud of doing."

"Shall we?"

The guiding leader nodded, and the two of them faded into the clouds as Sol's rays flickered off the gold chain dangling from Benn's pocket.

Benn emerged from the grassy field several blocks from Tori's home. He knew the field well. He watched Nolan play football here many times. Then turning his head to look over his shoulder, he saw the bleachers that wouldn't be constructed for eight more years. There, underneath them, stood Nolan embracing Tori. Benn sighed. He was present that day, silently standing off to the side, absorbing the echoes of their emotions. It was the first time Benn realized he loved her. He had imposed this love upon Nolan, giving him the courage he needed months before to profess his love to Tori. Only, it was not Nolan, who uttered the words of love to Tori, it was his Guardian, singing a song beautifully accompanied by a chorus of Angels.

He put his hand into his pocket and pulled out the Black Hills gold locket. The sunlight reflected off the rose, glaring triumphantly back at him. Today he would confirm what he had known these last twenty-nine human years. He had crossed the line from protector to lover. No suppressed Guardian emotions could dim the burning that incapacitated Benn's Guardian heart for the second time.

He made his plan in the Rose Garden of Love. Each step examined carefully for any flaws. Each possible outcome considered, and the essential ending confirmed. Today he would execute his plan, one made to save humanity. One that only a few Guardians knew about and one Guardian would act on.

This plan wasn't the same as the one he followed before. He had to revise it to make it work. This time, he would merge his essence with the body of Nolan. He knew it would work; he had done it before the day Nolan stood at the altar. Benn had blended his essence with Nolan's body, reciting the wedding vows that weren't his to say.

In another life, he simply saved Nolan's life at birth and guided Nolan making Earth his home and Tori his life. He was to be a Watcher and nothing more, except, something in the eyes of Tori commanded his Guardian heart, and he fell in love with her. In that lifetime, just being near her at first or seeing her in Nolan's thoughts were enough. However, after time, it was no longer enough to watch from afar. His only solace was that he would see her again when the Creator called her home.

Still out of his reach, he would take comfort in being near her for all eternity. Yet ... this time, this new mission didn't end where Lexis left off. Now, Benn would act for the good of his people at the risk of his life force. From this day forward, Benn's essence was to be harbored by Nolan until the day the Creator called Nolan home. At that time ... Benn would face judgment for his unlawful actions.

He looked down at his feet to assure the marker was identifiable, and then he knelt next to a granite rock surrounded by sprigs of blooming flowers. It had been wedged into the earth two hundred years before Silver Lake came to be. With one pass of his hand, the rock levitated. He tore a piece of his robe's hem, and then gently wrapped the gold locket inside of the silk cloth. Carefully placing the cherished bundle securely in the hole, he lowered the stone. Here, the locket would remain safely for sixteen years, until the day he would profess his earthy love for Tori.

Benn strolled up the sidewalk and paused at the sound of an infant's cries. It was the same sound that called to him the day before. He heard many human children cry, but none held the significance that this one had. The melody buried within the cry played a song that captured Benn's essence. He knew a world without this song would become a dark place.

He continued forward, but he didn't enter Tori's home; instead, he materialized into the large three-story home to its right on Lake Street. At the top of the stairs on the second floor, lay a young woman in labor. Her tears were not as joyful as the tears of Tori's mother the day before. For inside the womb of this grieving mother was the still heart of a lifeless fetus.

Her visit to the doctor hours earlier confirmed their suspicions. Early on, this pregnancy developed complications. The woman knew her child wouldn't grow to full term, and she would deliver early. Her doctor tried to convince Lillian to allow him to perform a cesarean section to remove the dead fetus, but Lillian's heart couldn't endure the cold sterile environment of the hospital. Even if no life whelped from inside of her womb, this fetus was still a child. Her son, the one she prayed for many years to bear.

Her husband held her hand with love thick in his touch. He stayed by her side faithfully, feeling her grief. When it was over, he would tell her the dark secret he was hiding. After five miscarriages and now their second stillborn, he took it upon himself to make sure his wife ... that he, never suffered like this again.

"You're doing well, Lillian. I see his head. Just a few more pushes, and we'll be done."

Lillian screamed, her heart searing with pain greater than what her body suffered at this moment. "I'm sorry, Carsten."

He closed his eyes to fight back the tears. "What are you sorry for ... love."

"Because I can never give you what you need."

"You have given me your love. That is enough."

"But—" she winced, as another contraction rippled through her abdomen. "I—can't seem to give you—" Just then, Lillian fainted.

"Is she all right?" Carsten screamed, focusing his attention on the surprised midwife.

She moved to Lillian's side knocking over the small nightstand in the process. As she felt for Lillian's pulse, her eyes widened with relief. Carsten watched intently, sorting through his anxieties.

"It's strong and steady," she said. Then grabbing a blood pressure cuff from off the table, she wrapped it around her bicep. "Yes—her BP is normal; considering she's in labor."

"Then why did she faint, Miranda?"

"Mr. Stone, labor isn't easy. She'll be fine. Now let me help her finish this. The sooner it's over—the sooner she can begin to heal."

Then taking smelling salts from her med kit, Miranda placed it under Lillian's nose. Immediately, she awoke, consciously swatting at the midwife's hand.

"How do you feel, love?"

"I ... I'm fine. Please ... is it over?" she begged, grabbing her forehead. Her sweat felt sticky, matting her hair to her cheek.

"Just another push, dear—and it will be," the midwife spoke with hesitance in her voice. Carsten could see the doubt in Miranda's expression.

Lillian pushed once more with all of her strength, and then she fell back sobbing hard. Carsten touched her forehead tenderly, blinking as tears filled his eyes.

It was over, and the child was delivered. Lillian closed her eyes wanting to forget her pain ... to forget this moment. Then unexpectedly a loud cry jolted through the room. She opened her eyes to see the midwife standing slack-jawed in utter surprise. In her arms, she held the infant boy who was never to be—squirming strong and healthy.

"Oh, my God ... is he...?"

The midwife brought her mouth to smile. "Yes ... he's alive, Lillian ... he's alive!"

"Carsten ... Carsten, do you hear that? Our boy—he is alive! He's alive!" Lillian reached her arms out to take her son. An impossible reunion built of impossible dreams ... forged by a miracle.

31.
LET IT BE SO

Guardian Ream—present-day

Two members of the Council of the Twelve, Brielle and Dasia, had gathered unofficially to address allegations of illegal practices committed by many of its esteemed Guardians. To bring insight into the claim of heresy, these Guardians were summoned to the Great Hall on Sol.

"Guardians," Brielle began with an uneven tone of voice. "You have been called here today informally to be made aware of rumors that have plagued our ears. No one is on trial; we are just merely trying to sort out an apparent confusion of events." She nodded her head towards Dasia, confirming her opportunity to speak.

"The questions," Dasia said, "we will ask today are to be answered, we hope in truth, without the need to turn this into an official setting. Again, as Elder Brielle has pointed out—we seek answers to clarify rumors that are too strong to ignore. First of all," Dasia said suggestively. "It has been brought to our attention that some in this room may have ... shall we say, dabbled in time travel. Is this true?"

No one spoke immediately. Their eyes just darted back and forth from one another.

"Do I need to ask this question again?"

"Elder Dasia," Isaiah said timidly.

She sat straight up in her chair leaning forward. Then motioning slightly with her hand, she gestured to him. "Speak your cause, Isaiah."

"I come not because of your summons, but on behalf of my granddaughter."

"Your granddaughter?" Beck turned to face those present. "You do not have a granddaughter, Isaiah."

"Silence, Advisor," Dasia ordered. "Allow Isaiah to speak."

He looked firmly into Beck's eyes. "Elder, I do have a granddaughter."

Beck interrupted again, ignoring Dasia's order. "Excuse me, Isaiah, for my ignorance; however, you have never bonded. How do you propose to bring about the offspring you claim to be your granddaughter?"

"Isaiah," a voice spoke out from the back of the court chamber. He recognized it to be Guardian Malachi.

Beck could see the same nervousness in Isaiah's eyes that he knew were present in his. Mataya held a good poker face that she credited to her superior mental skills.

"If you are speaking about the human girl named Raina—then do you not remember that the Sentinel redeemed her from the evil's clutches—giving her back the life she lost? True, she has not received the same security in her new life as hoped. Is not that the reason we all agreed with Elder Mataya, forming the Secret Council to assist in her plan of protection? However, this Council has no evidence that any misgiving has befallen her since our efforts began. Where do you acquire the information that has cost all of us our place in the realms of Heaven?"

Isaiah's eyes darted toward Mataya. "They do not know, do they, Elder?"

She looked away condemned. "No, Isaiah. What I charged you and Enoch to complete was my decision and mine alone. Malachi and the rest were kept in the dark just as Beck has been."

Beck shot her a worried look. Her words triggered a memory that he had forgotten.

Isaiah insisted with eagerness. "Please, allow me to continue to state my request. I believe it shall answer your questions completely." Isaiah looked around the room as if he was waiting for the others present to grant their permission for him to speak. It was clear that he had taken all in the room by surprise. Their expressions confirmed their desire to hear what Isaiah was going to say.

"Very well," Brielle allowed, hesitant of what the Guardian's next words would be. "What do you have to request?"

Isaiah stood tall. He knew what he was about to say wouldn't be received well by Beck or anyone else in the chamber. He didn't care; Isaiah needed his cause pled before all, and his desires to come true.

"My granddaughter's new life is in peril. I cannot stand by as commanded and watch her die. After her first death, when her life was restored, she was not the one she was before, and now every Guardian must acknowledge her suffering and rescue her."

"What do you mean by saying that her life is in peril? Who are you talking about?" Elder Brielle asked, trying to hide her own guilt in the matter. Her private compassion for Josiah had put her in a compromising position as well.

Had it not been for Elder Dasia's petty fondness for the Guardian laws, no one would be assembled here today. Daisa began her own mission when she stumbled upon the absences of Elders Torrey and Josiah. It was the Head Elder's demonstration in his Council meetings that first caught her attention. Then when she witnessed Elder Torrey remove him from session, she became suspicious.

Dasia's investigation was directed toward Advisor Beck. He was not as careful as he believed he was being when he traveled from his home to the brook. Although Dasia was never able to accompany him there, and she had no proof of what he was actually doing, it was clear his intentions were not molded after Guardian fashion.

She had witnessed Elder Torrey behaving in the same manner. She secretly followed him for several days, acknowledging his less than exemplary behavior as well. Daisa didn't understand what he was doing in his search for the brook, as the song of the stone in his pocket never sang to her.

It was only a matter of time before she learned that Mataya was walking in forbidden realms—but Dasia had no idea they were created by Mataya. Although time travel is forbidden, Daisa performed her own travels in the name of the law. What she discovered in Earth's past greatly alarmed her. The very thought of a Secret Council acting beneath the law for the benefit of her people was incomprehensible.

Her invitation granted to the Watchers Malachi and Sariel to join her at this meeting was purely voluntary. Daisa couldn't uncover any misgivings on their behalf that were punishable by the laws in her realm.

Dasia had served on the Council of the Twelve for a hundred years. There was only one other time during her servitude that she witnessed the secretive workings of a

Guardian. Two human years ago during Josiah's trial and now today in this room.

"I speak of the human girl, Raina," Isaiah said impatiently.

"That human is of no concern to any Guardian," Elder Dasia interjected. "Her life ended, Isaiah. Surely, you have not forgotten that. Through grace alone, it was given back. Her purpose has been fulfilled, and she is no longer the vessel."

Isaiah barely noticed the Elder's interruption. He continued speaking, for time was of the utmost importance, and there was no need for senseless questions. "... in this new plan she suffers once again. Her second life has not been without trial and dangers. The evil that controlled the ones who opened the Abyss, still lurk in the darkness taking what pleases them. That evil now taunts Raina, and I cannot bear to see this anymore.

"She is not due the darkness that has followed her. I request that she be brought to the plane she walked before Markian and Dinah attacked her. I am asking you to release her and to release Josiah of his word. You must bind the two of them together and end the suffering now. Their cries have reached Heaven, and their tears overflow the brook. You know this, Beck," he said, turning his head quickly to stare into Beck's eyes. "Tell us the truth. Share with this Council the healing waters you have taken charge of."

"Isaiah," Beck spoke sharply, angry at the fact that he had just exposed the brook. He was even angrier with himself for not realizing Isaiah had knowledge of the brook. For the safety of all, no one should know the secret of the Brook of Tears. "She was a human vessel before, and so shall she be now. She is not your granddaughter. That notion is impossible. I know in the dream realm Great

Elder Mataya created, you were instructed to watch over the human girl's descendent. However, that does not give you a birthright claim, Isaiah. Do you forget that?"

"Beck," Brielle interjected again. "You have been instructed to hold your tongue. Now please, do not interrupt again."

"You are incorrect, my friend," Isaiah announced smugly. "She may have housed the Sentinel in the previous life; however, what you do not know is that a new course of action has been completed. Per Elder Mataya's orders, I have bonded with the human Rebekah. My actions have created a new life. Raina's mother bares an essence in her soul. Raina is indeed now a Guardian offspring."

"Mataya," Beck said alarmed, "what is he saying?" Then he recalled her words, that late hour when she came to him in the brook. *"I made a decision concerning the child's welfare and our plan without consulting you."*

Then he knew what had happened in his study that morning when she became rigged, and separated from their conversation. Mataya had drifted between two universes again. In one universe, she acted against his instructions taking matters into her own hands. In the other, she stayed true to the course they had set. Her mind continued to change their plans, always interfering with what Beck needed to happen, and Mataya wanted to happen.

"Mataya, no," he whispered. He had hoped that Isaiah wouldn't confirm his suspicions.

Mataya winced at Isaiah's statement. She hadn't told Beck of the changes in their plans. He was just as stunned to learn them as Dasia and Brielle were.

"What are you speaking of, Isaiah?" Dasia inquired, still alarmed, and quite curious.

Before Isaiah could speak, another voice echoed from the back of the room. Boldly, Benn got up from his chair, looking at the two Council members directly in the eyes. Torrey's warning to never cross over again was ignored.

"It appears that although we are all in this room together, our causes were not the same. Some may have wanted the best for Elder Mateo, the human Raina, and our Head Elder—but clearly there were other motives that drove us to forsake our Guardian ways." He paused, glancing at Elder Torrey who remained hidden in the shadows.

Torrey had used his newly discovered talents for his own protection. Invisible to all of those in the room except Benn, he had bowed his head ashamed. No matter what his intentions were, Torrey was wrong. When the request for his appearance to this meeting arrived, Torrey ignored it. The chance of their arrest was too great and Benn counted on him too much. With the stones, Torrey could maintain some control as Benn walked between the realms of Earth's past and future to secure the body of Nolan. Once it was done, Torrey was sure the other timelines would dissolve, and the course he set would confirm the new beginning. The beginning, he believed was the true course. What Torrey didn't realize, is that Elder Mataya and Advisor Beck, also believed their timeline was the true one. As Isaiah had said, it appeared that their causes were not the same. Each may have wanted the best for the human Raina and their Head Elder, but clearly, there were other motives that drove them to forsake their Guardian ways.

"What do you mean?" Beck shouted, raising his hand as to instruct Elder Brielle to hold her order for his silence.

Benn continued full of confidence. "Forty-five years ago, I saved the life of my Esprit de corps while in his mother's womb. After many years had passed, I fell in love with his mate."

Elders Brielle and Dasia shot him a look of horror. The thought of more Guardians becoming ensnared by human emotions and acting upon them was alarming.

"That is preposterous," Beck interjected, his voice crying out louder than the other Guardians who agreed with him. "You have crossed the line by loving the mate of another."

"Please, allow me to continue, for I have done much more than to love a taken woman. Because I loved Tori, I allowed human emotions to blind my judgment. This cost my Esprit de corps his life. I did not sense Markian's evil intents approaching, and he was victorious." Benn's essence shuddered when he felt the many responses from those in the room. His story was better left untold, except his love had to be known. "The human Raina suffers now as her mind is under attack. I could not stand by any longer and see what resulted from my ignorance. Her mother, Tori, perished unjustly because of my selfishness.

"When I was presented with a way to change my mistakes, I could not ignore the opportunity. While Elder Mataya and yourself, Beck, worked to correct the changes her dreams caused by searching through the parallel realms, I created another timeline."

"What did you do?" Beck shouted, calculating what Benn's actions may have done to his and Mataya's plan.

"Elder, I went back in time, to the day of my Esprit de corps' birth. Instead of just saving Nolan's life in the womb of his mother Lillian, I entered his infant body. My plan allowed me to be raised near Tori in constant vigil."

His efforts stabilized Mataya's wild imagination, and now, Benn's statement proved that her will to hear her brother's thoughts in her mind were stronger than his efforts and sense of duty.

Mataya sighed. "Oh, my." At this moment, Benn's action seemed more dangerous than those her mind created. She realized immediately what Benn had done. Carefully skimming the faces in the room, she waited for their minds to calculate what Benn's actions meant to all of them. "Why?" she whispered amazed.

"I did this so I could watch over Tori, so no evil would find her. While it was your intention, Elder Mataya, to plant the essence of the unnamed entity within Tori's womb to throw off the evil one, I planted the seed of my essence through Nolan. The human child carries my essence and thus, the Guardian gene. I am sure that those present in this room are not clear on your instructions, Mataya."

"What instructions?" Brielle and Beck demanded to know at the same time. Mataya shook her head. Her secret dealings would now be exposed and understood by all in the room. There were no more secrets to be kept, and now her brother's fate once again rested in the hands of the Council.

Benn continued confidently. "Since Mataya encouraged the bonding of Isaiah to the human Rebekah, their offspring who is Raina's mother, also carries a Guardian gene. Tori is part Guardian, and this makes Raina a Guardian as well. Isaiah and I have bore daughters of our essences."

Beck looked around the room at the many faces Mataya had already evaluated in her hidden fear. Shock and disbelief embedded upon their expressions.

"I agree with Benn," Enoch voiced. "Why should Raina suffer twice? Has not the evil come against her before and cried in victory? Tori and Raina are of us. We need to provide for them as we would our own."

Beck's mind raced, sorting through the new information. His actions too, were exposed. He and Mataya would suffer the same fate as Enoch, Isaiah, Benn, and Elder Torrey.

"All right, Enoch," Brielle spoke up. "What will you have this Council do?"

"Save Raina from the evil. Do not allow our children to suffer."

"Enoch, we are saving Raina," Mataya confirmed. "Do you not stand watch over her? Have we not guided the dream realms to be in our favor?"

"Yes," Isaiah answered before Enoch could, "except her life needs more than our guidance."

"What does she need?" Brielle asked, already knowing what Enoch and Isaiah were thinking. "Her life has been restored. You should have not interfered." She glanced at Dasia who remained horrified, and unable to speak.

"You are wrong, Councilman; it was not the life she deserves. She is one of us. Let her be allowed to—"

"Enough," Dasia ordered.

"No," Isaiah interjected. "There is never going to be enough. The evil found the human despite Lexis' plan. Josiah guarded her, but the evil prevailed because of the weakness of Markian and his daughter. They may be in Deimos, but the residual effects of their actions traveled through the universe. This Council of secret members agreed to manipulate the earthly outcome by watching the human child and protecting those who were not Esprit de corps. We were careful, yet the evil one once again has come up against us. For eighty-four human years, we have acted carefully, to preserve the vessel for the Sentinel. And now," he said, turning slowly from one Guardian to another, "Enoch and I have sacrificed our Guardianship to bring about this plan. We gave up the possibility of living in the outer courts of Heaven. And now, the evil comes against us again, and we do nothing.

"Is Enoch's near ninety years on Earth worth nothing? The human females, Netamae, Rebekah, Tori, and now Raina served a great cause for us. Their purity and honesty have been valuable. The actions of the others and me need to be redeemed. The Watcher Talib was destroyed, sadly in the service to our cause. Do we now dishonor him by forgetting what that cause is? Raina's life evolved far greater than a human vessel. She is now born of Guardian essence. She is one of us."

"I concur." Torrey exited the shadows. Those in the room stood amazed that another had entered the room unannounced. Elder Torrey moved around the large room, and sat not in his normal chair at the council table, but in the witness section. He proudly joined many Guardians whose roles expanded from Watchers to protectors. Torrey stared quietly, examining the others summoned to this courtroom. To his right was Beck, Jaleel's aide. Next to him sat Great Elder Mataya. Torrey noticed how she looked pale and withdrawn. He wondered what could possibly make a Great Elder look so distraught. He swore for a moment that Beck might have grasped her hand in his. He dismissed the quick touch and continued to view the others.

Beside Beck were seated three Watchers, Malachi, Isaiah, Enoch, and to his amazement, his mother. She sat bewildered next to the Benn. The lump in his throat was hard to swallow when he looked into her eyes. He saw the pain he sensed was always there since his childhood.

"Elder Torrey? I must say this is a surprise to receive your visit. Tell me please." Dasia paused, glancing at the members of the Secret Council, "how have you come to enter this room without our knowledge? When this meeting was started in your absence, the chamber doors were locked."

"You know the answer to that question. Is it not written that nothing is hidden from a Great Elder?"

"You are indeed correct about the prophecy. However, please tell me for those who are void of understanding. How it is that you have come here today? What do you know of the intellect of a Great Elder's mind?"

"I come here requesting the right to speak. For I know the human Raina now bares the essence of my twin and not that of Lexis."

At that moment, sighs and gasps flooded the room. Evi screamed, burying her head into her hands. Her selfishness also cost her son. She knew this the moment she sensed him hiding in the shadows. Evi had hoped he remained dim to her workings, and that the stone from a tiny cabin over eight decades ago did not sing the song of truth.

"And," Torrey continued, "if the relevance of Guardian genetics has no bearing here today, then you must know more of Elder Mataya's plan. For in her workings, my sister and I were separated at birth. A Great Elder was raised on Earth, subjected to the humans' vile and foul thoughts. Her mind was tainted as she witnessed their massacres and ignorance. What purpose is there to destroying our own kind with humanity? Our existence has been marred by cross breeding. What will become of us now?"

Enoch jumped from his seat in protest. "Council, our actions have indeed damned us, and our punishments we will accept, knowing what we did—was right. However, please understand that what we did must not be judged too hastily, and our secret workings should not be ignored. Our intended cause was for the benefit of our people as well as Earth."

"Your intended cause only disrupted the even balance of our nature, Enoch," Torrey interjected.

"No, it has not. The even balance is how we work together. It is the cause that drives each of us. Please," he begged, looking around the room at the others, "my great-granddaughter needs to love. She needs our Leader, Josiah."

Enoch, too, took his turn studying the expressions of his fellow Guardians. He didn't see any reassurances in their eyes. He had sealed his fate, and that of Raina's wasn't confirmed.

"Despite what many of you believe, only he can save her now. He is the one who can reach into her mind and pull her free from the evil and the dimension the evil has created. Allow Josiah to expose himself and bring her back. I have tried and failed. The power of the cavern is too much for me. Josiah can save her, of this I am sure."

Dasia stood up perplexed at what she had heard. "Enoch, we cannot overlook what has been discovered in this room. I cannot even begin to assess the ramifications of what each of your actions has done. I would never have dreamed such disrespect for the Creator's will, could be born of a Guardian's mind and desires. Each of you acted without waiting on the Creator's decision. My fellow Guardians—and those words as I say them—bring a foul taste to my mouth. You are all guilty and must be held over for trial."

Mataya stood up, fighting off the tremors that shot through her celestial body. When she spoke her voice quivered and her words slurred. "Council, it is I who has brought this destruction down upon my people. I freely admit that I did whatever was in my power to instruct those in this room to do my bidding. In my desire to hear my brother's thoughts, I did whatever was necessary to secure his life. It is I who should be punished in this courtroom today."

"Mataya ..."

A soft and powerful voice echoed through the room. Instantly a white mist formed, and began to swirl around the room. The stones in the pockets of Torrey's and Beck's robes began to hum, almost dancing to the elegant rhythm. As the musical mist settled, there before them stood the Sentinel.

Her voice, filled with glory, and omnipotence darted through their minds. *Human or Guardian judges and standards will try no one in this room today. The Creator will judge what has come to pass, when He deems the time appropriate.*

Their actions seemed more heinous to each of them in the face of the Sentinel. Her appearance brought about a reality each had shunned for their own wants and needs. Each Guardian remained silent, too paralyzed by the Sentinel's power to move. She looked sternly into the eyes of each one present in the room. Her words of instructions flowed precisely at the same time into the mind of each Guardian.

The course each of you has chosen to follow must conclude without the Creator's assistance. As you have acted irrationally and without His guidance, therefore, He will likewise act by ignoring your plea. It is clear that some of those born into the race of Guardians have indeed followed in the shoes of the humans by forsaking the omnipresence of the Creator. It is He, who allows life and new creations.

Do you stand before me, Isaiah, truly believing that any offspring created was by your hand only? And you, Benn, do you believe that you have the strength to choose life and death? Your essence will not inhabit any life form that has not been sanctioned by the Creator. Nolan's life is not yours to command. It is God who grants life and receives it back.

Benn felt his essence wail within, as a peculiar sense of power flowed through him weakening his celestial body. The grunt of Isaiah next to him confirmed that, he too, felt the first of their punishments inflicted upon them.

The Sentinel turned her head to face Mataya and Beck with a condemning stare. *Do you, Mataya, believe that the realms, which you play in, were yours alone? And, Beck, the beauty, and existence of the Brook of Tears are far beyond any mental comprehension you have of its meaning, and the performance of the Stones of Fayruz. Did you really believe its magnificence was controlled and kept by you alone?*

Your ignorance equals the same foolishness that allowed the Angels to fall from grace. Their actions caused the Great War to erupt and many battles were fought in the town of Trevor on Earth. The two of you will be held accountable for the deeds that have interrupted the finely fashioned balance of Earth.

She moved once more to stand solely in front of Torrey. *Elder Torrey,* she finally instructed. *You are the product of the environment that Mataya's thoughts, and the misinterpretation of a scroll, has brought forth. Because of a scroll not counted worthy to be honored, you have* been denied the privileges of your birthright. You must use the qualities of survival that your mind had practiced in the absence of your sister to continue.

Your efforts to assist Benn in his horrific plan to control the life of Nolan; will be examined more thoroughly at another time. For now, you will spend your days guiding your sister's essence until she has reached maturity and the plane she was intended to walk by the Creator.

When she finished directing Torrey, the Sentinel moved down the rows of witness chairs once again, to speak to the ones responsible for leading so many Guardians astray.

It is by each of your current actions that I order you, Great Elder Mataya, Elder Beck, and Elder Enoch to continue as you have chosen. Do what you must to save the human Raina from Tarik's torment. When you have completed your mission, you will then stand before the Creator for judgment. It appears that each one of you before me has forgotten the time and manner, in which the Creator answers the prayers of His children. Has history not taught you that victory does not come from carnal hands, but from God's spirit!

Her words brought a crushing blow to each Guardian's mind. Judgment indeed was at hand and the worthiness of their missions truly proved now to be selfish acts. The Sentinel stepped forward, almost gliding across the room until she stopped in front of Evi.

She gasped, anxious because of the one who stood before her. Closing her eyes, Evi tilted her head backward. The Sentinel's expression remained dull as she spoke to Evi with closed minds. Whatever words the Sentinel had spoken immediately strengthened her. This Guardian would finally find the peace her heart had missed since the day she gave up her child.

Gracefully, the Sentinel began to pass in front of each Guardian again giving them private words of instructions. Some wore faces of relief, while the others knew where their fate would lie. When she reached the last Guardian, she turned strolling back toward the center of the room. When she spoke, her voice sounded more powerful than it had before.

I charge you this day to evaluate your behaviors, and I chose some of you to become accountable for their actions before the others. The rest of you shall return to your studies and await further instructions from me.

Then, with the wave of her hand, the Guardians one by one, began to disappear until only Mataya, Beck, and Enoch remained.

What you need to do, do quickly, she ordered. *The Head Elder must be the one to save the human. Offer your guidance as needed, except remember; only he has the power to save Raina. You will find him in an old church not too far from Silver Lake. I believe, Beck, you know the place I speak of to you.*

Beck nodded his head in confirmation. He had indeed visited the church before in another timeline.

May God's speed go with each of you today. Even though you have chosen to turn you back on the Creator, trust assured, His blessing still goes with you.

Then in a soft hum of a melody, she faded with the developing mist, and was gone.

32.
IGNORANCE OR TRUTH

Earth Realm—present-day

While on his way to his study on Sol to check in on his duties, Josiah passed a large brick church set off the road. The urge to enter the early 1840s church became overwhelming. Inside the historical church, the choir was practicing for tomorrow's services. The traditional hymns rang harmoniously throughout the building.

Josiah discreetly moved through the church until he reached the vestibule on the third floor. He chose this spot because it opened to the pipe organs, and he could see the choir members below. Positioned around the room was antique furniture and old statues from the church's early years. Without any warning, he was interrupted by the appearance of two Guardians who had approached him from behind an old altar.

"Who are you?" Josiah asked curiously. "Why do you lurk in the shadows?"

"We need to speak with you about a secret mission," Mataya said.

"I do not understand what you want from me, I do not know who you are."

"Josiah, you know who I am."

He hesitated to answer. There was a familiarity about the one before him. Her beauty resembled the Elder he imagined bonding with in the Abilene Chamber. A vision he immediately dismissed that chilling day when the tender thoughts of his Raina came to mind. He attempted to discern if evil intentions emanated from the tall slender entity. His memory recalled exactly who she was. Failure to remember her would be an impossible notion, as a Guardian's mind contains vast amounts of intellect. Every memory and every thought the Guardian harbored could be retrieved very quickly, so quickly, that time itself couldn't be measured.

An act he did out of guilt for letting his Raina go, Josiah tried to bury the facts of his visit to the Abilene Chamber deep inside his mind. He hoped to forget what he agreed to for Earth's safety. To relive the decision he made to stand by, knowing Raina would perish instead of taking her away with him tortured Josiah greatly. Now for humanity's sake, once again, they both needed Josiah to act without selfishness.

A strong feeling of anticipation grew wildly out of control within his essence, and Josiah had to get a hold of himself. There was no time to allow those corruptible human emotions to rule over him. Abruptly, his mind began to race, shunning the emotions.

Her features and her voice seemed familiar, but she couldn't be the Great Elder Mataya. Her presence, her being, appeared to be too good-natured that night to conceive such trickery and misconception facing him at this moment.

"No, you are an impostor," he insisted unexpectedly. He had not meant to say the words. Somehow, he offered them too readily. He knew then that his thoughts were open and not completely his own.

"Josiah, our minds merged once before. You must remember what I told you. Please, Josiah. Try to concentrate. You know what thoughts I imposed upon you. It is imperative that you remember the things of the past."

"I know nothing of your thoughts," he interjected loudly. "Yes, I linked once with the Great Elder Mataya, and her omnipotence coursed through my essence. Our thoughts were briefly one, indeed. I could never forget her presence ... her utter state of being. For this reason, I know she is not you."

"Josiah, please open your mind for a moment, and allow our minds to link ... once more. I will show you what your mind has forgotten. I will show you why I am here today."

Cautiously, Josiah chose to put some distance between them. He began backing away from the dusty altar.

"No. If you have words to speak to me, then do so openly. I will not allow you to touch me."

"Very well, Josiah. I must say that it pains me to see the distrust your human mind has concealed within your essence."

"It is not distrust ... but service to the Creator that keeps me from being lured into your wickedness."

"Young Josiah." Mataya lowered her eyes, rebuking his ignorance. "I assure you that there is no wickedness inside of me. I am filled with a sense of duty—just as you are."

"Then, is it duty or evil that brings you to this sacred place?"

She raised her eyes in affirmation of her cause. He must understand the ramifications of the issue at hand. "It is human love, my young Guardian."

"And what do you know of human love?" he retorted, annoyed at her persistence. A stance he believed to be another form of trickery.

Mataya took a step forward and reached out to touch the large statue that separated them. Her petite fingers rested gently against the smooth bronze finish of the Peita sculpture. Her energy began to pull the molecules from around them lighting the dim vestibule.

"I know much ... as much as you. For it is the human love intertwined with your essence that I carry in my mind. Do you so easily forget that our minds were one, Josiah?"

"I have not forgotten the mind that called so innocently to mine. That mind would never pose such fallacy, or even attempt to destroy the credibility of the Creator with lies."

"As I said, it is distrust that keeps you from believing me. Discern the moment, my young Guardian. Allow your essence to once more absorb my omnipotence," Mataya urged.

The organ began to play a new hymn. Josiah marked the passing of time by the tone of the earthly music he loved so well. The music, until then, he deprived himself of enjoying. Since he lost his Raina, he refused to take pleasure in any of the earthly treasures he found so delicately within her.

The room grew brighter by the glow of Mataya's power. Her determination to bring Josiah up to speed and win his confidence fueled the channel of electricity accumulating around them. Josiah sensed her eagerness, feeling the warmth of her energy flow over him.

"You are wasting my time. Tell me now what you want from me. End this charade, and spare the good people in this building from your unjust actions."

"All right, Josiah. I will entertain your human emotions and doubt for the time being. However, you must listen well, and allow me to have my say, for what I have to tell is very important."

"I will be the judge of your credibility. Just tell me what has brought you here."

Mataya looked at the male Guardian to her right. Beck exchanged glances to be courteous. He knew what she was thinking, but this was supposed to be an impossible task, for her thoughts should have been closed to anyone who was not a Great Elder.

Beck was unique. He knew her thoughts and interacted without spoken words. A power he obtained from the Stones of Fayruz permitted his mind to endure her vigor and for his intelligence to surpass that of a normal Guardian. This became a key element in his plan to give back the Head Elder the love that he lost.

The Brook of Tears contained many wonders including the Stones of Fayruz. The energy and empathy enveloped within the Stones of Fayruz sought out young Beck. His pure nature and compassion for the brokenhearted entities he saw daily called to the compassion of the brook. It gave him a supremacy that Beck acquired so easily and used with great restraint.

Now Beck would need to apply some restraint with their situation. He could simply use the power of the Fayruz stones and force his thoughts upon Josiah—controlling his mind as he had done with Mataya. With this power, Beck made her to forget her visits to the brook. He could impose the same power on Josiah compelling him to obey their instructions without any hesitation or regret. His actions indeed were a crime that would be well worth the punishment ... if the punishment truly served the purpose. Such an act wouldn't solve their problems now. They needed their Leader to act of his own accord and for his own reasons. They were the same reasons that matched Elder Mataya's agenda and brought her to this church. Reasons ... that persuaded Beck to keep his secrets and not abuse the vigor cascading through his essence.

"Do you remember the day you returned to your study and found a tattered piece of parchment on your desk?" Beck asked.

A chill crept through Josiah's essence. He remembered this day quite clearly. It was on this day his beloved was nearly killed by the evil one in the woods. He had gone to her house impersonating Josiah. Then he lured Raina into the woods by her home and proceeded to take her back in time. There, he plotted in the past to kill her undercover of the time continuum. He believed Josiah wouldn't discover his deed if done in a different era.

It was on this day he arrived nearly too late. When he found her, she was in a wretched state, suffering from a fractured wrist and severely in shock. Josiah had healed her, and then giving into pity and the despair of his failures, he fogged her memory, making her forget the dreadful ordeal. Had he not gone back to his study, against his better judgment to read the parchment a second time, then Raina's life wouldn't have been endangered by the evil.

Josiah answered hesitantly, remembering the fearful expression on Raina's face. "I do. Why do you ask? How do you know of the parchment?"

"Because, Josiah—I placed the parchment in your study," Beck said.

Josiah's anger began to swell until he felt a surge of energy discharge from his essence. "Why did you do that?"

"I did that because I needed some kind of evidence to warn you of what was to come. I needed to recall certain events to your memory."

"How would the parchment become the evidence you needed? What is it you want from me?"

"Please, Josiah, allow us to proceed," Mataya pleaded. "We do not have much time."

Beck continued his request, wanting to reassure Josiah of his intent. As he spoke, he moved fluidly across the room. Then stopping in front of an old cherry wood desk, he waved his hand above it. Instantly, the top right drawer opened. Beck reached in, pulled out a white cloth, and began unfolding it. He removed the tattered parchment, presenting it to Josiah.

"Take this and examine it. You will find your essence has touched it. This is the same parchment from your study."

Josiah moved cautiously, in a slow even glide toward Beck, putting some distance between him and Mataya. As soon as he touched the parchment, his fingers tingled emitting a faint blue glow. Josiah knew the parchment was indeed the one he held from that frightful day.

"How did you get this?"

Beck grinned. He heard the inquisitiveness of Josiah's mind calculating the truth of his claim. "I simply took it back after you left your study for Earth. I told you, I needed some evidence to make you believe. Do you recall what the parchment recited?"

"Of course I do. However, how did it get to this place?" he said impatiently, desiring for this conversation to unfold their mysteries.

"Good, then your memory will serve its purpose."

"For what?" Josiah questioned intently. "Tell me how you got into my study twice and why you felt the need to remove the scroll once you left it?"

"Josiah, you seek signs to prove what your mind already knows. I will explain many things to you. Please, allow your mind to be open to the truth. Allow your benevolence for the humans to match your passion for servitude to the Creator. Much of what I say may seem bizarre ... and unworthy of truth. I beg you to decipher the good and know that what I speak of the Creator has permitted to occur."

"Then proceed, and I will judge what is worthy and permitted by God."

"Very well, Josiah," Mataya said softly. Her lips formed the words for Josiah's benefit; however, Beck already knew her request. "Please, Beck, will you continue."

"The parchment I left told you of the story of Lexis and those who sought out his daughter. You correlated the events of the scroll to that of your friendship with the human girl, Raina. Fortunately, you allowed nothing else to enter your mind. You did not investigate any further, how the parchment got there or question its authority. This, I counted on, for if you acted with haste, then all would be lost."

"What are you speaking about? What would be lost?" Josiah asked.

Beck dismissed his questions, continuing without answering him. "Once you realized that your Raina's life was in peril, you concentrated on the evil around her. Thus, the evil one saw only your intentions, while my intentions were hidden from him.

"As Mataya executed her plan for the vessel's survival in another realm, I discovered that Markian's daughter, Dinah, was traveling through time to locate the Scroll of

Sychar. I worked diligently to thwart her plan contacting key Guardians in the time continuum who knew of the scroll. Then I began manipulating the events and actions of those charged with the safekeeping of the Scroll of Sychar. I altered their memories and responses to their duties."

Josiah became alarmed. Beck's actions proved to be no more worthy of praise than the actions of Markian.

"If you knew of the efforts of Dinah, then you should have stopped her. Do you stand there proud that you have fogged the minds of innocent Guardians? Do you even care what the ramifications of your actions have had on those poor individuals?"

"Josiah?" Mataya spoke, wanting to clear his thoughts of deception. "Beck meant no harm, and none was done to any Guardian. He merely covered their actions to throw Dinah off track. The ramifications of her success far outweighed any of our actions. Do you not see ... if her plan succeeded, all would have been lost?"

"All was lost," he scowled. "I lost Raina and Earth was ravished by the evil duo and those Demons they raised from the pit. Despite the Sentinel's efforts to restore Earth, the damage was done."

"Josiah, you misunderstand my role. I have acted for the commonwealth of all Guardians and humans. It was not my intent to change the future, but to help guide it in another direction. If I could have alerted you to what was to come, and you defeated Markian and Dinah before the Abyss was opened, then Mataya's plan to enter the past would have been unnecessary.

"Unfortunately, even though I knew what previously unfolded, I did not work fast enough, and I failed. Leaving you the scroll was not enough of a clue to warn you. At that point, our only choice was to continue through with Mataya's plan. I was cautious because her realms at times were unstable, and they looped with one another. Controlling the needed outcome was difficult and risky. For us to carry forth our goal we needed the help of many other Guardians. Too many, I feared would learn of our actions. It was not my guilt that I was concerned for, but for their safety and security in the realm of Heaven."

"How can you say that, Beck? You deceived and distorted the time continuum. When you had the power to stop the evil you looked the other way. Your actions are heinous."

"No, Head Elder my actions preserved Earth while we waited for the Sentinel to mature. Do you not understand that the evil one just saw your actions and not the plan I was forming? That plan has now begun to unfold with Elder Mataya's assistance. She risks much to act for our worthy cause ... for your cause, Josiah."

"Worthy cause? You speak in twisted riddles. If you have something to say, then tell me now," Josiah demanded, feeling his patience for the two of them wearing thin.

"Josiah, you must understand. Beck and I have traveled through time. Our mission is to change the events of the past for a brighter future," Mataya insisted.

"Impossible," he interjected. "That is not permitted. You have violated our laws once again. You deserve damnation in Deimos."

"Yes—however, it is a risk we are willing to take. What we did had to be done in order to save those who have been harmed by the evil one."

"The only one harmed was Raina. She is not your cause, nor is she your fight."

"As I have said before, Josiah. You misunderstand our actions. We fight for more than your human friend, Josiah. We fight for the life of my brother Mateo, as well."

"Your brother." Josiah snarled clinching his fist. "Is a traitor to our kind. He received just punishment for his deeds."

Mataya bowed her head, absorbing Josiah's desire for vengeance upon her brother. "Do you not remember at his trial, he acted without true knowledge? Are you so filled with hatred that you cannot forgive one such as him?"

"There is no hatred within my essence," he declared angrily.

"You lie to yourself, Head Elder," Mataya interjected strongly.

"No," Beck corrected softly, "he is filled with sorrow and loneliness. It cries to me day and night. Your tears, Josiah, fill the brook. The Stones of Fayruz can no longer cleanse the pain and soothe the waters from your tears. That is why I cannot stand by and watch as my Leader suffers."

Josiah stood restless, observing the two offenders before him. His position required him to arrest Beck and Mataya and charge them with the crimes that they committed. Their sentence for their unlawful acts was an eternity on Deimos. However, his embarrassment concerning the words Beck spoke kept him from acting upon his required duties.

The truth is that Josiah did cry. As much as he didn't want to admit it to anyone, his tears of sorrow for the loss of his dear sweet Raina spewed regularly. The time span that elapsed didn't calm the pain searing through him. His Guardian heart suffered as much as the human one he fabricated a night so long ago. The night he acted upon love ... willing to risk his life for the tender touch of his Esprit de corps.

"I do not understand what you are speaking of." Again, he lied to himself. His superior mind already knew where this conversation was taking him. He faced the truth he buried a lifetime before, the truth that poked at his heart and ravaged his thoughts daily.

"Josiah, I live up to the name that has been given to me. I am the Dweller by the Brook."

Josiah sucked in a needless breath, feeding off a human response that forced itself to surface.

"I learned very long ago how to pass from the present to where the brook exists. I am the Keeper. It is my job to maintain the brook's purity. I sift the stones that diminish the regrets of the Creator's children. I hear the causes of the damned within the layers of the brook's waters. It is I who recites the prayers of others to fight for the regrets of those called unworthy, so that the stones may drain the sorrow, and replenish the mist with hope."

Beck gestured toward the stain glass window, pointing with his index finger. All at once, a mist formed enveloping the window. A soft humming sound danced in the room emanating from the mist. It formed tiny musical notes that danced in the shadows on the floor.

"Josiah, do you think it was a coincidence that you saw visions of Raina while on Deimos or that parts of her future were hidden from you? I am responsible for what you saw in the burning wasteland. Our actions changed the outcome of Raina's life and hid her future from you and Jon. Do you not see? Her future was not destined and since it kept changing she had no future for you to see."

"How do you know about that? I have told no one."

"Because, Josiah. I opened the atmosphere of Deimos. I was the one who allowed her dreams to reach you."

"Impossible!"

"Is it, Josiah? Are you not standing before me now? Were you not unjustly tried in a court of deception? Did you not feel the burning sand upon your feet and the coarse wind scraping against your skin?"

Josiah was stunned at his knowledge. No one who was ever been sent to Deimos returned, no one ... except Josiah. If Beck didn't have a part in his return, then he would have no knowledge of the darkness of Deimos.

"You know this to be true, Josiah. A tiny hole remained open, and you followed the light to Earth. It was no coincidence. I visited Deimos and brought Raina there with me. Through her love, I was able to create her dreams that freed you. It is this love that allowed me to free her mind from Deimos the day she collapsed in the observatory."

"Deimos," he yelled. "What are you talking about?"

"Josiah, have you not realized what is going on here. The evil one Tarik is stalking her mind. He manipulates her memories and dreams, forcing her to endure his torture. Tarik is destroying her mind and her body by pulling her into his mystical realm. During one of his attacks, he took her to Deimos in an attempt to have her life force destroyed by the planet's power.

"When she lay unconscious on the floor of the observatory, he forced her mind to become trapped in the realm of Deimos. The evil one has taken her to many realms full of terror toying with her rationality. It is a game he enjoys playing until she meets the fate he desires for her demise. Had I not rescued her that day and brought her to the brook, Raina would not have survived."

Mataya had remained very still, waiting for confirmation that Josiah understood and accepted their appearance. When his mind comprehended their message, then he would become part of their plan.

"How—tell me how you did that! Tell me how he controls her mind!"

"Come with me, Josiah, for this is a long story—a story that I will tell you gratefully. Nonetheless, you must join me in the dream world. Please come with us to the Brook of Tears. For it is there that you will fully comprehend what mission Elder Mataya and I have sanctioned."

"Did you snare Anani in your trap—sending her in your place too? She warned me of the evil actions; however she vanished before she could assist me."

"No, she acted on her own."

"Then how did she know?"

"Please, Head Elder." Beck motioned for Josiah and Mataya to follow him.

At his command, the mist parted from the window, and Sol's rays streamed in elegantly unveiling a stairway. Mataya was the first to approach the stairs. This was nothing new to her. She walked them before, when Beck summoned her from the Abilene Chamber. Her first few visits were easily forgotten as the result of a form of protection for Beck's retreat. When he was sure of her dedication and knew of her acceptance, then he allowed her to recall the brook. Until then, she thought her visits to be mere hallucinations from the lack of her brother's thoughts in her mind.

She knew Mateo wasn't himself. His mind became dark spots within her mind. Many times, she witnessed episodes of his forgetfulness, choosing to overlook them even when she had found him in a daze. When he recovered from his episodes, Mataya acted as if nothing had occurred.

There were many warning signs that she didn't see. Even as Beck brought her to the brook, he didn't miss the absence of her mind either. The unity these twin Guardians shared was severed by greed and hate.

As they ascended the stairway leading to the garden, each Guardian's concentration wore thin from the anticipation of the moment. Mataya had the future of her brother on her mind, while Beck had Mataya's safety as his primary concern. Josiah's thoughts were engrossed in the events of the past and those that were to come. None of them sensed the appearance of another hidden in the shadows of the church.

Anani was not the only one who looked after her friend. Jaleel took the warning of the mysterious visitor very seriously. He was keeping Josiah under careful observation following his every move. Tricks he learned from Great Elder Yakira had helped him to keep his essence from being detected by the other Guardians. Perhaps some of his people would classify this deed as a matter of deception with no acceptable excuses. In Jaleel's mind, however, the possibility of punishment for this abomination meant nothing to him.

He and Josiah had vowed in their youth to defend one another's honor and lives against opposing forces. Of course as children, they knew no evil and their honor was defended though fairy tales. As they grew and became adventurous, their travels had brought them to many worlds where the cultures of these worlds were foreign to them. A few times, their overeager desires to experience thrills of the commoners put them in dangerous situations. It was then that their pledge proved its worth. Now, in their adulthood, dangers found them when they were not looking. Too much sorrow and grief had touched their lives. Emotions and events once thought never to enter the life of a Guardian had indeed inflicted them.

Quietly, Jaleel scurried up the mystical staircase behind them. Still hiding in the shadows, he spied a row of trees off to his left. Then using the sound of the rippling brook to disguise his footsteps, he took the group's moment of distraction to dart toward the tree line. He moved swiftly, determined to be ready to assist his dear friend Josiah if needed.

Josiah looked around amazed and stunned, if a Guardian could be, at the world that surrounded him. Never had he imagined a place such as this full of peace and love. The brook Beck created by God's plan was filled with tranquility felt through the heart of a human and not the essence of a Guardian.

Beck led Josiah to the Brook of Tears. As they approached, the white mist formed, ushering the regrets of troubled souls into the water. The Stones of Fayruz parted to accept the discontentment and renew the hopelessness.

Jaleel fought hard against the temptation to expose himself. The existence of the brook overwhelmed him with the magnificence it contained. Though he was not touching a stone of Fayruz, he could feel the battle within it, to defeat the sorrow and spread the peace. It occurred to him, that what he felt in Josiah's dorm holding the mysterious ooze stained rock compared to the sensation of this place.

"Do you see, Josiah, the wonders of this place? I created this magnificence from a dream, and now it thrives as an access way for the disheartened entities. From out of this brook hope and love regenerate. Together they form the musical notes you see above the water. Then the songs stemming from each note reach the outer realms of Heaven. They bring love and peace with them as they float through the universe."

"Tell me," Josiah asked amazed, "Beck, how is this possible? How can what you speak be true?"

"It is not our place to question, Josiah. You know as the Head Elder that one should just simply believe."

"I do believe in many things. Nonetheless, your story is wild and born out of your insanity."

Mataya frowned. "I told you he would not believe. His heart is too damaged."

Josiah corrected her in a sharp tone. "You know nothing of my heart, Mataya."

"I know more than you think. It is broken because of me."

"I do not understand what you mean by that, Elder."

"Josiah, it is I who has brought this discord down upon you. In my weakness, I have allowed my desires to change your world. Had I let well enough alone, you would not be suffering now."

"Elder, you are insane. You have not affected me in any way."

"No, Head Elder, you are wrong."

"What do you mean? I demand that you explain yourself to me!"

"What she means, Head Elder," Beck interrupted, "is that she feels responsible for the terrifying visions you are having. Her will to change the outcome of her brother's fate fractured the realms of many worlds. My plan was to stop Markian before he attacked ending the need of the Sentinel's premature arrival. However, against her knowledge her power acted upon her imagination and created new timelines." Beck glanced back and forth from Josiah to Mataya. He knew how much his words pained her. "We have been searching for clues to point us to the true course. Our mission is to end the various timelines and stop the fluctuations. Unfortunately, we find we are not acting alone. It is unclear to us the intentions of the other's causes, but much interference to the time continuum has occurred. This had put the human Raina and your essence in jeopardy. Our actions allowed the lives of others to be lost. The death toll did not stop with the humans. Good Guardians have also lost their lives for our cause."

"What have you done?" Josiah gasped horrified. His body tensed, prepared to defend himself.

Alarmed by his friend's disposition, Jaleel lost his concentration and jumped out from behind the trees. Great Elder Mataya immediately noticed his appearance. Her sudden actions and thoughts caught Beck's attention. Before Jaleel could even confront the group of Guardians, Beck saw him.

"Councilman Jaleel," Elder Mataya shouted, taking a step toward him. Beck instinctively pushed her aside to protect her. He sensed no malice from Jaleel, but his presence clearly was not welcomed.

Josiah said nothing, looking back and forth from Jaleel to Mataya and Beck. Emotions of surprise and anger both surfaced. He came to the realization that neither Guardian, including himself, stood sinless at this moment. Each one had acted for their cause, believing it to be worthy. When in actuality, deception and selfishness ruled their judgment, blinding them from the intended cause of the Creator.

"Councilman Jaleel, what is it that brings you here today?" Beck questioned, evaluating his intents.

"Do you even need to ask me that question?" Jaleel snapped sarcastically.

"Yes, I do, Councilman, considering that you are trespassing."

"Tres—"

"Enough," Josiah urged. Then looking sternly at Beck and Mataya, he spoke with authority. "Tell me why we are here."

"Head Elder," Beck replied, stepping closer to him, "I will explain what you need to know—but please, keep an open mind."

"Do not tell me what to think," he retorted. "I will evaluate the truth myself."

"Fine," Beck said harshly. Then he glanced at Mataya before fixing his eyes on the other Guardians before him. "Mataya intended to go back in time to guide Lexis by placing his daughter in an ancestor of Raina. It was her hope that the timeline change would throw off Markian's detection of Raina on Earth. She believed after making the essence switch from the infant Raina to her great-grandmother—that Markian and his daughter would not look for her in the past. This seemed reasonable, as there were to be no clues in the present indicating that she ever existed in Silver Lake.

"However, she ... we—have encountered another form of evil that plotted against us. The entity's name is Tarik, and he was more intelligent then we imagined. We believe Dinah brought him to Earth during her search for the Abyss. His origins lead us to the planet Adrastea, and that is where Dinah uncovered the Scroll of Sychar.

"When a Watcher was killed during his service as protector, we knew that Tarik had found Lexis' child, and her death was emanate. Unfortunately, we were not prepared for Tarik's attack. He killed Raina's natural great-grandparents, Clemet and Naomi before we could manipulate the timeline once again. The Watcher Isaiah saved the infant Rebekah from drowning after Tarik's henchman failed to kill her as well." Beck paused, recalling the look on Mataya's face as she recited the account to Beck. "Mataya's mind then created another realm whose timeline included taking the baby and allowing a Guardian to raise her. Mataya's new plan proposed placing the essence of an unannounced Guardian in Raina's grandmother Rebekah, once again concealing the ancestry line. Mataya then retrieved Lexis' child from Earth, and the Sentinel was brought here to this brook for her protection. In our designed timelines, the unnamed essence has also found refuge in this brook."

Josiah's stance loosened. Their words were too shocking to conceive. Beck sensed Josiah's dismay, but continued to explain their actions.

"More Watchers were placed on Earth to keep the infant safe to insure our plan. Guardian Enoch, at the urging of Mataya, married his Esprit de corps Netamae Burrows. She was Naomi's friend, and they adopted Raina's grandmother Rebekah. Together Enoch and Netamae raised her as their own child in Earth customs, as she harbored a secret essence within her. When Rebekah grew, she took her husband Isaiah. He too was a Guardian in disguise and not the human as in the original timeline.

"When the appointed time arrived, Isaiah's human image bore a child with Rebekah. If the child developed both an essence and soul as with Lexis' original timeline, then all the better. The existence of another essence would add more protection for the child. As planned, Mataya still placed the unannounced essence in their child who was born Raina's mother, Tori."

"Oh, no." Josiah's knees weakened.

"Yet, again the realms where inflicted by the evil when the Guardian child's mother sought her out in a moment of despair. Somehow, Tarik followed her to Earth in the year 1930, and figured out our plan. We have confirmed that he acquired the assistance of other Guardians to complete his mission."

"What we did not know," Mataya spoke up, "was in the original timeline Raina's father was an Esprit de corps. His destiny then, and still is, a mystery to us. Human love is powerful, and we did not know that Benn, who was the one assigned to guard over Raina's father, fell in love with

Raina's mother, Tori. Before Markian struck and killed Nolan, Benn fled from grief and anguish because of his actions. Upon seeing Nolan's death, he went into exile because of his sins and failures."

"I am on the Council," Josiah interjected, "I know nothing of this event taking place."

Mataya shook her head. "You would have no reason to, Josiah. The timelines changed in the parallel universe. His actions went unnoticed because he changed history more than once."

"Impossible!" Jaleel looked at Josiah for confirmation that Beck's words were incorrect. That confirmation never came.

"Please, Councilman, allow me to continue," Beck requested. It was clear he was becoming annoyed by the constant interruptions. "Mataya and I worked to secure the future of Raina and Mateo for our own cause. We calculated each realm Mataya created, coercing them to fuse together at the right moment. Our actions were supposed to bring us to the end of our plan, except it did not work. What we did not know is that another also worked for the safety of the unnamed essence. Hidden from us was the fact that the unnamed essence's twin brother realized he was a Great Elder."

"Twins," Josiah whispered.

"Yes, she was a twin. Her brother acquired knowledge of what played-out in one of Mataya's timelines through the assistance of a Stone of Fayruz."

At the mention of unique stone, Josiah instinctively padded his robe pocket. Jaleel knew what it was that Josiah had sought.

Beck had not stopped talking; completely unaware of what was going through Josiah's mind at that moment. "... this Guardian sought after his own desires to have his twin returned to him and his parents. Guardian Benn fell weak with human love and acting in secrecy, he went back in time to change the outcome of his mistake. Benn believed in doing this that all would be made right and the realms would fuse together. He did not act alone, for the twin's brother Great Elder Torrey aided him. However, his actions and those of male Guardians have not benefitted any of the realms and have just added to our problems."

"Elder Torrey," Josiah mumbled softly. Now it seemed clear to him why the Councilman took him out to the garden. He had another motive other than the Head Elder's reputation. If Josiah had left his seat that day, then his actions would have a negative effect on the plan Torrey was concluding.

Josiah spoke harshly, to reprimand the fallen Guardians. "I am horrified to hear of your actions. I cannot even begin to comprehend the effects your carelessness has caused. Your sins are great, and your punishment will not be swift. Why did you not hold your places, and remain faithful to the Creator's plan and commands?"

"Damn us all you want, Head Elder, for it is your right and obligation to our people to do so. We have disobeyed the Creator casting aside His divine plan for our own. We must be held accountable by the laws of our people, and sent to Deimos as our punishments. However, the true sentencing will come when the Creator judges our essences, and He condemns us. We accept this fate for our actions, except, we cannot stop now. The evil has come into the future, tracking down your Raina, and now holds her mind captive in realms resembling human dreams."

Josiah moaned. "No."

"I speak the truth, Elder. This is why we have come to you. We know she has pulled you into her dreams, needing your assistance. I know you have discovered this. The young Guardian Anani has shown you this, has she not?"

Josiah felt another blow to his world. Had he become so oblivious, wrapped upon in the human desire to have his Raina, that he couldn't see the actions of those around him? How could he have been so dim to her power, and blind to her secret actions? Josiah cursed himself for not seeking out the entity's identity. Had he fulfilled his obligations Anani would never have jeopardized her essence to help him.

"What does the child have to do with your actions?" Josiah questioned, with uncertainty in his voice. Anani was indeed just a child. He felt a desire to guide her when her parents first ceased to exist. Only his time on Earth distracted him from his obligations, making Raina the only thing that mattered to him.

Mataya stepped forward, closing the gap between her and Josiah. "Anani admires you greatly. She felt your sadness and grew humanly concerned for your well-being. At first, she acted on her own by going to Earth to watch over you. It was not long before she had seen the changes in her roommate. Perhaps, it was not a coincidence that her roommate was Raina. When she saw the episodes of her dreams affect you as well, it grieved her essence."

"Yes," he finally admitted. "I have been uncertain of what is really happening, except I know Raina needs my help."

"Indeed, but you will not prevail while it is her mind calling to you. The Tracker knows how to manipulate our minds, and that is why you fail. Anani thought she could attempt the task of assisting your mind to enter Raina's dream. She knew you could fight the Tracker Tarik in his realm. And when you beat him, he would be destroyed, and your Raina would be safe. However, he discovered Anani's actions—"

"What? Is she well?" Josiah asked fearing for Anani's life.

"Yes, Josiah. He sent her to Sol where she is unharmed. Her mind appears dim to the past—but she is well. We are not sure why he spared her, as his reasoning remains a mystery to us."

Josiah became intrigued by the thought of a solution to save Raina, yet his anger for the discretions of the Guardians remained strong.

"Tell me about this power, Beck?"

"When you have accomplished our goal, then the evil will meet his fate and the destinies we were all meant to fulfill will resume."

"What am I to do?" Josiah asked weary.

"Listen carefully, Head Elder," Beck began.

33.
DREAMS

"Please, tell me about the dreams, Raina?" he questioned, wanting to try to gather more information. If Josiah could figure out how the evil caused them, then it may give him a greater advantage when the time came to rescue her in her dreams.

Raina looked away. Her heart was full of honesty, but the truth was too hard to utter.

"Raina, I will not laugh—if that is what you are afraid of."

"No." Her smile faded as she looked away.

"Tell me please, what is it?"

"Really, Josiah ... it's nothing, okay?"

Josiah's mind searched for any reason he could offer Raina to make her feel more comfortable. He hoped that if she felt secure than Raina would share what she was hiding from him.

"No, it is not all right. Raina, I hope you understand that I do not doubt you. It bothers me that you will not talk to me."

"Please, Josiah ... really it's nothing. Can't we just leave it at that?"

"Sure," he said disappointed. "If that is what you want."

Raina could sense his dejection. Her silence had hurt him anyway. "Please, don't be upset with me, Josiah?"

"Raina, I could never be upset with you. Why do you think that I would be?"

"I don't know. You just seem ... so distant today. I feel as if I may have offended you somehow?"

"Hey now," he said, reaching out for her hand. "I am sorry if it seems like that to you. I did not mean to give you the wrong impression of me. You can never say or do anything that will offend me."

"I guess I'm just being silly," she said, bringing her eyes up to meet his eyes. "Do you promise that you won't try and analyze my dreams—if I tell you about them?"

"Raina, please ... do not worry about whether or not I will analyze your dreams. I would not be so rude. I am not one of those doctors from the hospital."

"I know ... I just don't want you getting any notions that I belong in a padded room, or I'm emotionally challenged."

As sincere as he could be, Josiah brushed his fingers along her cheek. The gentle motion of his hand sent shivers down her spine. Josiah smiled at her reaction, feeling pleased he had affected her in that way. He knew better than to encourage this behavior from her, so he slowly pulled his hand away regretting that he had to do so.

She could never know what they once shared in another lifetime.

"Raina ... please understand that I do not believe you are suffering from any type of mental disease. Your blackouts were real, even if the latter brain scans were inconclusive. Something put you into the hospital, and it was not your imagination."

"Are you sure about that, Josiah? Are you sure that you're not hanging around with someone who's crazy and deranged?"

Josiah closed his eyes and sighed. What could he say or do to convince her that she was normal? "Raina—I thought we were past this and that we had already established my opinion of the whole matter?"

"I know what you believe, Josiah. It's just that there is so much happening right now."

"Please, come and sit with me," Josiah said, motioning toward the rock wall that lined the entrance to Fox River Park. "I think we really need to talk about what is going on with you."

Then taking her hand into his, Josiah led her across the road to the long earth-tone colored stones fastened together by mortar. Carefully placing his hands around her waist, he lifted Raina up—setting her down gently on the uneven layered rocks. Josiah scooted up on the wall and sat next to her. His human mind urged him to tell her everything he knew about her life and her dreams—but his Guardian senses warned him to remain silent.

"Raina ... when I saw you in that hospital bed, I found myself feeling very alone. It did not matter that we had known each other for just a few weeks. I was very worried about you. I believe with all of my heart that something made you ill, and if that illness is still affecting you, I want to help you. However, I cannot when you do not trust me."

"Josiah," Raina said in a high-pitch tone, "I do trust you. I trust you with my life, don't you know that?"

"It is not the question of if I know that ... but do you know that?"

"Of course I do."

"Then please, do not shut me out."

"Josiah, I am not shutting you out. I just don't want you thinking that I'm crazy."

"Raina, I told you already that I do not believe you are anything close to unstable."

She cupped her hands together nervously rubbing her palms with her fingertips. "I know," she whispered.

Josiah took in a deep breath. Then putting his arm around her, he pulled her body into his. Raina closed her eyes feeling a sense of security in his presence. He had already done so much for her. Without hesitation, he dropped his studies to fly across the country to a strange city. He vowed to be her crutch to lean on, but he carried her instead ... without complaint.

Raina snuggled her head closer into his chest. She felt extremely at peace when they were together. A special attraction to him went beyond the good friendship they shared. How could she tell him what feelings danced in her mind, or what magic kept her heart beating?

"The other night, when I fell asleep with my head on your lap, it was the first time in months that I didn't dream about the cave. But still nothing about my dream seemed abnormal." Raina smiled and laughed nervously. "I dreamt we were walking in a beautiful garden. Everywhere I looked; there were lavender roses and stargazer lilies. Tall sunflowers brighter than any yellow I could imagine towered over them. It was almost as if the sunflowers guarded the flowerbed.

"I was beginning to feel normal, that's if I even know what normal is anymore. Last night when you stayed at the lake fishing with my dad, the awful dreams came back. For some reason, they were different ones this time."

"Different, please tell me how so, Raina?"

"Well, I didn't dream of the cave or the plane crash. I felt afraid, but somehow it didn't seem like it was my fear."

"Raina, I do not understand what you are getting at?"

"That's it. I don't know if I understand it myself."

"Try and describe the dream for me."

"It was so different than any dream I ever had. I felt calm and relaxed. I was in a large room, furnished unbelievably with chandeliers glimmering from the glow of burning candles. There was a ballroom dance and the room was full of people. Over the music, I could hear voices and it sounded as if they were speaking in Italian. The women were dressed in beautiful floor length dresses that flared when they walked. The clothing made me think that I was in the early 1800s. I wore a gown just as graceful as the other women did. It was amazing how the blue silk shimmered in the light." Raina's expression changed, bringing a smile to her worried face. "As I walked further into the room, I began to recognize the composition as a piece from Beethoven. I became really excited and pushed my way through to the center of the room. Oh, Josiah, it was magnificent. I wish you could envision my dream.

"There I was a few feet away from Beethoven. I wish you could have heard him; he played with such determination and passion. I could've lost myself in the moment listening to him perform. I couldn't help myself, my arms flailed in the air as my fingers slid down an imaginary row of piano keys. When he finished, I turned to follow him and I bumped into a man. As I begged his pardon, I caught the look in his eyes, and it was you, Josiah."

Josiah stared at her breathless. He had attended many of Beethoven's performances. Never had his essence been distracted from the marvelous sounds of Beethoven's talent, until one night, just before Beethoven had become very ill. Josiah was lost in the moment, just as he was every time his Esprit de corps performed. This night his essence moved carelessly through the room dancing on the musical notes. Then without any warning, he floated into a young woman who stood a few feet from the piano. Her presence captured Josiah's attention, and he immediately stopped to gaze upon her. It was the only time a human, other than his Esprit de corps, caught his attention. There he was invisible to the woman, and yet she stared at him with two extraordinarily bright blue eyes.

"That is certainly an imaginative dream, Raina. What happened next?"

She grinned awkwardly. "I awoke, I guess, at least I think I did. All I know is that it got extremely dark and quiet. It seemed to last for hours, until the loud clanging noises."

"Clanging noises? What do you mean? What was it that made the noise?"

"It was people sword fighting, I think."

"Wait, sword fighting? Are you sure of this?"

"Yes, I know what I heard. It was easy to make out what the noise was."

"Where were you in this dream?"

"I'm not sure where I was, but I could hear the clanging of metal and men screaming. There were crying women running to the fallen men, and children gathered in the streets watching. Some were dressed like Roman soldiers."

"Roman soldiers," Josiah said hesitantly, "are you sure of that?"

"Yes, I am. The Roman men were wearing white tunics and helmets that covered their faces like in the movies. They had very large shields that they used to block the arrows and swords of the other people."

"What else did you see in this dream?"

"Well, I dreamt that I left the wooden house and ended up in a courtyard. There were about a hundred men fighting, and I tried to run away. I came across two men, and one of them was on the ground. The other man was ready to run his sword through him, but a third solider came and stopped him. Then those two men started arguing. I tried to run past them, but the other solider still lying on the ground caught my foot and pulled me to the ground next to him. I began to scream as he pulled out a knife and was going to stab me. Before I knew it, the one who stopped the killing had wrestled me free. In the fight, his helmet came off and rolled across the street. I'll never forget the look on your face at that moment."

"My face, what are you talking about?" Josiah questioned, not believing what she was saying.

"Josiah, the soldier who rescued me was you."

Raina could hear him gasp. Josiah remembered that night as if it was still happening. In his human image, he argued with his Esprit de corps, trying to convince him not to take the life of his enemy. Josiah was too caught-up in the moment of the atrocity to see the future.

While he pleaded for the fallen soldier's life to keep his Esprit de corps pure, the enemy grabbed the slave woman and tried to murder her. As Josiah attempted to rescue her, his Esprit de corps slay the man with his sword. Josiah stood there stunned if he could be, holding the shaken woman in his arms. Her sapphire eyes cried both tears of sorrow and tears of relief. They pulled his concentration away from his sense of loss, as the connection he shared with his Esprit de corps was broken.

Josiah may have saved the life of a stranger, but the life of his Esprit de corps was now over. He chose to stray from his purpose when he slay the soldier. It was not his life at risk—the fallen soldier was hurt, and death chased after him. He could've simply walked away. Instead, his Esprit de corps chose a new path—forsaking the Guardian who watched over him, and took a life unnecessarily.

"It was the same in the hospital," she continued. Raina was unaware that Josiah barely heard her talking. He was lost in the memory of that horrid night, recalling the tenderness he sensed from the slave woman. "When you stayed with me all night long, I felt so safe. I guess I never really thanked you for that."

Josiah inhaled deeply, trying to regain his composure. "Raina, you do not need to thank me. You are a good friend to me. I just did what friends do for one another."

Eager to explain herself she scooted her body upward so she could look into his eyes. "No, Josiah—you do so much more. You came halfway across the United States to visit my family. I could've traveled alone."

"Well, you would not be a good friend if you had left me sitting in my dorm over spring break."

"You're just saying that."

"No, it is true. Just what do you think I would be doing right now if I was left there alone?"

"Studying, I suppose."

"What, do you think that there is nothing else I could be doing?"

"Precisely. All you do is immerse yourself in books or hang out with me. Not that it's a bad thing, of course."

"No, I do other things, as well."

"Really, like what?" she challenged.

He stuttered, reaching for some excuse to give her. "Well ... I ... I."

"Yeah, that's what I thought." Raina snickered confidently.

Josiah gave up searching for false examples. The truth was a secret, and his human mind could never think past Raina. Josiah frowned, wishing he could change the subject. Raina was very in-tuned to him and there was nothing that he could say to plead his defense.

She must have sensed his embarrassment, because she stopped laughing. Her face lost its gleam, making Josiah regret his transparency. He couldn't resist, and raised his hand to touch her cheek. At once, she cupped her hand over his, pressing his hand tighter against her face and smiled.

Like many times in her past life, Josiah found the power of the moment. Words during these times meant nothing to them. The connection they once shared seemed to be reaffirming its bond. Then removing his hand from her cheek, she brought it to her lips and tenderly kissed the tips of his fingers. He leaned in slowly, taking her hands into his returning the kiss. Josiah swore Raina blushed as she leaned back smiling.

"We should get going," Raina said, looking at her watch. "My mom has dinner waiting. I think she baked me a cake."

"What is the occasion," he asked, and then immediately gasped in surprise. Today was her nineteenth birthday. He had forgotten all about it, in such a human frame of mind.

As they began to walk down the road, Josiah quickly knelt and picked up a handful of gravel. Once back at Raina's home, he would mold them into a unique space diorama—consisting of vibrant colored planets—that represented the way he saw the universe through his emerald-green eyes.

Even though he was proud of himself for such a quick recovery of the occasion, he couldn't shake Raina's dreams or his memories. Was she truly there in Beethoven's home watching him dance with the music, or running for her life during the Roman war?

34.
SEARCH AND DESTROY

Earth Realm—dream-state

As Raina predicted, Tori had baked a cake in her honor. Her mother's secret recipe for butter cream frosting added to the beautifully created yellow and gold sunflowers that elegantly encompassed the chocolate cake. After a delicious tortelli alla zucca dish with fresh grilled streaks and the traditional birthday song, Josiah, Raina, and her parents retreated to the sun porch for Raina to open her gifts.

"Oh, Dad, this is the one I wanted. I looked all over the stores, and this camera was sold out. Where did you find it?"

"If I told you, then I would be giving away all of my secrets. Your mother knows too many of them already. I guess this one will be mine only." Her father winked laughing.

"Well, I have a few of my own, dear." Tori chuckled, handing Raina another package. She took it and quickly tore the wrapping paper before Tori could sit down.

"Mom—how did you get this?" Raina asked, completely stunned by the shadow box she held in her hands.

Inside the frame were three sections separated by dividers. Pictures of her great-grandparents, Enoch and Netamae, lay decoratively placed in the first frame. Along with their pictures were cherished mementos of thimbles and hairpins that belonged to Netamae. Beside them was an assortment of Enoch's lucky fishing lures and his hundred-year-old pocketknife.

In the section to the right were pictures of her grandparents, Rebekah and Isaiah. Miniature wooden carvings of animals and furniture made by Isaiah surrounded them. The backdrop for the pictures was embroidered doilies beautifully stitched with lace trim that Rebekah had handmade.

Tori had made sure to include a couple of family pictures, and some of her riding stargazer in the lower section. Many of her riding ribbons and her lucky belt buckle lay in a triangular pattern next to the pictures.

As Josiah examined the heirloom, the faces staring back at him brought about a deep sense of curiosity.

"Your gift is next, Josiah."

"It is not anything as glamorous as the shadow box, or as cool as your dad's camera. I thought that you might like it though."

"Well, I can't believe you even knew it was my birthday. So I'm sure anything you give me will be cool."

Raina was more careful at tearing the paper than on any of her other gifts. The look in her eyes as she opened the diorama was nothing like Josiah had ever seen before.

"Is it okay, then?"

"It's more than okay. Josiah, this is perfect. Where did you ever come across this? I have never seen anything like it before."

"I made it. As you can see, there are a few flaws. I am really not that handy when it comes to crafts."

"Oh, no. It is absolutely beautiful. Thank you, Josiah. I can't believe this. The planets look so real. The comets and the stars jump right out at me."

"Well, I am glad that you like it then."

"Of course I do. Look at this, Dad. Have you ever seen something this magnificent?"

"No, I haven't. But it will go nice with your space collection in the attic."

Josiah looked up intrigued. "Space collection?"

"You should take him up stairs and show it to him, dear."

"I will—come on, Josiah. Let me take you to 'Planet Raina'."

"Planet Raina?"

"Yes, at least that is what my mom calls it. Right, Mom?"

Tori grinned. "Between her fascination for sunflowers and outer space, I am never sure where we will find her. So, I named the attic 'Planet Raina'. You'll see what I'm talking about when you get up there."

Josiah followed Raina up the stairs to the third floor attic. As soon as Raina turned on the light switch, the constellation appeared brightly on the ceiling. In the corner was a lamp that emitted shapes of stars and plants through the lampshade. From the ceiling hung models of rocket ships and shooting comets. The room truly resembled a planetarium.

Josiah particularly noticed the accuracy of the constellation Raina made from past school projects. She had everything laid out perfectly by dimensions and point of references.

"Wow, Raina, this is amazing. How did you ever come to make this?"

"I told you in Hemet that I was fascinated by the stars."

"Yes, but I never imagined you were this intrigued."

"You say that like it is a bad thing."

"No, of course not. It is just that this is incredible. Your star charts and constellations are extremely accurate. And look," Josiah said, noticing the telescopes by the window.

"Don't worry. I'm not a 'peeping Tom'. I used them to help with the layout. Hey–." Raina suddenly thought. "You said you weren't up on the whole stargazing thing."

"What do you mean?"

"Well, how did you know I had the constellations placed accurately?"

"I do spend a lot of time with my nose in books ... is that not what you said earlier at Fox River?"

"Touché." Raina smirked, as she walked over to the table by the window and leaned over setting her diorama down on it. As she straightened up, Josiah heard her utter a moan, and then watched helplessly as she hit the floor.

"Raina," he screamed, running across the attic to reach her. "Raina, what is wrong? Raina, do you hear me?" He scooped her up into his arms terrified as her body shook and trembled. More moaning sounds escaped between her clenched teeth. Just then, Josiah heard the loud thumps of her parents rushing up the stairs.

Nolan knelt down next to his daughter. "Raina!"

"Nolan, what's wrong?" Tori screamed before she got a clear view of her daughter.

"Tori, she's seizing. Call an ambulance now!"

Tori turned and ran back down the stairs. Josiah thought he heard her stumble half way down the steps. If she fell, she never let on.

"Josiah, what happened to her?"

"I do not know. She was fine. We were talking about the constellation, and then she collapsed. What is happening to her?"

Nolan pulled her free from Josiah's arms to lay her on the floor. "She is having a seizure," he replied, taking her pulse.

"Why?"

"I don't know!"

Tori returned, running up the steps as fast as she had going down them. "The ambulance is on its way! What's wrong with her, Nolan?"

He didn't answer her; instead, he looked at Josiah with a blank stare. "Josiah, go and get my black bag by the front door."

Josiah immediately got to his feet and headed for the steps. He realized his shell's legs were trembling as bad as Raina was. They made the flight of stairs difficult, but he couldn't let his shaky legs slow him down. By the time he was back up in the attic the siren of the rescue squad boomed loudly in the distance.

The next few minutes unfolded like a terrible movie. Josiah felt at a loss to help Raina not knowing what was happening to her body. Her mother appeared as horrified as he was, but Nolan played-out the part of a doctor. He worked quickly not showing any emotion a father would have under these circumstances.

Slowly the minutes blended into hours as the night dragged on since Raina collapsed. Josiah sat around the visitor's lounge waiting for news of Raina's condition. Every now and then, Tori would try to show some optimism to a quick recovery after each update from Nolan. Josiah could see the concern in his eyes and knew Tori's hopes had no foundation.

By eleven o'clock that evening, he and Tori were allowed to join Raina in her room in ICU. Nolan was able to persuade the charge nurse to allow them to wait at her bedside, instead of in the visitor's lounge. Tori sat in the chair Nolan had pulled over to the head of the bed for her. Exhaustion weighed heavily on her face, and no amount of hugs from Nolan could change that.

Josiah grabbed the chair across the room and carried it quietly to the other side of Raina's bed. Taking her hand into his, he bowed his head resting it on the bed rail and prayed. Nolan continued to recheck her vitals, disputing her treatment plan with the attending physician. He argued with Nolan over ethical obligations and conduct. Point made, Nolan was her father not her doctor.

"You should get some rest, Josiah," Tori's voice burrowed its way into his thoughts.

A quick glance at the wall clock told Josiah it was three o'clock in the morning. "I am not tired. Thank you."

"Perhaps not, but you need your rest, too. I will wake you if there are any changes."

The fact that he didn't need sleep wasn't an issue. Even in Raina's grave condition, he had to continue in a human façade. "Sure," he mumbled, but he didn't leave Raina's side. He continued to sit there frustrated—contemplating the words of Anani.

You must find Raina in her dreams and pull her back to this reality. Since her mind is controlling her bodily functions, and she is not ill by true human standards, your powers cannot heal her until you have accessed her mind and destroyed the connection the Demon has with her.

"I cannot do this," he muttered to himself, too loudly. Securing her hand into his tighter than before, he tried to clear the anxiety from his mind and think only of pleasant thoughts.

Unexpectedly, Josiah found himself pacing back and forth restlessly within the dimly lit cave. How he got there this time was a mystery to Josiah. He had not felt the damp air move in around him, and his essence didn't fall victim to the horrid pain and emotions that incapacitated him during the previous episodes. There was no warning that he would find himself here in her dream. The last thing he recalled was the sterile ICU room filled with only gloom. He didn't call upon the power of the Stone Fayruz to send him to her. Had he known what it could do, he would've used it long ago.

Josiah was conscience of the fact that he stayed all night by her bed, listening to her father's directives and waiting for Raina to call to him. Yes, it was the same as in California. Her brain scan showed massive brain damage, warranting surgery. The risky procedure most likely would be ineffective at curing her current condition. Even the realization that her body would remain in a coma on artificial life support was clarified, for those whose hope was too strong to grasp the truth and seriousness of her medical condition.

Very faintly, Josiah heard the voices of her parents flowing through the creaks in the cave wall. Most of their words were mumbled and unclear, but he understood the gist of the conversation.

Nolan pegged Josiah for one of the unrealistic hopers. He saw the look in Josiah's eyes as he held the hand of his unconscious daughter. The look was no different than from in California, except this time Nolan knew Josiah somewhat more than he had initially. He understood that his daughter felt the same for this young man as well.

"He doesn't understand, Tori, what is happening here," he whispered. "The boy is living in a pipe dream."

"Nolan, he is just being optimistic. Raina has to pull through this, she just has to."

He tightened his embrace around her, not his wife, too. "Tori, this isn't like the last time. There are no faulty machines this time that we can blame for her condition. Our daughter is very ill."

"What are you saying, Nolan?"

"I was wrong. We were all wrong."

"Nolan, you're scaring me," she said anxiously.

"Tori, we couldn't diagnose what had made Raina sick the last time. When the scans came back inconclusive because of the dysfunctional equipment, we assumed that some form of bacteria had invaded her blood stream, causing her to collapse. This time the scans show us the same diagnosis. Honey ... Raina is very sick."

"Just a minute." Tori pulled away from Nolan, beginning to panic. "What are you saying?"

"Tori, I got a call from the hospital in Hemet two days after Raina came home. All of their diagnostic evaluations and equipment servicing confirmed that the medical equipment was not faulty. The initial scans upon her admission were conclusive."

"No—no—Nolan, you're wrong. The antibiotics and the blood transfusions cured her the last time. She obviously just had a relapse. Tell her doctor to order the same medication and follow the last treatment plan. She'll be all right then."

"Tori, that treatment just masked her illness. It won't work this time, honey."

"Why not," she shouted, giving in to the fear that waited to overtake her senses.

Josiah heard Tori screaming at Nolan in the dream world and flinched. He knew that the Demon was succeeding. He closed his eyes in disgust, and then he opened them again trying to focus on the Raina that was here with him in the cave. Even his Guardian mind grew weary trying to concentrate on the events in the cave and the true condition of Raina out of the dream world.

"Josiah, are you all right?" Raina asked, concerned by his change in appearance.

"Yes, I am just lost in thought."

Tori's cries continued to spill over into the cave adding to the already horrific emotions damning Josiah's cause.

"Honey, please, get a hold of yourself," Nolan said. His voice sounded callus and heartless.

"Get a hold of myself. Nolan, for the love of God, you just told me that my daughter is dying!"

"Tori, please, you'll wake the boy. He just fell asleep a few minutes ago. Let him rest."

"Why didn't you tell me the hospital called?"

"Because I watched Raina, and she seemed fine. She sprung back too fast to be as ill as her diagnosis led us to believe. I just didn't think she was sick."

"You should have told me," Tori interjected, feeling the anger pressing for its escape.

"I didn't want to worry you. I was doing all that I could."

"Doing all that you could. Doing what—watching our daughter die?" Her words sounded harsh, but Nolan knew the love behind them.

"No, I was running some tests of my own."

"Running tests, what do you mean?"

"I took some hair and blood samples from Raina when she was sleeping. I sent them to the lab in Madison and had the samples tested for every illness in the book as well as toxicology panels."

"Toxicology ... what were you thinking?"

"When she first arrived in the ICU at General, she showed signs of a drug overdose."

"Our daughter doesn't use drugs."

"Tori ... Pasadena is a big city sitting right alongside L.A. She could've been subjected to something without her knowledge. The apartments in Hemet were old, and the lead paint had never been removed. But those labs came back negative."

"Nolan, your prognosis has to be wrong. Our daughter has to pull through this."

Tori's pleas for her daughter's health went unheard by Raina. As far as her mind knew, she truly was in the cave and not dying in a hospital bed.

Josiah continued to pace like a caged lion as he tried to concentrate and shut out the voices from the other side. He had not discovered how to enter this dream and he didn't know what it would take to leave it. He only knew that he had to find away to take her from there. That night in her living room when she slept in his arms, he just simply wished to search out her soul, and it was honor for his people that had stopped his kiss and brought him back to reality.

Emotions seemed to play a part in crossing between the dreams and the waking world. His thoughts that night were full of love, as they are now. However, tonight the emotions of love struggled with the emotions of pity and grief. In the need for her safety, he could find no sense of honor.

"It has to be something else. Something that I am missing," he murmured to himself.

"What did you say?"

He ignored her question, still evaluating how he got there, and how the Demon brought her there so easily without any warning.

"It has to be some kind of portal he uses. An object he has possessed."

It was then when Raina saw a determination in Josiah's eyes that she recognized from another time.

"The stranger! Yes, the stranger."

"What stranger, Josiah?"

"No one," he scowled. Josiah chided himself for speaking too freely.

This was Raina's dream. The thought of her being conscious enough to realize that or to know she had the same dream before was idiotic. He had to concentrate on what he had seen during his visions in this place. There was the stranger he saw the last time. He had to be the same one Raina thought was her great-grandfather. Then he remembered the stranger in the cave who held a shiny object into the air.

"Yes, the shining light. That has to be it!"

"What light? Josiah, tell me what we're looking for?" she demanded.

"A clue ... I do not know—a message or a sign to show us the way out."

He couldn't stop his essence from absorbing her fears and reacting upon them himself. The moment was becoming too overwhelming for him. His shell couldn't contain the massive amount of energy and molecules within the cave. His shell shouldn't truly exist in this place, but the power of the Tracker was strong. He controlled every element around them. If he was real in this realm, then there was the possibility that a part of Raina was real, too. Josiah sickened himself, knowing that now his weakness was becoming another danger for her. His endurance was already thin with the splitting of his essence. The amount of energy it took to maintain the two shells was incredible.

"What do you mean the way out? Can you be more specific? Where do you think we are?" she asked, curiously.

"Yes—no, I am sorry. I am not sure what we are looking for. I will just know it when I find it. It has to be here somewhere in all of this junk," Josiah shot back angrily. In a growing rage, he continued shifting through the massive amount of artifacts stacked in a pile on the cave floor.

Then picking up a vase, he launched it across the cavern. The sound of the crystal shattering startled Raina, and she cowered to the ground screaming. Josiah immediately froze, feeling his shell's endurance weakening further.

He sensed her fear and knelt down next to her trying to concentrate on projecting the emotion of compassion toward her.

"I am sorry. I did not mean to make you afraid. It is just that—I am—" He lowered his eyes in shame. "I am not the best at handling situations like this. Please, forgive me."

Raina nodded, trying to hide her anxiety. "It's okay."

Josiah grinned, pretending he was calm. She must not know how badly the intensity of the moment was affecting him. He felt the strands of his human shell fraying from the power of other tormented souls lingering in the cave. If he didn't get a hold of himself, his essence would release destroying the cave and his precious Raina. The thought of her perishing by his own hand devastated him. Once, when she harbored the Sentinel he knew Raina could withstand the release of his essence. Now, her human body was defenseless against the forces that gave Josiah life.

The beeping sound, too faint for Raina to hear, continued to remind him that her fate was in his hands.

Since he entered into the realm, her heart rate had dropped. Even as she huddled in the corner, her anxiety was not enough to increase her heart rate in the real world.

When he raised his eyes to meet hers, Josiah moaned, facing the possibility of defeat. The bloody discharge from her ears and nose had seeped over into the dream world. Her realities were overlapping, and her body was dying in both realms. This was no longer a trick of the Demon's to encourage cranial surgery. Her body was dying, and Josiah could do nothing to save her. The evil had penetrated the castle walls, and Josiah's kingdom was crumbling.

"What are you looking at?" Raina questioned, perplexed at his expression.

With a smile, he extended his hand toward her to help her up from the ground. "Nothing. I was just lost in thought trying to find a way out of here."

Just then, Tori's screams invaded the cave. "Nolan— look!"

Josiah froze, waiting to hear what had concerned Tori. Until now, he hated the fact that her words flowed over into the dream world. Now he realized it was a helpful form of communication to monitor Raina's earthly condition.

Nolan released Tori, moving to Raina's bedside. His body jerked the bed in his haste to examine his daughter.

"Nolan, what's happening to her?"

"She's bleeding out!" Nolan gasped, reaching to press her call light.

"How are you going to do that?" Raina asked, diverting his attention away from the outside activity. "We don't even know where we are?"

"I just need to find the key to this place."

She looked at him confused. "Josiah, there is no keyhole to use a key on."

"I am sorry. I did not mean an actual key. I need an item that does something it is not suppose to. That will help us find our way out of here."

"What do you think it will look like?" she questioned, kicking a gold challis lying on the floor.

"It is like a—"

"What about this?" Raina asked Josiah, tugging at the locket tucked into her shirt.

"What is that?"

"It's a locket. My great-grandparents gave it to me before they died."

Raina held it out for Josiah to look at. The gold object within her hand emitted a glow that her eyes couldn't see. Josiah recognized the glow immediately. He couldn't mistake the residue left by his essence.

"The back window was welded shut, and my great-granddad said that he couldn't fix it. However, that wouldn't be true because he was a genius at everything. There must have been a reason that he didn't truly want to fix it. So, one day I fiddled with the spring, and it popped open. When I did, the room lit up with this amazing bright light, and the locket played a beautiful song. I wanted to cry because it sounded so amazingly familiar."

Raina pressed on the snap, and the clicking noise popped in Josiah's ears. It made the same sound two human years ago, when he created it for her.

Anxiously she held out the paper toward Josiah. "This piece of paper fell out of it. I knew it was old, but I couldn't read it because it was drawn over. For some reason, the squiggly lines looked familiar, too ... but I don't know why. I must have seen them before ... except I don't know where I would have."

He felt the power of his essence emanating from the locket he recognized as the one he made for her in the

Garden of Love on her seventeenth birthday. Then closing his eyes, Josiah broke the hold the power of his lingering essence had on him. He opened his eyes again concentrating on the tiny piece of paper Raina grasped tightly in her fingers. His skin barely brushed against hers when immediately, he saw the long forgotten blue light surge from his fingers.

It increased with an astounding sensation of warmth that traveled up his arm. Josiah's body began spontaneously trembling. The parchment he held allowed the desires of others to come true. With one wish upon the scroll, he could have all he ever wanted as long as he was truly determined to receive his desires.

"Espérer," he whispered. Josiah was terrified that he held such power in his hand. If the wrong person touched the scroll and made a wish, all humanity could fall. "Where did you get this?" he demanded, rebuking the blue light.

"It was in the locket," she said, glancing back to the locket in her hand. Her voice trailed off, and she stood still staring at the locket.

He became apprehensive of her sudden change in demeanor. "Raina, what is it, what is wrong? Raina, talk to me."

"The picture," she mumbled, raising her eyes to look at him. "How did you do that?"

He looked at her puzzled. "Do what, Raina?"

"How did you put this picture in here? Where did you get this from anyway?" her voice now sounded fearful.

"What picture?" he questioned, taking a step closer to her. Raina handed him the locket, so Josiah could see what she was looking at. His heart skipped a beat, and his surprise was clear to Raina.

"This is Dewitt Beach in Silver Lake. I was never there with you. Tell me how you got this picture. How did you put it into my locket?"

He answered slowly, staring at a picture of him with his arm around Raina at the beach. "I did not make this."

"Josiah, wake up!" Nolan grabbed onto the shoulders of the shell left motionless in the hospital room to push him out of the way. From inside the dream realm, Josiah looked up at the cave wall where the sound of Nolan's screams were coming from.

The hospital bed jerked to one side as two nurses arrived to assist Raina. Josiah was barely aware of the movement in either realm. He wanted to hear why Nolan was so fearful.

Raina looked into his pale face afraid. "Are you—all right?"

"I do not know," he whispered doubtfully. He examined his hands watching as the blue glow magnified, now consuming his hands. He heard the beeping sound warning that Raina's heartbeat changed again. Josiah began turning his palms upward, waving his hands in a fluid motion. He threw the scroll onto the ground afraid he couldn't stop the transition.

"Raina, run!"

"That light—where is it coming from? What is happening to you?"

"Raina, run—get away from me now!"

"What's happening here?" her screams filled the atmosphere with her negative energy.

He didn't answer her. At this moment, his mind was consumed by the many reasons for why the light had appeared. If he didn't control the blue light, then all would be lost and his energy surge could unwillingly kill Raina.

"Can you hear me?" Raina yelled, staring at the fading body of Josiah. Afraid that he was now something else she needed to fear.

"Son, get out of my way," the doctor ordered.

Josiah realized then, that he was not in the cave anymore. His whole essence was now in the shell propped against the chair that once sat next to Raina's bed.

"What is wrong with her?" Josiah shouted, trying to collect his bearings.

"Josiah, listen to me," Nolan urged. "Just go out to the waiting room."

"No," he begged, "tell me what is wrong. What is happening to her?"

"Josiah—go," he ordered again, checking Raina's pupilary reaction. "Tori, take him please!"

More members of the medical team came running into the room. One grabbed the stethoscope from around Nolan's neck and began taking Raina's blood pressure. The other opened the crash cart anticipating what medical items might be needed.

"Her BP is 90 over 68," the nurse hollered out.

Josiah shouted over the nurse's report. "No, I want to stay!"

Nolan looked up from cardiac strip—his voice was shaky. "Josiah—Raina is very ill. We need to help her now. You're just in the way!"

Tori moved to Josiah's side. She grabbed his arm upon her husband's instructions and tried to lead Josiah from the room.

"No, I have to stay," he begged, pulling away from Tori.

"Honey, please," she pleaded, "let them work. They need the room."

"No, I need to be here, in case she calls to me!"

Nolan shouted impatiently. "Josiah, my daughter is in a coma! She won't be calling for you. Now get out of here before I call security!"

Josiah looked at Nolan hopelessly. They didn't understand, nor could he explain to them what was happening to Raina. He hesitantly took two steps toward the door to comply—when he felt the cold grow over him. His shell began to convulse, and he collapsed to the floor. His body wailed and shook horribly.

"Nolan!" Tori screamed kneeling horrified next to Josiah's trembling body.

Nolan looked up from Raina's heart monitor, devastated that her heart rate dropped again. He could barely see the top of Tori's head over the edge of the bed at first. He gasped as his blood rushed through his body making his heart jump. What could be wrong with his wife?

Nolan darted around the side of the bed surprised at seeing Josiah convulsing on the floor. He looked back at his Raina knowing her fate. Josiah was a new victim now, and he needed medical help. He knelt down beside Josiah, assessing his airway and checking his carotid pulse.

"It's ... too fast," he mumbled to himself. "Josiah, can you hear me," he hollered. "Nurse, start an IV and let's get some medication onboard to stop the seizures!"

"What is the rundown?" Dr. Jon King, the new resident asked. Then he kneeled next to Josiah, opposite of Nolan.

Nolan looked up at his dying daughter and then back at him. "I don't know," he said weakly.

Dr. King began checking Josiah's vitals. "I got this. Go to your daughter," he ordered, knowing firsthand the emotion of helplessness. "Son, do you hear me. Can you understand what I am saying?" he asked, staring at the lifeless shell that resembled his son.

To the others in the room, he was just another doctor. To Josiah, he was quite possibly his sole reason for survival. Jon sensed the diminishing power of Josiah's essence. The shell he created was dying. If it ended its function, while Josiah remained inside, he too, would be lost. Jon needed to intervene, but not here. The humans must not be allowed to witness this intervention. Jon had to get Josiah's shell to some place where he could safely try to revive it.

"We need to get him to CT," Dr. King commanded.

Jon assisted the other staff of the Emergency Response Team who was not attending to Raina, to load the unconscious boy onto the gurney. The team began to push Josiah hurriedly from the room toward Radiology. As they darted down the hall, Jon acted to secure their moment of escape.

Jon's people forbade mind control, except Josiah had attracted too much attention to walk away unnoticed. As they entered the evaluator, Jon fogged the minds of the team of nurses and doctors. With one pass of his hand, he and the shell of Josiah's body faded from the elevator. Left standing seemingly unaware of the past few minutes was a group of doctors and nurses with an empty cart. When the doors opened, each exited completely oblivious to the tragedy happening on the third floor. Jon would have to risk returning later to fog the minds of the others.

"Josiah," Raina kept calling, searching frantically for some reason to answer her questions about what was happening to him. His fading body reminded her of the ghost stories she heard as a child. Raina wondered in the back of her mind if Josiah was truly a ghost. All of a sudden, Raina saw a dark flash dart across the room. She recognized the pungent odor of the Demon. The wretched beast lunged at the remaining image of Josiah, encircling him with his scaly arms. Josiah collapsed to the ground, locked in the black mass.

"Josiah—Josiah!"

She watched Josiah's now visible body thrash about on the musty cavern floor. The dark figure's features were lost in the dim light, but Josiah's contorted face full of anguish could be clearly seen. His moans of pain and torment vibrated off the cave walls. Their meaning was beyond Raina's comprehension, yet they afflicted her. Each time Josiah received a substantial blow from the evil one, Raina's body received the negative energy. The techniques of the Demon's torturous effects were also seen on Raina's human body.

"Were losing her!" the nurse yelled to get the doctors' attention.

Again, her heartbeat fluctuated, becoming slower. With each assault sustained by Josiah to his essence, both Raina and he felt the effects.

The Demon reached for the locket, dangling from Josiah's fist. He grabbed it trying to yank it free from Josiah's grip. Under normal circumstances, the chain should have snapped, but this one remained strong.

The despicable growling noise of the Demon vibrated in Raina's ears covering any sounds Josiah made. The attacker intentionally blocked his commands for her to pick up the brown paper from the cave floor. He knew, too well, what was written on the scroll. If one word was uttered in this realm, he would be destroyed and the realm with him.

"Raina—grab the parchment and run!" a mysterious voice shouted, rippling through the cave.

"No!" The Demon raised his hand shooting a bolt of electricity at Raina. It hit her, throwing her body into the pool of stagnant water at the eastern end of the cave. The cold water immediately began to make her tremble.

"She's crashing!" Nolan reached for the drug box. He grabbed a vile of medication and injected it into the IV tubing.

Tori remained still in the corner of the hospital room. Her daughter's life was failing, and she knew any minute that it would be over. Her tears began to fall hard obstructing her view. The insanity of the moment was playing tricks on her mind. She could've sworn that her dead grandfather stood hovering over the dying body of Raina. His face looked strained and his eyes didn't hold the beauty she had remembered seeing all of her life. Then the figure smiled at her and disappeared.

In the cave, Raina swam frantically trying to get out of the pond. Her screams no longer echoed, and her heart began to fail from the cold temperatures. Still struggling, she thrust her outstretched fingers out of the blackened waters looking for a cliff or something to pull her out with safely. Raina felt a sense of relief as she clutched onto something warm. Her mind told her it was someone's hand. A helpful stranger perhaps, coming to her rescue. She felt his arm wrap around her wrist pulling her body through the layers of liquid. Before she knew it, she was on the cold rocky ground coughing and struggling to breathe.

"Raina ... Raina?"

She heard the voice calling to her. It was so familiar and comforting, but she couldn't see where the voice was coming from. She wiped the murky debris from the foul water out of her eyes, and then focused on the voice.

"Raina, you are okay—just breathe."

She inhaled deeply, trying to catch her breath as the calm voice instructed her. The cool musty air stung, smelling like sewage and death.

"Come on, we must hurry," the man's familiar voice instructed, still demonstrating its calm tone.

Raina staggered to her feet, feeling around her for something to hold onto.

"Do not worry, child, I have you," Enoch said in a soothing tone. He took hold of her arm, and then began to lead her through the underground passage. The wind howled, blowing strongly against them. Her frail frame shuddered from the fierce current of air as she fought desperately to keep up with her savior. Feeling her pace lessen, he tugged her along more forcibly. There was no time to concentrate on being gentle. Enoch knew that time was running out, and their adversary would find them soon.

"We must hurry, Raina, I sense that he is coming."

She tried to move faster feeling every bit of her strength dissipate. "I'm trying. Where is Josiah?"

He didn't answer her. Then pulling harder on her arm, he forced Raina along through the corridors. Her body banged into the walls helplessly as they pressed on. She was almost too far gone with shock to feel the abrasions where the jagged rocks sliced through her skin. The earth began to shift beneath their feet, and Enoch felt the incline of the ground. Raina continued to struggle, losing her balance. She threw her arm out in front of her, managing to push off from the ground. Enoch scooped her up steadying her in the middle of the path.

Enoch's essence sensed the entrance was close, except he realized the evil entity was even closer. Just as the entrance came into view, a large dark colored eagle with glowing red eyes swooped down in front of them. His large talons extended five-feet wide, fully intent on capturing its prey in its massive claws. His enormous wingspan reached twenty-feet from the tip of one wing to tip of the other. The force of his flapping wings blew chunks of dirt and small rocks through the air.

Raina heard the demon bird's horrid scream, but her vision was obscured from the darkness.

"Duck, Raina!" Enoch screamed, pushing her to the ground.

She fell hard to the dirt floor, smashing her head against the sharp edge of a fluorescent colored rock. She rolled around on the ground in pain trying to get away from the eagle. It landed inches from her head clawing and scratching in the dirt. A cloud of dust flew into the air blocking Raina from Enoch's view.

Enoch screamed trying to shout over the eagle's deafening squawk. "Raina—run!"

Raina barely heard his words uttered because of the screeching bird's protest against his unwanted visitors. Designed to kill, this beast's sole desire was for his next meal.

Enoch hollered again, with urgency in his voice. "Raina, go ... go!"

This time the eagle was too close, and she couldn't hear his plea at all. Enoch grabbed some rocks from off the ground and began pelting the vicious feathered fiend in the head. Instantly, it turned its attention from Raina to Enoch. In a swift motion, the eagle lunged at him. Its wide pointed talons dug deep into Enoch's right arm, dragging him into his colossal claws.

Enoch thrashed, punching at the eagle attempting to free himself. He concentrated, trying to use his powers to strike back, except nothing happened. Another trick of the Demon's doing. Mind over matter was how he practiced his deception. Although Enoch couldn't see or feel his powers striking his assailant, Raina clearly saw the green light illuminating Enoch and the bird.

The room temperature changed, and Raina felt the cold hovering over her. She screamed scurrying to her feet, still fumbling in the dark. She remembered the glow of her locket and reached for her neck. Raina sighed when she realized the locket was not there, and she knew what this meant. The terror began to swallow her up into the Demon's clutches, and Raina became hysterical. The Demon laughed wickedly as he held her tightly, sucking all hope and determination to free herself from her mind. Tarik focused so intently on Raina, that he allowed the illusion of the eagle's vigor to fade.

Enoch realized that the menacing bird was not real, and that his essence indeed reigned within this mysterious realm of Tarik's. He pulled the energy from around him and drew in his strength from the cave's molecules. His essence manipulated the natural energy of the green light, and then he thrust it into the air. It collided with the eagle—then the energy engrossed his captor, and his feathers burst into flames. Enoch jumped away from the blazing fowl. Its squawk roared through the cave, as the eagle staggered around crashing into the walls. Enoch sprinted to the other end of the large cavern watching as the fowl was reduced to a pile of smoldering embers.

"No!" Tarik froze at the sight of his prized possession crumbled to ashes before him. "How dare you come into my realm and destroy my possessions."

In one leap, Tarik had Raina in his grip, shaking her in anger. He threw her into the cavern wall, admiring how worthless her human skin was at protecting her.

"No!" Tori's voice shot through the cave.

"She's not breathing," Nolan yelled, warning the members from the team who remained after Josiah was taken to Radiology. "Call a code!"

Nolan reached under the side of the bed, pulling a silver pin from out of a manufactured notch on the bed frame. At once, the head of the hospital bed lowered, shaking

Raina's head and arms. Nolan grabbed the cardiac board, and then rolled Raina over, hurriedly placing the plastic board under her.

"I've got this," a voice roared in his ears as Nolan felt his body shifting. "Nolan, we've got this."

Nolan recognized the voice. It belonged to his good friend and colleague Dr. Graham Reedman.

"Nurse?" Graham said, nodding his head toward the traumatized Nolan. "Take him and his wife out into the hall."

She grabbed Nolan's arm, but somehow he managed to pull away. "No, I need to stay!"

Graham removed the paddles from the defibrillator. "Nurse—now!"

The Demon picked Raina up again with his mental powers, twirling her body in circles in the air. Then he turned toward Enoch with a ferocious glaze in his eyes. Determined to fight and win, he lunged at him. Raina's body slammed into the jagged rocks and fell like a rag doll to the ground. She lay there dizzy and disoriented from the dark. Off in the distance she could hear thunderous crashing sounds followed by flashes of light. Bolts of electricity bounced off the damp walls, shooting sparks through the air.

Raina cowered on the ground, fearfully curling her body into the fetal position. She tried to protect herself from the chaos around her. Her chest felt like it was caving in from some type of pressure. She swore that her heart was on fire. The evil entity had succeeded in stealing her hope. Raina gave up and began to cry, praying for her life to end.

"Make this stop!"

Then mysteriously, she was no longer in the cave. Raina realized that she was lying on a forest floor. The air smelled of fish, and the call of loons beckoned for her attention.

Next to her laid a tiny sunflower. Raina strained to see its beauty through the red liquid caked in her eyes. With a trembling hand, she reached out to touch the flower. A faint aroma of angel face rose swirled past her, bringing a soft whisper in the wind. She heard the words quite distinctively as they flowed with a comforting tone.

"Raina ... Raina, I am here."

"Josiah," she managed to mumble through her parched lips. The name brought her a sense of inner peace and courage. She uttered the words so easily, as each vowel formed perfectly over her tongue.

The voice's response was drowned out by a loud thud behind her. The shaking earth scattered debris into the air. It fell upon Raina's body covering her in a blanket of ash. She watched horrified as the forest disappeared and she found herself lying on the cave floor again.

Then something sharp pierced Raina's chest, tearing her flesh. She screamed in pain swatting at the burning sensation swarming through the wound. Blood spewed from her chest, seeping onto the fluorescent stones. The coarse colored rocks began to shine brighter than before. This glimmering effect traveled along the cavern floor changing the exterior of each rock.

Enoch and Tarik still fought, fully intent on destroying one another. Locked in a battle of good versus evil, they were oblivious to the changing condition of the cavern floor.

Raina became alarmed as she saw the rock's appearances begin to transform. Desperate to flee, she strained to sit up and couldn't. Her body ached, and she was weak from hemorrhaging. The excruciating pain radiating from her chest stopped her from getting away from there. She began to panic, watching as the illuminating effects encompassed more of the rock littered surface.

It moved at a quick pace, darting up the east wall until it reached the ceiling. The clay surface drew in the strange colorful mass, allowing it to change into a liquid consistency. It began to ooze into the crevasses gouged through the walls, expanding inside of the hollow areas until they were full. Unexpectedly, the clay turned to mush, and the walls began to disintegrate, creating a rocky mudslide. Sections of the ceiling broke loose, dropping large chunks of rocks everywhere. They rained down to an unusual extent crashing around the fighting entities.

A boulder smacked Enoch on the shoulder, breaking the mental connection the duo shared. It was then that Enoch realized the cave was collapsing. He shot one more burst of energy toward Tarik, then Enoch dove to rescue his distraught great-granddaughter. He landed upright next to her supine body. Bending over he hoisted the nearly unconscious Raina to her feet. Carefully he pulled her closer into his body trying to shield her head and protect her from falling fragments.

Her face flopped against his chest, and she noticed a soft glow coming from above her head. Raina realized that it was the same locket her great-grandparents had given her. Through the soft glow of an etched sunflower, she made out the calming eyes of her rescuer.

"Grandpa?" she whispered, and then she collapsed, becoming unresponsive in his arms.

To Enoch's right, he noticed a vivid tubular shaped beam of light trickling through the crevasse in the south wall of the passageway. It shone brightly upon a series of metamorphic rocks, seemingly unchanged by the fluorescent light. Strategically placed in a zigzag pattern, Enoch recognized the circular shapes that resembled the same pattern as what was on the case of the scroll of hope. Enoch had no choice. He had to risk the possible misinterpretation of the pattern the light formed upon the rocks and advanced forward.

He hurriedly positioned Raina over his shoulder and began moving cautiously. He continued in a sequence of slippery steps and jumps landing onto the rocks that were sinking into the ooze. The crevasse in the wall opened wider with every step Enoch took. When he reached the last rock, he hurled himself into the air with Raina still propped over his shoulder. Just then, a strong force surrounded his body pulling him down. He and Raina tumbled violently to the ground.

"Raina," he pleaded, looking at his great-granddaughter still unconscious a few feet away from him.

Before he could call out to her again, the force tightened its clutches around him. Enoch felt the power draining from his essence. He cringed, recognizing the evil laugh of Tarik. The cloaked stranger of Raina's terrifying dreams had won. The darkness had succeeded to claim Raina's great-grandfather in the same mental prison he held Raina securely within.

Enoch's Guardian heart began to melt, and his sense of failure loomed deep in his mind. Human tears of love and defeat began to gush from his Guardian eyes. Enoch realized that even after his careful planning, he had fell victim to the evil that hunted Raina since her birth. This time the glowing sunflower wouldn't save them as he had planned.

Death would meet them in this mysterious realm of no escape. Tarik had indeed proven to be cleverer than Enoch thought. Even after he was injured and lost his prize pet, Tarik's tricks of mind control and illusions stole Raina's and Enoch's rationality. In their minds, they believed there was no way to escape and waited for death to take them. The meaning of the Espérer scroll meant nothing to Enoch now. The effects of Tarik's magic drained the scroll's memory from him.

The cavern floor continued to turn fluorescent colors as Raina's blood still poured upon the ground. The stones that Enoch used to assist in his escape sunk beneath the ooze and disappeared. The sludge that formed from the ooze still crept along the walls, now completely covering the cave. The ceiling continued to crumble, falling much quicker than before. Raina's body lay covered by the crashing debris. The ooze had surrounded her now, encroaching closer to where she was laying.

Enoch's tears found no end even when his human heart broke in two. His human form could no longer survive the pending doom and sustain his essence. If Enoch didn't flee and leave Raina there, his essence would perish. His Guardian mind told him what he needed to do, except the last reaming shreds of his humanity fought with right and wrong. Against his will, Enoch's essence converted back to his true form sending a burst of energy in all directions.

"No!" he screamed. Then he used his dying powers to rein back in the energy he released and sent it in the form of a whirlwind down the tunnel to his left. He lingered aimlessly in the cave waiting for the air to clear. His fabricated tear ducts were gone, but the human left inside of him shed one last tear.

Enoch sighed deeply as a single teardrop fell softly across the back of his hand. When it made contact with his celestial body, the teardrop turned an olive color emitting an intense light and a humming noise. The olive colored light illuminated the space his essence occupied, projecting shadows of musical notes dancing around him. The music that guided Raina so faithfully in her time of need came to their rescue now. The melody brought a song of hope. It was this hope that had filled Enoch's mind, renewing his power to fight back against Tarik.

Enoch charged his energy, propelling it through the olive colored tear soaking into his hand. Instantly, the olive light flashed around them, and the musical notes formed a sword. At Enoch's unspoken command, the sword flung through the air striking the stunned Tarik. He fell to the ground screaming as the music sucked his reason for existing from him. The song consumed the sadness and bitterness from Tarik's mind, destroying the hold he had upon this universe.

As Tarik lay dying, Enoch's essence immediately drew him to Raina. With emotions incomprehensible to a Guardian, he cradled her in his arms. Human compassion was how he would save Raina.

The magic of Tarik's realm began to dissipate and the cave disappeared.

"No!" Tarik squealed, as his realm faded. At that moment in the last chorus of the olive light's song, Tarik was gone.

The lake's waves sent a calming song into the sunlight. Enoch found himself standing at the edge of the water in his true form. His tears had dried, and his hope was renewed. For next to him fast asleep and uninjured, lay his great-granddaughter supine in the warm sand. The only sign of her previous state was a small drop of fluorescent ooze that had dried on the palm of her hand. It was so tiny that Enoch knew that no human would be able to see it. The urge to wipe it away slowly melted because of the sound of the music that echoed from within the spot of ooze.

Enoch turned around examining the glorious view. He rejoiced at their safety believing that he had succeeded in destroying Tarik's realm. Relieved, he knelt down next Raina and began to rub her forehead.

"Rest, my child. You are safe for now," he whispered, examining the green-crusted stone Raina gripped tightly in her hand. Enoch reach out to take it from her when Raina's body faded from before him. In her absence, the sand remained undisturbed. Enoch scooped up a handful of sand from where she lay, and let the grains slip between his fingers. As the sand blew in the wind, Enoch stood up to admire the view one last time.

From the beach, he could see the many realms running parallel with one another. To his right the cold wind gust across Silver Lake. The snow fell heavily, crunching under the feet of the workers. Their voices carried in the wind, clearly heard over the chopping of the ice. He almost shuddered as he heard the squeal of the train wheels coasting.

To his left he watched Raina as a teenager sitting in the swing. Beside her, a dark-haired boy with emerald-green eyes held her hand tenderly. He followed her eyes off to one side and found Raina swimming in Silver Lake with her father. Nolan's laughter filled the air as he challenged Raina to a race to the buoy and back.

Enoch turned once more to stand in front of his old Earth home. He watched himself stroll up the steps and sit in the rocking chair beside the only woman who could keep him on Earth. Lovingly, he grasped her hand in his and began to hum their favorite song. He watched as his wife closed her eyes, and then he smiled when her soul drifted toward Heaven.

This moment of peace brought more joy than imaginable. For at that moment echoing in the wind were three precious words. Enoch didn't have to witness what was happening to know the outcome in Raina's hospital room.

"There's a heartbeat!" Graham yelled. Nolan's knees weakened, and he leaned against the doorframe for support. His wife was oblivious to her husband's relief. She had not heard Graham's words with her face buried into Nolan's chest.

35.
ANSWERED HOPE

Dream Realm—present-day

Jaleel watched stunned as Jon knelt on the ground, holding Josiah's lifeless shell. Human concern consumed him, toying with his mind. For Jon to see his son in this state brought about unnatural emotions that he didn't know how to deal with. In his former days as a Guardian, Jon had watched many Esprit de corps whose fathers knelt in prayer over their dying children. He saw two outcomes from those tragedies. For as many children he witnessed healed, he also stood by the gravesite spiritually consoling the fathers of those who didn't survive. At this moment, Jon truly understood what human love was. All the sacrifices he saw fathers commit in the name of love, finally made sense to him. This willingness to risk one's life for another became very clear.

Jon knew from the dreadful barn fire, that he was able to heal his son once before. He hoped now that the energy within his essence was strong enough this time to heal him. He linked his essence with Josiah's essence, and his mind called out to his son attempting to communicate with him. Jon's concentration was poor and his emotional state hindered the connection.

Josiah, Josiah ... can you hear me? he pleaded from within his mind. *Josiah, you must listen to me.*

Jon felt Josiah becoming weaker during each attempt. Every moment he remained in the shell the chances of survival diminished. Jon's energy also began to dim as he shared his life force with his son. He feared that Josiah's shell would perish killing him, so he refused to pull his essence back. He hoped his energy would help sustain his son until he could be rescued from his fake humanoid body. Jon too, would make a father's sacrifice by acting with no regard to his own life. He became more fearful this time than he had the day of the burning barn. That day Josiah suffered from guilt, today he clearly was injured.

Josiah, focus on the sound of my voice. Josiah, do you hear me? Jon's voice spoke through his thoughts, trying to maintain his link with his son. *Do you know where we are, my son?*

Josiah just barely became aware of his father's intervention. *Father?* He thought, feeling his mind bogged down with the memories of Raina's terrified state.

The connection Jon had with Josiah was not nearly as strong, as he needed it to be. Josiah's mind fought for control to return to the dream world. Jon could feel his resistance as Raina's screams echoed in both of their minds.

Son—I know she is in danger, but you must let go. Josiah, you are dying. You must break your link with her. Josiah ... do you understand me?

"Jon—what is happening?" Jaleel pleaded, watching as Jon and Josiah quietly sat still like statues.

Father? Josiah thought, hearing his friend's voice muffled in the distance. He realized that he was no longer occupying his shell in the cave, even though he still heard the dripping water and felt the darkness's chill. *Where is Raina? I can hear her crying.*

I know, my son, so can I.

Jaleel placed his hand on Josiah's limp shoulder growing impatient for the well-being of his friend. He couldn't hear the conversation, except he sensed the urgency in Jon's essence. Jaleel knew his friend was dying, and he couldn't help him.

"Does he hear you, Jon? Are you sure that this is working?"

How did I get here? Josiah thought weakly. His essence felt drained and powerless. He could feel Jaleel touching his trembling shell—hear his father's words in his mind—but he felt as if his essence was still standing by his beloved.

I am not sure, his father answered. *Your human shell on Earth is perishing. I removed it from the hospital room and brought it to this place. Jaleel is here with me. We are still in the hospital in the lower level of the building. We have been hiding down here waiting for you to come around.*

How did you pull me from the dream world?

I am not sure that I really have, Josiah. Your mind keeps fading from me. Briefly, I see the cave in your mind. You are standing next to Raina and a stranger. However, as fast as that vision comes, it disappears. When that happens, I lose my connection with your mind all-together.

I know who the stranger is, Father. His name is Enoch. He was once a wise Elder who traded his essence for the sake of another.

Son, what are you talking about, your words make no sense?

He acts of his own accord, Father, to help Raina. Judgment will be upon him, and there is nothing that I can do to help him.

"Jon, have you reached him, yet?" Jaleel inquired, still anxious to know what was happening. "Is he aware of your link to his mind?"

Josiah, the universe is immense. The realms support many entities. Are you saying you did not recruit his assistance?

No, I did not. He appeared to me when I was fighting to rescue Raina.

Son, I have been trying to communicate with the remnants of your essence that became trapped in your shell. It has been a long time. Josiah, your essence is so weak. How did you ever survive?

Josiah didn't answer his father's question. He was not sure how he ever made it from the cave alive during any of the dreams. His mind raced, trying to sort out his reality from the dream world.

What happened to my earthly shell? Father, why was it perishing?

"Jon, tell me, is he all right?" Jaleel demanded, growing tired of Jon's silence.

"Yes, Jaleel. He seems fine, at least for the time being. He has heard me, except he is extremely confused."

"Does he know what is happening?"

I do not know, Jon continued, answering Josiah's thoughts and ignoring Jaleel's questions. *I felt your essence weaken, and I went looking for you. I found you on the floor of Raina's room. Her father was trying to help you with the assistance of some other hospital staff.*

Josiah became alarmed. *They saw me collapse. Does anyone know my shell is not real?*

No, they do not. I fogged their memories.

Father ... no! Josiah's mind cried out. He couldn't bear to have his father punished because of his weaknesses.

It will be fine, Josiah. No one who came to your aid remembers the episode. It is as if it never happened.

Nevertheless, I was in her room talking to them, Father. When she pulled me into her dream, my shell was left there.

It is all right, my son. Her parents seem to remember that you went back to Raina's home to get some rest and to give them some time alone with her.

You can create scenarios as well? Josiah interjected, surprised at his father's capacities.

Yes, I can. My mind link with Elder Mataya's mind has taught me a few things.

Father, I feel so different.

I know, Josiah. Your essence has been in a great struggle and is damaged. The pull that the cave has on you is tremendous.

Am, I dying? Josiah asked, sifting through his mind to hear his father's answer. There was no hiding the truth. The linking of their minds joined their thoughts and energy.

I do not know what will happen, Josiah, should I release you. I have never found myself subjected to such a situation as this before.

I need to see Raina. I need to make sure her mind is safe. Let me go back.

I do not think it wise at this moment. I have told you. I do not know what will happen when I release you from my essence. I do not know if you will go back there at all. I am not sure how the cave draws you in the first place.

Father, it is not the cave that draws me there—it is Raina asking for my help.

Does she know who you are?

No, I am not real to her. She is aware that I have powers; however, it is still just a dream to her. Father, I have to go back, I can hear her screams.

I know, I can still hear her as well, he replied, unaware of the mist that began to form around them.

Do not fear, he will not perish. The thoughts of the Great Elder Mataya rushed into their minds. *Release him, Guardian Jon, and I will heal him.*

Jaleel jerked, startled by the Elder's sudden appearance.

Jon didn't hesitate to comply. His link with the Elder Mataya had already proven to him that she contained a vast amount of energy consisting of many powers Jon had never known existed. When his mind linked with Mataya, she had opened Jon's mind, allowing him to understand who and what the Sentinel was. Jon released his son, and Mataya immediately linked her essence with Josiah's essence. His power had begun to return to him, and Josiah felt his strength increasing.

Josiah, do you feel well?

He answered hesitantly, completing a mental check of his mind and essence. *Yes, I do.*

Very well then, Mataya replied, pleased at her success. *Your work is not finished, Josiah.*

What must I do, Elder Mataya?

Josiah, the task you set out to complete is still undone. Your Raina is not yet safe. Enoch rescued her just before your father found you. As you fought Tarik, he led her from the cave, taking her to Silver Lake. The Demon's connection was temporarily broken when Enoch destroyed part of his cave. Enoch thought she was safe, however, Tarik immediately redesigned his horrid realm and has reclaimed Raina's mind. We must concentrate on saving Raina. Enoch had only temporarily separated her mind from Tarik—he will regain control again—permanently destroying her if we do not stop him.

No! I cannot let that happen. Josiah's mind screamed so loudly that Jon heard the echoes in his mind, too.

Josiah, Mataya said forcibly, demonstrating her power, *your human emotions will not help this situation. You must learn to control them.*

What do I need to do?

You are the only one who can answer that, Josiah.

"What is going on, Jon? What is the Great Elder saying to Josiah?" Jaleel demanded.

"He must go back, Jaleel. Raina is still in danger."

"No, you cannot allow him to do that, Jon. He is too weak. Even I could sense his essence failing, and I was not linked to his mind."

Jon looked at his son lying there almost healed from near death. He feared the outcome, but Jon knew what Josiah had to do. "Jaleel, he must go back. It is the only way to save her."

"No, Jon, you have to stop him. He is much too weak."

"Do not fear for his life," a voice spoke from the shadows.

Jaleel and Jon turned to look where the voice was coming from. Jon recognized the Guardian from Josiah's mind. It was Elder Enoch. His arrival startled Jon and Jaleel, except Mataya seemed unaffected by his visit. She continued her conversation with Josiah, assuring him of his victory.

"Elder Jon, Councilman, Jaleel," Enoch said addressing them confidently, "it is a great honor and my pleasure to meet two very prestigious defenders of our people."

"Who are you?" Jaleel questioned defensively, moving his position to stand in front of his fallen friend.

"My name is Enoch. I am a Guardian, such as you. I have come to aid Josiah in the rescue of my great-granddaughter."

"Your great-granddaughter?" Jaleel asked, confused by his appearance, and statement. "Who is she, and what concern is she to us?"

"My great-granddaughter is Raina, Councilman."

"What ... you are mad? Raina is human."

"Councilman, I neither have the time nor the patience—to explain what evil has been at work here, and the battles we have fought—to claim what belongs to the Guardian world. Josiah and I must leave now for the sake of this realm."

Enoch moved to approach Josiah. Just as he bent down to touch Josiah's arm, Jaleel pushed him away. Enoch retaliated by charging at Jaleel and slamming his celestial body up against the wall. Jaleel thrust his energy outward, striking Enoch until he lost his balance and staggered sideways. Then seeing his opportunity to strike again, Jaleel raised his hands into the air. Just then, a bolt of energy hit Jaleel throwing him to the ground.

"Enough," Elder Mataya ordered, still positioning her hand in front of her, ready to react again. "Councilman, you will stand down. There is no time for this, we must hurry."

"No, Elder, I will not let you take Josiah. He is too weak to go back to the dream world."

"Councilman, you have no choice in the matter. Enoch and Josiah must go back to the dream realm now." Elder Mataya turned to face Enoch who still stood ready to defend himself. "Enoch, you may proceed with your plan."

Enoch knelt down by Josiah's shell touching his shoulder. "Yes, Elder, I will. I promise I will watch over him, Jon. Trust me; his safety is as much of a concern to me as it is to you two. The livelihood of my great-granddaughter depends upon him."

Jon moved taking a step away from Josiah. "I believe you, Elder."

"So, we are just going to stand here waiting to see if Josiah lives?" Jaleel retorted, still humanly angry over the situation.

"No, Councilman," Mataya corrected, "you and Jon are more important to this mission than you realize."

"What do you mean?" Jaleel asked, glancing at Jon, and then back to the eccentric Guardian.

"Councilman, Jon has proven to have great strength. Yet, he alone cannot achieve the outcome that we need. You and Jon must combine your powers maintaining a mental link with Josiah."

"That is impossible, Elder Mataya. I do not have the capabilities to do what you have asked."

"Jaleel," Mataya snapped at him, "have you not found yourself in the mind of Great Elder Yakira? Has she not shown you the wonders that one's mind can bestow upon another?"

Jaleel was cautious to admit that his mind did indeed experience the mind of Yakira. He knew that Elder Mataya was aware of the link that occurred on Prometheus to discern Josiah's innocence. To think that she knew of their relationship worried him. Too many times, Yakira and he risked exposure to be together. To confirm their indiscretions would condemn them both before the eyes of the Council.

"I have," he replied, humanly nervous.

"Then you know what strength of concentration is required. You do understand the elements involved, and I am sure you have gained the knowledge to direct your essence and your thoughts."

"What does that have to do with rescuing Josiah?"

"Councilman," Enoch spoke up, "you and Jon will remain here in this realm petitioning for Josiah. Together, with the joining of your essences, you two can maintain a link with him. Jon has already heard the echo of the dreams and can communicate with Josiah in the dream realm. Your combined powers will create a gateway into the Demon's realm. By using that gateway, you can pull Raina from Tarik's dream world, sending her mind back into her body. As you do this, you two will also bring back Josiah."

Jon closed his eyes and sighed. He understood what was expected of him and what would be lost this day. "Elder Enoch, you place a lot of confidence in young Jaleel and me. Can you be sure that all of you will not perish?"

"Yes, I can be sure, Jon, of their survival"

"Then explain to us how you can guarantee their safety." Jaleel interrupted, rolling his eyes in frustration of the moment.

"Because, Councilman, I have made the wish upon the Scroll of Espérer." Then touching his shoulder, he and Josiah faded away leaving Josiah's shell unoccupied.

"Elder Mataya, I fear I am not strong enough to do this."

Mataya grinned. "Jon, fear is not for Guardians."

"I am not so sure of that, Great Elder."

"I will not leave you two. I will stay here, Jon, and assist in any way I am permitted.

"Permitted to," Jaleel retorted, "what does that mean? Have you not caused enough calamities to fall upon my friend by sending him back to that place?"

"Jaleel," Jon said sternly, "mind your tongue. It seems much more is at work here than you realize. If the Demon Tarik is to die this day, it cannot be by the hand of Mataya. Have you forgotten that it is forbidden for a Great Elder to take a life?"

"No," Jaleel whispered. At that moment, he realized what might come to pass. They were truly alone to fight for the lives of those that meant so much to him. Mataya may be able to offer her strength, but her powers couldn't be used to help destroy the evil.

Josiah detested the cave and its creator. The cave was filled with the bleakness of Tarik's evil essence. Tarik had proven to be a worthy adversary in skill alone, however, Josiah's compassion and determination was stronger.

"Do you recognize this area, Josiah?"

"No, Enoch. I have not been in this part of the cave before. I never got past the first sections of catacombs."

"I do not think this is a new location, Josiah. I think that this is the same realm, just altered in some way because of the cave collapsing before. Do you see the colors on the wall?" he asked, looking around them focusing in the dark.

"Yes, except I do not recall them being green before."

"They were not this color green before Raina's blood shed upon the ground."

"Is she hurt, Enoch?" he questioned fearfully.

"I am not sure. She was injured until I took her to Silver Lake. Once we left the dream, she appeared to be well. However, I do not know what Tarik has done to her since his new attempts to pull Raina back into his realm."

Enoch and Josiah continued forward following the narrow winding passageways. The further into the cave they ventured looking for Raina, the brighter shade of green the walls became. The ooze seeped down the chipped and flaking stone like lava, flowing onto the ground. It accumulated into numerous thick sticky globs, pooling together into puddles on the floor. Josiah and Enoch had to be careful about where they were stepping, forcing them to walk down the center of the cave. Josiah took pity on the rodents who were trapped in the gooey substance, cringing at the squealing sounds they made, squirming to be loose. Their terrified moans of pain reminded him of what he knew Raina was facing.

As they moved throughout the tunnels, Enoch and Josiah crept along trying to be as stealthy as possible. The loose gravel on the cave floor shifted from the impact of their weight crunching and popping under their feet. The noise made their footsteps too loud as they shuffled along. With each crunch, Josiah feared he would be Raina's demise.

"I can smell him ... he is close," Josiah informed Enoch. The Demon's odor lingered with Josiah day and night since his first visit to the vile realm.

"Yes, Josiah, the odor you speak of is sulfur. It smells like his flesh is rotting."

"Enoch, this odor is normal for the tunnels. It gets stronger closer to the center of the cave; however, it seems more pungent today. Do you know if he was injured in your struggle with him?"

"Yes, I did injure him during our confrontation, but I believe you had a good go at him before he turned on Raina and me."

Josiah winced. "I had him pinned down, but he overpowered me. Somehow, he hurled me into some fowl smelling murky water. As I swam to the edge to get out of the water, a large serpent jumped out of the water and grabbed a hold of me. It tugged with great force pulling me into the deep water. I became entangled in the stringy kelp. As much as I hated feeling confined, I believe the kelp disguised my appearance. After a few passes, the serpent apparently gave up on me and left. When I surfaced, the cave was collapsing around me. I do not know if Tarik was injured by the falling debris or not."

Just then, a screeching noise bellowed throughout the cave. Its high pitch pierced their ears.

"Shhh," Enoch said. He stopped in his tracks holding his hand in the air. "Did you hear that scream?"

Josiah stopped instantly, listening for the scream to sound again. Faintly, he heard it himself. "It sounds like a woman's voice. It appears to be coming from over to our left."

"Yes, I believe you are correct. That is where I hear the sound of running water coming from. He must have Raina locked in the passageway over there."

Josiah sighed sorrowfully. Tarik did seem to like his stagnant water. Josiah didn't doubt that Raina was near. His essence begged to save her, except his mind feared to see what condition he would find her experiencing.

"Enoch, do you see what I see?"

"Yes, there appears to be a new passageway in that direction. We should go and investigate it."

In unison, they both turned toward the direction of where the woman's scream originated. The entrance to the new set of tunnels narrowed forcing them to stoop low as they walked. When they exited the tunnel, they found it opened into a large hollowed-out room.

"I have been here before," Josiah said, pointing off to his right. "I recognize the artifacts piled in that corner."

Enoch looked toward the direction Josiah was indicating. He saw several mounds of glass and silver vases stacked together. At the base of the mounds were many open chests. Some were filled with gold challises and coins, heaping over the sides. Others were packed with parchments and jewelry that sparkled in the dim light, trickling through a crack in the walls.

"Josiah, do you know what these artifacts are doing here?"

"No, but I have an idea as to why they are here. Tarik dwells in the dreams of others. I think he steals their riches as he destroys their minds."

"Help me," a voice whispered in the distance.

Josiah's head snapped to follow the voice. There huddled in the corner as always, sat Raina. Again, her appearance was more than Josiah could bear to look at. He started to move toward her, stopping a few inches from a pool of ooze.

"Raina," he said gently, reassessing the best way to hurdle the ooze to reach her.

Raina didn't acknowledge Josiah. She appeared to be in a daze, mumbling something to herself, but to his relief, Raina wasn't crying. The waterfall behind her rushed violently splashing the water against the walls. It traveled along a crevasse in the wall, dripping down near Raina. Her clothes were soaked, and her beautiful golden locks were matted and snarled. Josiah recognized the debris in her hair to be from the serpent's pool. It repulsed him to see his poor Raina covered in the revolting sewage.

Another scream in the distance magnified inside the cave. Josiah could barely make out the words.

"Nolan!" Tori felt her heart jump inside of her chest. "Nolan, she's coming around."

"Who was that?" Enoch said, startled by the voice. He took a defensive stance—ready to protect his great-granddaughter.

Josiah halted, alarmed by the scream. He recognized the woman's voice as Tori's voice.

"Nolan, come here," Tori screamed again. Her voice traveled throughout the room. It crossed over into the dream realm sounding gargled to Enoch, but Josiah understood the words clearly.

Enoch flinched. "There it is again. Can you make out what it is saying, Josiah?"

Josiah's eyes went wide as disbelief rolled across his face. "Yes, I can. It is Tori, Raina's mother."

"My granddaughter? Where is she? I do not see her," Enoch said. His eyes darted back and forth in the dark. "What is she screaming about, Josiah?"

Josiah glanced back at Raina who was still huddled unresponsively in the corner. "Tori is not here. Her screams are coming from the waking world. They are truly from Raina's reality."

Unexpectedly at the sound of Nolan's voice, Josiah gasped. Enoch watched his eyes glaze over as Josiah stood there motionless with his hands at his sides. His facial expression was the same as Raina's was. The screams stopped, but Enoch knew something had stolen Josiah's attention.

"Josiah, what are you looking at?"

"What is it?" Nolan shouted back, surprised by Tori's urgent tone of voice. "I am coming!" Nolan leaped out of the chair, rushing to Raina's bedside. The agony of seeing his little girl lying there with a tube inserted into her nose sickened him. The IV in her arm almost seemed acceptable—because it simply carried medication that could be discontinued—when the IV was removed. Her feeding tube was life sustaining. If she didn't recover completely—then this artificial item used for nutrition would become part of her necessity of life.

He sighed disgusted at the thought of the quality of life she would lead—if her every breath were to rely on a machine. A machine that could malfunction and end her life as quickly as it had begun.

"Raina," the voice spoke, spilling over into the cave. Josiah watched as Raina raised her head and then looked in the direction of the voice. He felt some relief to see a form of response from her.

"Raina ... honey, I am here for you," Tori whispered, above the sound of the oxygen machine. Her voice cracked, nearly crying at the sight of her daughter's movement.

Raina moaned, blinking her eyes incoherently. She was lost between her reality and the dream world. In reality, the hospital room was spinning, and the voices around her seemed muffled. She couldn't hear them clearly over the sound of the water dripping off the cave walls. It all seemed too real in her mind to ignore. Raina's body shivered from the chilled effects of the musty damp cave. In her dream, her clothes were still wet from plunging into the stagnant water. She thought that Tarik was going to drown her when he held her under the water, but for some reason he had let her go and quickly exited the pool.

"Raina, it's Mom. Do you hear me, honey?" Tori asked frantically, taking her daughter's hand into hers. "She feels so cold, Nolan."

Raina moaned again, still blinking because the light in her eyes were too bright. The cave had been dark, and her eyes adjusted to the blackness. Now the light in the hospital room burned her eyes, making her vision blurry. She closed her eyes again, and when she opened them, she saw Enoch approaching from her right side. At the sound of crumbling rocks he stopped, crouching to the ground.

"Josiah, do you still hear the voices?"

"Yes, Enoch, they are as concerned as we are at this moment."

Just then, the earth began to tremble, forcing the wall behind him to shift. Several jagged-shaped rocks fell from the ceiling crashing to the ground a few feet away from Raina. She didn't seem fazed by the noise.

"The cave seems to have suffered structural damage from our last engagement. The ceiling is weak. We need to get her out of here now, Josiah," Enoch said.

He moved forward slowly trying to lure Raina away from the crumbling wall. He feared that she was going to be crushed by the falling rocks before they could save her. Enoch called out, trying to keep his voice low, so that the Demon wouldn't hear him. Enoch could sense Tarik's presence, but he didn't think that he was so close to them. He was sure the demon would attack them immediately.

"Raina, listen to me."

She must have heard Enoch because she looked up. "Grandpa?" she questioned, with a hoarse voice.

"Raina, get up and come to me."

"What?" she asked confused.

"Raina, come here, please," Enoch demanded, with urgency in his tone of voice.

He motioned with his extended arms for her to follow his command. Raina started to stand up, and he thought she was going to listen to him. Then all of a sudden, she stopped and looked upward.

"Dad?"

Enoch followed her eyes upward to see what she was looking at. He became distracted at the sight of the huge shadowy figure, as his instincts told him it was not his great-granddaughter's father.

From behind Enoch came loud popping noise as an explosion of flying rocks and debris flew through the air. The force of the explosion sent them all tumbling to the ground. Before Enoch could get to his feet, the reaming section of the wall collapsed. It pinned Enoch under several huge boulders and chunks of crusted rock. Immediately, a bright warming light charged through the gaping hole in the wall.

"Enoch!" Josiah yelled, diverting his attention from the ceiling to the pinned Guardian.

Josiah glanced once more at Raina then got to his feet and moved to rescue Enoch. Cautiously trying to side step the sticky ooze, Josiah found himself trapped in the center of the cave. The path to reach Enoch had closed because of the gooey florescent ooze. Josiah began to suffer from his human-acquired fear, realizing that the path to reach Enoch was obstructed.

"Enoch, hold on. I am coming to help you."

"No, Josiah. Get her out of here now!" He held up his arm motioning to Raina with his hand. "Raina, please go to Josiah. He will take you from here."

"Raina," her father said. He shook her shoulder trying to get her attention. When she didn't respond, he grabbed her hand squeezing it within his. "Raina it's Dad, can you feel my hand?"

"Grandpa, I love you," she said. Tears formed in her eyes as she looked at the fallen Enoch.

Her confused voice lingered in both worlds. She raised the arm her father held to wave back at Enoch, watching him wave goodbye to her. She didn't know in her delirious state that he was motioning her to go with Josiah. She managed to catch her bearings and tried to stand up pleading with Enoch to stay.

"Grandpa, don't go. Please stay with me."

"What did you say, Raina?" Tori asked, confused by her daughter's words.

"Grandpa, please stay with me. It is so dark here," she insisted in a daze, calling out in the cave's dream world. Her words in the actual reality sounded gurgled and confused.

A noise ricocheted through the sound of the settling debris, and Raina looked up again staring at the ceiling. She blinked, trying to clear the dust from her eyes. More rocks fell throughout the cave just narrowly missing her and Josiah.

"Raina!" Enoch hollered, more frantically than he had before. "Raina, do you hear me?"

Enoch lay there unable to loosen the rocks that had mysteriously pinned him. He felt their immense weight crushing his human image. Barely able to turn his head, he struggled to look into the light. A movement on the other side caught his attention. He almost felt a sense of peace filtering in through the light. Then he saw them standing there. He couldn't hear Jon's or Jaleel's words, but he knew they were there to help. If he could just get Raina's attention and direct her to look at him, then he could guide her to the light. If she walked through the hole in the wall to the other side, he knew sure that she would be safe.

"Josiah," Enoch begged, hoping to make him look his way. For some reason, Josiah had stopped trying to reach him or Raina. He just stared blankly at nothing at all. "Josiah, can you understand me? Look at the wall. Josiah—hurry!"

Josiah either chose not to respond or couldn't respond. This concerned Enoch more, as he could feel the negative energy building in the room. The human emotion began to grow stronger and wildly out of control. If Enoch had not practiced living as a human for the last eighty some years, surely the emotions would have crippled his mind. He would find himself giving up until he faded away in the Demon's darkness.

"Raina," Enoch shouted again, hoping to break through to her. "Walk toward the hole in the wall. The light will make you warm." Enoch was sure the idea of warmth would coax her into the hole.

"I can't leave. My mom is calling to me."

"Yes, you can. She is outside of here. Go toward the light, Raina. She is waiting for you on the other side."

Raina pointed up to the ceiling. "No, I hear her up there."

It was then that Enoch saw the shadowy figure for what he really was. The evil Demon hovered over Raina, clinging to the cave's ceiling like a perched bat. His expression was sinister, and he growled like a rabid dog.

"No, Raina. Do not listen to him," Enoch instructed. "Go toward the light, and tell your mother that I love her very much."

She looked downward from the Demon to the shimmering light. "I'll tell her, Grandpa," Raina mumbled.

Tori's voice sung through the chamber destroying everything Enoch was trying to build. "Honey, Grandpa isn't here."

"Josiah, help me," Enoch ordered, trying to make Josiah look at him. "Tell her to go toward the light. Josiah, do you hear me?"

"Yes, he is, Mom," Raina managed to answer her mother, "but he wants to go away now. Mom, ask him to stay. I miss him so much." Then her voice trailed off into another incoherent rant of mumbles.

"Raina, your grandfather is—"

"Tori." Nolan shook his head. "She is delirious. She doesn't understand you right now, dear."

"Oh, Nolan, will she be all right?"

"Mom, I'm so ... co ... cold. I have to get these wet clothes off."

"What?" Tori asked, baffled by her daughter's murmur. Then processing what she said, Tori responded uncertain of the whole situation. "Raina, you're not wet."

"Tori," Nolan said, correcting her again, "she's not herself—just yet."

"Nolan, what's wrong with my daughter?"

He wanted to sooth his wife's anxiety, but he knew that he couldn't. "Tori, she's confused from the illness and her high fevers. The seizure medication makes her delirious."

"How long will this last, Nolan?" Tori exclaimed, growing more concerned for Raina's welfare with every passing second.

"A few hours ... a few days maybe."

"A few days!"

"Relax, dear. Her delusions are not an uncommon result, considering what she has been through the last couple of days."

"Oh, Nolan, what if she doesn't get better?"

How could he be honest with her now? Tori had been through too much, watching her daughter lying in a near death state. He couldn't possibly give her more grief than he could handle at this moment. Against his better judgment, he lied to her.

"She will, I promise."

In the dream, Raina looked off to the side of the cave, focusing on the motionless Josiah. Enoch watched a smile grow across her face.

Yes. He thought to himself. *Finally, we have a connection to her mind.*

"Muahaha!" The Demon laughed, hissing wickedly at Enoch, as if he had known his thoughts.

Just as Enoch was about to call after Josiah again, he heard a new noise from behind him.

"Enoch, do not move," Josiah cautioned him, recovering from his trance. "Raina, please listen to me. Do as your grandfather says—"

Then before he finished speaking, something flew past Josiah, forcing him to duck low. The gust of wind caused by this mysterious object shook the cave. Raina lost her balance falling a few inches from the pond. The impact of her body crashing against the ground sent a vibration rushing through the cave floor. The serpent appeared from the murky pond, leaping in and out of the water. It began to swim close to the edge, snapping its claws in the air. The serpent was trying to latch onto Raina. She lay there seemingly dazed with her eyes fixed on the scaly creature.

"Raina, get away from there! Come to me. You can do it, just try," Enoch begged, feeling his essence growing weary.

Then at that moment, several more chunks of rock broke free from the unstable ceiling tumbling to the ground. As the dust cleared, Josiah cringed. What he feared the most had come true.

"Enoch!" Josiah stood there helpless to assist him.

There was nothing now that Josiah could do for him. Raina was his primary concern. He had to get her out of there before it was too late.

"Raina, please," Josiah urged, trying to encourage her. "I need for you to leave now. I promise your great-grandfather and I will follow after you in a few minutes." This was the second time in his life that he evaluated Raina's white lie scenario.

"Josiah, I know ... but I want you to come with me now," Raina insisted, in what Nolan believed was a continued state of delirium. For him to see his daughter tormented in this delirious state tore at his heart.

"I will join you when you get outside of the cave," Josiah prompted. "I promise you this. Just please ... Raina, go toward the hole in the wall. Your parents are waiting for you."

"Grandpa, if I go, will I see you again?" she called out to him, as she searched the pile of rocks looking for him.

Enoch didn't respond to her, so she asked him her question again. This time she was nearly shouting. Her babble in the real world began to increase at an alarming rate scaring Nolan.

"Grandpa, didn't you hear me? Will I see you again?"

"Yes," his voice finally replied, echoing from behind the mountain of rocks, "we will see each other in the light. Your mother and father are calling for you. They are outside, Raina. Now, please go to them. Hurry, Raina, while they are still there. Now go!"

"No, Grandpa, I want to stay. I want to see Grandma. Where is she?"

"Raina, she is not here. You must go now and leave this cave!"

"Grandpa, please, come with me," she still pleaded. "I miss you so badly."

"Raina, please," Josiah insisted, no longer mimicking Enoch's voice. "Go outside where it is bright and warm. Your mother and father are waiting for you. You have been gone for a long time. They miss you."

Raina turned to look back at the light. She could feel the warmth penetrating her raunchy smelling clothing. She hesitated knowing somehow, there was safety outside the cave. But in there were two people she cared for very much. Her confusion blocked out the snapping noise of the creatures clenching jaws. With every leap, he seemed to be getting closer to her.

"Raina, hurry!"

He watched fearfully as the serpent launch itself so high that it landed on the stone wall, snarling with vengeance. "Get away from her!"

Frantically, he evaluated the encroaching ooze that had surrounded him. His chest felt hollow when he realized that the ooze had sealed off his path for escape. A brief sensation of relief washed over Josiah as the serpent slid back into the pond.

"I can't go, Josiah. My grandfather is here, and you're here. I have to stay."

"No, you have to leave, Raina. You have to leave now. This place is too dark. There is no happiness here for you."

"Mom," she said. Her voice sounded so loudly that it echoed deep inside the cave from the hospital room.

"Raina ... Raina. I'm here, honey."

Her mother's cries still flowed over into the dream. Then faintly Jaleel and Jon heard Tori's cry drift into the hospital basement. Jon bowed his head in pity.

"Jon, what was that?"

"It is Raina's mother. I have heard her pleas in Josiah's mind. I did not realize you heard her, too."

"How is it that we can hear her? I thought you said the realm was a dream. We are not in it. How is this possible?"

"I am afraid that the dream realm is collapsing. The Demon's power has shifted and echoes of that realm are blending with ours."

"What does that mean, Jon?"

"We have to get them out of there." Jon sighed, beginning to feel defeat. "You must get Josiah's attention."

"Yes, Jaleel," Mataya agreed. "You have to see if you can find them through the opening."

"I will try. Tell me what I need to do, Mataya."

"Concentrate on Jon's thoughts to find the opening. When you have found it, then you must concentrate on Josiah's thoughts. When you locate him, communicate with him. Warn him of what is about to happen."

Jaleel did as Mataya instructed. He focused all of his thoughts on Jon's, until he found the opening. *Josiah,* Jaleel called after him, peering through the hole into the darkness. *Josiah, you must leave there now!*

Josiah snapped his head to the right, only now seeing the figures that caught Enoch's attention before. "I am coming," he answered, barely aware that the words were in his mind and not coming from the cave. He had no idea that his essence was growing dimmer. His concentration was too consumed by his concern for Raina's safety and the realization that the ooze trapped him.

Josiah? His father attempted to call into his mind, focusing on the vision in Jaleel's thoughts. *Our energy is growing weak, and Tarik's realm is beginning to close in around you. Josiah, do you hear me? Push her out of the cave. The realm is collapsing much too fast. Jaleel and I do not have the strength to maintain the molecules. You have to leave there now!*

Hurry, Josiah! Our plan is not working. Tarik has played some trick upon us. Every time your father tries to increase his power, Josiah, your essence seems to fade. Tarik is controlling this dream, not us.

All of a sudden, Tarik's despicable laugh roared throughout the cave. "Ha, ha, ha! Did you really think that your worthless and scrawny minds could fool me? Do you not realize what you are dealing with here?"

Josiah's voice roared over the sound of rushing water that seemed to grow more earsplitting with each laugh from Tarik. "Raina—run now!"

It became more urgent now than ever before to get her out of this dream. The Demon had caught them all at their game, and his plan appeared more efficient than theirs did. His laughs of confidence continued to boom off the crumbling walls. The vibrations of his laugh shot through the cave, forcing many fissures to develop in the walls. This allowed the water from Tarik's river to flow through it at an alarming rate.

Raina just lay there with a blank expression. She was staring as the water poured out of the cracks. Even as it cascaded across the dirt floor, she didn't move. It traveled slowly at first, turning muddy as it bubbled across the rocks and uneven terrain in a zigzag pattern. As the water increased in volume, the level in the cave began to rise several inches gushing over Josiah's feet. Raina scooted her body upward until she stood hunched over, resting on hands on her knees. Josiah realized that the accumulating water was quickly approaching the pond in the center of the cave. Soon the water would flow over the large stone wall that encircled the entrance to the hole. When it reached the top of the wall, the water would run into the pond making its water level rise as well. Eventually, the serpent would escape his prison and make the cave his domain. There was no kelp or weeded areas to provide cover to anyone trapped in the cave. The beast would find his prey easily and strike merciless without warning.

"Josiah, what's happening here?" Raina said frightfully, shifting her feet in the cold muddy water. "Josiah, don't you see that the water is rising?"

"Raina, answer me," her father screamed. His voice shot through Josiah with an aching chill.

"Nolan, please, not again?" Tori cried, watching the cardiac monitor register the slowing rate of Raina's heartbeat. The beeping alarm grew louder, crossing over into the dream world.

Tarik laughed wickedly, rejoicing at the sound of his near victory. Then he dropped from the ceiling, making a loud splashing sound. The water swelled pushing into the already unstable rocks—so that they moaned at the force of the water. Josiah could feel the earth beneath him becoming soft and mushy. The ground began to shift beneath his weight as it absorbed more of the water.

Then his feet sank into the cool mud. It sent a hideous feeling of gloom sprinting through his body. He gasped in despair as Raina began to shiver profusely from the temperature change within the cave. The water level had risen to Raina's waist, and Josiah knew if she didn't leave now the realm would consume her mind forever. He didn't understand how she remained so alert, as he could feel the world slipping away.

Jon felt the sudden change in the cave's molecules as clearly as Jaleel had. *They need to leave there now. Jaleel, can you still see them?*

Jaleel refocused his thoughts searching for Josiah's mind. All he could find was panic and turmoil. *No—Jon, I cannot.*

Try harder, Jaleel. We are losing this fight, Mataya ordered.

The serpent bellowed, realizing the water level of his prison was rising. He started making rapid passes in the pool, leaping up into the sky and surveying what would become his extended home. His hideous calls screeched through the cave amplifying with every pass.

Josiah's essence was draining much faster than even Mataya believed was possible. The plan of Enoch's should have worked. With Jon's capability of linking with his son's mind and Mataya's and Jaleel's assistance, they were sure of a victory. The portal their thoughts created should have been strong enough acting as a passageway between reality and the dream world. The mental link was their connection that allowed them to observe his actions in the cave. It was to be the trio's escape. With every thought of Josiah's, they were to watch the dream sequence played-out, waiting for the right moment to strike. Together their combined energy would distort the molecules causing a fracture in the dream. This was supposed to make the dream world become unstable, loosening Tarik's control over Josiah. When this happened, Josiah and Enoch were to flee with Raina through the mind of Jon and Jaleel. It seemed ingenious. The Demon would never feel their presence and be left off-guard by the surprise attack. But sadly, Jon and Jaleel couldn't control where their energy would expel. By the time they had realized this, their efforts had injured Enoch.

When Tarik materialized secretly into the cave, his superior mind quickly ascertained what the Guardians were doing. To ensure his win and nourishment from their pain, he shot his energy across the room. It damaged the portal Jon and Jaleel were using to communicate with Enoch and Josiah. Then the energy bounded back, exploding into the cave. The effect of the energy burst crushed Enoch with the collapsing wall killing him.

"Josiah, do you stand there with no response to my challenge?" Tarik taunted, mocking Josiah.

"I do not call this a challenge. You are a monster and your friend is the Devil. I will not encourage your behavior, Demon."

Tarik snarled. "There is nothing here to encourage. There is no strength left in you, nor is there an essence dwelling within Enoch. I too, felt his essence dissipate. I must say that I am impressed at how easily you mimicked his voice. Bravo, what a marvelous trick."

Raina turned her head toward Josiah, just now realizing what Tarik was saying. "Grandpa?" At that moment, she began to thrash and wail in the water, grasping her chest.

"Raina," Josiah screamed, "hold on, I am coming!"

The pain and burning her body felt in reality from before had returned. It seemed worse this time—as her body had not healed from the last episode when her heart stopped. Raina's ribs were breaking from the pressure of the chest compressions. The fact that she was conscious in the dream world—allowed her to suffer from the physical pain her body experienced while it was dying.

"Just give up, Josiah," Tarik growled. "You are fighting a lost cause. You will not win. Your kind cannot prevail against me."

"You are wrong, Tarik. I will win this."

"You, Josiah, are nothing more than a puppet to me. A glorious chance to experience, as your human friends say, 'play time.' Just ask Councilman Uriah, he will tell you."

"What?" Josiah spoke aloud, chiding himself for not keeping his thoughts hidden from the Tracker.

The Tracker laughed wickedly. "Oh, yes. I had almost forgotten. You will not be able to ask Uriah after all."

"Why do you say that, Tarik? You are not as strong as you pretend to be?"

"For being a Head Elder, your mind is dim. Did you not sense the loss of his essence in your world?"

"You ramble on with nonsense, Tarik. If I did not know better, I would say you were stalling for some reason."

"It is you, puppet, who is stalling. I killed Uriah for his unworthiness to my service."

"I do not believe you. What would Elder Uriah have to do with any of this, Tarik?"

"You have a short memory, Josiah. Do you not recall how determined he was to damn you to Deimos. Have you forgotten the inconsistencies in his accusations at your trial?"

Josiah's expression went blank. He had forgotten. "What did you do to Elder Uriah?"

"Do you really think that Markian acted alone? He was too foolish to get anything right. It was Uriah who condemned the people on that plane where your precious human friend perished."

"Tori," he whispered, "you were responsible for killing Raina's mother and all of those innocent people."

"No, not me. My hands are free from bloodstains. It was Uriah who forced the plane to crash. I am held blameless to that deed."

"What about Markian and his daughter? Were you behind their actions as well?"

Tarik laughed louder than before. "I may have encouraged them *a little*, except they were full of wicked seeds before Dinah brought me and my Master Toah with her from Adrastea. I just saw a moment of opportunity—and I took it. That pleased my Master greatly."

"You are a monster, Tarik. Your presence in my realm has done far greater damage than Markian or his daughter."

"If I were a monster, then I would not have dealt so fairly with my puppet, Uriah. I killed him straight away, allowing him to release his essence for retribution before I crushed his skull. There really was not that much pain. Of course, I know your kind does not really feel pain, so I helped Uriah experience just a little before his death. I know that you understand what I am talking about, Josiah. Did not the arrows from the Abyss sting your side and drain your power?" he asked, allowing his voice to echo throughout the cave. His laugh caused more loose rocks to shift and fall from the walls.

As Josiah feared, the water level had raised so much that the serpent was now free. Josiah saw its tentacles swishing in the water. As the serpent swam closer to Raina, Josiah tried to surprise Tarik by lunging forward to attack. Tarik suspected his childish moves and grasped Josiah in his energy. Terror consumed Josiah when he realized that he was helpless to free himself. Then his greatest fears began to develop. Raina let out another wretched scream and sank below the surface of the water.

"Raina, no Raina!"

He had felt her drown once before, and the thought of seeing her pale blue lips stole his faith for success. The link with his father became too weak to sense, and the reality that he and Raina were going to perish dominated his mind. He struggled with his last bit of energy trying to reach Raina. The water was polluted with evil, and the dark cave hindered his vision. The success of finding her was unlikely, but he couldn't let his Raina die like this. He struggled, trying to free himself from Tarik's energy.

"Do not fight me, Josiah. It will just make this worse on you. Look now, Enoch is dead and your dear friend, Anani, has lost her senses because of my power. How foolish she was to believe she could outwit me by attempting to assist you to enter my realm. She may never be the same again. And of course Raina is somewhere under this water. You know that her human lungs need air and now she has been deprived of this necessity."

Tarik began to rejoice at his victory letting his guard down. Self-pride became his downfall as silently in the water, the serpent struck. It leaped from out of the water and then clasped his jaws around Tarik, dragging him under the murky liquid.

Josiah felt the hold on him immediately vanish. He dove under the water where he believed Raina had sunk. He swam around franticly, but he couldn't find her. His essence was too weak to sense Raina making it difficult to find her.

He swam above the water once more to see if she had surfaced. It was then when he saw Tarik in the jaws of a second serpent being ripped to shreds by the two creatures. Tarik's screams sounded wretched, but they were a relief. With Tarik dead, Josiah could find Raina without worrying about fighting him, too.

"No! No! No!" Tori cried, as Nolan pulled her into his embrace. "She can't be dead. Nolan, do something, please!"

He buried his wife's head into his chest sadly. "I can't," he whispered.

"Oh, my God—why!" Tori screamed, not knowing her words carried over into the dream world.

Her pleas of desolation shoved a dagger of death into Josiah's heart. He tried to block out Tori's cry of despair, not wanting to believe his Raina had died. He pushed Tori's voice and the pressing thoughts of his father from his mind, so that he could concentrate. Fearfully, Josiah swam through the water looking for her body, desperately ignoring what was happening around him.

When the serpent attacked Tarik, his hold on the molecules stopped, and Jon was able draw back their stolen energy. The light grew brighter illuminating inside of the cave. Apprehensively Jon and Jaleel peered into the apparent empty cave.

Jaleel, you must go into the cave, Jon ordered. *I have lost my connection with Josiah.*

How? he asked confused.

Give me your hand, Mataya commanded Jaleel in her mind, lending the assistance she promised them earlier. *I will help you pass through the portal.*

Jaleel complied, reaching his arm up toward Mataya. The wise Guardian grabbed a hold of Jaleel's hand and projected Jaleel into the cave. In the hospital basement, Jaleel's celestial body shook violently as if a current of electricity had darted through him. He closed his eyes, and then his mind grew dim.

"Josiah," Jaleel called to him from inside the cave. In the distance, he saw Josiah bobbing up and down in the water. Jaleel dove under the water himself and swam to meet him.

"Josiah, we have to go now. The dream world is almost gone."

"No, I need to find Raina. Help me please, Jaleel?"

He reached sympathetically to touch his shoulder. "Josiah, she is gone. Her body on Earth can no longer breathe on its own. Her parents weep now, and the doctors have given up. We must go now or you will perish, as well."

Before Josiah could protest, Jaleel grabbed a hold of him, pulling him through the water. As they reached the hole in the cave wall, Jaleel attempted to push Josiah through the hole.

"No, Jaleel. Let me go. I have to find Raina."

"Josiah, we have to go. This realm is collapsing. I am sorry, but she is gone."

Josiah pulled himself free from Jaleel's hold. Then feeling his essence melting away, he dove under the water to begin his search again.

The water level had risen so high that it nearly covered the mystical opening that Jon and Jaleel made in the cave wall. All of a sudden, Josiah felt the water's temperature change. As it became very cold, the light that shinned through the cavern wall disappeared. The darkness began to overtake Josiah draining his last bit of will to live. On Earth, Josiah's essence had weakened and his shell in the dream world failed. Despite Jaleel's and Jon's urging to have Josiah leave the realm, he refused. His essence unknowingly became trapped within the shell and began to perish as his shell ceased to exist.

His last thought was a mysterious vision where he was swimming in a beautiful ocean. The dream vividly played-out in his mind, leaving him unaware that in Tarik's realm, the serpent charged through the water towards him. Just as he was a few feet away, Josiah's dream showed him that the serpent was near. He stopped swimming and froze horrified at what he was witnessing. In its mouth, the serpent held Raina's body between his large teeth.

Even in the darkness, Josiah could make out her ashen skin and blue lips. The serpent stopped instantly at the shattered wall and rose up high into the air. His magnificent body glimmered even in the darkness, displaying the uniqueness of his kind. With its slimy tentacles coiling like a snake, he removed Raina from his mouth and held her out to Josiah like an offering.

"A life for a life," it said in a velvety voice, too humanly sounding for such a bizarre looking creature. "Freedom for freedom, I grant you. The realms of my world and yours—cannot comprehend the vile actions of Tarik. He has held my people and me captive for so long—we know not where we truly should exist. For your perseverance, we thank you. Our freedom is granted by you this day. Take what belongs to you and leave this place now," the serpent ordered, changing the tone of his velvety voice.

Josiah reached out to take Raina's body. His hands shook as he grabbed hold of her. Hope filled his heart at once when he realized that she was breathing. Her incredible blue eyes opened, confirming her life was safe.

When she spoke, Raina's words sounded mumbled from allowing her fear to run over into her voice. "Don't leave me, Josiah."

He tried to assure her, pulling her weakened body closer to his. "I will not, I promise you."

Then staring into her delicate face, he saw the light that could fill his empty heart. The light that could renew his essence and absorb the love he hid deep inside of his Guardian heart. At that moment, Josiah's essence regenerated casting a blue light around them. On Earth, Jon felt an enormous amount of relief wash over him, and Josiah's essence was revived. The lifeless form he held in his arms began to glow.

Unaware of his essences' condition on Earth, Josiah could concentrate only on Raina in the dream realm. He couldn't deny her request, nor could he turn her away. If he continued now, his Guardian existence would once again be at risk. His people's judgment would be upon him and Deimos a certain destiny. At this moment, it was a risk that didn't matter anymore. Here in his arms was his Raina. Surely, he wouldn't be forbidden such a moment.

The emotion and intensity of what these few earth seconds held for them lingered so strongly between one another. His decision was no longer left to a Guardian mind or the fragility of a human heart. His essence took over, and Josiah fell into an ocean of peace and love.

Raina, he spoke softly into her mind then the cave went dark.

36.
LAST REQUEST

Guardian Realm—present-day

Josiah sat oblivious to the sounds of the garden outside his window. This morning his study seemed dark and lonely. Before him, his leather bound book lay opened on the mahogany desk. The ink from his pen rolled slowly over the damp parchment that wrinkled from his tears. Josiah felt as if his essence was suffocating. His breathing deepened to take in the artificial air filled with the stench of depression.

Why did he torture himself so? Josiah had spent the night in human form, fighting to steady his shaking hand. It seemed to tremble worse this time than during any of his other entries. Perhaps it was because during the night, he penned the final chapter. The book he titled "Espérer" meant hope, and hope is what he carried until yesterday. He ended the chapter in a poem that he read repeatedly, looking for another possible finale. Unlike most poems, this one told a grim story, and yet it answered a longing question. He read it once more hoping there was a possibility the poem alone could change his fate. With another deep breath, he began for the fortieth time reading it to himself.

Yesterday, I fought for the one I love, her heartbeat, thankfully in my arms. Tomorrow, I will say goodbye to the one I love, my heart will perish in my chest.

If there were one last token I could ask for, it would be for knowledge of the future. For the moment weighs heavy giving no answers and I can no longer live with guesses.

Our love was strong and the bond unbroken, only her mind knew not what it once had. The birds sang, and the Angels' choruses shouted, but their songs ceased to fill Heaven's space. My ears will no longer hear the song, and my eyes will grow dim and bleak. I must make it on my own now, for my life and hers has no place.

If I was granted one wish, I know what it would be, my life for hers gladly I would give. Call me weak for the love that binds me, but I will waste not one day. The portals of time know no boundaries and the will of the Creator no end. I must live with His decisions, waiting for when His plan unfolds, and He carries me away.

Josiah laid his quill down on the desk. Still breathing heavily, he picked up the picture he treasured of Raina. It was his favorite one, taken at Dewitt Park in Silver Lake.

Raina stood at the edge of the water as the Sun was beginning to rise. Behind her, the orange sky outlined the row of trees, casting a dark shadow upon them, placing a black imprint on the horizon. The tree line's reflection on the water gave the illusion of a mirror image. Each treetop was mimicked on the water with fine detail, appearing flawless in the eyes of Mother Nature.

The peaking Sun forced an orange canopy to cast its glow upon the water. It made the mimicked tree line expand further across the lake until it danced with the morning mist greeting the fishermen. The Sun's reflection had sent streaks of light across the top of the water. It shined a bright yellow, as the orange sky enhanced the horizon. He followed all of this fine detail on the picture until it came to one subject. The whole reason Silver Lake, Wisconsin existed.

Gently tracing the outline of her face with his finger, he closed his eyes. The truth came to him, winning over the irrationality that guided him these last nineteen years. Hope had a place in his life, although not where he wanted it to be. For no matter how much Josiah tried to control the future he knew it was not his to command. In the moment he accepted this, a new life began to unfold.

Josiah? the Sentinel's voice spoke softly in his head, pulling his concentration from his beloved's picture. She stood in all her radiance, perfectly posed like a statue. Her aura glowed brightly signifying her supremacy and her gentleness.

Sentinel? Josiah whispered, startled by her appearance. As he scooted out of his chair, he dropped the picture of Raina. He winced at the sound of the breaking glass as he knelt down onto the floor and lowered his head. Immediately he dislodged from his shell and appeared in his true form. The thud next to him as his shell hit the floor reminded him again how fragile humans were and how weak he was from their love.

Rise, Josiah, she commanded, gesturing to the kneeled Leader, *we are equals here in this chamber.*

What have I done to warrant your visit? he questioned, still staring timidly at her feet. He had hoped she would think it a sign of obedience or respect. In actuality, he couldn't bear to look at her face. The Sentinel's resemblance to Raina always overwhelmed him. He shifted his eyes to the faint glow on his right. The light reflecting off the broken pieces of glass confirmed that Raina's picture survived the fall untouched. For this, he was relieved, as it was the only true picture left from those days. He could simulate a new one, only the original offered him a comfort no other material item could.

You must be relieved that Raina lives.

Yes, I am, Sentinel.

You fought hard for her, Josiah. You always seem to be fighting for her.

It does seem that way. You must know—I will continue to fight her.

I know you will. You have been a most courageous Guardian. Even though you have not acted within all of our laws, I admire your determination to be there for her.

It is love, Sentinel, that gives me the determination to fight for her.

I know it is. Human love has indeed changed you, Josiah.

Do you believe that is a bad thing, Sentinel?

No, Josiah. You have demonstrated the love our Father has desired for His children.

And what does that love mean for Raina?

Her body will heal, Josiah. Soon it will return to its normal function, and she will live a happy life.

Then there will be no ill effects from Tarik's mind control?

No, the Creator will see to that. As we speak, she has regained consciousness, and her life support was removed.

Josiah sighed relieved.

Did you think she would not recover, Josiah?

I prayed that she would. I just did not know what the Creator had planned for her.

It is true that miracles do happen. You have seen that with your own eyes.

I know I have, Sentinel. However, what Raina suffered could not be explained by the humans' medical diagnosis. I did not know if her mystery illness—well if a miracle was enough for the witnesses.

It is enough. There will be no questions.

What will become of her now, Sentinel?

Mataya's episodes have caused many issues for us to consider. Fortunately, her dreams have now ended, minimizing the strain caused to our realm. I am pleased to tell you that the Secret Council has stopped its practices, and its members for now have returned to their normal lives in their realities.

Josiah needlessly sighed. *This is good, Sentinel. You must be relieved to see the realms returning to normal.*

No, I am not, Head Elder. I have found no relief yet. Mateo's freedom from Deimos is the only pleasant action I will commit. For my mission in this endeavor to repair the fissures in the timeline, only serve to give me great complications.

Complications, Sentinel? That astonishes me, to think that you believe this to be true.

Please, Josiah. She motioned with her hand. *Take your rightful place in this room. Kneel not before me, but stand beside me as my equal.*

Your Honor, I am not an equal. Your reverence far surpasses mine in every aspect of our essences.

Rise, Josiah. She commanded of him, now reminding Josiah with her thoughts of whom it was that stood before him.

Josiah took in another wasted breath. Somehow, this human reaction gave him strength to face the ghost of his eternal damnation. He stood up making direct eye contact. As feared, her features caused him great pain.

I must make this clear to you, Josiah. The Sentinel began, ignoring his solemn thoughts that were presenting themselves very strongly. *The life of Raina will not be the same, as you once knew. The life you created in Silver Lake vanished when Earth was renewed. The events of Mataya's dreams have taken place by the ill actions of her empty mind.*

The Creator will not allow the timelines of any realm to be altered again. The current situations of this realm and the others affected by the Secret Council's actions will remain as they are. Two good Guardians have lost their essence because of Mataya's over active mind. Since the timelines remain, theirs existences do not.

Enoch, Josiah interjected sadly. *He was a courageous Guardian, more courageous than I was. He sacrificed much for Mataya's cause.*

Do not forget the one you never met. The Watcher Talib, too, gave his essence for this cause.

You misunderstand me, Sentinel. I could never forget those who gave their existences to save Raina. They truly have more honor than I do.

Honor will hold no relevance in the timelines. For this reason, Nolan's life will continue on Earth in the course it was to follow before Benn interceded the second time. Benn's actions beyond his Guardian responsibilities are dissolved. The infant Nolan survived at birth because of Benn's healing powers, and nothing more. He will possess no essence, and his soul is secure.

The human female, Tori, on the other hand, is a different matter. Isaiah's life force will not have been inherited by Tori, as Isaiah's actions no longer have a bearing on her life. From the beginning, when Lexis placed the essence of Rayna within her body, her soul was affected. The infant's essence became part of her, cleverly hid within the human genetics. I know you sensed this when you healed Tori's mangled body the day Raina was born.

Yes, I did, Sentinel. I did not know what I had felt or saw in her eyes until just recently. I believe that is why the bond, the connection between the Tori and Nolan of the past, was so strong.

You are correct. That is why when the realms were returned to their natural state after Abaddon's reign, the Creator did not change the events leading up to the accident, except for Nolan's survival. Therefore, Nolan continued, and Guardian Benn remained distant from them.

I was intrigued, Josiah, to learn of his involvement and the self-destructive actions him and Elder Torrey pursued. I did not believe that Torrey would learn to use the Stone of Fayruz for such an act. He was just as selfish to use the stone for the creation of Benn's mission, as Enoch was to wish upon the Scroll of Espérer.

Sentinel, what of the Watcher Isaiah?

In actuality, he played no part until the urging of Elder Mataya. His essence will remain his and will have no bearing on Tori. The only spiritual ramification upon her life is the essence of Rayna. Isaiah has returned to Callisto to wait further instructions from me, as the other—

Tell me about Elder Torrey's sister?

It is easier, she replied sadly, *to return earthy timelines to their original course; however, the spiritual accounts of our world are not. The unannounced child, the secret Great Elder, has returned to her home. I retrieved her from the Brook of Tears where Beck watched over her after Mataya removed her essence from Earth.*

She has a great adjustment to make. She was conscious of her true heritage while hidden away in the brook and not allowed to live, as a Guardian should have. Elder Torrey and his parents will have much responsibility to acclimate her to the life she was to have. They will need to assist her in dissolving the human interference she was exposed to on Earth. She endured much as she dwelled in the bodies of Rebekah and Tori. The Sentinel paused, and Josiah felt her hesitation. A sorrow he never believed existed washed into his mind.

Sentinel? he asked, returning her hesitation with curiosity.

She smiled knowing he felt her moment of compassion that was also her weakness. *I do not know how much longer those Guardians of the Secret Council will exist in their realms. It has not been made known to me what Elder Mataya or Advisor Beck face. Her initial thoughts were portrayed without her knowledge. It was not until Beck realized what was happening and developed their plan that the Guardian world began to feel the effects.*

He believed he was acting in more of an effort to save than for selfish reasons. Their actions of faith for the words of unholy scripture, instead of in God, warrant severe punishment. In spite of this, our Father has a compassionate soul. His children acted on the love He desired for them to acquire. They have demonstrated this love, regardless of how inappropriate their actions were for seeking out the Scroll of Espérer.

The human emotions clouded their Guardian rationality and their judgment was not clear. They put their faith and trust in material objects and not that of the Creator. The Father understands what their motives were, and they realize what chaos their actions have caused. A simple prayer of forgiveness covers a multitude of sin. She chuckled. *After all, they acted to protect the one who was to be my vessel. Mataya, of course may have had more of a selfish motive to her actions when she convinced Evi and Tahir to give up their child. And then do not forget how she persuaded Malachi and Serial to join her. However, if Tarik had not continued to pursue the plan that Markian failed in completing, then no Watcher would be prosecuted now.*

Will Anani face prosecution for her involvement?

No, the child will not. She committed no crime. Your command, our command, was to mingle with humans more closely to grasp a better understanding of human emotions. Anani did just that. She chose Raina as her subject, and as far as I am concerned, she kept a close eye on a friend. The Sentinel smiled, suppressing another human laugh.

Josiah didn't return her humor because of the animosity he felt. It occurred to Josiah then that Tarik may have not acted alone. Before he could ask his question, the Sentinel answered him.

Yes, Josiah. Tarik did not act alone. It was he and his Master that took advantage of the Council's decision to remain neutral during the attack on Cressida. He is the one responsible for their destruction.

And what will become of Tarik's master? Josiah asked, with a hint of disgust in his thoughts. It troubled him to recall how his dear friend Anani, was left an orphan in Bianca's war against the people of Cressida.

The Creator will not allow him to prevail. However, like Earthlings, sin chases his kind and welcomes the evil intentions. If there were no evil then the children of God would not know that good exist. I assure you, Josiah, when it is time, his punishment will not be swift.

When will that come to pass, Sentinel?

It will happen when the Creator chooses to act. For now, we still have other issues that affect you, Head Elder.

Issues, Sentinel? What are they?

Your Raina is still in childbearing years. Since Rayna's essence, my essence, intertwined with Tori's soul, we have also become a part of Raina. Of course, you also sensed that, did you not?

Yes, I did sense that within her. I realized when I held her dying body in the cave that she was indeed filled with a power no human could harbor.

Then you understand that any offspring she produces will also harbor an essence.

I had considered that, Sentinel.

That essence would proceed to create a new form of being. The children may not exist well in either world. If her mate were human, this decreases the essence passed along to her children. As her bloodline continues in the human fashion, my essence will not exist in her great-grandchildren. However, if a Guardian were to bond with her, perhaps, one whose essences is as strong as yours, then the children may be born completely Guardian or human and have no place on Earth or the outer realms of Heaven at all.

The Sentinel watched Josiah's body closely, evaluating his demeanor. He remained standing very still, daring not to look away from the one who commanded his attention. Although his body complied, she mentally felt his struggle for control.

Josiah, she said, with a reverent tone that he could hear, not only in his thoughts, but also filling the room around him. *I have felt the horrible pain that strangles your essence and rules the life the Creator has given you. Your determination to be with the human girl cries to me daily. For your dear friend, Anani, has pleaded your case before me, and the Creator has heard her request.*

Josiah gasped deeply, as his mind strained to recall the sensation of his human heart skipping a beat. *What are you saying, Sentinel?*

The Sentinel felt him fighting to remain in control of his faculties, just as he had that day in Silver Lake for the sake of his Raina. No entity had ever retained as much control of their thoughts from the Sentinel as Josiah had accomplished on both of her visits.

To ensure that her offspring do not evolve, the Creator will grant you humanity in exchange for your essence. You have a choice now, Josiah. She paused, allowing Josiah's mind a moment to relax and absorb her words. He needed time to contemplate what her offer really meant to the both of them. *Do you understand what this means?* she questioned, with the compassion flowing into his mind. It was her way of reassuring him that she meant to be helpful in their communication, and not completely incapacitate his thoughts.

I am not sure, his mind whispered.

You will give up your essence and your existence on Sol ... never returning home. The faithful Guardian Lexis, too, gave his essence for the love of a woman. In the Creator's desire for human love to touch the essence of a Guardian, Lexis was granted a human body. Humanity gave him a wife and a child in exchange for life in the outer realms of Heaven. When his mission was complete, he died a human's death never seeing our universe again. He had neither soul nor essence, and now dwells where the Creator chooses. Do you truly desire such an outcome as this, Head Elder?

I do. He thought, still casting his eyes directly into hers. Raina's face stared back at him, reminding him of what he gave up so long ago.

And, is this what you choose?

Yes, Sentinel. I have learned to love, and I will miss my home, and my parents—however, my life was always meant to be with Raina. We both know this, Your Omnipotence.

You will give up much for your addiction to human emotions. It will be a high price to pay on your behalf, young Josiah.

I know this, Sentinel. It is a choice I am willing to make.

There will be no way back. Your essence will diminish. Your lungs will need the air that you manipulate to appear human. Do you understand that your assimilated heart will really function as a human's does ... and will stop when your human life has fulfilled its destiny? You will not live forever, Josiah ... but a few years in her presence.

A few years ... how many years will it be, Sentinel?

As many as the Creator deems fit ... just as He does with every other entity He has created.

Sentinel, what will become of Raina if the Creator should take me while she still lives?

That is not for me to say or for you to know. Only the Creator reveals the mysteries of Heaven to us. He alone can answer that question. You will risk much becoming human. Her mind warned him with authority and hidden pity.

I understand this, Sentinel. Nevertheless, the risks are well worth it. My life has no meaning now. I must be with Raina.

Your life has much meaning, Josiah, she scolded, wanting to remind him to put his life in perspective. This was something she felt he had not done since that spring morning he heard the lullaby. *You have allowed your mind to close itself to the beauty of our realm. There is much that you have forsaken and ignored about our people's traditions and customs. You have allowed yourself to forget what your heritage and your birthright have to offer you, Josiah.*

Sentinel, that was not my intention. Until I found Raina, I never considered another way of life, other than the one I was willed to live by my parents. It is a life that now consumes me with passion. You can read my thoughts, Sentinel, and you can feel my emotions. Do you not understand what it is that draws me to her? I must have that life to be complete. Please do not deny me my beloved Raina again.

Josiah, she warned, *to choose the life you wish with the human girl would make your old life here on Sol obsolete. Your existence in this realm will end. If you accept the new plan, there are many possibilities in what you request of the Creator for regret to enter your heart.*

I will risk it, Sentinel. If you can bring her back to me and allow us to feel what we had before, I will do this without hesitation or regret. I can find no other joy than to have her by my side again.

The Sentinel's face formed a grin. *Your human life will not be without pain and sorrow, Josiah. Do you not realize that you will become part of the race you despised in your youth?*

Sentinel, I no longer despise the human race as I once had. My mind was closed then and my eyes blinded to their true purpose. I have matured and learned that the Creator has given them life and values all of His children. There will be no sacrifice on my part that is too great. I do not feel that I would be making a sacrifice at all, Sentinel.

The life you had with Raina before I emerged is gone. You will have to start a new relationship with her and her parents. She paused, examining his expression. She could see the determination and human love that filled his eyes with hope and his mind with the gentlest emotions she had ever felt from a Guardian. *Josiah, please understand that you will be subject to new experiences and memories. Her old ones will not return, and she will never know what you once shared. Because of this, you must realize that a part of her is gone forever.*

What do you mean? he asked cautiously, trying to ascertain the meaning of her thoughts.

I am sorry, Josiah, except Raina cannot be allowed to know of her past timeline, or that she once harbored me. The joining of your essence and her soul has no relevance in this realm. Because of this, Raina may not return the feelings you are so eager to shed your existence for, Josiah.

His mind raced looking for the possibility of another outcome. In sadness, he found none. *Is there a chance that she will remember anything at all?*

Her life is new, as I have explained to you. The course she follows now is of the Creator's choosing. It is not for you or me to question or attempt to change its relevance.

Sentinel, I understand this, except my heart must ask. Do you fault me for this?

She smiled, and Josiah felt her warmth and sincerity flow through him. It reminded him so much of how the thoughts of Raina danced in his mind after he joined with her.

I do not fault you, Josiah. You may ask all that you desire, except the answers I cannot give to you. The Creator will answer your questions when He chooses the moment to expose His greater workings.

When will what you speak of come to pass? He thought restlessly. *How much longer will I have to wait to embrace her in my arms?*

The Sentinel felt the need to calm him for his fears were beginning to destroy the trust his mind had in hers. He heard her mind question herself, as to how she could reassure him when his mind begged in agony.

You may wait a very long time. Raina could choose another, and your life will not cross paths with hers.

No—that will not happen. I have felt her attraction to me. I know that she, indeed, loves me. I have seen it in her eyes and felt it in her touch. We will again have what we once shared.

Josiah, I warn you not to get lost in those human emotions. You must remember, Josiah, that tears are the essence of everything.

Sentinel, tell me please. When will I lose my essence?

When the Creator decides it is time. He will determine when the human life you desire will dissolve your essence. Until then, Josiah, you will exist in the life as your parents had created, you must continue to obey the rules and traditions of our people.

With that, the room went quiet, and the Sentinel left. Josiah picked up Raina's picture from the floor, clutching it into his chest. He leaned against his desk, balancing himself. The Sentinel's words meant much to him, and the anticipation grew wildly out of control. Then picking up his Espérer book, Josiah added another entry. This entry contained more hope within those words than any other writings he had ever penned upon the pages with his human hand.

37.
CHOICES

Josiah's world was turning on its axis and the Sun was beginning to rise on Earth. He wondered what the occupants of Silver Lake were doing now in this new dawn. Their human actions always seemed to hold a certain attraction to him. An attraction he blocked out during his days in California before he found Raina.

The walk through the garden brought many untamed emotions to Josiah's essence. His duty to his people as Head Elder fought with his human heart's determination. Once in his lifetime, the human aspects of his shell lingered with him as a very strong memory. Thus, the emotions and memories of his earthy encounters were not real to his essence. In time, Josiah became finely fashioned and in-tuned with his shell, an experience believed to be impossible. Josiah's mind didn't recall the memories of how his shell would react to certain circumstances, for his essence has learned in actuality to feel them.

This morning the flowers seemed to bloom with greater ardor than ever before. The song of the birds passionately added to the Angels' chorus, filling the garden with harmony and peace. Josiah had believed he would never visit his garden again. The pain of losing Raina had taken any desire to be here away. This garden of love was not meant to be tarnished with his feelings of desolation. Yet today, as he made his final decision, the garden welcomed him. To lose his essence for love seemed acceptable, far more honorable than losing it to Deimos. For unlike that barren planet, he would still feel emotions, and his memories would remain his.

He smiled as he stopped to look at the sunflowers and stargazer lilies. Then looking down at the lavender colored angel face roses, he chuckled. After all of these years, Raina's knight in shining armor would bring her the rose she requested to profess his love. He knelt down to smell the aroma of the lilies. Raina's thoughts once told him how she believed such a scent came from Heaven. She never knew how right she was in her beliefs.

Josiah ran his fingers over the rose petals. This sent the aroma swirling through the air, sealing his confidence for what he was about to do. He clutched several stems in his grip tearing them from the plant. Josiah stood up crushing them between his fingers until they turned into a lavender color powder. With one last gaze at the garden, he turned and faded away.

Josiah materialized at his parents' home. His mother answered the knock on their chamber door. She wondered what had brought her son there, so early in the day.

"Josiah, honey. Please come in." She smiled at him, stepping aside to allow him to enter.

Josiah noticed the entryway décor, and realized that nothing had changed since his youth. For a people who want nothing and can change things at the least bit of desire, her chamber remained the same. This was proof that his parents took only what was needed and never indulged in more than what was necessary to exist.

"Hello, Mother. Good day to you."

"And to you as well, Josiah. Tell me, what is it that has brought you here today?"

"I need to speak to you and Father. Is he in, Mother?"

His father's voice chimed in from behind him. "Yes, I am here, Josiah. What is it that you need?"

"Please, we should sit, Father. I have much to say."

"Is everything well with you, Josiah?" his mother asked. She was suspicious of his visit.

"All is well with me. In fact, it is better than well."

"Oh, Josiah, I am so glad to hear that," Kiersten said. She felt happy for her son's sake.

"I am not so sure that you will mean what you say, after I am done speaking with you, Mother."

Jon spoke, sharing his wife's earlier suspicion for Josiah's unannounced arrival. "Josiah, tell us please, what is on your mind?"

"I have received a visit from the Sentinel this morning. She has brought me news that is both exciting and sad."

Kiersten sunk down in the Victorian style chair she was standing by. Somehow, a mother's heart always knows when it will be broken. Josiah caught her expression, knowing his words were going to hurt. He stiffened, feeling his joy for the moment begin to fade. Jon took one look at his wife and knew she sensed something terrible. A glance toward his son, and he could see the gloom begin to fill in the features of his face. The smile he wore when he first arrived was gone.

"Josiah, what do you need to speak to us about?" Jon cleared his throat nervously. It was one human habit he picked up and was never able to dispose of it from his behavior pattern.

Josiah hesitated to speak. He just stared into the eyes of his mother. The ones that carried the same glossy look as they did the day Abaddon pierced him with his sword. He swallowed to clear his throat.

"As you were saying to us a moment ago, my son?" Jon asked, eagerly interrupting Josiah's thoughts. He knew whatever Josiah had to say, it was best to get it out into the open.

"Mother ... Father, the Sentinel came to me this morning with news. Until I looked into your faces, it was the happiest news I could ever hear. Now, the words I am about to speak will be the saddest ones ever uttered from my lips."

"You are leaving us, I can feel it," Kiersten said under her breath sadly. "She has called you away?"

Jon sighed at hearing the words. He didn't need the details to imagine what Josiah was going to say.

"No, Mother, she has not called me away, nor will she send me anywhere either. However, she has made an offer that brings me great difficulty."

"What is the offer, my son?" Jon questioned, closing his eyes. As much as human emotions intrigued him—now were not the time to experience them.

"The Creator has made His decision on how to handle the workings of the Secret Council. He is dealing with those involved in the time shifts and the human bred children."

"And how is He dealing with them?" Jon asked, not caring about anything other than what Josiah hesitated to tell them.

"He will not allow further interruption to the timeline or the realms concerning Raina and her family."

"What is his solution then for the Guardians and their essences?" Kiersten asked him, feeling as impatient as her husband was.

"The Sentinel did not tell me what the solutions was to be, Mother. I only know that Raina's life will remain as it is."

"What does that mean for you, Josiah?" Kiersten questioned, not sure, if she wanted to hear the answer.

"I have been granted a choice by the Creator. It is a right that I did not earn and cannot credit it to any wishes that were made upon the writings of the scroll of hope. This has truly been given to me when I have not deserved it at all."

Jon knew it now. The writings within the scroll answer the greatest desires of those who have proven themselves determined. When he learned that Enoch had acquired the Scroll of Espérer and put it into Raina's locket, Jon feared that Josiah too, would allow himself to drift further from the honor of his people. To know that Josiah was wise enough to understand where the true blessing came from, encouraged him. Yet, now he questioned Josiah's wisdom.

"What will this choice mean for you, Josiah?"

"Father, I have the opportunity to be with Raina," he said proudly.

"This choice is not without consequences, I am sure," Jon said sternly.

"You are correct, Father. My decision will not just affect Raina and me, but you two as well."

Kiersten looked at her husband both astounded and grieved. "Retirement," she whispered.

"I am sorry, Mother, except I do not understand what you mean by that."

His mother smiled at him. "After you left us on the mountain top, I asked your father if you could retire from the Council. He told me that my notion was an impossible thought."

Josiah sighed and then sat down in the chair by the piano. When he was a child, this chair became his favorite place to sit and listen to the sounds of Beethoven. Then burying his face into his hands, he began to question his decision. His heart told him that leaving his people for Raina was a fair trade-off. Now, when he no longer thought of just himself, embarrassment and shame set in. Could he really forsake his family for an earth-bound human?

"Your decision, Josiah?"

He looked up at hearing his name spoken. He had not acknowledged the words of his father. "Ah, what?" he had to ask.

"What have you decided to do then?"

He moaned loudly. "Until I had looked you two in the eyes this morning, I was shedding my existence for her. Now, guilt has made me see that I may have made a mistake."

Kiersten realized that her own selfishness for losing her son made him question his right to happiness. "What is wrong, Josiah?"

"Mother, Father. Until this moment, I pledged to leave my home for all eternity and join Raina. However, I see the pain in your eyes now, and I cannot endure hurting you."

"Son," Kiersten spoke.

These would be the hardest words a mother could ever say. She looked at her husband, admiring the man she had bonded with so long ago. Without spoken words, each knew what they were thinking. The love they felt could endure anything. It was strong enough to last an eternity. To know this love was magnificent. To think of someone being deprived of this special love seemed to be meaningless and a horrible crime.

"Do not allow us to be so selfish. Your father and I have made our life together—and we have had the best that the Creator could offer us. We will meet someday in the outer courts of Heaven, this I am sure of, Josiah. Go now," she said, drawing strength from her essence, "and claim what you have risked your life for many times. And at night, when you glance up into the stars, know that it is your father and I who are looking down upon you."

Jon stepped forward and hugged his son. "I will be waiting until we meet again. I can think of no other who I would gladly give up my son for. You deserve happiness, Head Elder. Our people cannot fault you for this."

Kiersten got up from her chair and joined her husband's embrace, fighting back her tears. "Josiah, I hear the Angels singing in harmony. We will rejoice from our world at your happiness. For there is no greater prayer that I can pray—or answer I can receive—than to see you happy again."

"Goodbye, my son," Jon whispered, and then he bid him farewell.

In that moment, Josiah found himself standing in front of his good friend. Josiah was sent to his chamber where he found Jaleel waiting for him by his father's command.

"Josiah, please tell me why have you brought me here?" Jaleel asked, confused at being beckoned against his wishes from his study.

"I wanted to tell you something."

"Tell me what?" Jaleel asked curiously.

The look in his expression told Jaleel what he was thinking. He knew it then, that Josiah had made his choice. Nothing in this world could hold him here. The beauty of what the Creator offered on Sol couldn't compare to the treasure Josiah found on Earth.

"I cannot believe—" Jaleel began to say, and then stopped at Josiah's urging.

"Please, Jaleel, do not dwell."

"I do not mean to. It is just the thought of never traveling or enduring an adventure with you again ... leaves me feeling empty."

"I am sorry, Jaleel. I know of the loneliness that you speak about to me. It haunted me daily when I lost Raina."

"Will it pass, or must I endure this forever? Do you even feel remorse at our parting?"

"I do, Jaleel ... I do. In time, you will adjust to my absence. This I promise you, friend."

"How can you promise me that when the time you have been apart is measured by two Earth years and still the emotions afflict your essence? There must be another way for you to do this without leaving our world behind?"

"If there is one ... it was not an option given to me, Jaleel."

"So ... then is it over—our friendship? Our childhood adventures gone?"

"No, Jaleel, I will never forget you ... this friendship will never cease to exist."

"But it will, and you know it. In time you will forget me ... that human heart of yours will stop, and you will die."

"Yes, except I may enter the realms of Heaven. There you can visit with me ... there I will not forget you."

"It will be a very long time."

"Jaleel, since when do you mark the passing of time? Look how quickly Benn and Enoch served their missions ... how quickly Raina remembered me in her dreams."

"Yes, and do you realize, Josiah, how quickly I will lose my friend?"

"Jaleel, what I am about to do is by my choice. Do you have any idea what I feel for her? There is no sacrifice here. It is my desire to be near her until the Creator calls us home."

"Josiah, you are giving it all up. There is nothing that she can give up for you."

"Jaleel, I give up nothing, and I ask her for nothing in return."

"I hope you mean that, Josiah, because I truly believe that is exactly what you will get."

"Then that is my choice, one that I am willing to make and live with forever. I once told you, Jaleel, that I wanted to see into her future to know that she was well. I will not have to see, because I will be a part of it now."

"It is a dim future, Josiah. Imagine the consequences."

"Jaleel, tell me. Would you not make the same choices and the same sacrifices for Yakira?"

Jaleel lowered his head. Josiah knew him well. The forbidden attraction he had for Yakira was great. Together, the two of them experienced much, but those experiences came merely from the result of passion. Their love could be broken if they allowed their minds to think it. Josiah had shown that this was not an option for Raina and him.

"I believe that I would. However, it is clear that she would not. Yakira has left me and her return is not certain."

"I am sorry, Jaleel."

"Do not be. What we had should not have been. We both realize that, and we will take no more risks."

"I cannot say that for my own life, you know that."

"Then this is goodbye, my brother?"

Josiah shook his head. "No, not goodbye."

"Then what do you call this?"

"I call this a temporary parting."

"Do not fool yourself, Josiah. There is nothing temporary in your actions. What you do will be permanent."

"No, Jaleel, nothing is permanent. God can change anything."

"I fear, Josiah, that He will not change your mind."

"This," he said softly, breaking eye contact, "God will not do."

Jaleel said nothing, pulling Josiah into his embrace. He cleared his throat, stepped back from Josiah and smiled. "Then until we meet in the outer realms of Heaven, my brother."

"Until then," Josiah replied, waving as he dematerialized from his study.

Josiah went to Earth to be with Raina. She lay sleeping in the hospital bed breathing on her own. The artificial life support that troubled her father was removed. In a few days, Raina would be released from the hospital. Her mysterious illness cured by the miracle of *modern medicine* and now she lives.

Josiah could tell she was dreaming. Needlessly alarmed, he wondered what filled her dreams. He rubbed his hand, and the magical lavender powder of love reappeared. He rested his hand on her forehead, and the powder drifted through the air. The secret to entering her dream was revealed by love—then concentrating on her thoughts—he effortlessly joined Raina in her dream. Together they were standing in the Garden of Love on Callisto.

Raina stood before him frightened and safe at the same time. She was a vision of loveliness and peace that Josiah believed belonged to Angles. With a questioning expression, she spoke softly.

"I don't know what it is that calls me to this place. I have felt the urge for some time now. Please tell me. What has been happening to me, Josiah?"

He looked away, feeling her pain consume his very essence. Josiah opened his mouth to speak, but he couldn't find the words to answer her question.

"The darkness is so strong, it consumes me ... yet there is something about you that pulls me into the light. What is it inside of you, Josiah, that shows me the light when the night is so frightening? Please, tell me what it is, that you do to bring back some peace to my life? I need to know."

Raina looked at him with pleading eyes. Her request was more than he could bear. Then reaching out for his hand, her fingers gently brushed against his. As he felt the fire that burned in her soul, he sighed in defeat.

"Even in the worst dreams," she continued, in almost a whisper, "I see you there. All my life, I have seen you there. And when I'm ready to be lost in the darkness, you appear with a bright light to guide me out of the cave. Don't you see, when I get there in the light, you're always there to embrace me. I can't tell you what I feel in your arms. How safe you make me. How do you do it?"

Josiah looked sternly at her, contemplating her words. He knew of everything her lips uttered. He knew there was some kind of connection left in the portals of time that sent his essence to comfort her. Even when he had no idea that he was doing it, Josiah was still protecting her. Could it have been by some miracle or plan of the Sentinel? Is this what she meant when she said Raina would always be safe?

Yet, the nightmares, as Josiah had felt, were real. How was it possible for him to be brought into her dreams? How did he know when to appear? Was it her mind that brought him there, or was it some other entity? He knew now it was their love. For as easily as he joined with her thoughts in reality, it was the same for her dreams.

"Please, Raina. Will you walk with me through the garden?"

"Yes, I will."

Then taking her hand into his, they strolled through the Garden of Love. The birds sang cheerfully, and the butterflies danced in the breeze. The garden's aroma filled the air with scents from Heaven. The sunflowers stood tall following the face of God, while the lilies and roses waved proudly. Each flower casts their fragrance strongly into the air.

She must know the truth now, before his essence faded away. She must know who he is and what they once shared. He gripped her hand tighter within his, tugging her gently toward the stream. He stepped gracefully from one rock to another, helping her cross the stream. Raina closed her eyes, laughing softly. She trusted him without hesitation. When they reached the other side, they were no longer in the garden. She opened her eyes to find herself standing next to the hospital room window. She looked around amazed by the transition. Her doubt began to return and so did her fear.

"What is happening?" she cried alarmed.

"Shhh ... rest easy, Raina. Close your eyes and relax. You are in no danger. I promise you this. Soon your dreams and your thoughts will make sense."

How much longer could Josiah hold back? Could he be patient, and allow her the time she needed to fall in love with him again? Would his Raina accept the life he offered her? Her life was too short, and the time lost between them too long. His essence gave into the human urges, and he lost his Guardian senses in the moment. Josiah pulled

Raina into his embrace, risking the answers he feared, yet hoped to hear.

Unexpectedly, a warm sensation moved across her cheek. It took Raina a second to realize it was his hand. Two very soft fingers caressed her face, gently touching the outer edge of her lip. Slowly exhaling, her breath blew past his fingers. Raina opened her eyes to find his meeting hers. The deep emerald-green eyes invited her stare, and she couldn't look away. Josiah didn't notice, for he was lost in the purity of her blue eyes. As he focused, he saw every detail of the lines in her face, the delicateness in her irises, and heard the increasing thud inside her chest. No words needed to be said, they both knew what this moment held for them.

The warmth of her sweet breath lured him in, and his lips met hers. There was nothing in this world that could compare to what they felt now. Josiah's hands no longer shook, but Raina's body trembled. Josiah pulled back, and his kiss stopped short. He knew her memory had not fully returned to her. One last shred of Guardian wisdom made itself known as Josiah tied to hide his hesitation. He smiled softly to reassure her. Raina returned the smile, brushing away the curl that dangled in front of his eyes.

The Sentinel made it clear, that their relationship was to be on the human level after the Creator commenced His plan. Raina was not allowed to remember her former life—the life that held the love Josiah longed to feel. To make the decision he was contemplating now, condemned him. He was to become human before he acted, and now, he had to fight the energy swelling inside him.

His powers were strong and his will to be with her determined. With just a simple breath in her direction, he could command her embrace or her kiss, whether willing or not. Before now, each day's purpose was to give them one moment to touch each other or to gaze into one another's eyes. He had to be strong ... he had to be patient, for her sake.

To claim her now would fulfill the burning desire to have her back again. However, he knew it wouldn't be the same love that they once shared. If Raina were to love him, it would be because she remembered the bond ... the joining his essence and her soul had once experienced. Her reactions must be of her own free will and given without doubt or hesitation. It must be because she remembered everything, and wanted all of him.

Raina's eyes projected the story. All excuses and purposes were washed away. Only the existence of their love would save them now. His essence began to escape, filling the space around them. Josiah had to be careful, for he knew this was a mistake. He was not the clumsy college junior who sat next to her anymore; something had changed during the night. Josiah made a decision and he was willing to face the consequences, no matter the risks.

The pull between them was strong, commanding their attention. No will was strong enough to fight the force pushing her toward him. Neither memory loss, nor powers on all the worlds, could slow the pounding of her heart. It finally beat ready to explode within her chest. The magnitude of their emotions and desires sent the blue energy dancing throughout the room. No more restraints existed and no more worthless excuses remained to recite. The whole universe came together in that one small moment. Raina's eyes announced to the world the story Josiah longed to hear. She knew who she was, and she now remembered her purpose.

She raised her hand, placing it gently against his chest. Her touch was like nothing he had ever felt before. Raina stepped forward, pushing her body into his. Her actions confirmed what all their emotions were announcing. Josiah closed his eyes absorbing the moment. As he opened them, her breathing had stopped, and all passable air had escaped his shell. Raina trembled as she held his gaze. Very gently, he laid his hand against her cheek. With one simple pass of his exquisite finger, her entire being was at his command. His touch was slow and deliberate. Her skin was soft and warm. The pulsing sensation of his touch tingled back through his hand. Never had either one of them experienced such a sensation.

Breathe, he commanded her, more so by thought than word.

Raina couldn't look away and leaving was not an option. All of her will and her thoughts were consumed by his touch. Then raising his hands, Josiah encircled her head pulling her face toward his. The seconds it took for his lips to reach hers seemed to take an eternity. Their lips touched again with force, holding each other tighter. They felt each other's desires casting aside any doubt or worries. Her heart beat with the expectant touch of his lips and the heavenly scent that filled the room. Her existence was consumed by the magic that encased them in their own universe.

Then gently, his essence drew her in, and their thoughts became one. Every memory he carried, every cherished moment that drove him to proceed without her, became hers. Josiah's determination to be with her and to save her from Tarik emanated strongly in his mind. She felt his pain from the terrifying moments on Deimos, and his heart shattering at the news of her death. Each arrow belonging to Abaddon that pierced his side, now pierced hers. As she felt the desolation that followed Josiah, he too, felt the fear branded into her mind from Tarik's realm.

Every moment he had left containing an essence, he must make sure it was used wisely. In one simple thought, he pushed the sadness and fearful memories from their minds. Her dreams didn't haunt her, and her screams didn't come. Raina had changed; her life had emerged from the darkness that lingered over her. For once, Raina was not afraid and didn't feel anxious or paranoid. All that remained was the attraction they once shared. The breathtaking moment of their first kiss and the closeness, they felt in her new life. It was here in Silver Lake, in this moment their lives would begin.

How could I have forgotten this? How could I have forgotten you? Raina asked softly, within the barriers of their minds. *This is incredible. Your touch and the sensation of our minds thinking together as one are unbelievable. I can feel your body and its movements. I can hear your voice in my head. You were holding back a part of your being from me. How could you ever contain such control of your essence?* Raina looked down and blinked her tears away. With the softest expression anyone could ever make, she looked up staring with eyes full of certainty. Softly she whispered in her mind. *Josiah, I need you. Promise me that you will always be with me.* It was more of a statement than a question.

Then her hand moved around the back of his head, coming to rest on his shoulder. Soon, their love must find a way to prevail in a world controlled by human thoughts and actions. A world where desires to practice humanity is the only form of power Josiah will feel. He pushed off his sense of duty, falling into the ocean of irrationality that became his friend. This morning had confirmed that she once again felt an attraction for her Knight in shining armor.

I would like that very much, his mind whispered back.

Then gently cupping her face in his hand, he kissed her moving his lips with passion. The cocoon around them began to glow, as it had never done before. In that one moment, all the reasons for their world to exist came together in their embrace. Their love lasted through two life times. One that was aware and one that was hidden away. There could be no other reason or purpose to have emotion in this world but to bring them back together again.

ACKNOWLEDGMENTS

I want to give a special word of thanks to my husband, Kurt, and my sons Aaron and Donovan, for your encouragement to finish this sequel. Thank you for still loving me while I became a permanent fixture at the kitchen table. I am truly blessed to have you as my family. You guys are my Stones of Fayruz.

Thank you to my father, Charles Bishop, who not only acted as Hemet's official tour guide, but also gave me a few pointers on this story. Thank you for your love and the pedestal you have put me on. I am proud to call you my father.

Thank you to my other mother, Judy Bishop, for being a wonderful inspiration and very special person. You are my father's rock.

Thank you to my wonderful people who gave of their time and talents for this project. Editor: Judy Mobile. Graphic Designer: Joshua Frazer. Medical Advisor: Dr. James Toniolo. Cold Readers: Darlene Lassig, Allison Miller, Olivia Solfest, Jenni Cable, Cybil Krenz, Pat Dunn, Vanessa Knautz and Amber Ferraro. For without every one of you, I couldn't make my story vividly reach my reader's hearts. Thank you for your support when the coffee pot ran dry and I took on a new undiscovered language that you had to decipher.

Judy, your guidance and direction has helped to take this novel to new levels. I cannot begin to express how appreciative I am to have you join this project.

Thank you, Josh, for capturing the beauty of the brook in your incredible painting. You have given such a wonderful visual of the Brook of Tears.

Dr. "T," thanks so much for taking the time to review my medical interpretations. Your expertise truly made my hospital chapters come alive.

To my "Super Hero" Cold Reader Amber. You totally got inside the story finding the holes in my plot and pushed me to step beyond my original story line. Truly, you have helped to make this story a success.

Darlene, your wisdom and awesome "Teacher" skills, has been an asset to this project. Thank you for all that you have done to enrich my story.

Allie, once again, you have taken the helm and guided this story to unimaginable places. Thank you for pushing me along. Wait until you see what your next birthday gift is. See you next September.

Jenni, thank you for your suggestions, input, and willingness to tackle the manuscript twice. You have done an awesome job helping me to shape the manuscript into wonderful story.

Olivia, I am so glad to have someone as insightful and determined as you on this project. Thank you for sharing your talent with me. I can't wait to read your book. Happy writing!

Cybil, thank you for your thought provoking questions and for reading the manuscript twice. You have helped to make this novel complete.

Charlene Lassig

Pat, thanks for your attention to fine detail and your assistance to make this novel outstanding. Thankfully, there will be no loons bellowing in this novel.

Thank you, John Anderson HM1-USN-FMF-Retired, of Kenosha, Wisconsin for the magnificent idea of miniature wood carvings for Isaiah's shadow box.

Thank you, Debra Scully, who keeps pushing me along and gives me the courage to believe in myself. Thank you for honoring my novel in your restaurant.

Thank you, Stevie Nilles, for your clever imagination and for being my awesome "Horse go to girl." If Stargazer were real, then I would give him to you.

I want to give a special thank you to Rosemary Sears of the Hemet Museum in Hemet, California, for your wonderful tour, and the information on the historical facts of Hemet.

Thank you to the volunteers at the Western Science Center in Hemet, California, for your hospitality, and wealth of knowledge.

Thanks to the staff at Palomar Observatory, Palomar Mountain, California, for brining the stars to our own back yard.

Once again, I have found that music is my inspiration to write through the night. Many thanks to the talented artists for all you give to your fans. Thank you to David Duffield, Jonny Duffield, Ian Anderson and Jamie Pena of the band "Leo" for capturing my heart with another new song. "Sing to Me." Thank you to Kenosha's own "Special Blend" Tony Serpe, Craig Carver, Jeff Horton, and Dan Eisenhauer for the sneak peak of your awesome song, "Don't Wanna Say Goodbye."

Many thanks to my other favorite artists for whom I owe my deepest gratitude. It is your passion for music and talent for those golden words that kept me motivated.
Munford & Sons, Trans-Siberian Orchestra, Jim Brickman, 30 Seconds to Mars, Owl City, The Overcomers-Wooded Hills Worship, Jeremy Camp, Cold Play, The Fray, Collective Soul, Phillips, Craig, and Dean, Michael W. Smith, Air Supply, The Goo Goo Dolls, The Editors, Benny Hester, Dallas Holmes, Bette Midler, Barry Manilow, Kenny Loggins,Twila Paris, Life House, Lover Boy, Rob Thomas/Match Box 20, Enirque Iglesias, El De Barge, Nelly, and the late greats, Keith Green, Rich Mullins, and Michael Jackson.

Thank you to our American Heroes.
Heroes come in many forms. They are the men and women of our Armed Forces who risk their lives for liberty and justice of the American people. They are Teachers who are our children's futures—our world's tomorrow. They are Firefighters who risk life and limb to enter burning buildings to save our love ones. They are Police Officers who put their lives on the line daily to protect and serve. They are Nurses who work endless hours to care for the sick, and Senators who do what is right even when it's not popular. Thank you, Senators Robert Wirch, Tim Carpenter, Spencer Coggs, Tim Cullen, Jon Erpenbach, Dave Hansen, Jim Holperin, Robert Jauch, Chris Larson, Julie Lassa, Mark Miller, Fred Risser, Lena Taylor, and Kathleen Vinehout for remaining faithful to the people of Wisconsin.

www.ingramcontent.com/pod-product-compliance
Lightning Source LLC
Chambersburg PA
CBHW020455020726
47493CB00001B/38